Y CC   R\

O. ....   CC. No. ...... 46.

Return	Date of Return	Date of Ret
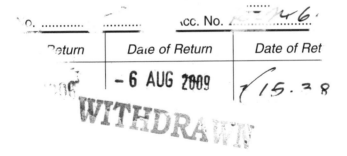	− 6 AUG 2009	15. ⌐ 8

WITHDRAWN

KILKENNY COUNTY LIBRARY

KK246027

MIND'S EYE

By the same author

White Devils

MIND'S EYE

Paul McAuley

KILKENNY
COUNTY
LIBRARY

WITHDRAWN

SIMON & SCHUSTER

LONDON • NEW YORK • SYDNEY • TORONTO

First published in Great Britain by Simon & Schuster UK Ltd, 2005
A Viacom company

Copyright © Paul McAuley, 2005

This book is copyright under the Berne Convention.
No reproduction without permission.
All rights reserved.

The right of Paul McAuley to be identified as author of this work has been
asserted by him in accordance with sections 77 and 78 of the Copyright,
Designs and Patents Act, 1988.

1 3 5 7 9 10 8 6 4 2

Simon & Schuster UK Ltd
Africa House
64–78 Kingsway
London WC2B 6AH

Simon & Schuster Australia
Sydney

A CIP catalogue record for this book is available from the British Library

ISBN HB – 0743238877
ISBN TPB – 0743238885

This book is a work of fiction. Names, characters, places and incidents
are either a product of the author's imagination or are used fictitiously.
Any resemblance to actual people living or dead, events or locales is
entirely coincidental.

The lyrics quoted on page 74 and 77 are from the Viceroy's 'Shadrach, Meshach, and
Abednego' (Dodd, Tinglin). The author and publishers have made all reasonable efforts
to contact the copyright holders for permission, and apologise for any omissions or
errors in the form of credit given. Corrections may be made in future printings.

Typeset by Palimpsest Book Production Limited,
Polmont, Stirlingshire
Printed and bound in Great Britain by
William Clowes Ltd, Beccles, Suffolk

KILKENNY COUNTY
LIBRARY C15.38
Acc No KK246074
Class No F
Inv No 18443
11. 11.05

For Georgina, always

NORFOLK,
28 NOVEMBER 1981

The day after Alfie Flowers's birthday, his tenth, his father picked him up from his boarding school and took him to the seaside. It was the last Saturday in November, frosty cold but bright and clear, and they drove with the Morgan's top down. The little red sports car was Alfie's favourite car ever, a hundred light years better than his Grammie's poky Austin Metro or the heavy old Rover that smelled of damp and always made him feel slightly seasick. Riding inside the Morgan's cramped, low-slung cockpit, sturdy dials gleaming in the varnished wooden dashboard and icy air ripping past the narrow windscreen, was almost exactly like flying in a fighter plane, and as his father hurled it around the curves of the B-road, Alfie pretended that he was a war ace, strafing enemies from the hedgerows.

Mick Flowers drove with casual expertise, his leather jacket zipped to the neck, his white silk scarf and blond hair raked back by the wind, telling his son that he had another assignment in Beirut, but it wasn't anything, an errand that would take no more than a couple of weeks. Alfie wasn't much bothered by the announcement. His father was a freelance photojournalist who spent most of his time in the world's hot spots, covering the endgame in Vietnam, conflicts in Rhodesia, Lebanon, Biafra and Cambodia (he'd been wounded in Cambodia), and the troubles in Northern Ireland. Because his father was away on assignments and his mother was no longer alive (a wild-at-heart Texas model Mick Flowers had met and married when he was working for London's high-end fashion magazines, shortly after giving birth to their only child she'd died in scandalous circumstances involving a drunken congressman and an illegal road race somewhere outside Amarillo), Alfie divided his time between boarding school and his grandparents' house outside Cambridge – his grandmother's house now, his grandfather having died of a stroke a year ago. Alfie sometimes wished that his father was more like the fathers of his school friends, a banker or company director or Army officer, someone with an ordinary job and an ordinary life, someone with a wife instead of a string of girlfriends, someone who didn't gamble away most of his earnings, who wasn't given to turning up without any warning, exhausted and dishevelled, filling the house with cigarette smoke and the tingling thump of rock music. But he was inordinately proud of him just the same, and clipped his photographs from newspapers and magazines and pasted them in a scrapbook alongside postcards and airmail letters from all around the world. When he grew up, Alfie was going to be a photojournalist too. There was no question about it.

'I'll be home well before Christmas,' Mick Flowers said. 'Cross my heart, et cetera. I'll help you with that kit your grandmother gave you. If you need any help, that is.'

It was the Airfix 1/600 scale model of the SS *Canberra*, the biggest Alfie had ever tackled. But two years after his first, badly botched attempt at assembling a Mark IX Spitfire he considered himself something of an expert at kit-bashing, and told his father that, except for the bow, which looked like it might be difficult to get exactly right, the assembly should be straightforward.

'We'll figure it out together, Chief,' Mick Flowers said. 'Deal?'

'Deal.'

They reached the junction with the main road; Mick Flowers aimed the Morgan at the flat horizon. When machine-gun stutters of sunlight exploded behind a row of poplars that someone had planted to make a windbreak, he glanced over at his son, saw that Alfie's eyes were tightly closed, and said, 'Flashing lights still giving you a hard time?'

They'd left the poplars behind. Alfie opened his eyes, shrugged inside his quilted anorak.

'If anything has happened since I last saw you, Alfie, fits or bad dreams, anything like that, I think you should tell me.'

Alfie shrugged again, stubborn, embarrassed and, most of all, ashamed. He didn't like to talk about his fits because it reminded him of the accident that had set them off, knotting up his heart with shame and guilt. He said, 'I'm getting better, Dad. Really I am.'

His father accepted the lie. Or at least, he didn't ask any more questions. The Morgan ate up the road with a steady roar. Trains of small white clouds appeared at the edge of the chill blue sky as they neared the coast.

A freezing wind blew off the sea, winnowing the marram grass on top of the dunes, skirling sand across the deserted car park, cutting straight through Alfie's anorak, school jumper, and grey flannel shirt. But he forgot all about the cold when his father opened the boot of the Morgan and presented him with a wide flat package wrapped in brown paper. Mick Flowers leaned against the car, blond hair whipping about his face, watching with a fond smile as Alfie tore open the package to reveal a diamond of bright red cloth, saying, 'I thought this would be as good a place as any to try it out.'

Ten minutes later, father and son were chasing each other along the beach, laughing and whooping as the kite caught the wind and swung high above them. Its taut red diamond thrummed as it dipped and soared; its long tail was studded with a dozen short lengths of plastic tubing that made an eerie keening sound as air played through them. With his favourite camera, a battered Nikon with a 21mm lens, Mick Flowers took photographs from several angles of Alfie leaning against the strong pull of the kite like a fisherman trying to haul in a prize catch; then he climbed on top of the crest of dunes and took a series of shots of the boy and his kite caught between the long, parallel planes of beach and sea. Later, in the darkroom of his rented London flat, he printed up one of these shots on high-contrast monochrome paper that accentuated the glare of the winter sun on the wet beach, and sent it to his son with a brief note memorializing the day. It was the last letter that Alfie ever received from him.

Alfie let the kite climb the ladder of wind until it was no more than a bright red dot pinned against the blue sky. He quickly learned how to make it slip sideways in heart-stopping swoops, like a nimble Spitfire or Mosquito avoiding German ack-ack, learned how to turn it into the wind and let it rise again, how to draw huge loops through the jolting air. But at last he grew careless and let it dip too low, and it stalled and dropped like a stone and crashed into the slate-grey sea. Mick Flowers kicked off his shoes and splashed into the water as Alfie tried to reel in the kite's dead weight, one moment scared that the string would break and his birthday present would be swept away, the next cheering wildly when his father snatched it from the top of a wave.

Breathless with excitement, father and son carried the kite back to the car, tied it to the rear bumper so that it could dry in the wind, and wolfed down the birthday tea that Alfie's grandmother had packed into a small wicker hamper. Fish-paste and watercress sandwiches cut in crustless triangles; sausage rolls with flaky, golden pastry; an iced sponge-cake stuck with ten sparklers which fizzed smartly but all too briefly.

The short winter day was nearly over. It was beginning to grow dark. Mick Flowers pulled a tartan blanket from the boot and told Alfie that they were going to build a fire — it would be a lot of fun.

'It's still officially your birthday, Chief. We have permission to stay out late and howl at the moon.'

Alfie, knowing what the fire was really for, felt a sudden dip in his stomach. He'd known all along that the day would probably end like this, but until now had managed to put it out of his mind.

The sun was setting behind a line of pine trees that hunched beyond the dunes. The empty beach stretched away for a mile on either side under a huge sky the colour of cut plums. Alfie helped his father build a small wigwam from driftwood and stuff it with marram grass and dry seaweed. Once lit, the fire burned briskly, tossing scraps of flame into the cold breeze, crackling blue and yellow as salty seaweed crisped. Mick Flowers produced a packet of marshmallows from the inside pocket of his leather jacket. He and Alfie skewered them on sticks and toasted them in the flames. The fire seemed to grow brighter as the air darkened around them. It was as if they were in a cave of light, an intimate space that invited confidences.

'I suppose we'd better get it over with,' Mick Flowers said at last, and took out a tobacco tin.

Alfie felt the knot in his chest, hot and hopelessly complicated. 'Dad, how long do we have to do this?'

'I don't know, Alfie. That's the honest truth.'

'Grammie says—'

'If we did what your grandmother wants and went to the doctors, they'd give you medicine you'd have to take every day of your life. This way is better, isn't it?'

'I suppose.'

They'd had this argument several times. It always ran along the same lines, and in the end Alfie always submitted. It was either Mr Prentiss's treatment or the hospital, and hospital would definitely be worse. Hospital meant obscure medical procedures. Hospital meant that strangers would find out what he had done – what he'd done to himself.

It hadn't seemed like anything at the time. A minor bit of trespassing, curiosity about what was hidden in the secret compartment in his grandfather's desk. It hadn't been his fault that he'd been hurt by what he'd found, not really. It had been a mistake, a horrible accident.

Last year, early in the morning of Christmas Eve, Alfie's grandfather had suffered a major stroke in his sleep. He had never woken up, had died later the same day. A week after the funeral, two men had come to clear out his shed.

This was no ordinary garden shed, but a kind of chalet set on tall, cross-braced wooden posts like the observation tower of a prisoner-of-war camp, its walls painted bright yellow, its roof pillar-box red. It stood in a copse of Scots pines, silver birches, young oak trees and rhododendrons at the end of the long, rambling garden of the Victorian villa where Alfie lived with his grandparents. A wooden stair ran up one side to the balcony where Alfie's grandfather had liked to sit and smoke his pipe while gazing at the view across fields and patches of woodland towards the level Cambridgeshire horizon.

Alfie watched from his hiding place beneath a big rhododendron bush, lying as quiet and still as a spy monitoring the activity of enemy agents, while his father and the two men moved to and fro inside the shed, their shadows appearing and disappearing behind its dusty window. He watched them come back down the stairs, each carrying two or three cardboard boxes, took careful aim with the cap pistol that his father had brought back from Singapore, one of the presents he'd opened with little enthusiasm the day after his grandfather had died, and carefully shot them over and over again. He was a sniper; he was the last valiant defender of a fortress overrun by its enemies; he was a detective thwarting desperate criminals. He watched as the two men, both of them much older than his father, stacked the boxes in the boot of their grey Jaguar, watched as his father shook hands with them, watched as they climbed into their car and drove off, and his father disappeared inside the house. He watched and waited until he was as certain as he could be that the coast was clear, then snuck through the scanty cover of the little copse to the shed and scampered up the stairs, his blood thrilling.

At first glance, nothing seemed to have changed. The two over-lapping, threadbare oriental carpets still covered the floor. The leather armchair where Alfie, as long as he promised to be extra quiet, had been allowed to sit and read while his grandfather worked, still slumped next to the black-leaded cast-iron stove that, stoked full of glowing coke, had grown so hot that when Alfie spat on it the spit danced around before vanishing with a satis-fying hiss. The stove was unlit now, of course, and the shed felt cold and damp, and smelled faintly but definitely of his grand-father's funny tobacco, a smell that touched something deep inside Alfie and made him feel sad and alone. The floor-to-ceiling shelves were still stuffed to bursting with piles of books and papers, and the photographs from his grandfather's time in Iraq still hung here and there, but his collection of ancient artefacts — fragments of unglazed pottery, clay tablets marked with neat rows of cuneiform writing, a clay lamp shaped like a slipper, stone and flint axes and hand tools and arrowheads, bone needles and pieces of bone incised with pictures of reindeer or horses, some bought at auction or from other collectors, some from archaeological excavations in Iraq where Alfie's grandfather had worked in the 1930s — had been cleared away, and the roll-top desk had been stripped of its familiar clutter of papers and stood bare and forlorn.

Alfie's grandfather, kindly, patient, sweet-natured and utterly remote from ordinary life, had worked there every day. Perched on the edge of a swivel chair, writing in neat copperplate with a green, gold-nibbed fountain pen pages of notes for his monu-mental, never-to-be-completed thesis, letters to other experts, and articles for publication in learned journals – Alfie's grandmother would later type copies of these, using an ancient black type-writer – or closely examining patterns on pieces of pottery or notches on fragments of bone with a huge magnifying glass whose cracked ivory handle had been thriftily mended with parcel tape, or making careful, minutely cross-hatched drawings with a set of Rotring pens on creamy sheets of heavy art paper. Now the stacks of notes and drawings, the neatly filed letters and every other scrap of paper had been cleared from the desk and its rack of pigeon-holes. Alfie tiptoed to the window and looked at the house through the bare winter trees, then tiptoed back to the desk like a burglar. There was something he simply had to know.

Last summer, barefoot, practising being as silent as an Indian brave, he had stolen into the shed just as his grandfather had been taking out a rolled-up sheet of paper from a compartment hidden inside the desk. The old man had calmly put the roll of paper away and had made Alfie swear, hand on heart, that he would not tell anyone about it, that it would be their own private secret, and that he would never, ever try to open the drawer and look at what was inside. Now Alfie reasoned to himself that it was his duty to see if the two men had taken this mysterious piece of paper. With his pulse beating in his throat, he pulled out the shallow central drawer, full of pencil stubs and half-used rolls of Sellotape, odd lengths of string and the metal rulers and the device like a compass with two points with which his grandfather had made measurements of his shards and stones and bones, carefully set it on the floor beside the desk, and reached inside the space into which it fitted and pressed the panel at the back. It yielded with a solid click and sprang loose; Alfie pulled it open and with-drew the rolled-up sheet of paper. It was yellow with age, and tied with a piece of black ribbon. There was also a soft leather pouch fastened with a drawstring – the pouch in which Alfie's grandfather had kept the powder that he'd added to his pipe tobacco.

Alfie remembered the clean thrill he'd felt when the secret drawer had yielded its treasure, remembered how he'd made a commando-style dash across the lawn and safely reached his bedroom, out of breath, his heart pounding. But he couldn't remember what had happened after that. There was a gap, a blank, and then he was lying in bed, feeble and confused, with his father sitting beside him.

Mick Flowers, angry and upset and, worst of all, trying to hide the fact that he was more than a little frightened, told Alfie that he'd had a fit after he'd tasted his grandfather's secret powder and looked at something he shouldn't have looked at. Alfie supposed that he must have untied the ribbon and unrolled the sheet of paper, but he couldn't remember doing it, and couldn't remember what he'd seen, either, couldn't remember if it had been a drawing or a diagram or a magic spell. Whatever it was, it had done more to him than give him a fit. It had put a twist in his brain. It had left its mark. That night, Alfie was possessed by vivid nightmares in which monstrous faces took shape from clouds of swirling dots and lines; the next day, he suffered another fit and, against the wishes of his grandmother, was taken to see an old friend of the family, Mr Prentiss, who devised the treatment that had more or less cured him.

A year later, Alfie still had the occasional minor episode. He'd get a funny taste in his mouth, sharp and sour as burning metal, and the world would jump like a bad splice in a film, but it was no big deal, not much worse than a stutter or a nervous twitch. He hadn't once been struck by a full-blown epileptic seizure like those suffered by the pale, nervous boy in the year below his at the boarding school. He didn't fall down and jerk about and make animal noises, and he no longer woke sweating and mute with terror from dreams of monsters that swam out of garish patterns, but although Mr Prentiss's treatment kept the bad fits and night-mares at bay, it didn't mean that Alfie liked it. It wasn't only that it reminded him of what he had done, but it was creepy and weird, too. He knew that it was necessary, but he also knew that he would never get used to it.

Mick Flowers glued together four cigarette papers to make a square, creased it down the middle, and dropped strands of tobacco in the bottom of the crease. He unwrapped a little cube of aluminium foil and crumbled a little of the rich black Moroccan hash into the tobacco, then reached inside his jacket and lifted out a small bag of soft leather that hung on his chest from a loop of soft black twine. With his back to the wind, he tugged at the drawstring that held the neck of the bag closed, took out a pinch of grey dust and sprinkled it on the mix of tobacco and hash, rolled up the joint and sealed it at either end with a neat twist.

Alfie watched this ritual with a hollow feeling. The little bag was his grandfather's, the very same bag that he had found in the secret compartment, along with the piece of paper. His grandfather had used the dust it contained to salt his own special tobacco mix, made up for him in a little shop on Charing Cross Road. Once upon a time, in a rare expansive mood, he'd told Alfie that the dust was the dried extract from a plant called haka, which had sprung up in the footsteps of Adam and Eve after their expulsion from the Garden of Eden, somewhere to the north of Baghdad.

Mick Flowers lit the joint with a snap of his Zippo, breathed in a deep, crackling toke and passed it to Alfie, who dutifully sucked on its wet teat. He'd been sick the first time he'd smoked one of these special cigarettes, but he was used to the rich sweet taste now. Without being told, he took the smoke deep into his lungs and held it there before exhaling. Mick Flowers watched sidelong, idly drawing dots and wavy lines in the sand with a stick. When Alfie had smoked the joint down to a nubbin, he passed it to his father, who pinched it in a little piece of rolled cardboard and took a final drag before tossing the roach into the glowing embers. Looking sidelong at his son, saying, 'Do you see them?'

Alfie nodded. He was staring into the heart of the fire, where sparks snapped and jumped among glowing embers. His father leaned in and stroked his neck, murmuring the incantation that put him under. Alfie knew that he was being hypnotized and slyly thought to himself that this time he would resist, or he would suddenly jump up and chase around the fire or run off into the dark. But it was easier to do nothing, to sit with the fire parching his face and the wind chilling his back while the familiar patterns crawled through the shivering heart of the fire and his father's voice rose and fell with the sound of the waves collapsing on the beach, a meaningless but soothing murmur . . .

Presently, Alfie passed from a light hypnotic trance into sleep. Mick Flowers stood, worked the stiff knee where a fragment of

KK246027

shrapnel was still lodged, and gathered his son's slack body into his arms. He kicked sand over the embers of the fire and carried Alfie through the dunes to where the little red sports car crouched. Behind him, the tide crept up the beach, touching and retouching with fingers of lacy foam the patterns he'd idly drawn in the sand. Then, with a sudden bold surge, it erased them and with another put out the fire.

The next day, Mick Flowers flew to Beirut. A week later, the flat he rented in London was destroyed by a fire. Three days after that, the British embassy in Beirut received an envelope containing his bloodstained passport.

His body was never found.

PART ONE
THE SEARCH

1

Alfie Flowers's past returned to him through the window of a 73 bus, in a flash of black light.

It was a sunny afternoon in London, the last week in May. Alfie had been photographing lichens on gravestones and trees in Abney Park, a large, overgrown Victorian cemetery that widened out in unexpected directions from its entrance on Stoke Newington Church Street. Volunteers were restoring it section by section, clearing graves of brambles and elder and sycamores, uncovering heaved and tumbled headstones, revealing new perspectives of sunlight. After several hours of wandering along paths softly heaped with fresh sawdust, Alfie, pleasantly tired, had snagged the prime position on the double-decker bus: on the top, the front seat on the left-hand side. The bus had almost immediately become stuck in a traffic jam because one of the utility companies was digging up the road and had reduced it to a single lane, but Alfie didn't mind. He wasn't in a hurry. He was a street photographer, a snapper of the city's unconsidered trifles and cast of eccentrics, scraping by on an exiguous income of royalties and residuals from pictures reprinted from his father's archive. He didn't have a schedule; currently he had no ties. There was no one waiting for him at home. He had all the time in the world. He sprawled in luxurious disarray on the front seat, sipping a banana-flavoured milk shake and watching people passing along the pavement on the other side of the street, which, where the bus had stalled, was pinched like a wrung neck.

That was when Alfie saw it. Bright as a shard of sun glancing off glass, except that it was black – a black circle splashed on the window of a restaurant, nagging at his attention, doubling into broad iridescent discs floating behind his eyelids when he tried to blink it away. It tickled his brain, woke old memories. It was an unscratchable itch, a sneeze that wouldn't come, a word lurking on the back of his tongue.

Some way up the street, in front of the trench where no one was currently working, the temporary traffic light turned green. The bus snorted and shuddered and started to move; Alfie blinked, gathered up his camera bag, stumbled along the gangway and down the stairs, jumped from the open platform to the pavement.

The splash of black on the plate-glass window of the restaurant, a Jamaican place painted yellow and green and red, seemed to swim and wobble, like the kind of optical illusion that keeps reversing its perspective. It reached out with a snaky maw, it was a tunnel or whirlpool hoovering up every speck of Alfie's sensibility. He took an involuntary step towards it and a van brushed past less than a foot away, sounding its horn. He danced back, saw a man in the black trousers and white shirt of a waiter come out of the passageway at the side of the restaurant, carrying a zinc bucket slopping suds.

Alfie's heart was suddenly pounding. There was the taste of burnt metal in his mouth. On the other side of the road, the waiter dipped a wad of steel wool in the sudsy bucket, wrung it out, and began to rub at the edge of the black circle. Alfie called out, asked him to stop please for just a moment, but his voice didn't carry over the noise of the traffic and the unheeding waiter continued to scrape away at the pattern, so he pulled his Nikon from his bag, jammed on the zoom lens, focused with trembling fingers, and fired off several shots.

By the time the traffic light changed back to red and Alfie was able to cross the road, the circle was already half-erased. The waiter, a slim young black man, watched him approach, a wary hostility beginning to harden in his gaze. Alfie was used to that look: many people, seeing his height, the breadth of his shoulders barely contained by his distressed leather jacket, the bland dish of his face under blond hair cut short in no particular style, assumed that he was an off-duty or plain-clothes policeman. A few days ago, while he had been waiting to cross Caledonian Road, a vagrant had wandered up and accused him of following him. Alfie made the mistake of looking around. The vagrant, bouncing on his toes, his fists balled up inside the pockets of his denim jacket, probably clutching a length of pipe or a sharpened screwdriver, eyes red and tender in bruised sockets from too much toking or snorting, leaned in close, his breath metallic and awful, saying, 'You can't fool me, man. I *know* you're police. I *know* you been following me.'

Alfie did what he always did in situations like that. He behaved like a policeman, staring straight into the man's face, asking him where he was going. The man's aggression evaporated in the glare of this frontal challenge. He averted his blood-charged eyes, meekly pointed with his elbow, up the hill, past the high white walls of Pentonville prison. 'I'm going straight on across the road,' Alfie said, 'so I won't be following you, will I?' Adding as the man began to shuffle off, unable to resist it, 'Mind how you go.'

Now, confronting the waiter's incipient hostility, Alfie fished a business card from his leather jacket and said, with what he hoped was a winning smile, 'I'm a photographer. A freelance photographer. Would you mind waiting for a moment while I take a picture of that?'

It was a thorny ring encircling a stencilled cartoon of an American soldier about to stamp on the head of a prostrate, large-eyed child. Dashes and circles, grids and sway-backed lines, zigzags like exploding lightning, several dozen bold, simple shapes interlocked like an insanely complicated clock mechanism, the whole thing about a yard across. Half-erased, it no longer had any power over Alfie. It was just a weird pattern framing a simple-minded piece of political graffiti.

The waiter studied Alfie's card, said doubtfully, 'I have to clean it off right now, we're about to open.'

Alfie reached into his pocket again, extracted the folded ten-pound note he kept there in case he needed extra persuasion and held it up, cocked between thumb and forefinger. 'For your trouble. It'll only take a minute.'

The waiter took the note, shrugged. 'Why you interested in this shit?'

Alfie was changing the lens of his Nikon. 'I'm interested in all kinds of things. People, the things people do, anything on the streets. Stand just a little to the left, could you, out of the light? Thanks.'

He took three shots, bracketing the exposure, took out the

little Olympus he used for candid photographs and took two more shots, just in case. The waiter told him that he hadn't seen anything like it before, he had no idea who had done it, it hadn't been there when the restaurant had closed up last night.

'Someone put their name to it, though,' he said. 'See?'

Alfie didn't, until the waiter pointed it out. Neatly printed beneath the cartoon, curved to fit inside the thorny ring, was the signature of the artist.

Morph.

'So you saw the first one on a restaurant window,' Toby Brown said, a week later. 'What about the others?'

'Basically, Hackney and Bow,' Alfie said. 'Elliot drove me around and about, and we managed to spot more than twenty of them. Four different cartoons, all in the same frame, all signed by Morph. But I found the best examples, like the one you're looking at, when I took a walk along the canal. It seems to be his favourite spot.'

It was the middle of the morning, the sun playing hide-and-seek among an armada of stately white clouds. Alfie and Toby were sitting in the scruffy little patio garden of Toby's basement flat. Alfie was nerved up because he had come here to ask his best friend to help him to look for Morph, find out who he was. He'd already tried to ask his grandmother if she had ever seen anything like Morph's graffiti, but it had been one of her bad days, and she had completely ignored the photographs he'd shown her. He'd shown them to his agent, too, had asked her if his father had ever taken pictures of graffiti – Lucinda had also been his father's agent, back in the day.

'Not that I recall, darling,' Lucinda had said. 'I can check the files, of course, just to be sure . . .'

'I'm sure you're right,' Alfie had said hastily, knowing that Lucinda had more or less complete recall of every one of her clients' photographs. She'd asked if this was a new project and hadn't looked convinced when he'd told her that it was nothing really, just something that had caught his eye. But she'd given him the benefit of the doubt and had changed the subject, telling him about a nibble from a German publisher who was thinking of reprinting a collection of Mick Flowers's early work as a street photographer in the 1960s, documenting London's street markets, greyhound tracks and coffee bars.

'I can't promise much in the way of an advance, darling, times being what they are, but I'll keep you informed.'

Alfie had managed to avoid explaining to Lucinda why he was so interested in Morph's graffiti, why he thought it might have something to do with his epilepsy and his father's disappearance, but he knew that if he was going to persuade Toby to help him, he would have to tell his friend the whole sorry story. He'd spent all last night nerving himself up, rehearsing what he was going to say and how he was going to say it, convincing himself that it was for the best, that it was the only way forward. Now, on the brink, he felt the yawning anticipation of a parachutist about to make his first jump, his palms pricking with nervous sweat while Toby frowned his way through the sheaf of photographs.

Toby Brown was a deep-dyed Grub Street hack a couple of years older than Alfie, slightly built, habitually dressed in black, and recently divorced; the basement flat was rented, its living room stacked with boxes of books he hadn't yet unpacked. He wrote interest pieces and movie reviews for local newspapers, hustled the occasional article or news story into the nationals, and reviewed every kind of book for newspapers and magazines. If you wanted an intelligent and entertaining overview of the memoirs of a minor cabinet minister, a popular history of the Third Crusade, a travelogue written by a best-selling author on his year off, or of the biography of a minor seventeenth-century courtesan, then Toby Brown was your man. Unlike most of his peers, he was neither a failed novelist nor an aspiring screenwriter. He believed hack-work to be an honourable profession, and earned a comfortable living by juggling multiple deadlines and tirelessly badgering editors for further employment. He and Alfie had long ago evolved a loose but profitable working relationship. When Alfie had to supply a couple of hundred words to accompany a photograph he'd sold, he'd ask Toby; when Toby needed a photograph to illustrate one of his pieces, he'd ask Alfie.

Toby said now, 'These are all by the same kid? Morph – that can't be his real name.'

'It's his tag – his street name, his handle, the name he uses to sign his pieces, his flicks. Elliot has a cousin who knows the scene. He says that Morph has been on the street for a month now, but no one knows who he is. No one has seen him, no one has talked to him, he doesn't hang out with anyone or use any of the tagger bulletin boards on the internet. But he's admired by the cognoscenti, even though he uses stencils to make his pieces, which I'm given to understand is usually frowned on. Hard-core taggers do their throw-ups and their four-colour burners – those giant cartoons with the balloon lettering? They do them freestyle. Morph uses a stencil, and always just the one colour, black. But even so, he's getting a good reputation. There's a talk-show host on a pirate radio station who's bigging him up.'

Alfie paused, out of breath, realizing that he'd been babbling and discovering that he didn't care. He was fired up by reckless exhilaration. He was ready to jump.

'"Hard-core taggers". "Bigging him up". You're getting very "street", Flowers.'

As usual, Toby's lopsided smile was clamped around a cigarette. He used up two or three packs a day. His black jeans and his faded black linen shirt, its sleeves rolled up above his elbows, were liberally speckled with cigarette ash. He had a pale, sharp-chinned face under a flop of disordered black hair. His dark eyes, set close together, regarded Alfie with fond amusement.

'I'm quoting Elliot's cousin,' Alfie said. He refused to be embarrassed. This was too important.

'Well, Morph may be famous on the street, but I've never heard of him. Why the interest?'

'Take another look at his pieces.'

Toby shuffled through the photographs again. 'I suppose they're not bad, as graffiti go. So this guy, this tagger, seems to have a political agenda. Is there anything else I should know? Because if you think I can turn this into a story, think again. Even with the anti-American angle, it's pretty thin stuff.'

'Forget the cartoons for a minute,' Alfie said. 'The cartoons aren't the point. Take a good look at the pattern that frames them.'

Toby picked up one of the photographs and held it close to

his face, held it out at arm's length, turned it around. 'I'm missing something, aren't I? What am I missing?'

'It doesn't do anything to you? It doesn't look odd, it doesn't jump out at you?'

'If this is about some kind of hidden image or message, you'll have to spell it out. Remember those optical illusions that were everywhere for a couple of years in the early 90's? A bunch of wavy lines that if you looked at them in the right way were supposed to turn into a 3-D picture of a bunch of galloping horses? You were supposed to relax your eyes, and it would somehow jump into focus, but I never got it. Same here. You're going to have to tell me what this is all about, Flowers. You're going to have to clue me in.'

Alfie sat back, took a breath. *Geronimo.* 'It's something from my past. And from my father's and my grandfather's pasts too.'

'From when your father was a spy?'

'He wasn't exactly a spy.'

'From when he was working for MI6 on a casual basis, then. What do these cartoons have to do with it?'

'It's the pattern around the cartoons.'

Toby scrutinized the photograph again. 'I still don't see it.'

'That's the point.'

'You'll have to be clearer, Flowers. There's a lot of static coming through. Try telling it from A to B in words of one syllable or less.'

'You know that I have epileptic seizures.'

Toby nodded. 'When you go away inside your head for a moment or two.'

'They're what's called clean absence seizures. The kind caused by classic petit mal epilepsy, except mine are atypical because they're not general seizures that affect the entire brain, they're focal seizures that affect only part of it. And they're accompanied by an aura, a weird sort of thunderstormy feeling. The aura, the weird feeling, is the focal onset of the seizure. I can feel myself going away. I can watch the part of my brain that's having the seizure.' Alfie realized that he was babbling again, and cut to the chase. 'I had a lot of tests when I was a kid. The doctors identified the part of my brain where the seizures were taking place. It's in the visual cortex.'

Soon after his father had disappeared in Lebanon, Alfie had suffered two major fits in a single day and had been admitted to Addenbrookes Hospital in Cambridge, where he'd been diagnosed with atypical partial epileptic seizures with secondary generalization and prescribed the sedative phenobarbitone. He was still taking phenobarbitone, was in fact chronically dependent on it, trying to keep the dosage to a minimum by supplementing it with benzodiazepine or clonazepam obtained from an acquaintance who worked in a drug-dependency clinic. He took Valium too, to maintain his equilibrium. He was an expert in self-medication, constantly monitoring and modifying his emotional weather.

Toby said, 'And this has what to do with these cartoons?'

'It doesn't have anything to do with the cartoons,' Alfie said. 'But it does have everything to do with the pattern that frames them. It has everything to do with what I see, and what you don't see. I mean, what do you see?'

'I suppose it looks a little like a crown of thorns.'

'It doesn't seem to move?'

'I told you, when it comes to spotting optical illusions, I'm not the sharpest ship in the harbour.'

'You see a static pattern. I see something alive. Something that pulses and spins.'

'Because of your epilepsy.'

'How long have we known each other?'

Toby Brown gave Alfie a serious look. 'Can I ask – no kidding around – are you okay?'

'Something like eight years?'

'Because you look a little on edge. More than a little, actually.'

'Eight years? Nine?'

'Around nine, I suppose.'

'I want to tell you something. Something I haven't told anyone else.'

'As long as you won't have to kill me afterwards, I'm all ears. Sorry,' Toby said, when Alfie gave him a look. 'I know. This is serious shit. What is it?'

'Some old family history,' Alfie said, and with a sense of falling through airy space told Toby about what had happened after his grandfather had died. The two men who had taken away his grandfather's papers and his collection of ancient artefacts. How he'd sneaked into his grandfather's study and looked at the sheet of paper hidden inside the secret drawer of the desk, and what it had done to him.

When Alfie was finished, Toby lit a fresh cigarette, snapping his lighter and bending to its pale flame. 'How can you be sure that it did something to you? That it wasn't just shock or, I don't know, grief?'

'I was all right before I looked at it. And afterwards, I had epilepsy.'

'But you don't remember what you saw. What was on this famous sheet of paper.' Toby was leaning forward, excited and pleased by Alfie's story, his close-set eyes shining with intelligence. 'It could have been a magic spell, or it could have been a picture of Barney the dinosaur.'

'I think it was a little before Barney's time.'

'The point is, what makes you so certain that whatever was on that sheet of paper has something to do with Morph's little artworks? How are you going to convince me that you aren't as nutty as a fruit bat?'

'This is going to sound nutty, actually, but Morph's graffiti affect me. Or rather, the pattern around them affects me. It's like the sun in my eyes, or fingers stirring around inside my head. It's a little like the aura I mentioned, the feeling I get before an attack. Also, I remember that my grandfather had a couple of flat stones, he called them plaquettes, that were incised with the same kind of patterns as the stuff Morph puts around his cartoons. And there's something else.'

Alfie rummaged in his camera bag, brought out a small flat box, and took off the lid.

Toby Brown leaned further forward and looked at the thumb-sized shard of time-blackened stone, framed with silver filigree, that nestled on time-yellowed cotton wool.

'That's very nice. But it doesn't mean we're engaged or anything, does it?'

'Tell me what you see.'

'I see marks,' Toby said. 'Dots over a wavy line. What is this, one of your grandfather's bits of stone? One of those plaques?'

'Plaquettes. No, they were taken away with the rest of my grandfather's stuff. This belonged to my father. He gave it to one of his girlfriends, the day before he disappeared. But the pattern on it is the same kind of pattern that was on my grandfather's plaquettes, and you can see the same kind of thing in the frame around Morph's cartoons.'

Toby sat back, favouring Alfie with his liquid, conjoined gaze. 'So, what are you trying to say? That these mysterious patterns not only caused your epilepsy but also have something to do with the graffiti patterns?'

Alfie twirled a finger next to his temple. 'I know, crazy as a soup sandwich.'

'You should definitely check your roof for loose pigeons.'

'She lived in Lebanon,' Alfie said.

'This girlfriend.'

'In Beirut.' Alfie paused, then said, 'I met her once.'

'Before you tell me the rest of the story, let's refresh our drinks.'

'I have a milk shake right here in my bag, thanks.'

'Of course you do. Bear with me while I get a refreshing beverage. It's a couple of hours before I usually indulge, but what the hell.'

After Toby had settled back in his chair, Alfie said, 'When I inherited my yard, there was an old caravan on the site. It hadn't been touched since my father disappeared. Since he died. He was something of a ladies' man, and he'd stashed letters from his various girlfriends there. I found them in a sugar tin. I suppose he didn't want one of his girlfriends rummaging around his flat and finding billets-doux from old flames. There were a dozen or so from a woman in Beirut, and I wondered if she might know something about what happened to him. So I played detective. I looked up a copy of the Beirut telephone directory in the Camden Library, spent a small fortune on long-distance telephone calls, and eventually got through to one of the woman's brothers. He told me that she'd married and moved to America, but wouldn't tell me where. I thought that was that, and I more or less forgot about it until she phoned me out of the blue, about a year later. She was in London, on holiday. We met, we talked about my father, and she gave me this piece of stone.'

Alfie remembered waiting for the woman, formerly Miriam Haddad, now Mrs Miriam Luttwak, in the lounge of the Savoy Hotel. Nervous and uncomfortable in his only suit, which seemed to have shrunk at least a size since he'd worn it last, at his graduation ceremony at Bristol University. He remembered that Miriam Luttwak had been older than he had expected, a trim middle-aged woman, hair piled high in a glossy blonde beehive, moving straight towards him through the clutter of plush armchairs and low tables. He remembered how she'd kissed him on both cheeks and said that he was definitely his father's son, she would have recognized him anywhere.

Over tea and scones, she explained that she had married an American doctor, a surgeon who had been doing voluntary work in the Palestinian refugee camps. When her husband's tour of duty had finished she had gone with him to America, to Boston. Before that, she had been working as an interpreter; she had worked with Mick Flowers when he had first come to Lebanon to cover the civil war, and they had quickly become close friends. She told Alfie that his father had stayed with her that last time in Beirut, that he had come and gone on business he would not tell her about, something that had involved another Englishman, although she'd never met her father's friend and didn't know his name. They had hired a car to drive to Syria, and that was when they had disappeared.

'The war was five years old then. It was a bad time for Europeans to drive alone through the country. I pleaded with him, Alfie,' Miriam Luttwak said, her gaze steady and serious. 'I told him to wait, I would arrange an escort. My brother was in the Christian militia, the Phalangists. With a little money it would have been possible to arrange an escort as far as the border. With a little more, to arrange for someone to help your father and his friend once they reached Syria. But your father said that it was a delicate negotiation, that if he turned up with a third party it would frighten off the people he and his friend were going to meet.'

'Where exactly were they going? Who were they supposed to meet?'

'I don't know. But I can tell you that when he left, he was carrying a lot of money in American dollars.'

'He was going to buy something.'

'I believe so.' Miriam Luttwak reached into her handbag and took out a small box, setting it in the middle of the low table between their armchairs, next to the silver teapot. 'A few days before he left, he gave me this. He said that it was very old. He also said that he wanted me to have it, for safe keeping. Later, when I knew that he would not be coming back, I had it mounted.'

Alfie picked up the piece of stone and ran his finger over the incised markings.

Miriam Luttwak watched him closely. 'You know something about it, I think.'

'My grandfather collected things like this. Very old things.'

'I think that your father and his friend were involved with tomb-robbers and smugglers. In the Middle East, people can make good money digging up treasures and selling them on the black market to collectors, or to agents who work for museums. Perhaps your father was trying to buy something important.'

Suddenly, unexpectedly, Miriam Luttwak tipped her head back. Alfie realized with a pang of embarrassment that she was crying, that she did not want the tears to ruin her make-up.

She drew a handkerchief from the sleeve of her jacket and dabbed carefully at her eyes, saying, 'He was very dear to me. He was quite the bravest man I knew, and a true artist with the camera. Every one of his photographs held a truth.' She sniffed delicately, folded the handkerchief away. 'I am sure you know that your father was famous for taking very few photographs. The other photographers would take a picture in black and white, and then shoot the same scene in colour, for coverage. Your father always used either one or the other. He said that some things demanded black and white, others colour, and it did not do to mix the two. He once rode with the Phalangists for three days, was involved in a battle that left two of them dead and five wounded, and in all that time he shot only two rolls of film. Another time, he came across some Christian youths celebrating over the body of a teenage Muslim girl. He was told by his escort that he would be killed if he took any pictures, but he took one anyway. He once told me, perhaps he told you this too, Alfie, that it was not worth taking a picture simply for the sake of taking a picture. That it was best to know when to take one, and when not to. He saw the world very clearly. More clearly than anyone else I have ever met. He had a poetic eye for the truth of the world — does that make sense to you?'

'Yes. Yes, it does.'

'You must keep this too,' Miriam Luttwak said, pushing the box across the table. 'His letters, I burned those before I married, you understand. And I am ashamed to say that I also burned the few photographs I had of him. But this, this is yours.'

'I can't take—'

'You will.' Miriam Luttwak glanced at her expensive gold watch and exclaimed that she had an appointment that she must keep. She and Alfie rose together, air-kissed awkwardly across the table, above the little shard of stone, and then she was gone.

In the scruffy, sun-dappled patio garden, Toby Brown said, 'And then what?'

Alfie said, 'And then I never saw her again.'

'I mean, is that it? She gave you this piece of stone, which your father gave her just before he disappeared, and you didn't try to find out what it was?'

'I knew that it was from something very old, I knew that the markings on it were like those on some of the Stone Age artefacts that my grandfather collected. What I didn't know was what it meant, and no, I didn't try to find out. I did ask my grandmother about it, but she told me that it wasn't her business, and it wasn't mine either. She told me to forget about it. She told me to let the past stay in the past, where it belonged. And for a long time that's just what I did. I was trying to maintain some kind of equilibrium in my life because stress increases the frequency of my seizures, and, frankly, I sort of forgot about it. And then I saw my first example of Morph's graffiti, and it all came back to me, all at once.'

There was a pause. An airliner dragged its roar above the fleet of clouds. A bird essayed a few experimental notes somewhere beyond the ivy-covered walls of the little garden.

At last, Toby said, 'So, how can I help you?'

Alfie smiled. 'Am I so transparent?'

'Why else would you have coughed up this painful confession?'

KILKENNY COUNTY LIBRARY

'I want to find this graffiti artist because he knows something about these patterns. Perhaps he can help me understand what happened when I looked at something I shouldn't have looked at. And what happened to my father. Perhaps . . . This is such a long shot that I don't really want to think about it, but if one of these patterns damaged me, perhaps there's another that can cure me.'

'And you think that I can help you find this guy.'

'I thought that your extensive contacts in the media might turn up something about him. If it's any help, I think he's from Iraq.'

'Because of his cartoons? I'm not so sure. There are plenty of people living right here who are against the invasion of Iraq. Alison marched against it twice. As she keeps reminding me, it did her sense of self-worth no end of good.'

Alison was Toby's ex-wife. Although they had obtained a no-fault divorce several months ago, she and Toby were still bickering as much as ever.

Alfie said, 'My grandfather worked in Iraq, before the war. That's where he became interested in ancient history, and I think that's where the plaquettes came from – the stones with the patterns on them.'

'Or he could have picked them up at an auction, or the local church jumble sale.'

'Also, Lebanon and Syria are next door to Iraq.'

And the drug that Alfie's grandfather had smoked, which had also been part of Mr Prentiss's treatment, had come from Iraq, but Alfie wasn't ready to tell Toby about that. He already felt that he'd told him too much.

'If you want me to help you,' Toby said, suddenly all business, 'you're going to have to let me do it my way.'

'Absolutely.'

'Leave these photographs with me. I'll get right on it.'

Half an hour later, Alfie was riding the bus home when his mobile rang. It was Toby. 'One of your photographs is going to be published in tomorrow's *Independent*,' he said.

Alfie felt a sudden knot in his chest. 'You're writing this up? Toby, that wasn't the deal.'

'I pitched an article about Morph, not you and your weird

family. The news-desk editor wouldn't take the story, but he asked me to send over your photographs. So I scanned a couple and emailed them to him, and he's going to use one to illustrate a piece about the results of an opinion poll about whether we should have invaded Iraq, the effect on the government's credibility, et cetera, et cetera.'

'And how will this help me find Morph?'

'First, it earns you five hundred quid, less my very reasonable commission. At some stage we'll probably need to bribe someone in Customs and Immigration to get hold of the names of all the refugees who recently arrived from Iraq, so don't turn your nose up at it. Second, it's possible that the photo will tickle Morph's ego. Maybe he'll ask for a copy. It'll be printed over your name, and maybe he'll get in touch. Any time you want to thank me, go right ahead. I won't mind.'

Alfie was wondering who else might be interested in the photograph – in Morph's graffiti. He was still in free fall, but now that the ground was rushing up to meet him there was no going back. He said, 'I suppose it's a plan.'

'It's *my* plan,' Toby said. 'How can it not work?'

2

Harriet Crowley's family had an affiliation with the British secret service that went back to the Second World War. Like most traditions in these brave new egalitarian times, that no longer counted for much, but because she'd helped Six unravel a nasty little affair in Nigeria three years ago, it took only a week to arrange a face-to-face meeting with her new handler. (The agent with whom she'd worked previously, a courtly, silver-haired man who'd possessed a colourful collection of bow ties and the driest sense of humour she'd ever encountered, had died of lung cancer last year.) But now, at eight in the morning, the new man was half an hour late, and Harriet was starting on her third cup of coffee and beginning to wonder if she was going to have to deal with the plague of glyphs and all it implied without any official help.

She was waiting in the corner of an Italian restaurant – tables covered with red and white chequered tablecloths scattered between fat pillars, the usual football memorabilia tacked to the wall behind the hissing Gaggia – in the basement of an office building close to Vauxhall Cross, the unlovely headquarters of MI6 that squatted beside Vauxhall Bridge like the offspring of an unwise coupling between an Aztec temple and a nuclear power station. Wearing her best trouser suit, a pearl-grey number from Karen Millen, blonde hair scraped back from her pale face, the temporary ID badge required for entry into the building clipped to her lapel, she was quietly anonymous among the dozen or so customers, just the way she liked it, reading her Penguin Classics edition of *David Copperfield*, taking a tiny sip of coffee each time she turned a page. She was used to waiting – it was a large part of her regular job – and she knew better than to phone and ask why her handler was late, or if he was even going to arrive. She decided that she'd give him another half-hour, if he didn't show then *que sera sera*, she'd have to try to chase down Morph on her own, to hell with the consequences.

He slid into the chair opposite Harriet's a few minutes before her deadline, calling to the waiter by name, asking for a glass of tap water. A tall man in his late thirties, sun-streaked brown hair worn collar-length, his face deeply tanned, a button-down blue linen shirt, sunglasses hooked in the breast pocket. A perfect specimen of the raffish public-school, Oxbridge-educated former special services type that haunted the Cross, telling Harriet, with a lazy smile that revealed half an acre of white teeth, 'I had the idea that the Nomads' Club was no more than a couple of crusty codgers left over from the good old days of the Empire. May I say how pleased I am to discover that I was very much mistaken.'

'I'm not exactly a member,' Harriet said.

'I understand you're in a flap about something or other. I can give you —' the man made a production of looking at his watch, a chunky number with so many dials and buttons that it might well have been the remote control for a nuclear submarine '— ten minutes. Fire away at will.'

'Do you have a name?'

'They didn't tell you? What am I thinking, of course they didn't tell you. I'm Jonathon Nicholl. My friends call me Jack.'

'I'll call you Mr Nicholl.'

'Do I detect a smidgen of hostility?'

'I was good friends with a charmer very like you a few years ago.'

'And I suppose he broke your heart.'

'Something like that.'

'Name the rogue and I'll call him out for you. Pistols at dawn on Hampstead Heath.'

'Or rocket launchers on the Millennium Dome?'

Jack Nicholl grinned. 'Whatever you like. Seriously. Was this heartbreaker anyone I would know?'

Harriet couldn't help being a little charmed by him — MI6 handlers were trained to be charming — but she knew that his charm was velvet over steel. She gave him her nicest smile and said, 'That's classified information.'

'Classified information is my business. And talking of business, I suppose we should get back to the matter at hand,' Jack Nicholl said, thanking the waiter when he placed a glass of water on the table.

'I have the samples right here,' Harriet said. She drew the A5 envelope from her compact leather rucksack and tipped half a dozen photographs onto the tablecloth, next to the little cut-glass vase which held a spray of silk flowers.

Jack Nicholl swept them up and with the brisk snap of a Las Vegas blackjack dealer turned them face down. 'I rather think you ought to be a little more discreet.'

'You asked me to meet you in public.'

'*Touché.* Suppose you tell me what they are.'

'Photographs of graffiti. Specifically, graffiti with an anti-inva-sion-of-Iraq flavour.'

Jack Nicholl showed his teeth again. 'I believe that "liberation" is the politically correct term.'

'Someone who signs himself Morph is putting them up all over East London.'

'And we should be interested because . . .'

'Because he's using a glyph to frame his cartoons.'

'Ah yes. I flicked through the files, of course. Very interesting and all that, but ancient history in more ways than one, isn't it?'

'I assume you read the file about the debacle in Nigeria. That happened just three years ago.'

'Mmm, and a nasty business it was too. But what isn't, in this line of work? So, what's the connection between your Nigerian adventure and this graffiti artist?'

Harriet had thought long and hard about that, making lists of names and dates, tangling them together with arrows. There were question marks beside most of the arrows. She admitted, 'I don't think that there's a direct connection. I think it has more to do with the source of the glyphs.'

Jack Nicholl considered that, then said, 'If that's true, it might cause complications, given the present situation. The glyph he uses, is it – what's the word?'

'Potent. Yes, it is. It's a version of the fascination glyph used in propaganda leaflets dropped over Occupied France during the Second World War. Without the drug, the effect is very weak, of course—'

'Of course,' Jack Nicholl said, raising one eyebrow.

Harriet couldn't tell if he was mocking her or not, and decided to give him the benefit of the doubt. She dug out the previous day's copy of the *Independent* and showed Jack Nicholl the photograph on page four. 'There's a possible complication. Someone else has spotted Morph's work.'

Jack Nicholl shrugged. 'It doesn't necessarily mean anything.'

'Look at the byline.'

'Alfie Flowers . . . Hmm, that does ring a dim and distant bell.'

'His father died during an operation in Lebanon.'

'Of course, the photojournalist. A man after my own heart, by all accounts. But his son isn't one of ours, and I don't believe he's one of yours, either, so how did he stumble into the picture?'

Harriet was impressed. Jack Nicholl's languid air disguised a sharp mind. 'As far as I know, he doesn't know anything about the Nomads' Club, but he was hurt by a glyph when he was a boy – an accident after his grandfather died. From what I understand, the accident could have sensitized him.'

Jack Nicholl thought about this. 'So Mr Flowers sees these graffiti and knows that they are unusual, but he might not know *why* they are unusual.'

'And then again he might.'

'Have you made contact with him?'

'Of course not.'

Clarence Ashburton and Julius Ward, the two surviving members of the Nomads' Club, had advised against it. 'There's no need to stir up that muddy little pond,' Clarence had said. 'We must respect the wishes of his grandmother,' Julius had said. Harriet had been certain that the two old men shared a secret that they wanted to keep from her, but she hadn't pressed them for an explanation. The Nomads' Club was a tangle of old secrets, failed intrigues, and half-forgotten conspiracies that no longer had any meaning. Secrets were about all that it had left.

Jack Nicholl said, 'Do you want us to make contact with him?'

'I think he might need to be watched, for his own good. If he goes looking for Morph, he might stumble into trouble by mistake.'

'What about the graffiti artist?'

'Obviously, he should be found as quickly as possible.'

'I suppose that "Morph" is his nom de plume. Do you have any idea who he really is?'

'He doesn't have a police record, but I do wonder if he might not have an immigration record.'

'I thought those shepherds or whatever they were had been wiped out long ago.'

'The Kefidis. They're no longer living where they used to live, but it's possible that some of them might have survived. And it's also possible that one of them might have made his way here, legally or illegally.'

'It rather sounds as if it's a matter for the plods over at MI5.'

'I no more want to share information with MI5 than you do.'

'Nicely put.' For the first time, Jack Nicholl looked at her with real interest. 'Well, I rather think we'll leave Mr Flowers alone for the time being. He'll have to look out for himself. Or perhaps the Nomads' Club can do something for him, as he's the son of a distinguished former member. As for Morph, I suppose I could put out a feeler or two. If I come up with something, I'll get back to you.'

Meaning, I'll call you, don't even think of calling me.

'Thank you,' Harriet said, and meant it. It was a lot more than she had expected.

'Think nothing of it,' Jack Nicholl said, and picked up the photographs. 'May I keep these? I'll tip them into a new file. I suggest you destroy the negatives or erase the jpeg files, of course.'

'I already have. And I've dealt with the graffiti, too.'

'Nothing too rash, I hope.'

Harriet took the can of black spray-paint from her rucksack and set it on the table.

Jack Nicholl laughed. 'I suppose that would work, wouldn't it?'

'I've been painting over every one I spot. Of course, there are probably plenty that I haven't found. There's only so much one person can do.'

After a beat, Jack Nicholl said, 'If that's a request for help, I can pass it upstairs, but I can't promise anything.'

'I thought it might be useful training for your latest recruits.'

'I'm afraid that all of our latest recruits are in language laboratories, learning Arabic. Have you asked for help outside the charmed circle?'

'I'm as eager as you to keep this under wraps.'

'Of course you are. Well, this has been an unexpected pleasure for me as well as you,' Jack Nicholl said, and pushed back his chair and stood. 'Please don't bother getting up, Harriet. I'll see myself out.'

3

Alfie's grandmother told him about his inheritance on his twenty-first birthday, eleven years after Mick Flowers had disappeared, and three years after leave to swear to his death had been granted by the Cambridge registrar. Alfie believed that his father had left nothing behind except for the Morgan sports car – sold long ago to help pay off gambling debts that had surfaced after his disappearance – a box of LPs and a wardrobeful of clothes at the house in Cambridge, and a set of photographic prints in his agent's files. Everything else that Mick Flowers had ever owned, including his archive of negatives and notebooks, had been lost in the fire that had gutted the flat he'd rented in London. So Alfie was surprised to learn, at his birthday lunch at an expensive, old-fashioned French restaurant in Bristol, where he was in his final year at the university, that for the past eleven years his grandmother had been looking after a patch of land his father had owned in North London. Land which was Alfie's to do with as he wished now that he had come of age.

'Your father won it in a poker game,' his grandmother explained. 'From a gentleman from Malta who I, believe, was later shot to death in a public house in the East End. Your father sometimes associated with very vivid types, Alfie. He was like your grandfather, he had a wild streak in him. But unlike your grandfather, God bless him, he never had the chance to grow out of it.'

Alfie's grandmother, Elizabeth Flowers, was a small, slender woman with a vivacious, gypsyish air, still attractive at sixty-five, her hair dyed glossy black, bangles on her wrists, a necklace of heavy wooden beads at her throat. She'd been a real beauty when Alfie's grandfather had met her during the Second World War, a demure knockout in her Army uniform. She'd been a driver then, chauffeuring high-ranking officers around London and the Home Counties, quite fearless in the blackout because she had acute night vision and could navigate the streets by starlight if necessary. She'd once driven for Field Marshal Montgomery, whom she remembered as quite the most bad-tempered man she'd ever met. She'd driven for General Sir Frederick Pile, Commander-in-Chief of Anti-Aircraft Command. She'd driven for a clutch of Yanks and an assortment of spooks. And she'd driven for Maurice Flowers, who'd been working at the SOE offices in Baker Street, and Maurice Flowers had fallen for her and she'd fallen for him. It had been a May–September marriage between a beautiful twenty-year-old and a fortysomething bachelor-scholar, but far stranger things had happened during the war. Elizabeth Flowers was briskly competent when she had to be, never more so than in the aftermath of her only son's disappearance, and always open-hearted and generous towards her grandson, but she had a sly, secretive side, too. Six months later, she would surprise Alfie again, when she invited him to meet the man she was going to marry – until that moment, Alfie had known nothing at all about her deepening love affair.

That evening in Bristol, she had another surprise for him, taking a *London A-Z* from her handbag and showing Alfie where his inheritance was situated: a sliver of land in Islington, next to the North London railway line. She laid two keys on the table. For the padlock which fastened the gates, she said – and for the caravan.

'Caravan?'

Alfie was having trouble taking all of this in.

His grandmother gave him a level look across the table. 'Don't get your hopes up, dear. This isn't going to make your fortune. It isn't much more than a patch of waste ground, with nothing on it but a caravan that's quite rotted away, and a kind of garage that pays a peppercorn rent. As yet, there's no planning permission for anything more permanent, but Islington is an up-and-coming area, and if you sold it to an honest property speculator, if you could find such a person, I'm sure you'd make a useful sum. But it's up to you to decide what to do with it. I've looked after it all this time, and now it's your responsibility.'

They agreed that they would visit it together when Alfie came home from university at Christmas, but Christmas was a month away, and Alfie discovered that he couldn't wait that long. He went up to London the very next weekend, trying to behave like an adult on a business trip – just going to inspect my property, don't you know – but feeling the same airy thrill that had possessed him when he'd made another clandestine trip to London several years ago, to look for Mr Prentiss's house.

It was raining in London, drenching down from clouds that sagged just above the crowded rooftops. Two in the afternoon and already so dark that the streetlamps were lit, communing over their own reflections in the wet roads. Cars sped by with their headlights on, splashing gouts of water onto pavements slippery with fallen leaves. Alfie's army-surplus grey wool coat was quickly soaked through and had easily doubled its weight by the time he found his way through a tangle of residential streets to the plot of land that his father had left to him.

It was squeezed between the back of a terrace of dilapidated four-storey Victorian houses and the cutting which contained the North London railway line. There was a pair of rusty mesh gates next to a small, temporary-looking building constructed from steel-framed concrete shuttering, with a roll-up door facing the street. Alfie's heart beat quickly as he turned the key in the heavy padlock. It popped open in his hand and he pushed the gates back and stepped through, feeling like a trespasser about to be menaced by a shotgun-wielding landowner. There was a wide pan of cracked, weedy concrete fringed on the railway side by brambles and leafless hawthorns and sycamores, black and dripping in the rain. A kind of garage stood at the end, a big open-ended shelter like a Dutch barn built of wood and corrugated iron where an old-fashioned red London bus was parked next to a caravan set on railway sleepers.

The second key opened the caravan door. Inside, it smelled of damp and mice. Mouse droppings lay everywhere on the cracked linoleum floor. The foam cushions of the seats at one end of the caravan had been deeply mined. The bottoms of the floral curtains were ragged. There were more mouse droppings on the Formica surfaces of the kitchen area. A dead mouse lay mummified in the tiny aluminium sink.

A newspaper lay on the folding table, its top pages brittle yellow lace. Alfie brushed off commas of dry mouse-shit, found a page where the date was still legible. Saturday, 28 November 1981. The day after Alfie's tenth birthday. The day Alfie had last seen his father.

Alfie locked the caravan and walked the boundary of his property, stood in the unforgiving rain and looked down at the railway lines. He discovered that he was happy. The property wasn't much, but it had been his father's and now it was his. He knew then that he would never sell it.

Elizabeth Flowers remarried soon after Alfie graduated. She'd met her new husband, Harry Walker, on a cruise along the Norwegian coast. He was an architect and a jazz buff, an energetic, gregarious man with a glass eye and a mane of white hair who played trombone in a pub band every Sunday and, as a party piece, was given to reciting poems by Tennyson and Browning that he'd been forced to learn as a schoolboy. Alfie liked Harry and liked his three sons too, but chose to live in North London, on his plot of land, rather than move into Harry's Victorian pile in Richmond. He bought a new caravan and had electricity and mains water laid in, and later bought a second, smaller caravan, which he turned into a photographic darkroom.

He'd been there ever since. Eleven years. He'd become a familiar sight in the neighbourhood. Slouching along in his worn black leather jacket, his camera bag bumping his hip. Thumbing through stacks of old magazines at the antiques market in Camden Passage on Saturday mornings, looking for examples of his father's early work. Eating special fried rice and spring rolls in the Golden Dragon Chinese takeaway on Caledonian Road, or spaghetti carbonara in the family-run Italian restaurant opposite Pentonville prison, or Thai green curry in his local pub. He was a regular at the pub, habitually snuffing out the candle stuck in its wax-covered bottle before sitting at the table in his corner, where he drank lemonade and lime in the shadows under shelves bowed with dusty, unread, unreadable books, and gossiped with other regulars – journalists, musicians, book dealers, men in the antique trade, men who inhabited the *demi-monde* of self-employment and scruffy bachelorhood. Undiscovered geniuses of the city exchanging gossip about rumours and conspiracy theories, doing bits of business with each other. Cash in hand. A favour for a favour. London characters. London geezers.

Living in a caravan on a piece of forgotten wasteland in the middle of London wasn't much fun in winter, but summers were a gift. In summer, the living was easy. In summer, Alfie's little yard was like a sliver of paradise glowing fresh and green among the sooty bricks and buckled streets.

Two days after his photograph of Morph's graffiti had been published in the *Independent,* nine in the morning, Alfie was lounging outdoors in his dressing gown, sitting in his plastic chair at his plastic table, sipping orange juice and munching a crois-sant. White clouds sailed the sky; the air was already warm. Birdsong in the hawthorns and the sycamores, butterflies fluttering around the dusty purple flower spikes of the buddleias that grew behind George Johnson's workshop, the thin scrape of a radio in one of the houses that backed onto the patch of land, the white noise of the city like a vacuum cleaner running in a far-off room in an enormous house.

The sycamores were taller, there was a Dennis F15 fire engine parked in the yard, and two double-decker buses now shared the big open-ended garage with Alfie's caravans – his tenant, George Johnson, who restored vintage Jaguars in the workshop next to the gates, had last year bought one of the obsolete Routemasters that London Transport was selling off cheaply – but otherwise the patch of land had changed little since Alfie had first seen it. Even without planning permission it was now worth a very useful sum indeed and because of the crazy spiral in property prices its value was increasing significantly every day. Alfie sometimes enter-tained a fantasy of selling up and buying a nice little flat, perhaps in one of those spiffy new developments in Clerkenwell, but the truth was that he was more or less content with his lot, especially on days like this, the city waking around him, birds singing each to each in the trees, the sun warm on his back. He was idly thinking that he'd take a stroll along the canal and see if Morph had put up anything new, ask any likely-looking kids what they knew. He'd phone Toby Brown first, see if he wanted to come along. Today might be the day when they found the end of the thread that would lead them to the graffiti artist.

Alfie knew that he might cause himself considerable grief by stirring up the past, but he was discovering that he didn't care.

He would be thirty-three this year. He was no longer young, and knew that he'd never be half the photographer that his father had been. He was technically proficient and he had a good eye, and occasionally, with a lot of luck, he managed to take the odd exceptional picture, but by now he knew enough about himself and his trade to realize that he didn't have the instinct of a truly great photographer, the perfect sense of the mood or immediacy of a situation or emotion or landscape and the ability to burn it into the heart of a shot. His father had had it; Don McCullin had it; Larry Burrows had had it in spades; Alfie didn't. Well, *c'est la vie.* He'd never kiss a princess, either, or become an astronaut, or a jet-fighter pilot. He was dug in here, protecting himself with an armoury of habits, maintaining his equilibrium, floating through life.

His last girlfriend had said that he was like one of those hermits that noblemen used to keep in a corner of their estates. She'd been making a joke, but it had the sting of truth. His biggest ambition at present was to mount an exhibition of his lichen photographs in some little bookshop, or on the walls of a café. In Antarctica's Dry Valleys, which were fantastically cold and lacked any form of precipitation, there were lichens that on a good day took in a single molecule of carbon dioxide, made a molecule of sugar, and exhaled a molecule of oxygen. Tiny stains on the rocks, thousands of years old, growing a millimetre each century. Like those lichens, Alfie had made a virtue of his marginal existence, but in the last week, while searching for Morph, he'd felt as if he'd been waking from a long sleep. For the first time in years, he'd begun to feel that the world was crammed with unfurling possibilities. For the first time in years, he'd begun to feel properly alive.

A car horn sounded outside the entrance to the yard. Alfie wandered over, holding his glass of orange juice, wondering if one of George's customers had arrived early. But then he saw the man in the pale blue suit and buttercup-yellow T-shirt who stood beside the silver Audi slewed in front of the gate, and called out, 'Don't waste your time. It's not for sale.'

Because there wasn't a week when some estate agent or property speculator didn't stop by and try to convince him about the benefits of selling up, or drop their business card in the box bolted to the gatepost.

'Mr Flowers?' The man held up a copy of the *Independent*, folded to show Alfie's photograph. He was in his forties, stocky and nicely tanned, his black hair clipped short, beginning to fade back from his forehead. 'Alfie Flowers?'

'That's me.'

'I'm Robbie Ruane,' the man said, smiling at Alfie through the gate's wire mesh. 'I believe that we have a mutual interest in Morph.'

'We do?'

'When I saw this photograph, I knew I had to track you down.' The man extracted a business card from the top pocket of his jacket and held it out to Alfie through the mesh of the gate. 'I run a little gallery in Brick Lane. Urban Graphics.'

Alfie suddenly felt exposed and vulnerable and foolish, his shanks bare beneath the hem of his dressing gown, the glass of juice clutched in his hand. He'd shown himself to the world, and the world had responded with this sharpie in his crisp suit and his paste-on smile.

'I wonder if I could talk to you about your photograph,' Robbie Ruane said. 'I believe that it's one of the pieces our mutual friend put up along the canal.'

'Do you represent him, Mr Ruane? Are you his agent?'

'Not at all. But, to be frank, I *hope* to represent him. Naive art, spontaneous art, street art that comes from the heart and the gut, art that responds to the anonymity of the city and the human condition – it's the next big thing. Very exciting, very provoca-tive, very now. I already look after a number of so-called street artists, and I'm very interested in Morph's work.'

'I'm sorry to disappoint you, but I don't have the first idea who he is.'

'Nor do I. Which is why I'm following up every clue I can. Which is why, when I saw your photograph, I simply had to talk to you.'

'Well, we've talked.'

Robbie Ruane waggled the card he was still poking through the mesh. 'I'm very eager to contact Morph. I'm even, because I'm so foolishly desperate, offering a finder's fee.'

There was something unsettling in the man's stare, a manic glint like that of a zealot, or a junkie desperate for his next fix. Alfie wondered if Robbie had been affected by Morph's pattern. If he was somehow sensitive to it, if he'd been hooked by it without knowing why.

'I'm a photographer, Mr Ruane. I think you've mistaken me for something else.'

'You found Morph's work and saw something in it, just like me. If you know anything, anything at all, I promise you that you'll be handsomely rewarded.'

Behind him, back on the plastic table outside his caravan, Alfie's mobile phone began to ring. 'I have to answer that,' Alfie said. 'And if I were you, I'd move that expensive car of yours before my tenant arrives. He has a short, sharp way of dealing with people who block the gates.'

As Alfie walked away, his whole back tingling, Robbie Ruane called out to him, saying that he'd leave his card, saying that they'd talk again, very soon.

The mobile had stopped ringing when Alfie reached it. He picked it up and checked the answer service, watching with a flood of relief as Robbie Ruane slid into his car and drove off. Toby Brown's voice said in his ear, 'I've got a couple of hot new leads, Flowers. Call me back.'

Alfie called him back.

'You know the industrial estate in Kentish Town?'

'Which one?'

'Regis Road, where the big UPS building is.' Toby sounded excited and out of breath. 'Get over here, quick as you can.'

'You've found something, haven't you?'

'Don't even think of walking, and don't get a bus. For once in your life take a minicab. Tell the driver to find Pronto Delivery, the far end of Regis Road. And tell him to get a move on. If you don't get here soon, they'll all be gone.'

'What will be gone?'

'Don't be late,' Toby said, and cut the connection.

Pronto Delivery occupied a warehouse unit in the far corner of a triangular industrial estate that was bounded on two sides by a

tangle of railway lines. When Alfie arrived in the minicab Toby
Brown was waiting for him outside the gates, smoking with furious
concentration. Saying, as Alfie paid off the driver, 'You're late. Why
are you always late? And don't forget the receipt.'

'What's this all about?'

'Come and take a look.'

He led Alfie down the road that ran beside the prefabricated
warehouse. Alfie told him about Robbie Ruane, and Toby said
that he sounded like an asshole, but harmless.

'I called my agent,' Alfie said. 'She's going to ask around, see if
he's who he says he is.'

'I wouldn't worry about him.'

'Suppose he finds Morph before we do?'

'Why would he? He hasn't found this,' Toby said, leading Alfie
around the corner of the warehouse into a yard where more than
a dozen white vans were parked. A gang of men in boots, oilskins
and heavy rubber gauntlets were washing them, scrambling about
with hoses and buckets and brushes, scrubbing at their sides,
sluicing them down.

Toby lit another cigarette and told Alfie that he'd heard about
it first thing this morning. 'The courier who delivered a piece-
of-shit biography for review is a friend of mine. Well, not exactly
a friend, but he comes around to my place just about every day,
there's no end to the books people want me to review, thank
God, and we exchange the odd word. He told me about this
because he thought there might be a story in it.'

Some of the vans had already been cleaned, their white flanks
wet and gleaming and still faintly marked with what had been spray-
painted on them. Men were scrubbing down the others with industrial cleaner and big sponges, with hoses with brush attachments,
scouring the big graffiti, Morph's flicks, that were centred on the
side of each van. The wet vans steamed in the sunlight. Water ran
everywhere across the tarmac, swirling around the boots of the men,
the tyres of the vans. Islands of white foam drifted on cross-currents.

Toby said, 'He did every van in the yard. These are the last to
be cleaned up – you only just made it. What do you think,
Flowers? Are these the genuine article? Are they ringing a bell
in that weird brain of yours?'

Every flick was the same cartoon in black spray paint of a grinning mullah cutting the throat of a sheep marked US ARMY, and they were all framed by the same thicket of interlocked patterns, glittering like rings of shattered black glass, spinning, pulsing in and out, against the white sides of the vans.

'A very loud bell,' Alfie said, reaching inside his bag for his camera.

He squared off and focused on an untouched flick, concentrating on the cartoon of mullah and sheep in the centre, its frame pulsing, pulsing with the pulse beating in his temples, in his eyes.

Toby said, 'I've already snagged a spot in the local rag. A recap on our boy's exploits, a couple of meaty paragraphs about the latest outrage. Two hundred easy quid, less the drink I owe the guy who tipped me off. We'll split it half and half.'

'You can keep it,' Alfie said, and took the shot, took another. It was like trying to focus on chains of sunlight burning off the heaving skin of the sea. He zoomed in and out. He bracketed exposures. He took general shots of the men working on the vans. The pulse was right inside his head now.

When Alfie had shot off the entire roll of film, Toby said, 'There's something else you need to see,' and led him into the warehouse, where a young black man was slinging boxes stencilled MEDICAL SUPPLIES – URGENT – FRAGILE into the back of a freshly washed van. Toby stepped up to him and asked where Barry had got to.

'Office, innit,' the man said, and threw another box into his van.

The office was a long hut that stood behind stacks of empty pallets. A sign, *No Entry For Drivers*, was taped to the half-glassed door which Toby opened without knocking. Two black women sat in front of computer monitors, talking into their telephone headsets and typing; a heavy, balding black man in shirt and braces looked up from his clipboard. This was Barry. Toby introduced Alfie and said that he needed another squint at the tape.

'Police took the original,' Barry said, feeding a cassette into a video player, 'so it's lucky I made a copy.'

Alfie said, 'You have him on video?'

'We have security cameras inside and out,' Barry said. 'The little bastard spray-painted the lenses of two of the cameras that cover the yard, but he missed the third. My boss is over at the firm that's supposed to monitor the cameras, giving them hell because no one noticed.'

'Two minutes-plus of the artist at work,' Toby told Alfie. 'Roll the tape, Barry.'

But when Barry switched on the little TV that sat next to the video player, Alfie, already primed by Morph's flicks, found that the black-and-white flicker hurt his eyes. He looked away, and Toby sighed and said, 'Try freeze-frame, Barry. Right there. Cool. Can't you at least glance at it, Flowers?'

Alfie risked a glance. A grainy still shot from a corner high above the triangular yard, deep shadows and the roofs of parked vans shining like radioactive tombstones.

'Just there,' Toby said, and tapped the lower right-hand corner of the TV screen with his forefinger.

Alfie bent closer to the TV. A pale smudge resolved into a face looking up at the camera. His mouth tasted like the inside of a kettle. Was that a hand holding a spray-can, etched against the pale glimmer of the van's flank?

'That's the best shot,' Toby said. And then said, in a different voice, 'Flowers? Are you all right?'

Alfie felt a presence behind his eyes, an assassin stepping out of the darkness in his skull, flowing forward. He jerked away from the TV and then he was sitting in a chair, his head tipped back, looking up at the raddled ceiling tiles of the office. People were crowding around him, and someone, Toby Brown, was saying, 'He gets turns like this sometimes. He'll be okay if you let him get some air.'

'I'm okay now,' Alfie said.

'You really don't like TV, do you?' Barry said.

'You looked like you'd been struck by lightning,' Toby said. 'And then you fell straight down.'

'Just be grateful you didn't get the full monty,' Alfie said. He washed down half a phenobarbitone and half a Valium with a couple of gulps of cold mineral water from a bottle that one of the women gave him. A needle of bright pain vibrated behind his left eye, but

otherwise he felt fine. When they were outside in the sunlight and
the bustle of the gang of van cleaners, he said to Toby, 'I'm not
sure if that was worth the price of the cab. Is that the best shot of
him you have? Because, frankly, it looks like anyone.'

Toby shrugged. 'Maybe the police will enhance it with their
battery of powerful computers and put out an all-points. But I
doubt it.'

'I suppose Elliot could try to do something with it,' Alfie said.

Elliot Johnson, George's nephew, was a freelance web-site
designer. He also helped out various members of his family with
their various bits of business, and helped out Alfie, too, when he
needed to digitize his photographs.

Toby said, lighting a cigarette as he walked, 'I guess it's worth
a try.'

Alfie said, 'I suppose Morph hit these vans because they go all
over London. Like mobile billboards advertising his prowess. But
why this particular courier company? It's way off his usual beat,
and he would have got greater coverage if he'd hit UPS, which
is just up the road. They must have a hundred vans.'

Toby shrugged. 'UPS vans are painted brown – the cartoons
wouldn't show up so well. And I imagine security is tighter at
UPS, too: it's a twenty-four-hour operation, harder to crack.'

'I suppose.'

'The point is to make sure that he knows you're interested in
him. There's a minicab office on Fortess Road. You need to get
back home to print up those photographs, and I need to get back
home to write a couple of paragraphs of deathless prose. What
are you doing on Monday evening, by the way?'

'I'll have to check with my social secretary.'

'Have her cancel everything. There's a party you need to go
to.'

'Because?'

'I've been a busy boy. Seeking Morph here, seeking him there,
seeking him every-fucking-where. Among other things, I've been
listening to that pirate radio talk-show host, the one who was, as
you put it, "bigging up" Morph. It seems that Morph has been
booked to appear along with a bunch of other spray-can artists
at a wrap party for – you're going to love this – *The Elemental.*'

'You're kidding.'

Alfie had worked briefly as unit photographer on the set of *The Elemental*, a low-budget, direct-to-video horror movie. But he'd quit after just two weeks, when he'd realized that the director had no intention of paying his expenses, let alone the fee he'd been promised.

'To quote someone or other,' Toby said, 'it's a small world, but I wouldn't want to paint it.'

4

The next day, a Sunday, Alfie took the train out to Kew to see his grandmother. This was his routine after she had moved into the care home. Last Sunday, when he'd tried to ask her about Morph's graffiti, had been one of her bad days. She'd been withdrawn, locked inside her head, refusing to look at his photographs, ignoring his questions, growing agitated when he'd pressed her. He was hoping that today would be better; when he'd called the care home just before setting out, the nurse had said that his grandmother had been very talkative at breakfast and had just taken a short stroll around the garden.

Alfie's grandmother had grown increasingly eccentric after Harry Walker had died. By then, Harry's three sons had all married and moved out of the big house in Richmond, and she had been living on her own. Gradually, most of the rooms had fallen into disuse. She hardly ever went out, and spent most of her time in a reclining chair in a corner of the sitting room, puzzling her way through romance novels or listening to the radio, while beyond the French windows the lawn grew lank and mossy, and the rose bushes she'd spent hours pruning, mulching and spraying against black spot and aphids knitted great tangles of canes. Often, her only topic of conversation was the past. Her childhood, the war, her courtship with Alfie's grandfather. Increasingly, she mistook Alfie for her son – for Alfie's father. An itinerant builder persuaded her that the drive of the house needed urgent repairs, and charged her two thousand pounds for a couple of hours of work. Luckily, she paid him by cheque, which Alfie managed to stop before it was cashed, but it cost nearly a thousand to clean up the sump oil that the man had sprayed over the drive's perfectly good tarmacadam. She had never been very interested in housework, but now dust silted everywhere, pots and dirty dishes festered in greasy water in the Belfast sink of the big, quarry-tiled kitchen, and the fridge was a repository of limp vegetables and experiments in

advanced mycology. Alfie arranged for a local woman to come in
twice a week to clean and do the laundry. He bought his grandmother a microwave because he had bad dreams about the gas
cooker. She'd turn on one of the rings and forget to light it and
wander off . . . Alfie and Harry's three sons took turns to try to
persuade her that she should find a smaller place or think about
sheltered accommodation, but she refused to talk about it. 'I'm
perfectly happy here,' she'd say. 'I have everything I need. Why do
you want me to move?'

The crisis came when Alfie got a call from the police. His
grandmother had been found wandering in her slippers and house-
coat in a street two miles from her house, so confused that she
didn't even know what year it was, let alone where she lived.
After she was diagnosed with early-stage Alzheimer's, there was
a family conference. Alfie and Joe, Harry's oldest son, assumed
joint power of attorney. The big house in Richmond, which
Harry's sons would inherit when Alfie's grandmother died, was
rented out; the income from this, together with the interest on
the substantial sum she had salted away after she'd sold the house
in Cambridge, was more than enough to pay for her place in a
residential care home.

It was a model of its kind, a rambling Victorian pile set well
back from the road, with a long gravel drive between pleached
lime trees and a large, landscaped garden. Every room had its own
en suite bathroom. The kitchens were spotless, the menus imaginative and varied, and there was a small shop where the residents could buy sweets and cigarettes, magazines and newspapers.
Trips were organized to the seaside and the theatre. There was
ballroom dancing in the spacious lounge every Friday night. There
were art classes, lessons in flower arranging and local history. The
place was as well-appointed as any four-star hotel, but no one
ever planned or looked forward to staying there.

Alfie's grandmother lived with the other disabled and confused
residents in a long, single-storey annexe at the back of the house,
rooms opening on either side of a corridor with polished brass
handrails fastened to its walls, and doors wide enough to allow
access by the wheelchair-bound. At the brightly lit reception area,
the young, smoothly plump Antiguan charge nurse confirmed

that Elizabeth Flowers was in a good mood, and Alfie found her sitting in her reclining chair by the window. Her white hair, no longer dyed, was fanned loosely around her shoulders. Alfie had brought a box of pastries, as he always did, and she ate an apricot turnover with a kind of absent-minded delicacy while he told her about his adventures in the last week. He wasn't sure how much she understood. She lived entirely in the past now, retreating further and further from the present as the memories and skills that she'd acquired in her long life were progressively lost to her disease.

She had long ago forgotten who Alfie was, confusing him with either his father or his grandfather, but this time she did look at the photographs, and seemed to pay attention while he explained how Morph's flicks affected him. On some visits, as now, she seemed to be reasonably alert; on others, like last Sunday, she would stare off into an unimaginable distance without saying a word. Worst of all were the times when she clung to Alfie's hand in mute distress, tears leaking from the corners of her eyes, when she seemed to be aware of what was happening to her but was unable to articulate her horror, and Alfie was unable to comfort her. Today, she listened and nodded, and when he was finished she said, 'I don't know why you're telling me all this, Michael. You know it isn't any of my business.'

'What isn't your business, Grammie? What was Michael involved in? Was it something to do with pictures and patterns like these?'

'Now you're trying to . . . you know, like the men.'

When she couldn't find the word she wanted, she wrinkled her nose in frustration, and Alfie could see for a moment the little girl she'd once been.

'The men?'

'With their top hats and rabbits.'

'Magicians?'

She nodded.

'I'm not trying to play a trick on you, Grammie.'

'Don't think you will,' she said, with a touch of her old sharpness.

'I wouldn't dream of it. Really. Did Maurice have any pictures like this?'

Alfie had looked for his grandfather's papers when he had helped to clear out the house in Richmond, hoping to find souvenirs of his grandfather's time in Iraq. Diaries and photographs, details of archaeological digs. He had hoped to unearth the manuscript of the thesis that his grandfather had worked on after he had retired, or a sheaf of his careful drawings of shards and sherds, but it seemed that everything had been cleared away by the two men who had visited the house after the funeral. All Alfie had found was a packet of letters and postcards dating back to his grandmother's courtship with his grandfather, sweet nothings exchanged by two lovers separated by the business of war.

His grandmother said, 'You must give it up, Michael. You have your little boy to think about. He needs his father now. He needs to be made well again.'

Alfie realized that his grandmother was repeating an argument she'd had with his father twenty years ago. He said, 'Was it something to do with these patterns? Take a look at them again, Grammie. Please. Tell me if you recognize them. Tell me if Grandad, if Maurice, ever showed you anything like this.'

A sly look stole over his grandmother's face. She smiled and put a finger to her lips and said, 'You won't catch me out like that.'

Her voice was light, girlish. Her eyes were bright. She still had most of her own teeth – both sides of Alfie's family had little need for dentists. She had her good bones and her good health. Her mind was being erased, but her body carried on regardless, blindly renewing itself.

Alfie said, 'How am I trying to catch you out?'

'I've never once let you down in that respect.'

Alfie wasn't sure if his grandmother thought that she was talking to his father now, or to his grandfather. He said, 'I know you haven't. But just this once, I need to know if these are the same patterns.'

'I didn't tell them.'

'Tell them what, Grammie? Tell who?'

'They wanted everything, but I had to keep something, Maurice,' his grandmother said. 'You wrote so beautifully about your adventures in Iraq and your work, I couldn't let them have everything. That wasn't so very wrong of me, was it?'

'Do you mean the letters? The letters Maurice wrote to you?'

The bundle of letters was kept with two photograph albums and other mementoes in a box file on the table by his grand-mother's bed. Every week, a volunteer would visit her and attempt to spur her failing memory by asking her to tell stories about the people in these old photographs. Sometimes Alfie would do the same thing. Now he pulled the letters from beneath the photo-graph albums, unpicked the knot in the ribbon he had tied around them four years ago, and showed them to his grandmother, fanning them out in front of her face. Torn envelopes with green and red stamps that bore the profile of a dead king. Lined blue paper, tissue-thin airmail forms torn along their creases. Ink faded to brown. Words or phrases or whole sentences blanked out here and there by the censor's black pencil. Alfie showed them to his grandmother but she looked at them blankly and shook her head when he asked if these were all she had kept from the two men who had come for her husband's things.

'I couldn't let them have everything. Say you'll forgive me. Please say you'll forgive me . . .'

Alfie told her that he would, of course he would. He felt filthily ashamed, knowing that he'd asked too much of her, but he also felt an eager spark of excitement. They walked around the gardens. His grandmother tried to name every flower she saw. Some of the names were right. At the end, after he had given up trying to make her understand that he would come and see her next week, she said suddenly, 'I never let them down.'

'Who didn't you ever let down, Grammie?'

'In all this time I never once let the nomads down.'

'The nomads? Which nomads? Who are the nomads?'

'I never once,' she said, and kissed Alfie on the lips, and clung to him so hard that when he disentangled himself from her grip he was frightened that he would break her bones.

The train that Alfie rode back into the centre of London was crowded with kids and pushchairs and parents laden with bags and backpacks bulging with polar-expedition amounts of kiddie kit. He leaned in a corner at one end of a carriage, sipping a lukewarm banana milk shake while the little three-unit train dragged itself over the bridge across the Thames, groaning as it picked up speed, spitting sparks as it shuddered along tracks elevated above the red roofs and treetops of Chiswick, through Acton, Kensal and Hampstead, past walls covered in scrawled tags and the exuberant explosions of three-and four-colour throw-ups. The interior of the carriage was also covered with tags, and the naive felt-tip assertions of school kids. *Marcus is a batty boy. Maxie = Lorraine.* Someone who called himself Venger had signed his name over and over in fat pillows of red ink, and the window beside Alfie was defaced too, its margins frosty with names scratched into the glass in angular scripts. Assertions of ownership. Advertisements of secret identities in secret codes.

Alfie slumped in his corner, a large, somewhat shapeless man, like a bear that hadn't been properly licked into shape by its mother, his blond hair a disarrayed halo, wearing a red check shirt and baggy black elephant cords, his bag clutched to his belly, his large feet in strap sandals. He had prehensile toes, long and double-jointed, thatched at their second joints with pads of dark hair. He was thinking about what his grandmother had said. He'd taken half a phenobarbitone tablet and a whole Valium to calm himself down and his thoughts moved slow and sure from point to point, station to station.

He was certain that his grandmother had recognized some-thing familiar in the pattern that framed Morph's cartoons. He was certain that she had seen something like it before, that it had set free a clutch of memories about her husband, his artefacts, and the interminable thesis on which he had laboured for so many years. He was certain that he'd been right all along, that the pattern around Morph's cartoons was definitely linked to his grandfather's work, to the piece of paper that had been hidden in the secret compartment in the desk in his grandfather's study. Also, he was pretty certain that his grandmother had kept back some of his grandfather's papers, that she had hidden them from the two men who had cleared out the study. It was possible that she'd kept nothing more than the letters he'd brought away with him, but he thought it unlikely because the few lines he'd read at random when he'd first found them, feeling like an amateur burglar trampling on family secrets, had contained no more than the usual endearments between two new lovers, how much his grandfather had enjoyed the Coward revue and the walk along the river afterwards, fond memories of their picnic on Hampstead Heath, how he looked forward to returning to London and seeing his 'naughty elf' again – the ordinary stuff of life refracted through the rose-tinted lens of love. Still, Alfie knew that he would have to read through them all, and he would also have to check through the rest of his grandmother's stuff. Everything to do with the house in Richmond was stored in Joe's attic; he'd probably have to look through all of that, too.

The documents and papers which Alfie hadn't had the heart to throw away after his grandmother had moved into the rest home were stuffed into a plastic crate that he kept in the caravan he used as a darkroom. Telephone bills and gas bills and electricity bills; cheque books and statements for accounts long closed; bills for repairs to the house in Cambridge; a scrapbook bulging with recipes clipped from newspapers and magazines; a box of postcards; schoolgirl essays and three Letts diaries; the deeds for the clothing shop her parents had owned before the First World War; a plastic bag full of sepia and black-and-white photographs of people in funny clothes and hats. Alfie spent most of the evening reading the letters and looking through everything else. Laying it all out on the floor of his caravan, bent almost double as he sat on the edge of the couch and sifted through papers fanned on the overlapping oriental carpets his grandmother had given to him when she had sold the Cambridge house, moths flattening themselves on the window behind him, his shadow moving across the low ceiling of the small caravan, the radio on the crammed bookshelf muttering to itself, a mug of raspberry tea forgotten and long gone cold beside his bare feet.

A fine, bitter-sweet sadness seeped through Alfie as he sifted through the litter of documents and bills, his fingers stained with the peculiarly clinging dust that old paper generates. The photographs were especially poignant. Men and women crowded gleefully together to fit into the gaze of the camera or posed alone with formal stiffness or with theatrical or comical flourishes, smiling or frowning at him out of a vanished past, frozen in particular moments that had lost all meaning. Several appeared again and again, in different costumes, at different seasons, sitting on a pebbly beach, standing with their bicycles in front of a wide cornfield, under an arbour of blowsy roses. Alfie supposed that they were friends and relatives of his grandmother's, but he didn't recognize any of them. Here was a birthday card to his grandmother from someone called Essie, who had signed herself 'your true best friend now and always'. Here was the death certificate for his grandfather, folded into an envelope with the bill from the undertaker, a bill from the florist, and a bill from the caterer – Alfie remembered sitting under the table in the dining room, hidden behind the stiff pleats of the starched white tablecloth, eating little sausage rolls one after the other and watching the legs of the people who had come back to the house after the funeral pass to and fro. Here was an order of service from the funeral, with a piece of paper, a bill from a safe-deposit company, slipped inside it. Alfie stared at this for a long minute before he realized that he had found what he had been looking for.

5

Harriet's instructions took her to the edge of the *London A-Z*, to Enfield and a small café in the middle of a short row of shops hunched in the thunder and diesel wind of the A10's busy dual carriageway. Her handler, Jack Nicholl, had arranged the meeting with an MI5 agent, Susan Blackmore, and an informer in the Kurdish community. 'She'll be very protective of the guy,' Jack Nicholl had said. 'If anything looks funny to her, she'll blow the meet and I won't be able to fix you up with another. So be cool, and do everything she asks.'

Harriet allowed Susan Blackmore to pat her down in the café's toilet. The MI5 agent searched Harriet's handbag and confiscated her mobile phone for the duration.

'If I see any sign that my man is going to be followed, I'll call this off at once,' she said.

'I understand.'

'And I'll also call it off if I think someone is eavesdropping, using a video camera, or taking photographs.'

'You don't have to worry—'

'And I will sit in while you talk with him. That's not negotiable.'

'Of course.'

Harriet bought two coffees and followed Susan Blackmore to a table outside the café. The MI5 agent was in her late twenties, only a year or two older than Harriet. She wore her mouse-brown hair in a ponytail pulled back tightly from her pale, scrubbed face, and was dressed in her street uniform of supermarket denim jacket, tracksuit bottoms, and trainers. All she needed was a baby in one of those all-terrain pushchairs and a clutch of plastic bags from Iceland or Costco, and she could have blended into any high street or social security office in the country. She smoked with a stabbing motion, telling Harriet, 'He's already risking his life for me. He doesn't deserve any trouble from the Friends in Legoland.'

The Friends was MI5's nickname for MI6; Legoland was what they called Vauxhall Cross. Harriet knew all about the rivalry between the two main branches of the British secret service – MI6 thought that MI5 agents were little more than jumped-up police; MI5 thought that MI6 agents were public-school amateurs playing games for glamour and glory – and made what she hoped were the appropriate soothing noises, saying that she realized that she was being done a tremendous favour, promising that she wouldn't compromise the informer. 'I just need to ask him a few simple questions about a young man I believe is living in his community.'

'This graffiti artist.'

'If your friend doesn't know anything about him, that'll be the end of it.'

'Am I allowed to know anything about this young man of yours? Such as why you want to find him, or what you'll do if you do find him?'

'I don't know very much myself.'

Susan Blackmore gave Harriet a shrewd look. 'You're not actually with the Friends, are you?'

Harriet, wondering what Jack Nicholl had told this woman, said carefully, 'The case seems to cross several boundaries.'

Susan Blackmore smiled for the first time since they'd met. 'Exactly how much were you told about my man?'

'I know that he's a Kurd, that he's originally from Iraq. He was on one of the Mukhatarat's death lists and escaped to Turkey, he got into some kind of trouble there, and fled to this country and claimed asylum. For the past five years he's been living here as a bona fide political refugee.'

This was what Jack Nicholl had told her over the phone. He'd also said that he was pretty busy right now, but perhaps in a day or two they could get together . . .

Susan Blackmore said, 'He's also a poet. A nationalist poet, with a strong following back home. Do you know anything about Kurds and Kurdish politics?'

'I was sitting in a restaurant in Islington a few years ago, on Upper Street. It was May Day, a parade went past. There seemed to be about half a dozen different Kurdish communist and socialist parties taking part.'

'There's an awful lot of them, all right, but they all have, fundamentally, the same goal. The Kurds are an ethnic group whose homeland includes parts of Turkey, Syria, Iraq and Iran. They've been campaigning for an independent Kurdish state ever since the end of the First World War. Various groups in Iraq staged an uprising after the first Gulf War, and there has been about twenty years of civil war between the Turkish government and the biggest of the separatist groups, the PKK,' Susan Blackmore said, pronouncing it Peh Ka Ka. 'The Partia Karkaris Kurdistan, the Kurdistan Workers' Party. After he was arrested back in 1999, the PKK's leader ordered a peace initiative, and at the same time the Kurds were given more human rights, in part because Turkey is desperate to join the European Union. But it's a very fragile truce, and the liberation of Iraq has complicated things. The Turks want to assert an old claim on the oilfields in northern Iraq; the Kurds believe they can finally establish their independent state. And the armed wing of the PKK, which evolved into the KGK, Kongra-Gel, the People's Congress of Kurdistan, sees a chance to establish its influence. It's just now ended its ceasefire and resumed its terrorist activities in south-east Turkey. We have an interest in all this because Kongra-Gel gets a lot of its money from the heroin trade.'

'How does your man fit into this? Which side is he on?'

'The Friends really didn't bother to tell you much, did they?'

'I suppose they expected you to do the job for them.'

'I suppose they did. Well, apart from his poetry, he's also the brother-in-law of the leader of a political movement based in south-east Turkey that's campaigning for the peaceful establishment of an independent homeland. He has a part-time job in a bookshop off Green Lanes, which is where he heard about a little group of hotheads who wanted to assassinate his brother-in-law and create a martyr, a figurehead for Kongra-Gel's nasty little war. He came to us, we helped the Turkish government deal with the would-be assassins, and for the past year he's been feeding us tips and gossip about the micropolitics of various little Kurdish gangs and associations in London. He's an excellent source,' Susan Blackmore said, giving Harriet a cool, hard look, 'and I want to keep him sweet.'

'Either he's found out something about the man I'm looking for,' Harriet said, 'or he hasn't. That's all I care about.'

'I'm sure he's found something. Of course, whether or not it's useful is another matter.'

'Let the buyer beware,' Harriet said. 'I don't have a problem with that, and if you don't have a problem with me asking him a few questions, why don't you give him a call?'

'The way it works is that I only call him if I think there's something phoney about this little get-together,' Susan Blackmore said. 'You can relax, by the way. I believe you're kosher. Your handler, he's a different kettle of fish, but let me worry about that.'

'Why are we meeting him here? Was it your idea or his?'

'I don't think Enfield is anyone's idea of anything in partic-ular. It's one of those places that just sort of happen, like the state of my kitchen. Why we're here, my man works in the bookshop more for love than money. He has a day job as a fork-lift driver in one of the trading estates nearby,' Susan Blackmore said, looking at her watch, 'and he should be here in five or ten minutes, as soon as he starts his lunch break. Meanwhile, we can relax and enjoy the local ambience.'

Harriet fetched two more coffees. Fifteen minutes later, Susan Blackmore's informant arrived in a battered blue Nissan saloon with a brass tissue-box holder on the rear shelf and a brace of pine-tree air fresheners dangling from the rear-view mirror. He was older than Harriet had expected, streaks of silver in his black hair, a hawkish face, the kind of stubble so impacted that no razor could touch it. His name, she learned, when Susan Blackmore introduced her to him, was Şivan Ergüner.

'We do this quick,' Şivan Ergüner said. 'So no one sees us.'

'If you didn't want to be seen with us,' Susan Blackmore said, 'you should have asked to meet somewhere really clandestine. The Tower of London, or, I don't know, the zoo.'

'I've been to the zoo,' Şivan Ergüner said. He had a charming smile. 'Except for the penguin house, I was not impressed. And the penguin house, it does not even have any penguins.'

'You look tired,' Susan Blackmore said.

'Do not worry, it is not the strain of my work for you. I had

a double shift yesterday. Another reason why we do this quick —
I have to go to work.' Şivan Ergüner turned his smile on Harriet.
'So, you want to know about this graffiti artist who calls himself
Morph. Can I ask why?'

'He's making a nuisance of himself. Have you found out who
he really is?'

'I do much better than that,' Şivan Ergüner said. He asked if
he could borrow a cigarette from Susan Blackmore and held her
wrist steady as he bent to the flame of her lighter, all the while
looking at Harriet with his soulful dark eyes. There were flecks
of hazel and gold in them, and he had lashes to die for. 'It turns
out I know the boy. He used to come in the bookshop.'

Harriet, who knew that informers had a habit of passing on
what they thought their handlers wanted to hear rather than the
truth, said, 'Are you sure? Do you have proof?'

'You said that you would bring photographs of his work. May
I see them?'

Harriet pulled the envelope from her rucksack and showed
Şivan Ergüner the photograph of one of Morph's pieces of graffiti.
The man studied it briefly, and said, 'Yes, yes, that is his.'

Harriet said, 'Who is he? Where does he live?'

'I do not know him as Morph, but as Musa. Musa Karsu, that
is his real name,' Şivan Ergüner said, smiling at Harriet and at
Susan Blackmore, enjoying their attention. 'He did some work
for a poster for the Turkish Workers' Communist Association.
Susan knows of them, of course.'

'They're mostly harmless,' Susan Blackmore said.

Harriet asked Şivan Ergüner if Morph — Musa Karsu — still
worked for the Turkish Workers' Communist Association. She
asked if he knew where Musa Karsu lived, what he looked like.

'He is sixteen, seventeen, not quite a boy but not quite a man
either. I would say ordinary-looking, black hair, brown eyes.
Nothing special to look at. Not so tall, perhaps a little overweight.
I would guess about your height, Harriet. His family was from
Iraqi Kurdistan, the so-called safe haven in the north of the
country. From somewhere in the mountains, I don't know exactly
where. You know, he and his father had a journey a little like
mine. They left Iraq last year, and were living in Diyarbakir, this

is a city in the south-east of Turkey where many Kurds live, and many refugees from Iraq, too.'

'They were sheep herders,' Harriet said. 'Once upon a time.'

'Ah, you know about that? Anyway, soon after they are living in Diyarbakir, Musa's father is arrested by the Turkish police, who think that he has something to do with Kongra-Gel. You know about Kongra-Gel?'

'I've been brought up to speed,' Harriet said.

'They are criminals who have little support among the people,' Şivan Ergüner said. 'They get money from smuggling drugs and guns, and the police think Musa's father is involved. They are wrong, but they must torture him to find out that they are wrong. And after they release him, I think it was about six months ago, he comes here as a political refugee, and brings Musa with him.'

'How can I find him?' Harriet said.

Şivan Ergüner shrugged. 'How do you find any of these poor lost boys?'

'An address would be a good start.'

Şivan Ergüner shrugged again. His shrugs were liquid, very eloquent. 'What can I say? He came here illegally, with his father, and he's trying to claim asylum. But there is a problem, because his father died. His heart, it attacked him. And Musa is still a minor, he is frightened of your authorities. He is frightened they send him back to Turkey, or put him in one of your lovely immigration centres while they work out what to do with him. So he drop out of sight.'

'Does Morph – Musa – does he have any other relatives?'

'Here? I don't know. I don't think so. He came with his father, and his father died. This was not too long ago, I think. A month, two months, no more than that. He used to come in the bookshop sometimes. I remember that he was always drawing. He can't help himself. He drew on anything, he drew all the time. Faces, mostly, and patterns like this one,' Şivan Ergüner said, tapping the photograph. 'He would even scribble on the newspapers we put out in the bookshop. You have to take the pencil out of his hand to make him stop. So, why do you want to find him? Are you angry because he makes these funny pictures against the Americans?'

'I want to find him before other people do,' Harriet said. 'People who might mean him harm.'

'What people? Americans?'

'Actually, yes.'

'I find that hard to believe,' Şivan Ergüner said, and held up a hand, forefinger and middle finger crossed. 'You British and the Americans, you are so very close as this. Not that I mind so much, because you get rid of Saddam, and soon I will go home. Yes, it's true, Susan. I must leave you. It's a bloody shame, no?'

'He likes to tease,' Susan Blackmore told Harriet. 'Ignore him. It's just for effect.'

Şivan Ergüner mimed pulling an arrow from his breast, and winked at Harriet.

'If you don't know where Musa is living now,' Harriet said, 'perhaps you can tell me where the Turkish Workers' Communist Association has its offices.'

Şivan Ergüner laughed. 'The Turkish Workers' Communist Association – such a grand name! – is five or six kids who meet in the cafés or the football club. They mostly argue among themselves, and write letters to the newspapers, and put up posters or tear down the posters of their rivals.'

Harriet looked at Susan Blackmore and said, 'Can I have their names?'

'I'll talk to you afterwards.'

Meaning, Harriet knew, there's absolutely no way I'm going to tell you, because it would risk exposing my surveillance operation.

'There is one more thing,' Şivan Ergüner said. 'I hear Musa has been hanging around with a pirate-radio DJ who wants to make him famous.'

'And do you have a name for the DJ?'

'Sure. He calls himself Shareef when he broadcasts, but his real name is Benjamin Barrett.'

'And where does this Benjamin Barrett live?'

'The pirate station he works for is Mister Fantastic FM. And that's all I know.' Şivan Ergüner looked at his watch, a fake stainless-steel Rolex, and smiled winningly. 'It's been lovely talking to you ladies, but I must go back to work.'

After the man had climbed into his rusty Nissan and driven off, Harriet and Susan Blackmore looked at each other and burst into laughter. Harriet said, 'Is he for real?'

'If you looked up James Bond in the Argos catalogue, you'd probably find Şivan's photograph. The reason he left Turkey wasn't anything to do with politics: he was having an affair with the wife of one of his brothers-in-law – the man those hotheads wanted to assassinate. I'm fairly sure that he's sleeping with the daughter of the man who owns the bookshop, but his information is usually prime grade, the finest ore. He loves to gossip, and loves to tell me all about it. I'm going to miss him,' Susan Blackmore said, 'if he ever makes good his threat to go home. I hope he does, actually, because if he stays here, sooner or later he's going to hack off someone who works for one of the gangs that run the heroin trade.'

'If this turns out to be useful,' Harriet said, handing the MI5 agent her business card, 'I'm going to owe you big time.'

'If you need any help,' Susan Blackmore said, 'call me. Six likes to think it has all the goods on the refugee communities, but if you want to catch up with your man we're your best bet.'

Harriet said, with her nicest smile, 'Are you trying to recruit me?'

'The offer's there, if you need it. It was good to meet you, Harriet. I really hope that you find what you're looking for.'

6

The Holborn Safe Deposit Centre occupied the vault of a bank that had stood at the southern end of Hatton Garden until it was hit by a five-hundred-pound bomb at the height of the Blitz. The vault, buried fifty feet deep in London clay, survived the blast, and in 1951 was converted to its present function. It was used by many of Hatton Garden's jewellers to store their stock each night, as well as by several hundred ordinary customers who deposited their valuables, important documents, and family keepsakes in its boxes, secure in the knowledge that everything was fully insured by Lloyd's underwriters, and the vault itself was protected by an impregnable box of reinforced concrete and steel plate, and by the very latest security and surveillance equipment.

Alfie learned all this from a leaflet that he found on the table of the safe-deposit centre's ante-room. He was waiting for the manager to return after phoning both Joe Walker and his solicitor to confirm that Alfie had power of attorney over his grandmother's affairs. Fifteen minutes passed; twenty. The little ante-room – breeze-block walls painted white, a worn green carpet, a battered table, two plastic chairs – was as cheerless as a police cell, and Alfie, expecting to be thrown out on the street or worse, gave a guilty little start when at last the manager came into the room. But the large, unsmiling man, wearing a pinstriped suit and club tie apologised for the delay, said that everything was in order, and led Alfie to a counter where a young woman checked his passport, had him sign his name in a leather-bound register, and said that Mr Kelly was already waiting in the vault.

Alfie had been unable to find the key to his grandmother's safe-deposit box, but this wasn't a problem. All he had to do was pay a small fee, and the lock would be drilled out. The young woman zipped Alfie's credit card through a reader attached to a telephone and gave him a receipt, and the manager led him through a steel-framed portal, like the hatch of a nuclear bomb shelter, into a disappointingly small, brightly lit space lined on three sides with the faces of the steel safe-deposit boxes, a neat, gunmetal-grey jigsaw puzzle of small and large squares and rectangles. Mr Kelly, a sprightly old man with brilliantined yellow-white hair, used his battery-operated drill on the lock, and stepped aside.

The steel-lined space behind the little door was about twice the size of a shoebox. Two manila folders lay beneath four stacks of small diaries bound in red or blue cloth, each with a year lettered in Indian ink on its spine, each decade's-worth bound with elastic bands that had long ago perished.

Alfie refused the manager's offer of the use of a viewing cubicle, said that he wanted to take everything with him. The manager found him a Marks and Spencer carrier bag for his treasure trove, and said, as they waited for the little lift that led to the world above, 'You understand that because we had to drill out the lock, the rest of the rental period has been voided. Fortunately, only a few months of the twenty-five-year contract remained.'

'What would have happened if I hadn't found out about this?'

'We always attempt to contact the customer when the rental period expires. If we are unsuccessful, we open the box, auction anything of value, and take our costs from the proceeds.'

'So it was lucky that I discovered the contract when I did. In a few months you would have opened the box anyway . . .'

And found a pile of worthless paper, and most likely thrown it all out.

'If we do have to open a box, sir, we always do our best to contact the customer. Please give me a call if you want to renew the rental,' the manager said, and wished Alfie a good day as the lift door opened.

Alfie took a taxi back to his place in Islington. He felt like a spy smuggling secrets across a border, and resisted the temptation to look at any of the diaries or open the folders until he had locked the caravan's door and drawn the curtains across its windows.

The diaries were written in a neat copperplate script that Alfie immediately recognized as his grandfather's, beginning the day that Chamberlain declared war on Germany and ending forty-one years later, on 23 December 1980, just before Maurice Flowers suffered his fatal stroke. The two folders were more immediately promising, for both contained sheaves of papers photocopied from informal notebooks that he had kept while supervising two separate archaeological excavations in northern Iraq in the late 1930s.

Alfie took half a Valium to mash his excitement, and leafed through the contents of the first folder, which described an excavation that had taken place in August and September of 1936, some sixty miles to the west of Mosul and the site of the ancient city of Nineveh, uncovering the church and other buildings of a small Christian community from the fifth century. There was a log of the daily progress of the dig, annotated by terse comments about the beastly heat and dust storms. One entry noted laconically that a group of bandits had been repelled by 'sustained gunfire for a period of a quarter of an hour, which came near to exhausting our ammunition'. There were details of payments to the workers, and to the traders who had supplied food and water. There was a carefully executed plan of the dig, and pen-and-ink drawings of various finds.

And there, among sketches of clasps, brooches and pins, several small knives and an unornamented crucifix, was a meticulous rendering of patterns of hash marks and dots sprayed among riverine curves: some of the elements that Morph used to frame his cartoons.

Alfie felt a fist in his stomach. Felt a tingling pressure at the back of his head.

According to a brief note at the bottom of the drawing, it was part of a larger design or glyph incised into the face of 'an anomalous stone I believe to be very much older than the structure into which it was incorporated'. There was no mention of this stone in the diary entries, but tipped in among the photocopied pages were a few browning photographs. A young man on the back of a camel – Alfie's grandfather in his youth, wearing puttees and baggy shorts and a pith helmet. A gang of men in burnouses using a crude hoist to lift a stone from a pit. A panoramic view of a stepped excavation, men working with crude picks and shovels on its different levels. An old man with a lined face, a long wild beard and a dignified expression, holding a large clay tablet against his chest. Four European men in pith helmets posing stiffly beside a large piece of stone that lay on its side in a trench, irregularly rounded at one end and cracked diagonally for half its length. Alfie's grandfather was a head taller than the other three, who looked to be in their teens.

On the back of this photograph was written, in a spiky script not Alfie's grandfather's, *Maurice, Clarence, Julius and David ~ Four Nomads, and an Anomalous Stone.*

Alfie remembered what his grandmother had told him yesterday – that she had never once let the nomads down. He also remembered that Mr Prentiss's first name had been David. He stared at the photograph for a long time, but couldn't decide which if any of the three youths posed with his grandfather was a youthful David Prentiss. He couldn't make out any markings on the face of the stone, either. Judging by the absence of shadows, the photograph had been taken at noon, and it was slightly overexposed.

The second excavation had taken place two years later, in a small valley in the Zagros Mountains of northern Iraq. There was a detailed map showing the location of the site, and a plan of the second church, twin to the one uncovered on the first expedition and of a similar age. This time the diary entries mentioned unseasonable rain and fog, and attacks on the baggage ponies by wolves. There were several sketches of fragments of a glyph found on something called Anselm's stele, badly eroded but almost certainly identical to that carved into the anomalous stone found at the first site, and the expedition had also discovered something completely unexpected beneath the church: a system of underground chambers with paintings and carvings 'of some considerable antiquity' on the walls. Maurice Flowers had made careful drawings of some of these, and among his renderings of ibexes and antelopes were 'examples of the elements of large abstract patterns': hash marks and grids and sprays of dots, zigzags and jagged rainbows, and nested curves like a child's drawing of a flock of seagulls.

Alfie couldn't help wondering if the piece of paper he'd found in his grandfather's desk had been an exact copy of one of those large abstract patterns.

He studied the detailed map of the three underground chambers, read an account of a failed attempt to clear fallen rocks blocking a passage that might once have led to other chambers, and discovered that there were pages missing from the journal, gaps in its day-by-day narrative. There was another small cache of photographs: a grainy view of snow-capped mountains; a picture of a lumpy meadow backed by a steep cliff; the same meadow stripped of vegetation and littered with carefully dug holes; four weathered pieces of stone stacked in a kind of pillar. And, in a chamber lit by a slanting column of sunlight, Alfie's grandfather standing next to a tall stone with a rounded top. It was just possible to see that there were markings on the face of the stone; although Alfie couldn't make out any real detail, even when he studied the photograph with his magnifying lens in shadowless tungsten light, he was willing to bet his entire yard against a child's sandpit that the markings were a complex pattern made up of the same set of elements as the cave paintings and the carvings on the anomalous stone and Anselm's stele, the same elements found in Morph's graffiti and on the fragment of stone that his father had given to Miriam Luttwak.

Alfie's long bare toes flexed rhythmically, gripping at the tufts that fringed one of the ancient oriental carpets, as he thought it through. Heavy black curtains were drawn across the windows behind him. A lamp glowed at his elbow, its light mellowed by a yellow and crimson silk scarf (left behind by his last girlfriend) draped over it.

Maurice Flowers had discovered complex patterns, which he called glyphs, on stones and in cave paintings in two places in Iraq. Alfie didn't know much about cave art, but supposed that the paintings were very old – much older than the church which had stood above them – tens of thousands of years old. Years later, exposure to a similar pattern or set of glyphs had damaged his brain. Had given him a form of epilepsy, and made him sensitive to the set of glyphs that Morph used to frame his cartoons. Those cartoons were anti-American, which suggested but did not prove that Morph was from Iraq. But the drug which Alfie remembered his grandfather smoking, and which Mr Prentiss had prescribed as part of Alfie's treatment after his disastrous trespass in his grandfather's study, had definitely come from Iraq. From a plant called haka, which grew somewhere north of Baghdad.

There was no mention of haka in the photocopied pages of the journal that Maurice Flowers had kept during that second excavation, and nothing to indicate that he believed the glyphs to have anything other than a historical significance. That discovery must have come later, but how had he realized that haka and the glyphs were in some way connected? Perhaps someone else had discovered that conection, Alfie thought – one of the 'Four Nomads'. One of them had almost certainly been David Prentiss, but who were the other two? Were they still alive? They must be in their eighties now, but it was possible . . .

Alfie was paging through the third volume of his grandfather's diaries, looking for and failing to find any mention of the Nomads, when his mobile rang. It was Toby Brown.

'I hope you're at home, Flowers, because I'm standing right outside your gates.'

'Jesus – the party.'

Alfie had forgotten all about the wrap party for *The Elemental*, and Morph's promised appearance.

'I've got a minicab here, so don't be too long putting on your glad rags.'

'Give me five minutes.'

After Alfie's caravans had been burgled for the third time, his tenant, George Johnson, had helped him construct a place where he could stash his valuables. There'd once been an inspection pit running the length of the garage. Alfie and George had placed an old office safe on its back at the bottom of this, welded a dozen steel rods to either side of it, and filled in the pit with three tons of ready-mixed concrete. A manhole cover set in the floor of the garage between the two caravans gave access to the safe's door. Alfie used a crowbar to lift it up, unlocked the door and heaved it open, and stashed the folders and diaries, wrapped in the Marks and Spencer carrier bag, inside. It wasn't as secure as the Holborn Safe Deposit Centre, it wasn't insured by Lloyd's of London, but it was the next best thing.

In the minicab, Toby Brown asked Alfie if Elliot had managed to make anything of the video grab of Morph's face, saying, when

Alfie told him that he'd only given it to Elliot that morning, 'How else are we going to recognize the guy?'

'You said that Adrian Welch is paying a bunch of graffiti artists to do some kind of performance piece. If Morph's there, we'll know who he is as soon as he goes to work.'

Alfie had decided not to tell Toby about his grandfather's journals and diaries. That was family business, a kind of parallel investigation that didn't have anything to do with the search for Morph. Instead, he told him what his agent, Lucinda Edelman, had found out about Robbie Ruane.

'I must say, he's something of a rogue,' Lucinda had said, when she'd phoned back that morning. Her husky contralto was that of a twenty-year-old siren from some old *film noir*; in person, she was a painfully skinny woman in her sixties, her hair cut in a page-boy bob and dyed deep glossy chestnut red, her face pale with powder, her lipstick vivid as a wound. She wore vivid clothes too, shocking pink Chanel, Liberty scarves, leopard-skin shoes, much gold jewellery. She lived a short walk from her offices on the King's Road in a mews house in Chelsea with her partner, a woman some thirty years younger, smoked clove-flavoured Russian cigarettes in an amber cigarette holder, and could drink most men under the table – she'd secured some of her best deals by outdrinking unwary picture editors and advertising executives. In the 1960s, she had represented half the fashion photographers in London; now, although most of her clients were dead, she was kept busy looking after their estates, and she also took on their relatives, as she'd taken on Alfie, without making it seem that she was doing them a favour.

She told Alfie that Robbie Ruane was a dealer who had made several important discoveries, but that he also had a reputation for fleecing naive young clients with outrageous contracts and deductions. 'He's being sued by two of his clients right now. Also by his insurers. It seems that he sold a painting after it had been supposedly destroyed in a flood. And he also has a habit of telling his clients that he was forced to sell their works at much lower prices than those which he actually receives.'

'So, basically, he's a crook.'

'The funny thing is, he doesn't need to be. He has plenty of money. He bought up and later sold scads of the early work of the Brit Art crowd – apparently he still has a very fine Damien Hirst vitrine. If he is a crook, it isn't out of necessity. It's because he's born to it.'

'You sound as if you admire him, Lucinda.'

'If there wasn't a rogue or two in our kind of business, darling, things would be simply too boring for words. And besides, it keeps the trade on its toes. But you, my chick, must have nothing to do with him. I won't stand for it.'

After Alfie had told him all this, Toby said, 'This is good. This gives us an in.'

'It does?'

'Of course it does. We find Morph, and we warn him about Robbie Ruane. Plus, of course, we ask him for an exclusive interview, to be published in one of the Sunday broadsheets.'

'Although we don't have any such thing lined up.'

Toby shrugged. He was jackknifed in the rear seat of the minicab, sucking on a cigarette and blowing smoke through the open window, a compromise with the non-smoking driver. 'We can say that it got spiked in favour of something else. Happens all the time. The important thing is to get the guy talking. And also, please don't get in a fight with Adrian Welch.'

'Why would I want to get in a fight with Adrian Welch?'

'Because he owes you money. Because you have this dumb idea that the world is a just place, and all sins must be accounted for. Be cool. This is more important than a few hundred quid.'

The wrap party was in deepest Hackney. There were parts of this blighted borough where the middle class had dug in for the duration: painstakingly restoring Victorian villas, patiently picking litter from their front gardens every day, organizing Neighbourhood Watches and petitioning the council. But this wasn't one of them. This was still a piece of London's Wild East, a spavined cul-de-sac lined with abandoned sweatshops and warehouses awaiting demolition or conversion into trendy live/work units. It was eight in the evening, the cloudy sky bruising with dusk, just dark enough to have triggered the streetlamps. Three burnt-out cars sat in a row on their wheel-rims. A supermarket trolley stood on top of a mound of fly-tipped builders' rubble. Two shabby men stood in the shadows of a narrow entryway, faces pale as chalk. One was chewing mechanically, dribbling some kind of dark liquid as his mouth worked.

Music boomed into the cool gritty air at the end of the cul-de-sac, where floodlights shone like a row of baby suns above the brick wall of the yard of a two-storey factory building whose windows, unlike those of its neighbours, were unboarded. It had been bought by a couple of young architects, urban-pioneer types who had converted a staggeringly cheap, completely wrecked property in an ungentrified no-go post-industrial area into a cool living space that doubled as an advertisement for their practice. They also rented out the yard and the ground floor to production companies who used it as a location for TV cop dramas and movies about Mockney gangsters played for cheap laughs by slumming RADA graduates. Tonight, it was the venue for the wrap party of *The Elemental*.

As he climbed out of the minicab, Alfie realized that the music playing inside the yard was some kind of cut-up or dub mix of the movie's theme song, an old-style reggae number by the Viceroys that drew a hopeful comparison between the plight of oppressed Rastafarians and the three prophets who had survived Nebuchadnezzar's burning fiery furnace. The writer/director/producer, Adrian Welch, had played it on set before the beginning of each day's shoot 'to put everyone's head in the right place'. *The Elemental* was about a fire elemental a bunch of teenagers had called up by using a Ouija board or reading something aloud from an old book – Alfie wasn't too sure. It was that kind of movie, made up of bits of other movies just like it. Alfie hadn't lasted until the end of the shoot, but he believed that the teenagers began to die one by one in horrible ways involving fire until the two survivors found the counter spell, or realized that the salamander could be blown up with metallic sodium. Something like that, anyway.

A DJ was doing some fundamental work on the song. Isolating a brief section of the bass guitar, and playing it backwards and forwards while bringing up the chorus, letting it lose itself in a chamber of echoes, stretching a plaintive line into a kind of were-wolf wail . . .

While Toby tried to pay off the minicab driver and light a fresh cigarette at the same time, a black cab pulled up, brakes squeaking, its engine making the familiar loose knocking sound, like an overeager clock. A young woman wearing little more than a white T-shirt cinched with a gold chain climbed out and sashayed through the gate, her hips tilting back and forth. 'Thank God for show business,' Toby said with a lecherous leer, as he and Alfie followed her into the party.

At the far end of the floodlit yard, the DJ, a black kid wearing fat headphones, spidered over his decks as he tortured the reggae song to death. *Shadrach was a dreadlock, Meshach was a dreadlock, also Abednego.* The high sweet voices of the Viceroys ringing out loud and clear for a moment, before drowning in a swamp of scratches and echo that shivered the air above the party-goers. There was the usual crowd of media people – actors and friends of actors, young novelists and film-makers and fashion-istas who genuinely believed that having famous, rich, or famous and rich parents was a handicap, and various liggers and hangers-on, most of them wearing at least two items of black clothing – salted with a spattering of beautiful young things in Goa chic, cheap ethnic clothes and expensive sunglasses. A group of sulky peacocks from Planet Goth lurked in a corner, among them a stunning girl as tall and slim as a supermodel, with purple hair, purple eye-shadow and purple lips, wearing fishnet stockings and a broad, studded belt instead of a skirt. Technicians wore T-shirts with the slogan *I Survived The Elemental* in fiery lettering across their chests. The lead actress, wearing a vintage puffball dress and bright red lipstick, was talking with an older couple, a silver-haired gentleman in a blazer and a plump woman in a flowery dress and a cartwheel hat – they had to be Adrian Welch's parents, who'd fronted the seed money for the five-minute demo which had won the movie funding from the National Lottery fund.

Alfie, in his scuffed black leather jacket and the white shirt and black trousers he'd put on that morning for the visit to the Holborn Safe Deposit Centre, fitted right into this eclectic crowd. As did Toby, in his usual uniform of crumpled black and fag ash. He snagged a bottle of Corona from one of the oil drums full of crushed ice, saw that Alfie had spotted Adrian Welch, and said, 'Remember, if you're going to talk to him, try to be nice.'

'I should ask him how Morph got himself invited to this.'

'Just don't get us thrown out before we find the kid.'

Part of the yard was penned off with a line of interlocking crowd control barriers hung with posters for *The Elemental*, the monster's snarling face composed entirely of CGI'd orange flames. Behind this makeshift fence, Adrian Welch, an aging trustafarian in blond dreads, long white cheesecloth shirt and combat pants, was chivvying a group of taggers who were eyeing the party-goers with contempt and suspicion. Their body language pure Travis Bickle: *You looking at me, fool?* Most wore hoodies and base-ball caps or woollen watch-caps pulled so low that they seemed to lack foreheads, and baggy jeans or military-surplus pants with thigh pockets big enough to hold a couple of spray cans. Several had pulled their hoods over their baseball caps for added anonymity. They wrote their tags on every flat public surface they could find and dreamed of covering entire trains from top to bottom in four-colour throw-up burners, but the actual act of tagging was private, furtive, anonymous.

Taggers never used their real names. Their tags were part of their street armour. Secret identities, superhero costumes. But now, with plastic carrier bags full of spray cans sagging between their brand-new trainers – when he'd been chasing after Morph on his own, Alfie had learned that taggers didn't carry their works in anything that cost money in case they had to make a run for it and leave everything behind – the taggers stood exposed in floodlight glare, nervous as unshelled hermit crabs. Behind them were a couple of pasting tables laden with aerosol paint cans and fat felt-tip pens, and a row of big, stretched canvases the size of front doors propped against the yellow brick wall of the yard. One of the kids was chewing gum with his mouth open. One was wearing shades with blue lenses. One had wrapped a red and white chequered scarf around his mouth and nose, like a Palestinian street fighter. One, the oldest of the bunch, stood with shoulders hunched and hands shoved in the pockets of a red leather jacket speckled with flecks of dried paint. All of them were pretending to ignore Adrian Welch, who had finally got them to line up so that he could make a pan shot with his Sony digital video camera, telling them in his *faux* Essex accent to relax, to hang loose and have fun, to do their own thing. His girlfriend, a tightly wound blonde in a slinky black minidress, trotted along the line, handing out video grabs of the monster from the movie, just in case the kids hadn't noticed the posters.

Toby took a quick swig from his bottle of Corona, leaned towards Alfie, and said, over the incredible noise of feedback, 'Which one do you think is our boy?'

'If he really is from Iraq, I suppose he has to be one of the white kids. But definitely not the one at the end of the line.'

This was a skinny, blushing boy who was obviously from some nice, middle-class suburban home, wearing baggy jeans at half-mast, a mesh T-shirt, and a skull-and-cross-bones doo-rag tied around his forehead, and trying to radiate a stone-cold hip-hop killer attitude.

Alfie pointed to the trio of council-estate kids who stood with their narrow shoulders hunched around their ears and the hoods of their sweatshirts drawn so far over their heads that only the tips of their noses were visible, and said, 'Those are definitely home-grown, too.'

Which left the guy in the red leather jacket, or, Alfie's most likely candidate, the guy masked by the Palestinian scarf, who noticed that Alfie was staring at him and gave him a sulky fuck-you glare. Alfie looked away, and saw through a gap in the crowd Robbie Ruane, wearing a fawn suede jacket and white T-shirt and watching through tinted Versace wraparounds as Adrian Welch turned through three hundred and sixty degrees, camera to his face, panning across the white canvases, the crowd of onlookers, the sullen group of taggers.

Toby was asking Alfie if he was okay.

'See that guy in the sunglasses? That's Robbie Ruane.'

'Uh-oh.'

'If one of those kids is Morph, one of us is going to have to cut him off before he reaches the prize.'

Adrian Welch told the taggers, 'Freestyle, guys, anything you like as long as it takes off from the salamander.'

'Sally-what?'

'*Say* what?'

Two of the council-estate kids elbowed each other, pretending to crack up.

'The fire elemental,' Adrian Welch said. His voice loud and clear in a moment of silence from the sound system. 'The monster in the photos you've been given. The one on the fucking posters.'

'*That's* not a monster.'

'We show you a *real* monster, no worries.'

The council-estate kids went into a huddle while the rest of the taggers grabbed pens or shook spray cans before slashing bold lines across the virgin white canvases. Palestinian Scarf worked at the tip of a felt pen with a taped razor blade, splaying it out, then turned to his canvas and made a big arc, and then another, defining an ellipse that he began to ornament with a fringe of dashes and dots like jumping sweat, Keith Haring-style, drawing them out to the edge of the canvas and leaving no room for Morph's trademark framing.

None of the other artists were producing anything like Morph's cartoons, either.

Toby, working on his second bottle of beer, asked Alfie what he thought. Alfie shrugged.

'I agree,' Toby said.

The graffiti artists were all hard at work now, rattling their cans, spraying outlines or filling them with bold splashes of colour, feathering lines with delicate shading. Their shadows, flung across the canvases by the bright arc lights, aped their movements. Most of them were working in black and red and yellow, although one kid was filling his canvas from edge to edge with an interlocking pattern of green and blue cubes – ice cubes, each with a tiny, vivid red flame at its heart. Adrian Welch crabbed up and down the line, the DV camera glued to his face, his girlfriend guiding him by his elbow. The air was full of the sharp-sweet smell of acrylic paint and propellant. A few of the party-goers were watching or taking pictures with digital cameras or mobiles, but most ignored the show. The DJ was still working the reggae song up and down. *Rastaman invisible, invisible yeah, some kind of miracle, oh no no.* One canvas stood untouched, its luminous white rectangle floating at the far edge of the line.

'None of those guys are our guy,' Toby said. 'At least, none of them are working in the famous style.'

'Maybe he's late.'

'Maybe he doesn't exist. Or maybe he's in jail, or his mother wouldn't let him out so late. Looks like the pirate-radio shock jock got it wrong,' Toby said.

'It looks like we have wasted a perfectly good evening,' Robbie Ruane said. 'Hello, Alfie. I've been waiting for your call.'

'I have to talk to someone else,' Alfie said, and Toby managed to get in the art dealer's way as Alfie dodged past a couple of goths ransacking an ice-filled oil drum and threaded through the crowd to the crash barriers. He unfastened two of them and stepped through the gap, saying boldly, 'Adrian! I want a word with you!'

Adrian Welch was videoing the tagger who was filling his canvas with tiny ice cubes. Without taking his face away from his camera, he told Alfie that he'd talk to him later.

'It can't wait. I want to know about Morph.'

'I'm *working*, Alfie. *Comprende?* I'm filming this for a nice little extra on the DVD. Enjoy the party, why don't you?'

Alfie caught the man as he tried to walk off, clamping a hand on his arm just above the elbow (just barely resisting the temptation to grab a handful of his blond dreads), saying right in his ear, 'How did you get in contact with him?'

Adrian Welch lowered the DV camera and glared at Alfie. He was in his late twenties, the kind of guy who was good fun for an evening but would wreck your life if you let him into it, who'd grown up thinking that the world was his toy, that if things got broken there were always more things. Still, even though no one needed another half-baked piece-of-shit shocker like *The Elemental*, he had actually finished it. He'd found in the film business an ideal venue for his instant charm and unabashed hustling; all the evenings he'd spent getting blissfully wasted at all-nighters at the Coronet and the Prince Charles hadn't gone to waste after all.

'If this is about the misunderstanding over your fee, this isn't the time and place,' he told Alfie, and signalled to the man who'd worked as key grip on the shoot. 'Tom! Tom, a little help here, if you please!'

Tom, a beefy middle-aged man with a shaven head, looked at Adrian scornfully, then turned away.

'I suppose you didn't pay him, either,' Alfie said.

'If this is some kind of shakedown—'

'I want to know how you got in contact with Morph. Tell me about that, and you'll never see me again.'

'Who?'

They were shouting at each other over the airplane-crash noise of the sound system.

Alfie pointed at the blank canvas. 'Morph. The tagger who hasn't turned up.'

'Tell me about it.'

'How did you get in touch with him?'

'He got in touch with me. Or, wait, it was his manager.'

Alfie said, thinking of Robbie Ruane, 'His manager?'

'It's what he called himself. Fellow by the name of Shareef. A friend of Frankie Fingers over there,' Adrian Welch said, pointing across the crowded yard at the DJ. 'They both work for the same pirate station, which is how Shareef heard about this. He told me that his man was the most famous tagger in London, and I told him to bring him down. Except that he hasn't. And that's all I know, so if you'll excuse me,' Adrian Welch said, shaking himself free of Alfie's grip, 'I have work to do.'

As Alfie headed across the yard towards the DJ, there was a sudden blare of air-horn noise, louder than the music. Everyone turned to look at the gate as the first of the sheep bolted through it, stopping dead in its tracks when it saw the people staring at it, other sheep jostling in behind it. Black-faced sheep, recently shorn, pale and skinny and knock-kneed, with yellow eyes and twisted horns.

Several people laughed, clearly thinking that it was part of the festivities. Adrian Welch swung around, the DV camera still up at his face, as another air-horn blast drowned out the reggae for a long moment and something went off with a flash right outside the gate. People flinched, shrieked, cheered. The sheep scattered in every direction with startling agility, pursued by a billowing cloud of green, sweet-smelling smoke. Letters were stencilled in black spray-paint on their flanks, one letter on each sheep. A couple of men chased a sheep lettered with a U. A sheep lettered with an O bolted under one of the tables, knocking it askew, scattering spray cans and pens. A sheep decorated with an exclamation mark grabbed the hem of the lead actress's puffball dress between its yellow teeth; she pulled back in panic and fell flat on her backside when a long strip of red material gave way. The three council-estate kids in hoodies backed away as a sheep lettered with an N trotted towards them. One of them aimed a spray can at it. Robbie Ruane muscled to the front of the crowd, raising his little Ixus camera to his face. The reggae gave out with a screech as a couple of sheep – an S and an A – cannoned off the DJ's decks. Adrian Welch, grinning hugely, was pointing his camera here and there while people ran from the sheep or chased after them or watched the knockabout comedy with studied cool.

Alfie ran through thinning green smoke towards the gate. He was absolutely certain, no question, that Morph had made an appearance after all. Outside, an ancient Land Rover completed a three-point turn and drove off. The two lowlifes he'd seen earlier chased its red rear lights, running with strange stiff cartoonish gaits. The vehicle accelerated and squealed around the corner at the end of the road; the two men followed. Alfie pulled his notebook from his camera bag and wrote down the Land Rover's number, just like a real detective, then went back inside to find Toby Brown.

7

'George won't be pleased,' Toby said. 'They're shitting all over the place back there.'

'Sheep shit's fairly clean, as shit goes,' Alfie said. 'Like pellets. We can sweep it out when we've made our delivery.'

'This is more like green slime,' Toby said, glancing in the rear-view mirror as he drove. 'Those are some pretty nervous sheep, Flowers. You'll have to hose down the whole van after this, and scrub it out with a couple of gallons of disinfectant. *Strong* disinfectant. And listen, what if the guy who owns the Land Rover isn't the guy who owns the sheep?'

'Why wouldn't he be?'

'Or suppose he doesn't want them back.'

'Why wouldn't he want them back? They're nice sheep. Famous sheep. Artistically significant sheep. Or they would be, if they ever managed to line up in the right order . . .'

'If he doesn't take them back, what are you going to do with ten sheep?'

'I'll dig a barbecue pit and invite everyone I know. I'll even invite you. But he'll take them back. Don't worry.'

They were driving George Johnson's battered Transit van east out of London along the A13, past what was left of the Ford works at Dagenham, past reefs of council houses, past retail parks, industrial parks, fenced wastelands where wrecked cars were piled in uneven stacks. The sheep jostled around each other in the back of the van, hoofs clattering as they scrabbled for purchase on the plywood floor.

Last night, at the wrap party, the DJ had refused to tell Alfie and Toby anything about Shareef or Morph – he'd clearly believed that they were police, looking scornful when Alfie had offered him ten pounds in exchange for Shareef's telephone number. The technicians had corralled the sheep in a makeshift pen lashed up from the crowd-control barriers, and Alfie promised the architects who owned the converted factory that he would find a good home for the animals. Luckily, they'd seen the funny side of the stunt. It helped that they were getting a puff in the *Evening Standard*, courtesy of the gossip columnist who'd been covering the party.

It hadn't been so easy to persuade George Johnson to find out who the Land Rover belonged to.

'It is more difficult than you think,' he told Alfie.

He was a short, burly man in his sixties, hunched in an over-sized oil-stained cardigan of indeterminate colour, its pockets sagging with the weight of nuts, bolts, and screws of every size, scraps of wire, and half-finished rolls of Polo mints. He'd become addicted to Polo mints when he'd given up smoking ten years ago, after a heart attack.

Alfie said, 'You make a phone call to your friend in the police, he makes his phone call to the DVLA. What's so hard?'

'If this was the old days, Alfie, you'd be right. But now, what with call logs and call monitoring and form-filling . . .'

'There's a McGarrett in it for your friend. And also one for you, of course,' Alfie said. 'Think about it.'

In the ticket-tout slang that Alfie had picked up from George, a McGarrett was fifty pounds – cash in hand, of course.

George pinched the tip of his tuberous nose between two fingers, twitching it back and forth as if trying to tune it to a radio station that would give him the answer. He was always fiddling with this fabulously sensitive organ, which, he claimed, could not only sniff out trouble or a bad deal a mile off, but could also predict the weather. He'd been renting the little patch of land on which his workshop stood for more than thirty years. He'd rented it from Alfie's father, and before that he'd rented it from Mr Chelab, the gentleman from whom Alfie's father had won it in a poker game, and before that he'd rented it from Ira Glass, who, according to George, had given it to Mr Chelab to save himself the trouble of having his arms and legs broken after he'd fallen behind on paying back the money he'd borrowed from Mr Chelab to set himself up in the haberdashery business. Ira Glass had bought it cheaply after the war, when the coach firm which had owned it had gone bankrupt, but he had never been able to build houses on it and make his fortune because he'd tried to bribe the wrong man on the council's planning committee, just about the only man on the planning committee who couldn't be bribed, which was why Ira Glass had spent a year in prison. That was where he'd met Mr Chelab, a crooked accountant who did a little work, now and then, for the Krays, which was why Ira Glass had so readily given up his property after he'd defaulted on his loan.

Although George rented just one corner of the yard, he exercised a kind of droit de seigneur over the rest, keeping the vehicles he restored as a hobby in the airy, open-ended garage, now and then asking Alfie if he'd mind if one or another of his extended family left a car or a van there for a few days or a few months. In return, George did the odd favour for Alfie. He'd found an electrician to run a mains cable to Alfie's caravans, for instance, and two of George's nephews had helped to dig the trench for the mains water pipe. Alfie, who knew that arranging an illegal vehicle-registration check was at least as big a favour as piping in water or cabling in electricity, said, 'I wouldn't ask if I didn't need it. And I really do need it badly.'

'You're still looking for that kid that does the graffiti?'

'Exactly.'

'I thought you had your journalist friend helping you out.'

'He's more of a book reviewer than a journalist. That's why I came to you, George. You're my last best hope.'

George popped a Polo mint into his mouth and sighed. 'Seeing as it's you, Alfie, maybe I can organize something. And listen, don't take this the wrong way or nothing, but don't you think you're taking this detective work a little too seriously?'

Alfie and Toby left the A13 and bumped along potholed roads through a shabby landscape neither city nor country. Scruffy fields growing thistles and corrugated iron sheds, a car-wrecking yard, a skip-hire business fortified with cyclone fences and razor wire and CCTV cameras, warehouse sheds that could have been phone centres, parcel depots, electronics factories, or private prisons. Articulated trucks and big vans roaring out of nowhere, rocking the Transit in their dusty wakes. Burnt-out cars rusting among elders and brambles. Hedgerows caught about with the tattered flags of plastic bags. Ditches clogged with pyramids of fly-tipped rubble. The boarded brick shed and canopy of an abandoned service station thick with swirling graffiti – none of it, as far as Alfie could see, Morph's.

This was bandit country, a lost place where pikeys organized dog-fights and bare-knuckle contests, and minor-league gangsters took out the opposition with shotgun blasts. Always electricity pylons marching away towards the low horizon. Always the sad sigh of traffic speeding in the distance. The Land Rover was registered to an address in this Bermuda Triangle, but few of the roads had names, and most of them led nowhere in particular, petering out at a gate to a junkyard or in a blighted clump of sycamores where someone had dumped dozens of black rubbish bags leaking some kind of toxic effluent.

At last, Alfie had Toby pull over outside a milk-powder plant and asked the security guard at the gate for directions. The man was able to put them right after an elaborate consultation with someone on the other end of his mobile phone. They doubled back and turned left at the abandoned service station, following a lane unmarked on the map, a dusty mane of dry grass in its centre, narrow passing places to the left and right in ragged machine-trimmed hawthorn hedges. The sheep complained at every jolt, scrabbling back and forth as the van swayed past a picture-postcard cottage with honeysuckle and white roses growing up one wall, past a fieldstone gateway framing the entrance to a track that arrowed away between freshly ploughed fields towards a farmhouse silhouetted at the low horizon. And there was a cast-iron sign beside an American-style mailbox on a post – West End Field, the address that George's contact had ferreted out of the DVLA.

It was a smallholding, basically a large field subdivided into smaller lots by post and wire fences. A decrepit Austin Maxi rusted on its wheel rims among rampant nettles beside a row of sheds, five of them, different sizes, each painted in a different primary colour. Four polytunnels gleamed side by side in the sun. There was a goat on a chain fastened to an iron stake hammered into the ground. There were chickens pecking about. In the largest of the subdivisions, sheep grazed disconsolately on threadbare grass.

There was a caravan with plastic pots of geraniums around the steps to its door, and a drab green Land Rover parked next to it.

'Stay in the van and keep the engine running,' Alfie told Toby.

'I don't think so,' Toby said, switching off the engine and opening the door. 'The van's so hot I'm sweating like a scouser in Dixons, and I stink of sheep. I think, actually, that after this I'll *always* stink of sheep. I think that I'm going to have to go off to some wild crag and live like a hermit, out of the way of ordinary society. So excuse me if I step outside and freshen my lungs with a cigarette.'

Alfie climbed out of the van too. They stood in front of it and looked at the smallholding, which simmered quietly in the sun. 'Maybe you should get back in the van just in case,' Alfie said. 'Or at least turn it around.'

'In case someone wants to start something over a few sheep?'

'In case it's the kind of place where the bodies are buried,' Alfie said, and walked up to the gate. He couldn't find a bell, so shouted out a hello, his voice a shocking intrusion in the meditative silence.

A man walked around one end of the caravan, a tall, bony black man in his forties, his greying hair trimmed close to his skull. He wore only frayed khaki shorts and flip-flops, and carried something that caught the sunlight when he gestured with it — a machete, what the Jamaicans called a cutlass. Saying, 'What can I do for you?'

'Mr Barrett?'

'Who wants to know?'

'Donald Barrett?' Alfie was trying his best to keep his gaze on the man's face, rather than on his cutlass.

'What's this all about? Why do you people keep harassing me?'

'I have your sheep.'

The man stopped a couple of yards from the gate and studied Alfie. He had umber skin, fox-coloured. A spray of freckles across his splayed nose. He said, 'My sheep are in the field right there. You don't see them, you're more of a fool than you look.'

He had a deep, calm voice and a steady gaze, but he also had his cutlass.

Alfie, feeling his armpits growing slippery under the inadequate armour of his black leather jacket, said, 'You sold or lent these particular sheep to someone called Morph. Ten sheep, freshly shorn, different letters painted on them? If that doesn't ring a bell I have them right here in the van. You're welcome to take a look.'

'I don't know anyone called Morph.'

'That's funny, because he turned your sheep into a cross between a work of art and a political statement.'

The man studied Alfie, then said, 'You really have sheep in that van of yours?'

'Ten of them.'

Toby said, 'I bet you can smell them from there.' He was standing beside the van, lighting his second cigarette from the butt of his first.

The man made a dismissive flourish with his cutlass. 'You're crazy, driving around with sheep in the back of that thing on a hot day like this. They'll die if you don't take them back to where they come from.'

'Well, that's why we're here,' Alfie said.

'I told you, I *have* sheep. I don't need any more, and I don't need any trouble either. You go away now. You have no business here.'

'I can help you put them back where they belong, Mr Barrett,' Alfie said, 'or I can turn them out in the lane and drive off, leave you to deal with them.'

'How come you know my name? You police? Or are you working for that woman?'

'What woman?'

The man said scornfully, '"What woman?" As if you don't know.'

'I'm not working for anyone. I'm just a concerned citizen who's worried about the welfare of your sheep. All I want to do is return them to you, and have a word or two about Morph. Or else my friend will open the doors of the van and let them go free.'

'I told you, I don't know any Morph.'

'Shareef, then,' Alfie said, and saw that the man recognized the name.

Toby banged on the side of the van. The sheep made panicky sheep noises inside.

'They're getting frisky,' Alfie said.

'Getting ready to run,' Toby said, and banged on the side of the van again.

'You don't want to do that,' the man said. 'That's cruelty to animals.'

'So is painting letters on their sides and setting them free in the middle of a bunch of media wankers,' Toby said. 'You're lucky we're not from the Hackney branch of the Animal Liberation Front.'

'I had nothing to do with that,' the man said.

Alfie said, 'Shareef isn't in any trouble, and neither are you, but only because we took charge of the sheep before the police or the RSPCA got involved. In return for our help, all I want is that you answer a couple of questions.'

The man beat the flat of the cutlass blade against his thigh, thinking about this. Toby waggled the handle of the Transit van's back door. The sheep clattered about inside, making the vehicle rock on its suspension.

'All right,' the man said. 'Anything to stop your friend tormenting those poor animals.'

'We'll give you back the sheep and you'll tell me about Shareef and Morph,' Alfie said. 'Deal?'

'I don't know from Morph. Shareef, I do him a favour, and this is what happens. Before I say another word, we should take care of those sheep,' the man said, stepping forward and unlatching the gate. 'Back your van up and let them out before they cook to death.'

After the sheep had been reunited with the rest of the flock (trotting in a crocodile file spelling OWSUAUTON! – only the exclamation mark in the right place), the man, Angus Barrett, offered Alfie and Toby tea. They sat on plastic lawn-chairs on a scruffy patch of grass behind the caravan and talked about Shareef while Angus Barrett dipped in a bucket of scalding water the chicken he'd beheaded and gutted with the cutlass (its head, oddly small, lay on the cut surface of a tree stump like a sacrificial offering) and ripped handfuls of dirty white feathers from its carcass.

He told Alfie and Toby that Shareef was his nephew. 'He came here yesterday. His father, that's my older brother, Donald, he own this place. I look after it for him. Shareef said that Donald had said he could borrow a few sheep. He said that he needed them for a little bit of publicity. Shareef, that's what he calls himself after he converted, his birth name is Benjamin, wants to be famous in the worst way. What he planned to do seemed like a funny idea, he claimed Donald had given him permission, so okay, I helped him out.'

'You helped him round up the sheep,' Toby said. 'And what else? Did you drive the Land Rover?'

Angus Barrett shook his head. 'I don't go into town if I can help it. Shareef came here with this big guy call himself Watty. The two of them drove off with the sheep, and they brought the Land Rover back late last night.'

Alfie said, 'What did this big guy look like?'

'Big. A bodybuilder, or a bouncer. Maybe both.'

Alfie said, 'He didn't look at all Arabic?'

'He was an island boy, like me. Drove a nice old Mercedes. Had a chipped tooth, I remember, which he showed the only time he smiled. He didn't say much, either. Anyway, I ask Shareef when he was going to bring the sheep back and he told me to chill, he'd bring them back the next day, first thing. I told him he better do just that, or he would be in big trouble with his father. Only he doesn't come back, of course. Instead, this woman comes around, asking questions, and then you turn up, also asking questions.'

Toby said, 'What woman is this?'

'I have her card,' Angus Barrett said.

He dug it out of the pocket of his shorts and handed it to Toby, who looked at it and read out, 'Harriet Crowley. Private Investigator. Do we know a Harriet Crowley, Alfie?'

'I don't think so.'

'She also wanted to know about this friend of Shareef's,' Angus Barrett said. The half-plucked chicken hung between his splayed knees. A snow of feathers stirred around his feet. 'But she have the smell of police on her, so I didn't tell her anything. She left her card, told me to call her if I thought of anything. Said there would be money in it, as if I was some kind of informer. She also said that I should think hard about cooperating with her, or else she would make sure that I got in trouble for transporting sheep around without a livestock movement order. Frankly, she pissed me off. So anyway, then you turn up, and you're looking for the same fellow. But so far you haven't yet told me why you want to find him.'

Toby showed him two newspaper cuttings – Alfie's photograph from the *Independent* and the half-page story from the *Camden Journal* – and explained what had happened at the party, said they wanted to follow it up with an interview. 'He's after publicity,' Toby said. 'And we're here to help him get what he wants.'

Angus Barrett picked at pin feathers in the lax white pimply skin of one of the chicken's drumsticks. 'You want to interview him, eh?'

'And his friend,' Toby said.

Alfie said, 'How about it, Mr Barrett? You'd be doing him a favour.'

'I've already done him one favour too many.' Angus Barrett pulled out a few more feathers, then said, 'You have something I can write on?'

Toby handed over his notebook. Angus Barrett wrote down a mobile telephone number. 'Maybe he talks to you, maybe he doesn't, but however it works out don't come back to me asking any more questions.'

'So,' Toby said, 'what are you doing here, Angus? Hiding out?'

Angus Barrett's smile showed every one of his teeth. 'You think I'm some kind of gangster, white boy? You t'ink I is a *yardie*? A rude bwyoh?'

'It was just that you said you didn't like to go into town, you said you thought we were the police . . .'

Angus Barrett laughed. 'All white people are police or immigration officers, and all black people are gangsters, is that it? The truth is, I'm looking after this place for my brother while I try to get my head together. I used to be a lecturer in media studies at the University of Middlesex, and all kinds of pressure got to me. The usual mid-life crisis, I won't bore you with it. I quit my job, my marriage was on the rocks, my brother said I could stay here. He has a couple of men who look after the sheep and the herbs growing in those tunnels — culinary herbs, for Donald's restaurant. The sheep also, it is hard to get proper mutton in this country. I give Donald's men a hand, I go for long walks, try to write my poetry . . . Sorry to disappoint you.'

'Apologize to the man,' Alfie said, 'for your unthinking assumptions.'

Toby Brown showed the nuked graveyard of his nicotine-yellow teeth. 'Fuck you, Alfie.'

'If you two gentlemen are going to work together in the future,' Angus Barrett said, 'you'll need to sharpen up your repartee. Now you'll excuse me, but I have to feed the livestock.'

As they drove away, Toby tossed his notebook and mobile phone into Alfie's lap, and Alfie called the number that Angus Barrett had written down. The phone at the other end of the connection rang and rang, a scratching in his ear, and at last a sleepy, congested voice said, 'What up?'

'Is that Shareef?'

'What you want?'

The van went past a car parked in one of the passing places. The driver was studying a map spread on the steering wheel, another victim of the Bermuda Triangle.

Alfie said into the mobile, 'I'd like to talk to you about Morph. About his piece of work last night, with the sheep, and his graffiti. Your uncle, Angus Barrett, gave me your number, and I was wondering—'

The connection had gone dead.

'Never let a boy do a man's job,' Toby said. He plucked his mobile from Alfie's hand and hit the redial button, saying as he steered the van with one hand, 'This is Toby Brown of the *Independent*. Am I talking to Shareef? No, that was my colleague. He takes the pictures and I write the stories. Perhaps you saw the piece about the courier vans in the *Camden Journal*? You did? Well, that was mine, the photographs were by my friend. He also did the very nice picture of one of your friend Morph's artworks in the *Independent*. You didn't? I can have a copy biked over right away if you'll tell me . . . No, I understand. Well, perhaps you'd like to check it out on the website. Yes, that's right. Yes, a longer piece. No, that story was bounced down to the *Camden Journal* because it was thought to be too local, but the very imaginative piece of work with the sheep is something else altogether. On its own, unfortunately, it isn't enough for the kind of article we want to run, which is why I'm calling. Yes, an interview, absolutely. So you're his manager, or his agent? I see. In any case, you can arrange . . . I see. No, I understand, but are you sure that . . . If that's how you feel, then we'll try our best, but you have to understand that space on the news pages is very limited, it will have to be something very special . . . I'm sure it will be. I look forward to seeing it. You'll need my phone number,' Toby said. He recited the number, told Shareef that he looked forward to speaking with him again very soon, and switched off the mobile, telling Alfie, 'And that, my boy, is how a real journalist works.'

'Bravo. When do we see him?'

'Not right away. What we have to do first is go to the Imperial War Museum, first thing tomorrow morning. Apparently, Morph is planning another stunt. A big statement. We write it up, the *Independent* publishes it, and then, when we've proved that we're serious, we get to meet Shareef.'

'It sounds like he's giving you the run-around.'

'He's a black kid,' Toby said. 'He's naturally suspicious of the media. Plus, he's having fun. If we go along with what he wants, we'll get what *we* want. So unless you have a better idea . . .'

'What kind of big statement?'

'He wouldn't tell me. I guess he wants to surprise us,' Toby said.

He stopped at the junction, stuck a cigarette in his mouth and lit it, and turned left, towards the A13. Hot air rushed through the open windows, but did little to shift the stink left behind by the sheep.

Alfie said, 'Do you think you can sell a story about this surprise?'

'That depends on how good a surprise it is. What about this mysterious woman? This private investigator? Think we should give her a call?'

'I think she works for Robbie Ruane.'

'Me too.'

'He expected to meet Morph last night, and when it didn't

work out he got this private detective to find where the sheep came from, just like we did.'

'If we're lucky, we're still ahead of the game. We have Shareef's mobile number, we've talked to him, we've sort of made a deal.'

'Meanwhile, this private detective is also looking for him.'

'Good luck to her.'

Alfie said, 'She'll have resources that we don't.'

'But we're smarter.'

'Shareef works for that pirate station, Mister Fantastic FM. Maybe we should try to find it—'

'You don't find a pirate station that easily.'

'They must have a studio—'

'All you need is a couple of decks, a mixer, and a microphone, and a feed to a low-power transmitter. You can set it up anywhere. In your kitchen, in your bedroom, in your garden shed. I already thought of that angle, Flowers, and believe me, playing Shareef's little game will be a lot easier. We're cooperating with him, we aren't harassing people who know him, we'll come off as the good guys. Which, of course, is what we are.'

'And if that doesn't get us anywhere?'

'Then we'll have to go after the pirate station. Or we'll look up Shareef's dad, this Donald Barrett, and ask him where his son lives.'

'Meanwhile, I guess we should take the van back,' Alfie said, 'and clean it out.'

'The Lone Ranger and Tonto are riding along a canyon,' Toby said. 'They make a turn around a bend and run straight into a bunch of Apache braves in full warpaint. The Lone Ranger turns to Tonto and says, "What do we do now?" And Tonto says, "What's with the 'we', paleface?"'

'I was hoping you'd give me a hand,' Alfie said, 'because I have an appointment at five o'clock.'

'And *I* have an appointment with my garden, a cool glass of beer, and an eight-hundred-page biography of a very minor seventeenth-century Italian poet. Who are you meeting, if you don't mind me asking?'

'It's family business. Nothing important.'

8

The man who had followed Alfie Flowers to the party had given Harriet the licence number of the Land Rover that had delivered the sheep, and she'd traced its ownership to one Donald Barrett. That part had been easy. But when Harriet had visited the smallholding just outside London that Donald Barrett had given as his address, it turned out that he wasn't living there, and its caretaker had stonewalled every one of her questions.

She'd already tried and failed to find Benjamin Barrett, a.k.a. Shareef. If he was one of the twenty-odd B. Barretts who rented a landline in London, he was among those who hadn't answered when she'd called, and none of the five Benjamin Barretts she'd traced through her contact in a credit-rating agency had been her quarry either. The pirate-radio DJ didn't appear to have a bank account, own a credit card or ever to have entered into a credit agreement, and he either used an untraceable pay-as-you-go mobile, or rented from one of the companies where Harriet didn't have someone willing to access the customer database for a small consideration. She hadn't had any luck tracing Musa Karsu, a.k.a. Morph, either. She'd learned from a contact in the Immigration Service that a seventeen-year-old boy by the name of Musa Karsu, and his father, Ahmed Karsu, had entered the country illegally six months ago. Ahmed Karsu, forty-one years old, a shoemaker, had claimed to have been tortured by the Turkish police; medical records and a report from Amnesty International had supported his case. He and his son had been given a flat in Harringay and awarded social security pending a final decision on their status, but Ahmed had died of a massive heart attack just five weeks ago, and his son was missing, placed on the 'at risk' register by Harringay Council's social services. The police were looking for him, but as Şivan Ergüner had said, how did you find any of these poor lost boys?

Harriet thought that it should be a lot easier to trace Donald

Barrett. He was a property owner, and almost certainly had a bank account and a credit history and all the other useful stuff that almost every adult accumulates. A quick search through her CD-ROM database yielded just over a hundred D. Barretts in the London area. She could waste a couple of hours plodding through the list, or she could narrow it down by some lateral thinking. From listening to his phone-in show on Mister Fantastic FM, she believed that Benjamin Barrett was pretty young; it was possible that either he was still living with his parents or he had moved out only recently, which would explain why he didn't have a credit card or a bank account. A relationship search on an on-line database that cross-referenced the electoral rolls for the past five years gave her just one address in London where both Donald Barrett and Benjamin Barrett were registered to vote. Harriet went doorstepping.

It was an imposing semi-detached house in Stoke Newington. The elegant black woman who answered the door turned out to be Benjamin Barrett's stepmother, and seemed unsurprised that a white woman was trying to find her stepson. He'd moved out last year, she said, but was vague about his exact whereabouts. 'Donald would know. He's paying the boy's rent.'

The number that the woman gave for Donald Barrett was engaged, but his work address was just five minutes away, a minicab company on Stoke Newington High Street. The dispatcher behind the grille in the tiny office buzzed Harriet through into a room where several drivers were waiting for fares, lounging in greasy armchairs, reading newspapers, playing a game of dominoes, all of them smoking furiously and ignoring the TV that muttered to itself in a corner. Donald Barrett's office was at the top of a flight of listing, uncarpeted stairs. He was a large, genial man, turning back and forth in the swivel chair behind his desk, his hands clasped across his belly, while listening to Harriet explain that his son wasn't in any trouble, but he had a friend who was an illegal immigrant and was just possibly mixed up in something murky. This took a while, because approximately once a minute one of the half-dozen phones on the desk would ring and Donald Barrett would raise a hand, its pale creased palm towards Harriet, and say that he had to take the call. Spinning around in his chair and staring out through the dusty bow window that overlooked the noisy road while he talked into the telephone, turning back, setting the phone down, smiling at Harriet and saying, 'Now, where we were?'

Harriet handed Donald Barrett a photograph of one of Morph's graffiti. 'The boy I'm trying to find has been spray-painting stuff like this all over this area. His street name is Morph; his real name is Musa Karsu. I need to find him, and I believe that he's a friend or acquaintance of your son, which is why I would very much like to talk to Benjamin. Just a few quick questions.'

Donald Barrett said, 'You say my son knows the person who did this?'

'That's the only reason I want to talk to him.'

A phone rang; Harriet waited while Donald Barrett answered it. When he put it down, she said, 'Your son won't get into any trouble, I promise. This is entirely about his friend.'

Donald Barrett thought about this. He bent over the photograph of one of Morph's graffiti, showing Harriet the horseshoe of bare scalp, creased with three folds, that divided his hair into woolly clumps above each ear, then leaned back abruptly, looking up at the ceiling, rubbing the outer corners of his eyes with his thumbs, saying, 'Excuse me. I felt dizzy for a moment.'

'Please take your time, Mr Barrett.'

'Spots before my eyes.'

'Did your son ever talk to you about Morph, about Musa Karsu?'

Donald Barrett gave her a cautious, considered look. 'You are working for the government. Customs and Immigration, something like that.'

'I'm a private detective,' Harriet said, placing one of her business cards next to the photograph.

'I suppose that if I don't help you, it will be more official, like the police?'

'Why I'm here, Mr Barrett, is to make sure it doesn't come to that.'

One of the phones rang. Donald Barrett picked up the handset and set it down on its cradle, silencing it. He said, 'They're a plague, these graffiti artists. I own a restaurant in Church Street, just around the corner. As a matter of fact, I am the secretary of the Church Street Shopkeepers' Association. I'm sure you know the neighbourhood, very nice, up-and-coming. We organize Christmas lights, we sponsor litter bins, we don't want the place blighted. These spray-paint vandals are one of the things we campaign against. Three times last month they attack my restaurant. Twice, one writes his name on the door in silver paint, and then someone puts something very like this —' he tapped the photograph with a forefinger '— all across its window. A week later, the same things are sprayed across the vans of a courier firm in which I have a share.'

'Pronto Delivery.'

Donald Barrett smiled. 'I see that you are "on the case". You follow up every clue.'

'I read about it in a local newspaper,' Harriet said.

Alfie Flowers had taken the photographs, and his friend Toby Brown had written the story. When she'd seen the article, Harriet had realized that the two of them weren't about to give up their search for Morph, and had decided to throw a little business in the way of an old friend, asking him to put a round-the-clock tail on Alfie Flowers.

Donald Barrett said, 'I report it to the police, of course, but they shrug their shoulders, tell me they are very sorry, but they can't spend all their time chasing after kids. You say the boy who does these things knows my son?'

'That's why I want to talk to Benjamin. He might know where I can find this boy.'

'Do you have children, Ms Crowley?'

'Not yet.'

'When you do—' Another phone rang. Donald Barrett picked up its handset, put it down. 'When you do, you'll love them with all your heart. You won't be able to help yourself. When they are little, they love you too, in the same way, but later . . .'

He paused, studying something inside his head. This big, proud man suddenly struck by a painful memory.

'When they grow up,' he said, 'they become their own person. They need you less. Their interests are not always your interests.

They have secrets, suddenly, things they do not want to share with you. What I'm saying is that Benjamin is my son, but he is also his own person. After his mother died, and especially after I remarried, he turned away from me. He refused to go to university, he chased his own dreams. I can't say that I like what he has chosen to do, but it isn't for me to try to stop him. I will admit that he has been in trouble with the police, but only for small crimes. But after he converted last year, it seemed to steady him.'

'Converted?'

'I raised him as a Baptist, and last year he decided to become a Muslim. I did not oppose it. After all, we are all God's creatures, and also, it seemed to help him to grow up. He has not been in any trouble for more than a year, he has become very interested in politics, and he has his radio work. I am proud of him. I thought that we were beginning to reach an understanding. Or at least, that is what I believed until you showed me this,' Donald Barrett said, tapping the photograph of Morph's graffito with a forefinger.

'Do you know which mosque he attends?'

Harriet thought she knew now how Benjamin Barrett, a new convert, and Musa Karsu, a refugee from an area whose population was almost entirely Muslim, might have met.

Donald Barrett looked at her across his desk. 'You say that he isn't in trouble.'

'I'm trying to find Morph. At the moment, your son is my only lead.'

'When he turned eighteen last year, after we had our argument about his going to university, Benjamin said that he wanted to move out of my house. He wanted his own place. I respected his decision. I gave him the deposit for a rented flat, paid the first month's rent, and told him that after that he was on his own. But of course, I end up paying the rent anyway, because he doesn't earn anything near enough from his radio work, and his schemes for getting himself famous so far have not worked out. Still, I am happy to help him. He is my son, and I believe that he was beginning to grow up and act responsibly. But if what you tell me is correct, it seems that he is still angry with me. He disrespects me with these silly spray-paint graffiti. The courier business, my restaurant . . .' Donald Barrett shook his head, made the tooth-kissing noise that Jamaicans use to show disgust. 'Would you think it petty, Ms Crowley, if I gave you his address? Would I be behaving as badly as he has behaved?'

'What's between you and Benjamin − that's your business, Mr Barrett. I wouldn't presume.'

Donald Barrett wrote on a piece of paper torn from a pad, saying, 'I'll give you this as long as you can tell me I won't be sorry that I did.'

Harriet met his gaze. 'I'm only interested in his friend.'

'That will have to be good enough,' Donald Barrett said, and handed her the piece of paper.

The address was a Victorian terrace in a scruffy street behind Green Lanes. Four bell pushes by the door; three ripe dustbins, a padlocked scooter, and a letting agent's sign board in the over-grown front garden. There was a piece of graffiti on the brick pillar of the gate, a hand-sized patch of the dots and swirling lines done in silver felt-tip. Harriet took out the spray can she always carried around with her now, shook it, and covered the pattern with several layers of black paint. Moving the can in little circles, making sure that she completely obliterated the pattern. A futile gesture, really − who knew how many of these Morph had put up around London? − but it made her feel a little better.

B. Barrett rented the flat on the top floor. No one answered when Harriet rang its bell; no one answered any of the other bells, either. The main lock on the front door was a three-lever mortice. Harriet used her picks and had it open inside a minute, used a flexible, credit-card-sized piece of aluminium to snub the Yale. Two bicycles leaned against the wall in the dark little hallway. A side table was piled high with takeaway restaurant menus, cards for minicab companies, yellowing envelopes addressed to former tenants, and several pieces of mail for Mr B. Barrett.

Harriet climbed the rickety stairs, snapped on a pair of thin vinyl gloves, picked the lock of the top flat, noting fresh scratches on the edges of the keyhole, and eased inside. The small living room had been thoroughly tossed. CDs and books − crime novels, books on Black Power and Sufism, commentaries on the Koran, books on comparative religious studies, a *Rough Guide to Turkey* – were scattered across the floor among drifts of polystyrene granules and feathers from eviscerated cushions. A sofa had been turned upside down and the fabric covering its back ripped away, exposing the wooden frame. Harriet traced a sour smell to the little galley kitchen, where containers of rice and flour and several kinds of bean had been emptied into the sink, and the fridge door had been left ajar. Everything in the bathroom medicine cabinet had been swept onto the floor; in the bedroom, the mattress had been pulled from the bed and ripped open, and the contents of the drawers of a cheap pine dresser had been tipped onto the floor.

The rotting sash window of the bedroom overlooked a two-storey red-brick extension and a small garden where an ancient apple tree stood among waist-high grass and weeds. What first drew Harriet's attention was a dense pattern spray-painted in black on the sagging back fence. Even at this distance she could see that it was one of Morph's graffiti. Then she saw that someone was standing in the alley behind the fence, a rake-thin man with a straggling beard and grey, shoulder-length hair, wearing an orange construction-worker's jacket. He stood quite still, staring up at the house, his mouth working mechanically.

For a moment, Harriet met his blank gaze, and then she realized what he was and bolted out of the flat, clattering down the stairs, tripping on a fold of loose carpet in the narrow hallway and knocking over the pair of bicycles when she tried and failed to catch her balance. She ripped the hem of her linen skirt and got oil on her hands when she untangled herself from the bicycles, left a smeary palmprint on the front door when she wrenched it open. At the gate, she looked left and right – and saw with a heart-freezing shock that the man in the orange jacket was running down the middle of the road towards her, leaning forward as he ran, his arms held stiffly by his side.

A low man. She hadn't seen one since the affair in Nigeria, three years ago, but there was no doubt about it. Luckily, she'd found a parking space right outside the house. She yanked open the door of her car, scrambled inside, locked the doors, and fired up the engine just as the low man rattled the handle, his slack face inches from hers, then jerking away when she stepped on the accelerator. She almost clipped a white people-carrier when she made a handbrake turn at the T-junction at the end of the road, slamming over speed bumps as she sped through back streets to the main drag of Seven Sisters Road. When she was certain that she wasn't being followed, she pulled over, shivering from the massive jolt of adrenalin. Her fingers felt huge and numb as she speed-dialled a number on her mobile, but her thoughts were moving smoothly; she knew exactly what the presence of the low man meant, knew exactly what she had to do.

Clarence Ashburton took for ever to answer. Harriet imagined the old man rising stiffly from his armchair, moving with painful slowness into the hallway, where the only telephone in the house, a black Bakelite antique, squatted like a toad on the leather-topped side table. When he at last picked up the phone, she forced herself to be calm, briefly telling him what she had seen, asking him to use the CCTV system to check the street and the back of the house.

'Are you certain it was a low man?'

'Absolutely. Please, Clarence, check the CCTV.'

She'd had the CCTV and a state-of-the-art alarm system installed a few years ago, after a burglary which she believed to have been commissioned by someone more interested in the surviving papers and records of the Nomads' Club than in Clarence Ashburton's antiques, archaeological specimens and keepsakes.

'It will take me a minute,' he said. But it was considerably longer than that before he picked up the phone again and told her that he could see nothing unusual on any of the cameras.

Harriet said, 'We've talked before about the possibility that Carver Soborin might try to come after the Nomads.'

'If he thought we had anything that would be of use to him, he would have visited us long ago. Besides, the man's safely locked up in an asylum.'

'It was definitely a low man, Clarence. Either Soborin isn't locked up any more, or someone else is using his signature glyph.'

There was a brief silence. At last, Clarence said, 'What are you going to do?'

'I'm going to make a call and organize some protection for you right now, and then I'll come over and check for unwelcome visitors. I should be there in an hour or so. Meanwhile, I think you should keep the doors and windows locked.'

'I suppose I should look out my revolver.'

'If anything happens before I get there – it isn't likely that it will, but if it does, don't try to be a hero. Dial 999 and ask for the police.'

'Julius isn't going to like this. He doesn't like his routines disturbed. Neither do I, as a matter of fact.'

'Lock the doors and windows. And leave your revolver where it is.'

Harriet rang a friend, Mark Mallett, and arranged around-the-clock security for Clarence Ashburton's house. Then she navigated the layers of Vauxhall Cross's automated phone system and reached Jack Nicholl's voicemail box.

'I need a face-to-face as soon as possible,' she said. 'I have good reason to believe that Carver Soborin has been let into the country, and I want to know why.'

9

Alfie decided to take a nap instead of cleaning out George's van, overslept, and was fifteen minutes late for his appointment with one of the archaeologists who worked at Franks House, the annexe in Hackney where the British Museum stored a vast collection of archaeological finds and ethnographic objects. When they met in the dingy lobby of the factory-like building, Dr Robin Cole waved away Alfie's attempt to apologize – presumably a few minutes were neither here nor there to someone whose business was the curation and study of objects many thousands of years old – and led him upstairs to a corner office with views of the roofs of the workshops and small factories strung along the nearby canal, tower blocks, and a distant church steeple. Alfie explained that he was thinking of writing something about his grandfather's archaeological expeditions while Robin Cole examined photocopied sketches from Maurice Flowers's journal and the fragment of stone, pointing out something that Alfie hadn't noticed before: traces of white pigment in the incised lines. The archaeologist was particularly interested in the paintings that Maurice Flowers had discovered on the walls of the caves beneath the ruin of the second church, telling Alfie that, if genuine, they were the first examples to be found in that region.

'Are you sure that you don't have a map, or a hint of exactly where these caves are?' Robin Cole asked. He was a trim, tanned, athletic man in his fifties, in a black polo-neck sweater and faded Levi 501s, a jeweller's loupe hung around his neck on a silver chain, blue eyes sharp behind gold-rimmed glasses.

There had been a map among the pages copied from the second journal, but Alfie had decided that he didn't want anyone else to know the whole truth just yet, no matter how much he might need their help, and told the archaeologist that he knew only that the caves were somewhere in the mountains in northern Iraq.

'Unfortunately, the originals of my grandfather's journals were lost,' he said. 'Those photocopies are all I have to go on.'

But this didn't deter Robin Cole, who for the next fifteen minutes asked all kinds of awkward questions about Maurice Flowers, his friends, and the two archaeological expeditions. Alfie, who had taken a brain-mashing dose of phenobarbitone and Largactil before he'd set out, to make absolutely sure that he didn't get too excited and throw a seizure, was hard-pressed to parry this interrogation, sweating beneath his black leather jacket, convinced that a faint but definite odour of sheep shit still clung to him even though he had showered and changed his clothes. As Robin Cole pressed him for details, he was tempted to cut to the chase, take out one of the photographs of Morph's graffiti from his camera bag, and explain what it meant to him, why he thought it was connected with the patterns his grandfather had found in Iraq. But the archaeologist would probably think that he was some kind of green-ink merchant, and he'd lose a valuable chance to find out why his grandfather was so interested in the glyphs, so he sweated it out, maintaining his cover story, stonewalling, saying that he had only just stumbled over his grandfather's papers, at last managing to ask a question of his own. Were there any other examples of patterns like the ones in the sketches?

'I remember that my grandfather was very interested in these patterns. He was working on them right up to his death, and I was wondering, is anything known about them?'

Robin Cole told him that this kind of abstract art was very common in Palaeolithic and Neolithic art, that the paintings of animals were rarer and far more important, especially considering their location. But Alfie wouldn't be put off, insisting that his grandfather had considered the patterns so important that he had devoted his life to studying them. At last, the archaeologist led him downstairs to a room where shelving units ten feet high held thousands of shoebox-sized metal drawers, each drawer labelled with a neatly typed card that sat behind a perspex shield neatly curved over at the top to form a handle. Robin Cole explained that the stacks contained thousands of fragments of Roman, Iron Age and Neolithic pottery, as well as some of the earliest examples of pottery from the Middle East and Northern Europe, and pulled open a drawer, saying, 'I think that we'll find what we're looking for right here.'

Because of his overgenerous self-medication, Alfie felt as if a cold, heavy toad was squatting on his brain, but his blood suddenly fizzed with excitement as he stooped to examine the fragments of pottery set in black foam rubber. The largest, a flat piece with a curved rim, was about half the size of the palm of his hand. Time had turned their coarse clay the colour of soot, but in the cool white fluorescent light the markings incised into them showed clearly.

Robin Cole asked to see the sketches again, briskly pointing out similarities between the markings on the fragments of pottery and the patterns carved into the anomalous stone that Alfie's grandfather had found in the remains of the first church, the patterns on Anselm's stele and in the cave paintings. He explained that the pottery was some 8,000 years old and had been donated by a private expedition which had unearthed it at Tell Abu Hureyra in northern Syria. The place had first been settled by people of the Late Palaeolithic Natufian culture, which 12,500 to 10,000 years ago had occupied a wide area of the Middle East extending from the Mediterranean shore to south-east Turkey, building round huts with stone foundations, harvesting the grains of wild grasses, domesticating wild dogs, and burying their dead beneath limestone slabs. Tell Abu Hureyra had been abandoned for a time, and then a much larger Neolithic settlement had been established, its inhabitants building mud-brick houses, cultivating wheat and other plants, herding animals, weaving cloth and, just before the site was abandoned again, making pottery and decorating it with abstract patterns.

'There are similar motifs in mobile and parietal art from both the Neolithic and Upper Palaeolithic,' Robin Cole said. 'In the Middle East, the Natufian culture left behind paintings and engravings of animals, people, and abstract patterns. And there are the famous examples of much older parietal art in caves in Northern Europe, Altamira, Lascaux, and so on, and of course the recent, very important discovery here in Britain, at Church Hole in Nottinghamshire. If your grandfather really did discover similar examples of cave art in Iraq—'

Alfie said gamely, 'From my distant memory of Latin lessons, parietal has something to do with walls.'

'Art on the walls of caves, yes, such as paintings or carvings. Or on large stones, like the one your grandfather found on his first expedition. There's a particularly fine example of large standing stones carved with geometric motifs from the Neolithic tomb at Gavrinis in Brittany.'

'So this kind of thing is very common.' Alfie was puzzled, trying to think around the toad in his head. If patterns like the glyphs were so very common, why didn't archaeologists know what they could do? Was it because they didn't know about the drug, about haka?

Robin Cole was saying, his eyes gleaming behind his glasses, 'Patterns like these are very widely distributed, and they are found in some of the earliest art made by humans. That doesn't mean that the examples found by your grandfather aren't interesting. Far from it. He seems to have discovered the first known example of Palaeolithic rock art in Iraq, and while I'm no expert, I don't know of any examples as densely worked as the patterns he sketched.'

'So they're like other patterns of a similar age, only more . . . intense.'

'Apart from that fragment of stone, do you have any other specimens? If you do, I'd love to see them.'

'My grandfather had a small collection, once upon a time, but I don't know where it is now. As I told you, even the originals of his journals have disappeared. Can you tell me,' Alfie said, choosing his words with great care, his palms prickling with sweat, 'what the patterns were for? I mean, apart from decoration, why were they made?'

'There's a question. Many of my colleagues believe that they were shamanic. Personally, I don't agree. These images certainly meant something to the people who made them, but we can't know what it is because we have lost the code.'

'Shamanic? Like trances, visions?' Alfie felt as if a lion or tiger – hot-breathed, dangerous, marvellous – had stepped into the aisle between the rows of neatly shelved drawers.

Robin Cole said, with sudden chaste severity, 'I'm afraid that as far as I'm concerned it falls into the category of what I call stories for children. If you're serious about attempting to find out all you can about your grandfather's discoveries – and I think you should, they may well be *extremely* important – I do hope that you won't waste too much time in pointless speculation about shamanism and mystical rites.'

'But, please, would you mind telling me something about it?' Alfie said, and saw that the archaeologist was taken aback by his sudden intensity. It surprised him, too, but he couldn't let this chance go. He felt as if he was a moment away from under-standing everything.

Robin Cole studied him. 'You said that this was something your grandfather was very interested in.'

'Yes. Yes, he was,' Alfie said.

'Was he in contact with other workers in the field? Did he discuss his ideas with anyone?'

The previous night, Alfie had skimmed through every one of his grandfather's diaries, but had failed to find any mention of glyphs, drugs, or his grandfather's adventures in Iraq. Unless, as he suspected, the letter N that occasionally appeared next to a date stood for *Nomads*, and indicated when his grandfather had met with the men who had helped him on those two excava-tions.

He said, 'I'm sure he was, but like almost everything else, all of his correspondence has disappeared. If you could tell me why some people think that these patterns have something to do with shamanism, it really would be a tremendous help in reconstructing his work.'

'Come with me,' Robin Cole said, after a moment. His sandals squeaking on the polished floor, Alfie followed the archaeologist down the length of the big room to the stairs, listening avidly while he explained that some scientists believed that the abstract patterns found in cave art were representations of phosphenes and form constants – entoptic phenomena generated by the human visual system independently of light from an external source.

'Phosphenes are generated by physical stimulation,' Robin Cole said. 'You can see them if you close your eyes and rub your eyelids. Form constants are generated within the visual cortex – the part of the brain that's directly stimulated by the retina. People see form constants if their state of consciousness is altered by psychotropic drugs, or by fatigue or pain or fasting – by anything that can shift their state of consciousness towards what's called the release of internally generated imagery.'

'Like dreams,' Alfie said, remembering the vivid nightmares he'd suffered immediately after his accident.

'Possibly, but I'm not an expert. The point is that these patterns are hard-wired into the human nervous system. As I understand the theory, there's a spatial relationship between the retina, the light-sensitive lining of our eyeballs, and the visual cortex. Light stimulates receptor cells when it falls on the retina, and that leads to the firing of neurons in the visual cortex. Form constants are generated by reversing this process – by stimulating the neurons in the visual cortex to fire, which in turn stimulates the retina. That's the first stage of a hallucinatory experience. The second is when the subject tries to make sense of the entoptic phenomena by translating them into familiar images, the third when the imagery becomes more vivid, often with the illusion of falling down a tunnel or into a vortex, and the hallucination displaces the real world. That much I don't have a problem with. It's underpinned by solid neurophysiological studies. But that doesn't mean that we should use it to interpret the significance of Palaeolithic art, to promote the idea that patterns and images in rock art are records of shamanistic vision quests.'

They had climbed a flight of stairs to a large, deserted room that reminded Alfie of the science laboratories in his old school, with long, wide benches, glass-fronted cabinets, trays, sieves, and bags stuffed with dirt. Robin Cole fussed with a huge bunch of keys, found the two which opened a door next to a sophisticated alarm system. Inside was the organic store, a windowless chamber kept at a constant temperature and level of humidity where delicate bone and ivory artefacts were stored in wooden drawers that would maintain their contents at the correct temperature for several hours if the air-conditioning failed. Robin Cole pulled one of these drawers from a stack, set it on a small table, and folded back its hinged lid.

'Wow,' Alfie said, looking at the three carefully shaped pieces in the drawer. The largest, a curved length of what Robin Cole told him was mammoth ivory, was carved with the images of a pair of reindeer.

'It's beautiful, isn't it?' the archaeologist said, unforced feeling softening his voice. 'The male is following the female, and their muzzles are raised and their antlers are tipped back in a characteristic swimming posture, as if they are crossing a river. Do you see how the flank of the female is densely cross-hatched? It's possible that it's meant to represent the thick winter coat. After crossing a river, that thick coat would be heavy with water and would slow the animals down and make them easier targets for hunters. But why isn't the male, whose coat would have been just as thick, similarly marked? Is the difference in representation because only females were targeted, or only males? We don't know.'

'Because the man who made this isn't here to explain,' Alfie said dutifully.

'Exactly. That's why our interpretation of all Palaeolithic art can only ever be no more than informed guesses or stories. And those stories will always be influenced by new discoveries, and changes in ideas about how early cultures developed and were organized. So early ethnographic analogies, invoking hunting or fertility magic, gave way to French structuralism, the space age brought an emphasis on archaeoastronomy, and the computer age a focus on prehistoric art as a means of storing and transmitting information. The current dominant theory – that many examples of prehistoric abstract art are records of visions experienced by people who had undergone drug-fuelled shamanic rituals – is merely the latest interpretation. It's no more true and no more false than any of the others, even though at the moment far too many naive students and scholars have jumped on the bandwagon and see entoptic phenomena and records of shamanic rituals and transformations everywhere in rock art, even in rock art which has no ethnography associated with it. In the end, all we can know about Palaeolithic art is that it was important to the people who made it. These were possessions that were highly valued by their owners,' Robin Cole said, and showed Alfie how one of the other items in the drawer, a reindeer scapula shaped into a spear-thrower and incised with the profile of a running horse, had been repaired after its shaft had snapped, how that repair had broken in turn, and slivers had been thriftily cut out of the reverse side to make needles.

Alfie meekly promised that he had taken this little lesson to heart, and Robin Cole said that he would be happy to help him with any other questions he might have. 'If you find out anything else about your grandfather's expeditions, especially if you find clues that point towards the location of these caves, please do let me know. Also, I have several colleagues who would love to talk to you about it. Things being as they are in Iraq it isn't possible to think of mounting an expedition at present, but in a year or two . . .'

Alfie hastily said that he had to be somewhere else, thanked the archaeologist for his time and trouble, and swam off down De Beauvoir Road in a happy haze of speculation, settling in a Vietnamese restaurant (it was seven in the evening, and he was suddenly ravenous), and jotting down everything that Robin Cole had told him about entoptics and drugs and shamans. Hunched at an end of one of the restaurant's long tables, his short, straw-coloured hair disordered, his bland face flushed with excitement, alternately scribbling in his notebook and dotting his vegetable noodles with fiery blobs of hot sauce and forking them up with absent-minded hunger. Making notes just like a real journalist or detective. Trying to fit fragments into a shapely whole.

The small piece of stone given to Alfie by Miriam Luttwak suggested that the patterns – the glyphs – had something to do with his father's disappearance. And Mick Flowers had been involved with the glyphs because *his* father, Maurice Flowers, had discovered them in Iraq, and later on, someone, perhaps Maurice Flowers, perhaps someone else, had discovered their effect on people who had smoked or otherwise ingested haka. Alfie wrote *Nomads* and his grandfather's and father's names in his notebook, and drew lines linking them in a triangle. Robin Cole had told him that it was possible that abstract patterns in rock art were entoptics, patterns generated by the human nervous system during the first stage of a hallucinatory experience. He'd gone to great lengths to explain that it was only a theory, not proven fact, but Alfie thought now of his grandfather's pouch of grey powder, the

powder he might well have tasted before looking at the piece of
paper from his grandfather's desk. He thought about the injec-
tions Mr Prentiss had given him, the laced joints he'd smoked
with his father. The patterns he'd seen afterwards, in fires. Patterns
that had been meant to accommodate him or immunize him to
the glyphs. Which were what? Intensifications of those patterns?
Potent combinations?

Alfie wrote David Prentiss's name, linked it to *Nomads*. The
two men who had come to take away his grandfather's things,
they must have been part of this too. Perhaps they were the
other two men in the photograph from that first expedition . .
. He wrote *Julius*. He wrote *Clarence*. He linked them to *Nomads*.
His grandfather was dead. His father was dead. And Alfie knew
that Mr Prentiss was dead, too, because he had gone to look for
the man three years after his accidental exposure to the glyphs,
after his father's disappearance. It had been during the summer
holidays, when his grandmother had gone up to London to
meet some friends, telling Alfie that she believed that he was
old enough to stay at home on his own and keep out of trouble.
Alfie travelled to London on the very next train after his grandmother's, feeling like a spy infiltrating enemy territory. He found
his way to Chiswick easily enough, but spent two anxious, frus-
trating hours walking around the streets without spotting Mr
Prentiss's white villa. In fact, he walked past it twice before he
realized that it was now painted pink, and the big tree in the
front garden was gone. And after he'd screwed up his courage
and rung the doorbell, the middle-aged woman who'd answered
the door had told him that the man he was looking for had
died three years ago.

Now, he wrote question marks next to *Julius* and *Clarence*. He
didn't know who they were, and he didn't have the faintest idea
how to find them. He supposed that he should look through the
diaries again, read every word, but he thought that it was unlikely
that his grandfather would have entrusted the key to these secrets
in an ordinary diary. He could ask his grandmother, of course –
she knew about the Nomads, it was possible that she would know
who the two mystery men had been, would know if they were
still alive – but Alfie knew that talking about her husband and

his research badly upset her, and he still felt guilty about his last visit, the way it had ended. He decided that he would only ask her about the Nomads if he ran out of leads; meanwhile, there was still the other half of the investigation, the search for Morph. Who, even if he wasn't from Iraq, definitely knew something about the glyphs. It was possible, of course, that his graffiti had nothing to do with patterns on cave walls or ancient lumps of stone. Perhaps he was simply recording what he'd seen after puffing on some especially brain-mashing joint or dropping a couple of tabs of acid or Special K. Perhaps it was no more than a coincidence, except that Morph just happened to have come up with a pattern that was potent. A pattern that attracted and held the eye. A pattern that tickled the part of Alfie's brain that had been damaged by his accident. A pattern denser and more vital than any to be found in the Palaeolithic and Neolithic art collected in the vast storehouse of the British Museum.

A pattern, Alfie thought, that worked backwards, from the outside in. Entoptics, form constants, were generated by the human brain. And if they were glimpses of the brain's wiring, wasn't it possible that the dense patterns of entoptics, the glyphs, somehow encoded basic human emotions and feelings? Fascination, fear, lust, hunger, whatever. Smoke haka and take a good long hard look at a glyph, and it would imprint itself on your brain, or trigger something already there.

For a moment, everything seemed an inch away from falling into place. He almost had it. But then the moment passed. He sat for a little while longer, and when he was certain that it wouldn't come back, paid his bill and lumbered off towards Islington.

He didn't see the man who had been sitting in a bus shelter across the road from the restaurant fold his newspaper and follow him.

10

A little after ten o'clock the next morning, Alfie arrived at the main gate of the Imperial War Museum to find Toby already waiting for him. The journalist stuffed the fat hardback he'd been reading in his bag, the kind of army-surplus khaki satchel that heavy-metal fans had favoured in Alfie's school, and said, 'You're late.'

'The place has only just opened. Have you spotted anything likely?'

'I thought I better wait for you and your X-ray vision.' Toby squinted up at Alfie and said, 'Are you all right, Flowers? You look like you won the Lottery and lost the ticket.'

Robin Cole had phoned Alfie just as he was about to leave, saying that he'd checked the museum's acquisitions records and discovered that Maurice Flowers had donated many of the finds from his first excavation, but they had been withdrawn during the Second World War.

'Do you happen to know,' the archaeologist had said, 'if your grandfather ever worked for or had any contacts with the secret services?'

Alfie had lied, saying that he didn't have the faintest idea, interrupting the archaeologist when he'd started in on what was obviously a long list of questions, saying that he would give him a call as soon as he found out anything of interest, but right now he was late for a meeting . . . Ringing off with the uneasy feeling that things were beginning to spin out of his control, but also wondering if the glyphs and the mysterious Nomads might possibly have something to do with his grandfather's wartime work with the SOE.

He told Toby, 'I suppose I'm a little on edge about this thing. Also, I spent two hours last night, scrubbing sheep shit from George's van.'

'Welcome to the glamorous world of investigative journalism.

Well, this is probably a wild-goose chase, but let's case the joint anyway.'

As they walked anticlockwise around the museum, Toby told Alfie that if he seemed more grouchy than usual it was because he was nursing some bad news and a worse hangover. Last night, over several bottles of red wine, he and his ex-wife, Alison, had had an intense discussion about what to do about the flat they jointly owned and in which she still lived. Something had to be done pretty quickly, because she had just quit her job at Amnesty International, and in three weeks would be moving to Oxford, to start a new job with Oxfam.

'It came out,' Toby said, 'that she's seeing someone. Some fucking poetaster who teaches Modern English Literature at Oxford Brookes University.'

'She's moving on,' Alfie said. 'Good for her.'

'She's moving to Oxford because of this fucker,' Toby said.

'That's right, keep everything all balled up in a nice tight knot.'

'This from someone with an advanced degree in how not to let go of the past,' Toby said, around the hand that cupped the flame of his lighter as he applied it to a fresh cigarette.

'Give me your opinion of this,' Alfie said, and handed Toby the printout of the video grab of Morph which Elliot had cleaned up with his battery of pixel-scrubbing programmes. Elliot had given it to Alfie in the pub last night, apologizing that he hadn't been able to do much with it, waving away Alfie's offer of payment but accepting a pint of lager. Saying, when Alfie asked him if he minded doing another little favour along the same lines, 'Sure, why not?'

Toby scrutinized the digitally enhanced screen-grab and said, 'It looks even more out of focus than it did before. I can't even tell if the guy is black or white.'

'Elliot thinks he's wearing something over his head. A stocking, perhaps.'

'A stocking mask. How perfect is that?' Toby said, handing back the printout. 'You're not the only one who's been working on this case. I've been doing a little background research.'

'You found out something. What did you find?'

'Let's see what our little maniac has been up to first. As long as it's at least as good as the stunt with the sheep, and it stays a slow news day, the *Guardian* will take the story. They might even publish one of your murky photographs. Which means that if Shareef is as good as his word, we'll soon be face to face with him, and maybe Morph too. Don't,' Toby said, after a moment, 'bother to fall on your knees to thank me, by the way. It was all in a day's work.'

'That's good. I mean, terrific.'

With a sudden uneasy sliding feeling, Alfie wondered what Toby could possibly have discovered.

'First, we have to find the fucking thing that Morph's supposed to have hidden here. Are you sure you didn't see anything that made your weird little brain itch?'

'It must be somewhere inside.'

They'd walked all the way around the museum, were standing beside the two fifteen-inch naval guns in front of the steps and columns of the building's entrance.

'That's great,' Toby said. 'Do you know what this place used to be?'

Alfie shrugged with one shoulder. His camera bag weighed down the other.

'It used to be Bedlam,' Toby said. 'Bethlehem Hospital, the place where they stashed all of London's head problems. Which means it's pretty fucking huge, and we don't even know what we're looking for.'

But after he and Alfie briefly queued for admittance behind a small crowd of tourists and a solitary veteran in a regimental blazer, Toby spotted Morph's latest artwork almost at once. It was in a corner of the large exhibits hall, where a collection of armoured vehicles and field guns, a vintage omnibus that George Johnson would give his right arm to own, and a massive green V2 rocket sat under a handful of fighter planes, the originals of the Airfix models that Alfie had assembled when he'd been a kid. There, fixed to the yellow brick wall of a niche where four neatly folded wheelchairs were stored, was a Perspex display case, divided into two by a shelf on which a stuffed rat wearing a miniature desert-camouflage jacket posed on a scatter of orange builders' sand in front of a photograph of a burning oil well. A model gun was glued to its pink paws and a pair of tiny wraparound sunglasses was perched on top of its head. In the space below the shelf was a large card on which was printed *Rattus Militus Desertus Americanus: Iraq 2004* in bold black lettering over a swirl of red squiggles and hash marks. It was signed, in familiar cursive script, *Morph*.

Toby asked Alfie if it was genuine. If it was pushing his buttons.

Alfie shook his head. 'The elements are there – the curves and squiggles and all the rest. But they don't add up to anything.'

'Maybe they aren't supposed to.'

'Or it could be a fake.'

'Well, it's definitely what we came here to find,' Toby said, and sloped off to look for one of the museum's attendants and raise the alarm.

Luckily, the press officer had a good sense of humour. Toby persuaded her to make a brief statement on behalf of the museum, and Alfie was able to take several photographs of the Perspex case before one of the curators removed it. It was lightly glued to the brick wall, and came away cleanly.

'Do mention that if Mr Morph wants his piece of art,' the press officer said, 'we'll be happy to return it to him if he gets in touch with us.'

Toby phoned his contact at the *Guardian*, got confirmation that the story would go in, and led Alfie to the half-decent café he'd discovered on his way to the museum. While Toby drank a mug of dark brown tea, ate a fried-egg sandwich, and wrote up the notes of his brief conversation with the public relations officer, Alfie sipped a gassy mineral water and wondered nervously what his friend had discovered.

Finally, Toby shut his notebook with a snap, lit a cigarette, fixed his close-set gaze on Alfie, and said, 'You're a dark horse, Flowers.'

'What do you mean?'

'I mean you didn't say that this was all about drugs.'

'I didn't. I mean it isn't.'

'That's not what my contact says. He says that pattern Morph uses to decorate his cartoons is made up of images you see when you get high. In the case of Palaeolithic shamans, that would have been opium, bog-standard hash, and something mysterious, lost to the mists of time, that's called hoama or soma. Ring any bells?'

'What contact? Who have you been talking to?'

Toby held up a minatory forefinger. The nail was badly bitten, and stained orange by nicotine. 'After you entrusted me with your story, I did some research on the interweb. I'm sure you've heard of it – it's something to do with computers, and sometimes it can be quite useful in ferreting out information.'

'So Elliot tells me. What did you find?'

'I Googled papers on prehistoric art, and a good percentage of what I found mentioned trances, shamanic rites, and the recurrence of basic types of entoptic images. These cave artists used to get high so regularly that they should have called it—'

'Please don't say it,' Alfie said.

'—The Stoned Age,' Toby said, straight-faced. 'And the things they saw when they got high were what are called entoptic images or form constants. I see from the way you're looking at me that you know something about entoptics. It's pitiable – like a dog that knows it's been caught out, and is waiting for punishment.'

'I only found out about them yesterday,' Alfie said. Actually, he *did* feel guilty about deceiving his friend, although he believed that he had just cause. His grandfather's journal had nothing to do with finding Morph. It was family business. 'I went to the British Museum – well, its annexe, actually, and asked an expert for his opinion on my little piece of stone.'

'Did you show him your photos of Morph's graffiti too?'

'I thought he'd think I was nuts if I tried to explain the whole thing.'

'Even though you are quite plainly as mad as a sock full of frogs in a microwave. So let me take a wild leap here. This expert took one look at your pebble and said, how about that, those patterns are actually entoptic images, and gave you a useful lecturette on why Stone Age art is full of them.'

'Actually, all he said was that it was *possible* they were entoptics. He also said it wasn't possible to know what any Palaeolithic or Neolithic art meant – why it was made, what it was used for.'

'You remember Jules? Jules Martens?'

'The guy who buys your review copies.'

'I also used to work for him, back in the day,' Toby said. 'He's the guy who book collectors turn to after they've given up on all the other book dealers. When there's one volume you absolutely must have to finish off your collection, when you've given up on eBay and have personally sat through auctions at Bloomsbury Book Auctions and Phillips and Biblion, when you've combed through every second-hand bookshop and trudged around every book fair, Jules is the man who can make you happy. He specializes in finding the unfindable, and he does it by having a small army of book runners in several countries who report back to him. Which is what I used to do, when I'd just arrived in London with the ink still wet on my First in English Literature and I was trying to find my feet as a freelance journo.'

Alfie had once bought something from Jules Martens: a photograph of Mick Flowers exhausted and unshaven in his special flak jacket with the extra pockets, cradling his favourite Nikon to his chest as he sprawled on a bare clay bank near Phnom Penh, Cambodia, in 1975. The photograph, taken an hour before he'd been hit in the leg by a sniper's round that had punched through the side of the jeep in which he was travelling, had been published in the *Washington Post* over a brief story about his close brush with death. Jules Martens had shown Alfie a yellowing copy of the newspaper and explained that one of his American contacts had tracked down the widow of the man who had taken the photograph, and she had agreed to allow Alfie to make a print from the original negative. Alfie had bought the copy of the newspaper and paid Jules Martens for the expenses he and his man had incurred while tracking down the widow because Jules had made it seem that he'd done Alfie a tremendous favour out of the goodness of his heart – it would have been rude and inconsiderate not to have reimbursed him. But when Jules had offered to look out for other items, Alfie had said thanks but no, thanks. He knew how the man worked. A little taste, and then you were hooked. He was terrific at what he did, no doubt about that, but he was also a sharpie, as urbane and professionally sympathetic as a plastic surgeon or a society drug dealer, and like them expert at spotting and exploiting vanity and appetite. Alfie hadn't wanted to become dependent on the man; hadn't wanted to become hooked on his father's past. Back then, five or six years ago, he'd still been in what his last girlfriend would have called denial. Back then, he was doing his best to maintain the steady, low-level hum of his equilibrium. So he'd paid off Jules Martens, had sent the negative back to the widow with a note of appreciation, and filed away the print he'd made and done his best to forget about it.

Now he said to Toby, 'You told Jules Martens about this? About Morph and everything else?'

'I had to give him a little background, but I didn't mention any names.'

'Did you tell him about my father, and my grandfather? About my family?'

There was a dry bitter taste in Alfie's mouth, as if a copper penny had been laid under his tongue.

Toby sat back, fixed him with his dark, close-set gaze. 'We've known each other nine years, man and boy. You were best man at my wedding. You ask me to help you out and, like it or not, that's exactly what I'm doing.'

'I told you what I told you in strict confidence, Toby.'

'You're been sloping around with all this secret family history hidden inside your head until one day you see this piece of graffiti and it all comes rising to the surface again, like a great belch of swamp gas. Suddenly, you have to do something about it. You have to find the guy who's been doing these graffiti, and when you realize that you can't find him by yourself, you decide to enlist my help. But you only want me to help you on your terms,' Toby said. 'You feed me partial information and treat me more like someone you hired than a concerned friend. Well, buster, fuck that shit. If you want my help, you've got to trust me to do the right thing by you, and you've got to realize that that might not always be what you expect me to do. And if you don't like that, go pay someone to do it the way you want it done, because I'm not going to do things any other way.'

It wasn't in Alfie's nature to stay angry for long, and besides, he knew that Toby was in the right. He said, 'As long as you didn't name names, I don't suppose there was any harm.'

'I didn't give away any sensitive information. Credit me with a little intelligence, Flowers. Assume that I know what I'm doing.'

'Okay.'

'And don't pull any more of that how–dare–you–step–over–the–line shit, or you're on your own.'

'Maybe you had better tell me about this expert that Jules Martens put you on to,' Alfie said. He was thinking that if he had to confess about finding his grandfather's journal, now was the time.

Toby lit a fresh cigarette. 'Jules has one of those memories that doesn't let go. He can tell you what he had for breakfast on a given day ten years ago. He says that he remembers the first word he spoke. And he remembers everything he ever bought or sold. When I showed him the photographs of Morph's graffiti, and gave him the story – the very carefully edited story – he put me on to a collector to whom he'd sold several pieces of crank literature. A fellow by the name of Roger Anslinger, a kind of free-lance scholar who lives off a trust fund. He's an expert on what he calls heightened states of consciousness: he's written a book on the anthropology of drug use, and is currently working on a learned dissection of virtual reality. He gave me this whole bit about how the path to heightened states of consciousness begins with dilated pupils, that the rods and cones in the retina at the back of the eye are outposts of the brain. "Pitched at the frontier between consciousness and reality." He has a *very* impressive library on every kind of drug, from sober medical studies to pulp shockers from the 1950s and 1960s with cool titles like *Psychedelic Sex* and *Drugged Into Sin*. There's a big section on shamanism, and he gave me the low-down on Palaeolithic rock art and entoptic images. Plus, of course, he has a booklet that Jules sold him. A piece of meretricious trash according to him, but not without interest to us.

'It was self-published by some maniac who was the self-appointed head of a cult that started up in the States back in the early 1980s, and broke up seven or eight years ago in scandalous circumstances. The usual horrors: brainwashing, drugs and free love, adolescent girls who used flirty-fishing – offering sex to strangers – as a recruiting technique. Not to mention the usual accusations of Satanism, sacrifice of babies, sexual abuse of children. The leader of the cult committed suicide soon after his commune was busted by the Feds, but at the height of his brief notoriety he published this,' Toby said, and drew from his khaki satchel a small sheaf of photocopied pages. 'This is the pamphlet that Roger Anslinger bought from Jules. He copied it for me.'

The title on the front cover, *The Quest For Haoma: A Personal Account, by 'Antareus'*, was hand-lettered above a naive drawing of a pyramid with the Eye of Horus above it, the kind of thing a reasonably skilled child might execute, except that it was encircled by unmistakable entoptic images. Wavy parallel lines, dots, riverine lightning strokes, interlocking arrowheads that appeared to flick back and forth as Alfie stared at them. The same kind of effect that made Morph's graffiti seem alive, made them seem to stand out from their background as if italicized.

Toby said, after a moment, 'Earth to Alfie.'

Alfie looked up, the taste of burning metal strong in his mouth, a dark tingling behind his vision. He said, 'These are the real thing. The ones in that display case back in the museum weren't, but these are.'

'Roger Anslinger said that they were special, too, but I just don't see it. I guess I'm not a heightened-state-of-consciousness kind of guy. But what *did* interest me,' Toby said, turning through the photocopied pages, 'was a brief reference to a couple of archaeological expeditions in Iraq which discovered patterns like this one, patterns which Antareus calls glyphs.'

'Glyphs – that's what my grandfather called them.'

'Antareus also mentions another expedition in Iraq, one that discovered a tribe of semi-nomadic sheep herders, the Kefidis. Their religious ceremonies involved use of the glyphs and a plant which was the source of hoama, or soma. The dates tally with what you told me about your grandfather's adventures, so I was wondering if this means anything to you,' Toby said, setting a page in front of Alfie.

There was a photograph at the top of the page. It was a bad photocopy of a blurry reproduction, but Alfie recognized it at once. Four men in pre-war colonial gear posing beside a big stone and the remains of a wall: the Four Nomads.

Alfie's premonition of a seizure grew suddenly stronger. It was as if something had sprung from the blackness inside his skull and was trying to force its way past him, into the light. He pulled the bottle of Valium tablets from his bag, shook one into the palm of his hand, reached for his glass of mineral water.

And then he was staring at shards of glass glinting in a spreading puddle of water on the floor between his sandals, and Toby was saying, 'Flowers? Talk to me. Tell me you're okay.'

'I'm okay.' The seizure had come and gone and Alfie was all right again, clear and empty. He dry-swallowed the Valium, apologized to the waitress who came over with paper towels and a dustpan and brush, and told Toby, 'I could do with some fresh air. Let's walk and talk.'

He felt a little spacey and about a step behind the rest of the world, but that was the Valium kicking in. Otherwise he felt alert and engaged and excited as he and Toby walked through the dust and exhaust fumes and slipstream wind of Lambeth Road towards Blackfriars Bridge. 'This Antareus,' he said. 'The man who wrote the pamphlet, the leader of the cult. His real name was Christopher Prentiss, wasn't it?'

'How did you know that? Wait, you knew all along. This is part of your man-of-mystery act.'

'I didn't know about the cult, I swear. It was sort of an informed guess.'

'Informed by what?'

'Tell me what Antareus wrote about this mysterious ancient drug, this haoma, and then I'll explain.'

Once again, he was thinking of the grey dust that his grandfather had smoked with his special tobacco mix. Haka: the same plant extract with which Mr Prentiss had injected him, the same extract with which his father had salted the joints as part of their private ritual. His last memory of his father was of the time on the beach when they'd shared a joint, and then he'd stared into the fire while his father had murmured Mr Prentiss's incantation . . .

Toby said, 'Actually, I got most of it from Roger Anslinger, and a couple of hours Googling around on the interweb. It seems that about four thousand years ago a pastoral people, the Indo-Iranians or Aryans, split into two groups. One group went south and settled the Indus Valley; the other remained in the original homeland in Central Asia, north of India and west of China. The earliest texts of both groups mention a drug used in an important act of worship. In the Indian *Rig Veda* it's called soma; in the Iranian *Avesta* it's called haoma. Most scholars believe that soma and hoama were two names for the same thing, but no one knows what it was.'

'But there are theories. Antareus had a theory.'

'There are a ton of theories,' Toby said. 'That it was a kind of alcoholic drink, or that it was derived from a species of rhubarb crushed and fermented in honey, or that it was a form of hashish, or some kind of vine. There's a vine from the Amazon – if you drink an extract of it, it really blows your head wide open. One guy, R. Gordon Wasson, proposed that it was the fly-agaric mushroom. He was a Wall Street banker and amateur mycologist who was friendly with Aldous Huxley. He made expeditions to Mexico and Russia, and became involved with a CIA research programme, MKULTRA, that trialled all kinds of drugs to assess their potential in clandestine operations and interrogations – everything from caffeine to LSD. The CIA was hip to LSD long before the hippies got hold of it. Anyway, Wasson was involved with all that, and he made a strong case that fly agaric was soma/haoma, although there's an equally strong argument that it was derived from a plant rather than a mushroom. Possibly ginseng, or harmel, or Syrian rue. Roger Anslinger favours Syrian rue. He told me that it grows in the homelands of both Indo-Iranian groups and said that its seeds contain psychoactive beta-carbolines, whatever they are.'

'What about Antareus? What was at the end of his quest?'

'He claimed to have discovered the source of the original soma/haoma – this tribe from northern Iraq, the Kefidis. Ring any bells?'

Alfie shook his head. 'Did he say exactly where they came from, and what this drug of theirs was?'

'Of course not. His kind never do. They believe they're working in the tradition of Paracelsus – you know, knowledge is power, and open source a sin against nature. There's a lot of bullshit in his pamphlet about the key to the one true path to enlightenment, but he doesn't give any clue as to what it might be. Because if he did, of course, he'd spoil the illusion. He certainly used these patterns and some kind of drug in his cult rituals, but apart from the name of this tribe, which may or may not exist, he was very careful not to let slip any actual facts. Maybe there's something useful buried among the usual crap about Atlantis and Stonehenge and the Pyramids, but just reading the stuff gave me a powerful headache, I don't really want to *think* about it. What is interesting is that there's a long passage about his father – how his father tried to stop him reaching enlightenment because he was part of a conspiracy dedicated to hiding the truth. Something called the Nomads' Club. Does that ring any bells?'

Luckily, Alfie didn't have to reply at once, because four police cars sped past them in a blast of sirens and flashing blue lights, and he had to close his eyes and press his hands over his ears until they were past.

'Another false alarm,' Toby said, as he and Alfie walked on. 'Hopefully.'

The cry of emergency vehicles was common all over the city, at all hours, of course – one of the birds that hung out in the scrubby bushes and trees along one side of Alfie's yard had taken to imitating a police siren, when it wasn't doing car alarms or telephones – but four of them, speeding past nose-to-tail towards the City of London, definitely seemed like an omen. A year and counting after the invasion of Iraq, the whole city was tense and anxious, starting at every little thing like a sleepless householder, waiting for something to happen . . .

Alfie said, 'The photograph you showed me – my grandfather had a copy of it.' He paused, waiting for Toby to ask where he'd seen this photograph, but the moment passed. 'On the back were four Christian names. One of them was Maurice, my grandfather. Another was David.'

'David Prentiss.'

'I think so. Also Clarence and Julius, I don't know who they are. But the four of them called themselves the Nomads.'

'So these guys were digging up stuff in Iraq back before the Second World War, and one of the things they dug up was the piece of paper that fucked up your brain.'

'Not the piece of paper. Whatever had been drawn or copied onto it.'

'But you don't remember what that was.'

KILKENNY
COUNTY
LIBRARY

'No, I don't. But a couple of days after I had my accident, my father took me to visit David Prentiss, to see if he could help me.'

Toby squinted up at Alfie. 'Maybe it's time you told me everything.'

'That's what I'm doing.'

Alfie remembered feeling a floating sense of detachment as his father had driven him to London in his grandfather's roomy, seasick-making Rover, as if everything was a movie he was watching inside his head, one that for the rest of his life he'd be able to recall with vivid clarity. He remembered that when they had pulled up outside the detached villa in the quiet residential road in Chiswick, his father had turned to him and told him that whatever Mr Prentiss did, however strange it seemed, it was to make him better. It would help him get past his little accident. And no matter what, Alfie wasn't to tell his grandmother about it.

'Are we agreed, Chief?'

Alfie nodded.

'Cross your heart and hope to die?'

Alfie remembered his father's forced cheerfulness, remembered how scared he'd felt when Mr Prentiss had opened the front door of the house after his father had pulled a brass ring set in the wall beside it. Mr Prentiss, very tall, very thin, corseted in a lumpy tweed suit, shook hands with Mick Flowers, saying, 'We're so pleased that you kept this between friends, Michael. A doctor would ask awkward questions, and prescribe inappropriate drugs.'

He examined Alfie from his remote height with wintry blue eyes, said that he must be the boy he'd heard so much about, and that they had both better come in.

As Mr Prentiss led them down the dark hallway, where a grandfather clock ticked loudly and steadily, as if dropping marbles one by one into a well, Alfie's father asked about someone called Emily, asked how she was.

'Unfortunately she has one of her headaches, and has taken to her bed.'

'And her daughter? I suppose it must be hard for her.'

'We won't talk about that, if you don't mind,' Mr Prentiss said. 'We'll go into the library. I have everything prepared.'

It was a square, dim room with two walls of books packed together on mahogany shelves. Behind a sofa covered in cracked red leather, French windows gave a view of the garden. A fire burned in the iron grate of the elaborate marble fireplace. Hung over it was a huge, age-darkened oil painting of a man armed with a spear and riding a horse at full gallop as he chased a lion across a stony desert.

'I see that you have noticed the painting,' Mr Prentiss said to Alfie. 'It's a portrait of my father, rendered by Dante Gabriel Rossetti. My father was a soldier in Abyssinia, and he really did kill a lion while he was there. The head of the beast in question once hung in the hallway, but alas, it had a bad case of the moth, and I had to make a bonfire of it. Have you ever had to burn a lion's head, young man?'

Alfie shook his head, uncertain if he was being teased.

Mr Prentiss's laugh was like the creak of a door caught in the wind. 'I would advise against it. Very hard to burn, the stuffed head of a lion, and the neighbours complained mightily of the smell.'

Mick Flowers told Alfie that he should go and play in the garden for a little while. 'Mr Prentiss and I need to talk.'

'I thought everything was agreed,' Mr Prentiss said.

'I want a word before we go through with it,' Mick Flowers said. 'I want to clear the air.' He stood with his arms folded, looking determined, and told Alfie that this would only take a few minutes.

It was early January, cold and damp and cheerless. A mossy lawn sloped between neatly dug flower beds stuck with the frost-nipped sticks of rose bushes to a row of arthritic fruit trees that stood in front of a red brick wall. There was a small greenhouse in one corner with lights burning brightly inside, harshly illuminating little bushes with grey leaves that grew in a trough of sand and gravel. There was a lattice-work iron gate in the wall, with a view of a path that ran along the bank of a wide river – Alfie supposed that it must be the Thames.

He watched a man row past in a skiff, bending and straightening, bending and straightening like a mechanical toy. He felt scared and angry and lonely. He'd done something stupid and it had hurt him. His father had told him that Mr Prentiss knew how to make him better, but Alfie knew that his grandmother thought otherwise. Grammie and his father had had an argument about it last night. Alfie had crept out of his bedroom to the head of the staircase and listened to the two voices behind the closed door of the living room. Grammie's voice quiet and calm and firm, his father's rising and falling – Alfie could imagine him striding about the room, as he often did when arguing with his mother. Alfie couldn't hear what they were talking about, but he knew with a clammy, sick feeling that they were talking about him. About what had happened. He sat in the cold dusk on the polished wooden stairs in his pyjamas, hugging himself, heard Grammie say that she wished Maurice had never become involved with those horrible things, it had taken over his life and now . . . Her voice breaking off, his father's voice muted and gentle, murmuring something comforting, her voice again, soaring on angry wings.

'Your son is having fits, Michael! Epileptic fits! We should call a doctor, I don't know why I haven't called one already. Suppose it's done something permanent to him . . .'

His father said something that Alfie couldn't make out. The conversation murmured on behind the closed door until Grammie said, very clearly and firmly, 'You should burn the filthy thing.'

'David Prentiss needs to see it first,' his father said, and Alfie didn't hear any more. He must have fainted or passed out, because he was in bed again, and his father was bending over him, silhouetted against the glow of the bedside lamp, telling him that everything would be all right, they were going to see someone who would fix him up.

But Alfie didn't trust the old man he'd been brought to see. He suspected that he had something to do with the two men who had come to take away his grandfather's things. He kicked stones through the lattice-work gate and stared at the cold river, feeling sick and miserable and utterly alone. Feeling as if the whole world had turned against him – and feeling scared too, scared of the old man, scared that he was going to do something to him that would be just as bad as looking at the piece of paper.

That was when the little girl came up behind him and said in a clear high voice, 'I know who you are.'

'Do you?' Like all boys his age, Alfie was usually indifferent to little girls, but this one seemed unnervingly confident and knowing. A small thin blonde girl in a calico dress, no more than four or five, staring boldly at Alfie, mischief gleaming in her eyes.

'I'm Harriet,' she said. 'I live here with my mummy and with my grandpop. And you, you're a spy.'

'No I'm not,' Alfie said. He tried to affect a casual scorn, but felt his face heat up. 'My father's a friend of Mr Prentiss. I'm just waiting—'

'A spy! A sneaky spy!' the little girl said, dancing about in a transport of unrestrained glee.

Alfie remembered Mr Prentiss appearing at the French windows and telling the little girl, 'You run along, dear. Go and find your mother. Master Flowers and I have a little business together. Do we not, young man?'

'I *caught* him,' the little girl said, proud and self-righteous.

'Of course you did. And you can be sure I will take care of him,' Mr Prentiss said, and beckoned to Alfie, who trudged the length of the lawn towards the house, a grim hot pressure at the back of his head, the feeling he had every time he'd been called to the front of the class to answer for some minor misdemeanour. He clearly remembered standing in the middle of the threadbare oriental carpet, feeling uncomfortably warm under his clothes, not looking at either his father or Mr Prentiss while the old man shut and locked the French windows and drew heavy velvet curtains across them. For a moment, the only light in the room was the sullen glow of the coal fire; then Mr Prentiss switched on a reading lamp that stood on a little table to one side of the sofa, among a clutter of photographs in silver frames.

Mick Flowers, at the edge of the pool of lamplight, his face half in shadow, smiled at his son and said, 'Don't be afraid.'

But Alfie was already afraid, his skin prickly hot, his pulse beating unpleasantly in his ears as Mr Prentiss bent stiffly over him and rolled up the sleeve of his jumper and unbuttoned the cuff of his shirt. The old man's hands were cold and dry. He rolled up Alfie's shirtsleeve and asked him if he had ever been injected.

Alfie stared at him, his mouth dry, his mind perfectly blank.

'You had a tetanus injection last year,' his father prompted.

'This won't be any different,' Mr Prentiss said. 'Sit down, just here.'

After he'd sat Alfie on a low stool, Mr Prentiss crossed to the other side of the room and came back with a small round tray which he set on the side table, moving several photographs to clear a space. He picked up a bottle of clear liquid from the tray, unscrewed its top, held a piece of cotton wool over its neck and inverted it for a moment, then wiped the cotton wool on Alfie's arm. Alfie smelled alcohol, felt the patch of moistened skin grow cold and dry, watched as Mr Prentiss picked up a small brown bottle and a hypodermic syringe with a glass barrel and a fearsome needle that caught a star of lamplight at its tip. The old man shook the little bottle and then, holding it upside down between finger and thumb, stabbed its rubber stopper with the needle of the hypodermic syringe and drew a measure of clear liquid into the glass barrel. Examining this with a critical eye, saying, 'If you would be so good, Michael.'

Mick Flowers stepped behind Alfie, folded his arms around Alfie's shoulders and held him tightly against his thighs. Alfie struggled against his father's grip, outraged by this betrayal.

'Look away,' Mr Prentiss advised, but Alfie watched from the corner of his eye as the needle of the hypodermic pressed against the pale skin of his arm. The skin dimpled, gave. Alfie felt a prick of pain and a coldness spreading under his skin as Mr Prentiss emptied the hypodermic, saw a bead of dark red blood rise when the needle withdrew. Mr Prentiss blotted the blood with a bud of cotton wool, massaged Alfie's arm with cool bony fingers, and said cheerfully, 'That wasn't so bad, was it?'

Alfie said, 'Is it over yet? Can we go?'

'We're not quite done,' Mr Prentiss said. He pulled up a wing chair and sat right in front of Alfie, catching his chin with one hand so that he had to look at the crystal that the old man dangled in front of him at the end of a loop of fine silver chain. It was long and thin and triangular, tapering to a sharp point at the bottom, its top girdled with small square facets and capped with silver. Spots of rainbow light flashed inside it as it turned to and fro about a foot from Alfie's face while Mr Prentiss talked in a soft, low tone, telling Alfie to watch the crystal, to concentrate on it as hard as he could, to imagine that there was nothing else in the room but the crystal . . .

Talking on and on without pause, the crystal swinging lightly to and fro, light flashing on its edges, colours running up and down inside it, the colours and Mr Prentiss's soothing chatter somehow running together, calming as a babbling brook in summer sunlight.

'All right,' Mr Prentiss said, after a while. 'You can let him go now.'

He seemed to be speaking from another room. Or rather, it was as if Alfie was in a space all his own, as if he was inside and outside the crystal at the same time. Mr Prentiss showed him sheets of paper with patterns made out of funny shapes on them, asked him to say if he saw anything moving in them, asked if he knew what they were, if they reminded him of anything.

'They're like the pottery. Grandfather's pottery.'

Alfie felt the words shape themselves in his mouth, but it was as if someone else was speaking. He wasn't scared any more. He felt comfortable and dozy, as if he'd been on a long tramp through the countryside and was waiting by the fire for Grammie to bring in crumpets and tea.

Mr Prentiss said softly, 'Do they remind you of anything else?'

'Sometimes when I close my eyes. And when I feel funny.'

Mick Flowers started to ask Alfie if he remembered what had happened, but Mr Prentiss said that it wouldn't be helpful to talk about it.

'What's done is done. What we will do now is make things better,' he said, and told Alfie that sometimes patterns like these could get inside your head, and stick there. 'They can upset the way you think. I think you have something like that stuck in your head, Alfie. I'm going to try to remove it. It isn't part of you, so it won't hurt. And then you'll feel much better.'

Mr Prentiss talked on and on, saying the same thing over and again in slightly different ways, his voice like water running over stones, a murmuring that no longer contained any words – at least, not any words that Alfie knew. He had a confused memory of staring at the banked fire in the fireplace and seeing things living there, swimming in the yellow heat like fish in an aquarium, or he was on a bridge and watching fish in the river below, smooth brown trout beating their fins as they hung in the slow current that made the green waterweed wave . . .

And then he woke up and found himself in the car, streetlamps and the lighted windows of houses going past in the darkness outside, his father smoking a cigarette as he drove, looking across at Alfie and asking him how he felt.

Alfie was puzzled. He felt fine. He'd fallen asleep, but now he was awake. He was fine.

His father looked relieved, said, 'You did well, Chief.'

'Am I better?'

'I hope so. Getting there, I think.'

'I feel funny.'

'That's part of the treatment, Alfie. It'll pass, and you'll feel like you always did.'

They visited Mr Prentiss twice more. Each time Alfie was injected with the clear fluid and made to watch the way that light sparkled inside the crystal as it swung to and fro. He saw the patterns swimming in the fire and afterwards woke in the car, on the way home. His bad dreams receded and he didn't have any more seizures. He couldn't remember when he had started the sessions with his father, and the joints laced with haka. He supposed it must have been in the summer holidays. And then his father disappeared and Alfie started to have seizures again, and his grandmother took him to Addenbrooke's Hospital in Cambridge, where he was found to be suffering from atypical partial epileptic seizures and was prescribed phenobarbitone. The drug reduced the severity and frequency of the seizures, but unlike Mr Prentiss's treatment did not abolish them completely.

'This drug,' Toby said. 'Did David Prentiss or your father ever let slip where it was from?'

'My grandfather said that it came from a plant called haka, which grew somewhere to the north of Baghdad.'

'Your grandfather told you about it? I though he died before you had your accident.'

'He used to smoke it,' Alfie said.

'He smoked it?'

'In a pipe. He used to mix this grey dust or powder into his pipe tobacco.'

'Are you sure he never mentioned haoma or soma? He didn't mention this tribe, the Kefidis?'

'I don't think so. Or if he did, I don't remember. It was a long time ago. But it has to be the same drug, doesn't it?'

Alfie and Toby were standing side by side on Blackfriars Bridge. Below them, the tide was running upstream, water flowing like brown silk towards Waterloo Bridge, the Shell Building and the utilitarian cathedral of Charing Cross. On the opposite bank, sunlight flashed on the upper curve of the London Eye.

Toby said, 'You haven't explained how you knew that Antareus was the nom de plume of David Prentiss's son.'

'The little girl told me,' Alfie said, remembering the third and last visit to Mr Prentiss's house. As on the first and second visits, he'd been told to play in the garden while his father and Mr Prentiss talked about whatever it was they talked about. He remembered daffodils nodding in the brisk March sunlight, the crooked sticks of the roses softened by new red leaves just beginning to unfurl. Remembered that the little girl had been hiding behind one of the apple trees, beckoning to him, telling him in a fierce whisper that she was playing spies.

'Mummy says I mustn't talk to you, but she can't stop me because she's lying down. She gets the most awful headaches. She gets sick and she has to lie down in the dark. So I escaped,' the little girl said. She was wearing blue dungarees and a yellow sweater. Her gaze was bold and frank.

'Why doesn't she want you to talk to me?'

'Because she doesn't like your daddy,' the little girl said, as if it was the most obvious thing in the world. 'I asked her if he was a spy, and she said that he was.'

Alfie laughed, it was such a ridiculous mistake. 'He isn't a spy. He's a photojournalist, a famous one. He takes pictures of wars and they're published in newspapers and magazines all over the world.'

'My mummy said that he wasn't to be trusted, and I said why not, was it because he's a spy? And she said yes. So when you came last time I couldn't see you, but this time she has a headache and I escaped. My daddy's famous too,' the little girl added. 'Only he isn't here now. He's in America.'

That's when Alfie had learned that the little girl's father was Christopher Prentiss, that he had gone away to do something very important and might not come back for a long time. 'That's why I have to use my mummy's name at school,' the little girl had said. 'Because they mustn't know who I really am.'

Alfie said to Toby Brown, 'I suppose Christopher Prentiss stole the drug from his father, along with copies of the glyphs, and ran off to America.'

'His father – David Prentiss. Is he still alive?'

Alfie shook his head. 'Actually, I think he died more or less when my father disappeared.'

'You have an odd look on your face, Flowers. Odder than usual, that is.'

'After my father went missing, the flat he rented in London was gutted by a fire. Maybe the people who disappeared my father and burned down his flat also killed David Prentiss.'

'Or maybe, because he was an old guy, he dropped dead of a heart attack.'

'Maybe they killed the other two Nomads as well. Clarence and Julius.'

'Check the newspaper archives,' Toby said. 'If David Prentiss was murdered, someone would have written it up. And if three old geezers were bumped off at the same time, it'll be on the front page.'

'Unless it was hushed up.'

'Why would it be hushed up? Or do you know something else you haven't told me?'

'I suppose I could check the newspapers,' Alfie said.

'What about Julius and Clarence? Do you know who they are? If they weren't bumped off by Smersh or THRUSH, they could still be alive.'

Alfie shook his head. 'The photograph was taken a long time ago. They're probably dead too.'

Toby lit a cigarette, shielding the flame of his lighter from the warm wind blowing along the river. 'So, we have these patterns, these glyphs, which come from Iraq. And we have this drug, haka, which may or may not be the mythical haoma or soma, and which also comes from Iraq. The glyphs are made up of entoptic images or form constants. Entoptic images are what you see when you begin to get high. Your brain loosens up and starts generating signals, and those are translated as patterns on your retina, which is the reverse of what usually happens. And the treatment you were given and the mumbo-jumbo in Antareus's nut-job pamphlet both suggest that for the glyphs to work you have to get high. Specifically, you have to get high on haka. Nothing else will work.'

'You're going to get mad at me again,' Alfie said.

'You have another confession.'

'When I took the piece of paper from the drawer in my grandfather's desk, I took something else as well. A leather pouch which contained the powder my grandfather used to mix with his pipe tobacco.'

'So you might have taken some before you looked at whatever was on that piece of paper.'

'I don't remember,' Alfie said, 'but I think I must have. Because otherwise the pattern wouldn't have affected me, would it?'

'You got high, and then some kind of glyph put the permanent zap on your brain.'

'That's what I think.'

'But now these glyphs work on you without the drug.'

'I'm definitely sensitive to them.'

'Because you have the permanent zap. In ordinary people entoptic patterns are hallucinations caused by drugs. But you're wired back to front. Entoptic patterns cause *you* to hallucinate.'

'Not any old entoptic patterns. Just the glyphs. That's why I wonder if what we found in the museum really was made by Morph. The pattern was made up of the right kind of things, but it didn't do anything to me.'

'Maybe Morph had an off day. Or maybe not all of his patterns are glyphs. The point is,' Toby said, 'that the pattern he uses in his graffiti does the business on you. It's definitely one of these glyphs.'

'Definitely.'

'So Morph knows about the glyphs too. The question is, where did he learn about them?'

'If he's from Iraq—'

'Which we don't know. He might be from the States, he might be a former member of Antareus's nasty little cult, or he might be one of their kids. Anyway, if Shareef lives up to his promise, we'll find out soon enough. Right now, you're going home and you're going to print up the photographs you took in the museum, and you're going to have them biked round to the *Guardian* lickety-split.' Toby wrote in his notebook, tore out the page and handed it to Alfie. 'Call this guy, he'll organize the courier. Meanwhile, I'm heading towards the very nice pub at the other end of this bridge, where I'm going to buy a pint of London Pride and sit in the sunshine and write up today's little adventure. And then I'm going to stroll over to the *Guardian*'s offices on Farringdon Road and drop off my copy.'

A tourist boat slid beneath the bridge, music thumping, its rows of benches almost empty. The brown river shone, sunlight glittering from its knots and whorls, its humps and eddies. Two barges at anchor beside the Oxo Tower swung gently to and fro. The buildings on either side of the river stood sharply against the blue sky.

Toby grinned at Alfie. 'Days like this, how can you not love this dirty old town?'

11

Harriet met her MI6 handler, Jack Nicholl, at the new restaurant in St James's Park, an egg-shaped wooden structure that emerged from a low grassy mound like a breaching whale. When she arrived, dead on time, she found him sitting at a small table at one end of the broad verandah that faced the lake, eating a boiled egg and buttered soldiers. A neatly folded copy of the *Guardian* lay on the table, next to his elbow. As soon as she saw it, Harriet knew that things weren't going to go her way. Jack didn't seem to be a *Guardian* kind of person; there could only be one reason why he'd brought along a copy.

He rose to greet her, apologizing for having already ordered his breakfast. He was wearing a pinstripe suit and a tie woven with a pattern of crossed AK-47s that was, no doubt, some girl-friend's gift. 'I have to hop over to Whitehall in half an hour, another briefing about the current preoccupation. Please, let me be Mother,' he said, and poured her a cup of tea. 'It's a pukka brew. Loose-leaf, none of your tea-bag nonsense. I take it you've seen today's *Guardian*, by the way.'

Harriet waved away a waiter who offered her a menu, and said, 'If you mean the article about the Imperial War Museum, it doesn't mean anything. And that's not why I asked for this meeting.'

Jack Nicholl smiled. 'But I rather think we should discuss it. Mr Flowers seems to be getting closer and closer to Morph.'

'There's another player now. And he's far more dangerous than Alfie Flowers.'

'We'll talk about Mr Flowers first.' Jack Nicholl dipped a buttered soldier in the hull of his egg, nipped off the yolky end with even white teeth.

Harriet said with a sinking feeling, 'I came here to talk about Carver Soborin.'

Jack Nicholl ignored this. 'The prank in the Imperial War Museum. Is there anything I should know that didn't make it into print? For instance, how did Mr Flowers and his journalist friend happen to find out about it? Have they been in contact with Morph?'

Harriet took a moment to overcome her anxiety. She couldn't set the agenda here; she was the supplicant. If she went along with this line of questioning, perhaps she could get a chance to turn things around, get back on track.

'I think they got in contact with a friend of his,' she said, and explained about the party at which Morph had been supposed to make an appearance, the stunt with the sheep, how Alfie Flowers and Toby Brown had returned them. 'I suppose they traced the Land Rover, just like I did. They had a long conversation with the man who looks after the smallholding, and got on the phone to someone as soon as they drove off. Unfortunately, I don't know who they talked to or what they said because they used Mr Brown's mobile, and by the time the man who was following them realized what was going on and managed to get a lock on the signal, the call was all but over. He heard someone saying something about making a big statement, then heard Alfie Flowers's journalist friend give out the number of his mobile.'

'Who was he talking to? Morph?'

'It's possible, but I believe that it's more likely that it was a friend of his, someone by the name of Benjamin Barrett. He's the son of the man who owns the smallholding where the sheep came from, and the Land Rover that was used to transport them. And according to the Kurdish informer run by your MI5 contact, he's a DJ or MC on a pirate radio station, Mister Fantastic FM, working under the name of Shareef. I Googled the radio station, checked out its web site, and found out that Shareef hosts a phone-in show. I listened to it yesterday. He spent ten minutes talking about Morph, his graffiti, and the political performance piece involving the sheep at the party, and told his listeners to check out a new piece of what he called protest art at the Imperial War Museum.'

'Is that how Mr Flowers found out about it?'

'They turned up at the museum at ten o'clock in the morning, when it opened. Shareef's broadcast was in the afternoon.'

Harriet had listened to it while driving to Clarence Ashburton's house, to check the new security arrangements.

Jack Nicholl said, 'You have a man following Mr Flowers and his friend. May I know who it is?'

'You never did come back to me with an offer of help.'

'What can I say, Harriet? I passed your request upstairs, I was told it would be considered, and I'm still waiting for a decision.'

'Meanwhile, I need to keep an eye on Alfie Flowers in case he stumbles over something useful, and I need to pursue my own investigations too. So I hired some old colleagues of mine to tail him. Don't worry, I'm paying them myself, it won't cost the government a penny. And I haven't told them a thing about the glyphs. As far as they're concerned it's a simple surveillance job.'

'Your "old colleagues" wouldn't be working for Mr Graham Taylor's private detective agency, would they?'

'You read my file. I'm flattered.'

'I believe they spend most of their time investigating insurance claims. Are they really up to this kind of work?'

'A large part of their work involves surveillance.'

'You mentioned something about getting a lock on a mobile phone signal. These people wouldn't happen to be using a frequency scanner?'

Harriet nodded.

'Mmm. I rather believe that became illegal after the Camillagate nonsense. It's a bloody nuisance, of course. Some hobbyist uses a scanner to eavesdrop on the Prince of Wales and his mistress, and all of a sudden we have to fill in a ream of paperwork every time we want to eavesdrop on *our* targets. But the law is the law.'

'If it worries you, get an order for an official tap on Alfie Flowers's mobile. And one for his land line too.'

'Oh, *I*'m not concerned about minor peccadilloes. But if I were you, I'd make sure that your friends don't get caught. I'm afraid that I won't be able to help if they get you into trouble with the police.'

'They know what they're doing.'

'Mr Flowers appears to know what he's doing too.' Jack Nicholl took a small sip of tea and blotted his lips with a corner of his napkin. 'It seems to me that you aren't entirely on top of this, Harriet. Or am I being unfair?'

'If Alfie Flowers arranges a meeting with Morph, I'll be right behind him. You can count on it.'

'If only everything in this business was as certain as you, Harriet.'

Harriet smiled. 'I'll take that as a compliment.'

Jack Nicholl returned her smile with interest. 'Feel free. So, what about this DJ friend of Morph's? Have you talked to him?'

'Not yet,' Harriet said. She explained that she had obtained Benjamin Barrett's address from his father, and that when she had broken into his flat she had discovered that it had been thoroughly searched by someone. She told Jack Nicholl about the man she'd seen in the alley at the back of the house, and the man who had chased her car down the road.

Jack Nicholl said, 'Are you certain that he was a low man? That he wasn't a crack addict or something similar? After all, this *was* near Green Lanes.'

'I know the difference,' Harriet said, remembering how, in Lagos, a gang of low men had run at her and the soldiers and police when they had gone to arrest Carver Soborin. The low men running out of the hot black African night, running headlong with that weird stiff gait, as if they were perpetually falling forward. Running without pause even when the soldiers had opened fire. 'It means that at least one British citizen has been turned. Possibly more – the man who followed Alfie Flowers to the party mentioned that when the Land Rover that delivered the sheep left the scene, two men chased after it. I didn't think anything of it at the time, but now I'm sure that they were low men too.'

'Let's suppose it's true . . .'

'Let's cut to the chase,' Harriet said. 'I know that Carver Soborin is here, in London, and I know where he's staying. It didn't take me long to find him, either. He always had a taste for the finest things in life, and that narrowed the search considerably. He's staying in the Dorchester with Rölf Most, the psychiatrist who owns the private psychiatric clinic to which he was committed after the Nigerian incident. Dr Most is a good friend of Carver Soborin's wife, who you'll no doubt remember is a Swiss citizen who skipped to her home country with most of mind's i's funds just before it was wound up. Dr Most was born in Switzerland too, emigrated to the USA and took up citizenship thirty years ago, sat on the boards of some of the same charities as Mrs Soborin, and like her was a member of something called the

Swiss-American Friendship Foundation. I think that he and Carver Soborin came to London because they are looking for Morph. They found out that Morph is linked to Benjamin Barrett, but so far he seems to have escaped them – as of yesterday, he was still broadcasting on his pirate radio station. They searched his flat and left a couple of low men to keep watch in case he returned to it, and I walked right into their trap. But that's not the point. The point is that the whole business has started up again. I think—'

'Harriet, please. There are civilians about.'

Harriet leaned across the little table and said in a fierce whisper, 'I think that Carver Soborin and Rölf Most want to find Morph and mine him for everything that he knows about glyphs. I think we have to find him before they do because it's quite possible that he could lead them to the source. The MI5 informer told me that Morph and his father claimed asylum after they came here from Turkey, but that they were originally from Iraq. It's obvious that they must have something to do with the sheep herders the Nomads' Club visited before the Second World War. If Carver Soborin and Rölf Most find him—'

'Dr Most is Dr Soborin's psychiatrist, not his business partner. Why would he be any part of this folie à deux? If that's what it is.'

'Carver Soborin became obsessed with the glyphs while he was treating Christopher Prentiss, and I think that Rölf Most has become obsessed too. That's what the glyphs do. They get inside your head. They change your mind. They're like a viral infection – they use us to reproduce themselves.'

'Like that poem about misery handed on from man to man. Deepening like a coastal shelf.'

'If you had seen what I'd seen in Nigeria,' Harriet said, 'you wouldn't be quite so flippant. Hospital wards full of children who had lost their minds. Children chained to beds to stop them gouging out their own eyes. Children who *had* managed to blind themselves. Row after row of catatonic children lying on mats, not even stirring to brush off the flies that clustered around their eyes and mouths. Wasting away because they wouldn't eat, and there weren't the resources to put them on drips. Dying of infected bed sores. Their mothers trying to get them to eat, to look at them. The poor women wailing, knowing that they had already lost their children, that they were the living dead. That's what happened the last time someone tried to use the glyphs, Mr Nicholl.'

Jack Nicholl absorbed the full force of her anger without flinching. He said, 'I've read the report, and I've no doubt that the reality was far worse. Unfortunately—'

'I haven't mentioned the smells, or the sounds. Have you ever heard the screams of a child that has used its fingers to gouge out its own eyes?'

'Unfortunately, it's out of my hands,' Jack Nicholl said, with a gesture that showed her that his hands were indeed empty.

Harriet had half-expected something like this, but the shock was still like a punch to her stomach. She said, 'Someone wants Carver Soborin and Rölf Most to find Morph, don't they? That's why MI6 isn't going to give me any help. That's why, after you've pumped me for everything I've discovered, you're about to warn me off.'

'I'm sorry.'

'Is it us, or is it the Americans?'

'Let's say that it is part of the grand alliance to bring democracy to every part of the poor old globe. And that's all I can tell you. I've already had my wrist slapped, actually, for putting you in touch with the Kurdish informer.'

'It has to be the Americans. And it's not official business, because if it was they'd be getting all the help you could give them.'

'We're trying to stay neutral,' Jack Nicholl admitted. 'And we certainly didn't tell Carver Soborin and Rölf Most about Morph. Perhaps a clipping service passed on the original newspaper story, perhaps they have their own intel. Anyway, they are here, and I have been told to ask you to keep away from them. My superiors would also like you to call off your search for Morph. We don't want an incident.'

'Would you call what happened in Lagos an incident?'

'If I could help you, Harriet, I would. But this has been taken out of my hands.'

'What's the CIA's role in this? Is it overt or covert? Do they have actual agents hotdogging Carver Soborin and Rölf Most, or is it someone from some proprietary company? More likely the latter,' Harriet said. Her thoughts were racing ahead of her. 'After all, mind's i was a proprietary company, a front for the CIA. And the chocolate milk drink it was testing in Lagos, the drink spiked with Carver Soborin's drug, the advertisements which contained glyphs, all of that was a CIA black op disguised as a commercial venture. Do you want something like that to happen here?'

'I've warned you to stay away,' Jack Nicholl said, dropping a twenty-pound note on the table and standing up. 'And with that, my job here is done. And so is yours, Harriet. That is, if you have any sense.'

Harriet realized that he'd chosen his words very carefully. She had been given a warning, but not an order . . . She stood too, saying, 'What will happen if I don't stay away?'

Jack Nicholl looked at her. His smile was back in place. 'I really did read those files,' he said. 'And I do admire the hell out of what you did in Nigeria.'

'Who is helping Carver Soborin and Rölf Most? Just the name, Mr Nicholl. It isn't so much to ask, is it?'

Jack Nicholl studied her, then said quietly, 'Check out a little scandal involving a private op in Peshawar, last October.'

'Peshawar as in Pakistan?'

'It was nice to meet you, Harriet. Please do try to stay out of trouble,' Jack Nicholl said. When he reached the bottom of the verandah steps, he turned and added, 'Good luck.'

And then he was gone, and Harriet was on her own.

12

Alfie picked up a copy of the *Guardian* first thing Thursday morning, found and read the story about the Imperial War Museum while walking back to his yard, and read it again over breakfast. Four short columns under one of his photographs of the bogus exhibit on the ninth page of the National News section, the piece headlined *Rat Invades Museum* and credited to Toby Brown's friend, the photograph credited to Alfie. They'd gone for the colour version, and although it had been slightly stretched to fit the space and the reds were just a shade too muted, it wasn't a bad reproduction; Alfie felt pleasantly optimistic as he puttered about, catching up on his chores while he waited for Toby to phone and tell him that Shareef had got in touch and arranged a meeting.

He spent a couple of hours scorching weeds from the cracks in the concrete apron of the yard with his flame gun, drank about a gallon of iced peach tea to rehydrate himself, ate a scratch lunch of pitta bread and hummus and olives. It was past two o'clock now, and although Toby still hadn't called, Alfie wasn't too worried. He'd tuned his radio to Mister Fantastic FM, and Shareef had just begun his phone-in show; presumably, the DJ wouldn't make his call to Toby until it was finished.

Alfie took the radio into his darkroom and listened to it while he tried to make a definitive print of one of his lichen photographs. Shareef wasn't at all bad, putting on a convincing ordinary-man-of-the-street act as he talked about police stop-and-searches: were they necessary in the current climate of fear about terrorism, or were they nothing more than another excuse to hassle minorities? 'I have my own opinion, but first I want to hear from you,' he told his audience. Sounding like any reasonably articulate North London young man, his voice pleasant, laid-back, as he coaxed shy or tongue-tied callers and sparred with hostile callers until they became too aggressive and he told them they were talking nonsense and cut them off, laughing when kids tried to hijack his show with breathless over-rehearsed raps, laughing at himself when he garbled an ad for the station, announcing that he was switching to a new topic, reminding his listeners about the big news yesterday – local graffiti artist Morph creating a sensation after he smuggled an anti-war piece into the Imperial War Museum.

'You heard it here first. Now you can read all about it in today's *Guardian* newspaper,' Shareef said. 'You know I don't normally big up the so-called "liberal" media, but just this once I'm asking you to go score a copy of that newspaper and check out how the establishment react when our boy Morph brought the voice of the street to the stuffy galleries of one of white Britain's top institutions.'

Alfie listened with pinpoint attention, his whole skin tingling, shaking a fresh print back and forth in a tray of developer while Shareef described the piece and translated the cod Latin tag for his listeners.

'The American Desert Army Rat, understand? Rats are unclean animals that spread plague and disease, and this particular rat spread the disease of Americanitis to the lands of our brothers. Picture him standing in front of a burning oil-well. We know what he feed on, sucking the oil from the ground with his two rat teeth like a vampire sucking blood from the neck of a virgin. We know that oil is why the war was fought,' Shareef said, the lilt in his voice growing more pronounced as he riffed on a familiar range of anti-Bush, anti-Blair, anti-war sentiments, inviting his listeners to phone in and comment, inviting them to phone up the museum and ask it to reinstate the piece, inviting them to write letters to the *Guardian*. 'I know that some of you disagree with my man Morph. I know that some of you have been disrespecting his pieces. Some of you have been sneaking about and covering them up, blotting them out. I want you to phone in too, tell me why you try to silence the voice of truth.'

Alfie found it hard to concentrate on his work after that, and besides, the crevices and fissures in the photograph of the lichen that he was printing up were beginning to seem a little like a glyph: luminous shards were lifting free of the lichen's crazy-paving surface, swarming everywhere in the dim red light of the darkroom. He lay down on his bed, the curtains drawn, fell asleep while listening to the rest of Shareef's phone-in, and was woken by the warble of his mobile phone.

'Well, he called,' Toby said. 'The fix is in.'

'Are we meeting him?'

'Tomorrow at four, at some gymnasium on the Kingsland Road.'

'And Morph? What about Morph?'

'Shareef says he wants to look us over first. See if we're worthy.'

'So we're no nearer,' Alfie said. He was sitting on the side of his bed, sleepy, cotton-mouthed, headachy. His short hair was pasted into knives by sweat, and his T-shirt clung unpleasantly to his back.

Toby said, 'We're one step closer.'

'Did you listen to his show? Shareef's, I mean.'

'He has some mouth on him, doesn't he?'

'I fell asleep while I was listening to it,' Alfie said.

Toby laughed. 'I didn't think it was *that* bad. I wouldn't be surprised if he didn't get a gig with some legitimate station soon.'

'I fell asleep while he was taking people's calls, after he talked up our piece about the museum. What I was wondering, did Morph call in?'

'It's a phone-in. Voice of the street and so on.'

'But why didn't Shareef let the guy he's so hot on promoting have his say? Why didn't he bring him in for an interview, or to read out a statement? Has he ever had Morph on his show?'

'And your point is?'

Alfie had first had the idea when he'd seen the fake pattern on the card in the display case. Now, after listening to Shareef's phone-in show, he was convinced that he was right. He said, 'First, Angus Barrett told us that Shareef took the sheep away with the help of a bodybuilder type who called himself Watty. And Watty can't be Morph, because the person caught on the security camera at the courier firm's depot is slightly built. He could be white or black, it's impossible to tell with that stocking mask over his face, but he definitely isn't a bodybuilder. Second, the stunt with the sheep could have been done by anyone. It didn't have anything to do with the glyphs. And third, the piece in the museum – the pattern on the card inside it was fake.'

'Are you saying that Shareef did the stunt with the sheep without Morph, and he did the piece in the museum too? What about the graffiti?'

'The graffiti are definitely the real thing, but the pattern on the card wasn't. I think we're dealing with two different artists. Morph – whoever he is – did the graffiti, but Shareef organized the stunt with the sheep, and the bogus exhibit in the War Museum. I think that Morph might have been friendly with Shareef once upon a time, but the two of them have fallen out, and Shareef is trying to cover it up.'

After a moment, Toby said, 'It's definitely the kind of thing we need to ask Shareef when we meet him. But you're going to have to think of a polite, non-confrontational way of doing it. Right now he's our only lead. We can't afford to piss him off.'

'I will. Meanwhile, I have some news of my own,' Alfie said, and told Toby that he'd spent some time in the *Guardian*'s archives yesterday, that he'd found a story about David Prentiss's death. 'He was badly injured by a hit-and-run driver, and died of a massive heart attack in the ambulance that was taking him to hospital,' Alfie said, remembering the way the tall, thin old man had looked down at him when they had first met. His tweed suit, his creaking laugh.

Toby said, 'You think this accident wasn't an accident? That someone ran him down deliberately?'

'He died on the same day that someone set fire to my father's flat. It's possible that the people my father was dealing with in Lebanon were responsible.'

'It's possible,' Toby said. 'But unless you have some hard evidence to link the two things, it isn't anything more than a coincidence. I think you should focus on our meeting with Shareef. Write down what you want to ask when we meet up with him, and we'll go through it tomorrow.'

After Toby had rung off, Alfie stepped outside to get a breath of fresh air. On the other side of the big, open-ended garage, George Johnson was doing some repair work on his RT bus. It had attended a rally somewhere in Epping Forest at the weekend, and although it had for once managed to return under its own power, it had been blowing steam through its radiator grille when it had finally laboured into the yard. Now the wings of its snub-nose bonnet were raised, the component parts of its coolant pump were laid out on an oil-stained piece of tarpaulin on the concrete floor, and George was standing at the workbench, using a wire brush to scrub oil from a big metal ring. When he saw Alfie emerge from the caravan, he walked over and said, 'You and your writer friend wouldn't happen to have got someone's back up over this graffiti merchant you're looking for, would you?'

'What's wrong, George?'

'It might be nothing, but then again it might not, which is why I thought it best to ask. What it is, there's a pair of geezers across the way in the park, dressed like tramps. Which is maybe all that they are, except that they were there yesterday, and they came back again first thing today.'

It was early evening, and the sun hung just above the rooftops of the houses that backed onto the yard. Alfie, looking through a gap in the trees and bushes that screened the yard from the railway, saw in the little park on the other side of the cutting a hard bright star twinkling among the swings and climbing frames of the playground where few children played these days. Saw the two men sitting on the tongue of the slide, leaning close together as they shared the can which had heliographed sunlight straight into his eyes.

'I think I should have a word with them,' he told George.

'I should come with you. Just in case.'

'I know who they're working for. It's nothing sinister,' Alfie said, and strolled out of the gates of his yard, crossed the railway bridge, and walked into the park.

The two scruffy, pale-faced men stood up as Alfie approached them, then turned on their heels and walked away with identical stiff, mincing gaits, like a pair of clockwork soldiers. Alfie called out to them, asking them to wait a moment, telling them he just wanted a word, and they broke into a run. They lowered their heads and tipped forward and ran, arms held stiffly by their sides, running out of the park, running down the middle of the street, running far too fast for Alfie, shod in sandals, to have any chance of catching up with them.

'Tell Mr Ruane I'm not interested in helping him!' Alfie shouted.

The echo of his voice came back from the houses around the park as the two men swerved around a corner and disappeared. A woman sitting on the steps of one of the houses looked up from the book she was reading. Alfie walked back to the playground and discovered at the bottom of the slide where the two men had been sitting dozens of the little packets in which cafés supply sugar, every one torn open and empty. Junkies, he thought, maintaining a sugar high. If that was the only help Robbie Ruane could afford to hire, no wonder he was so desperate to find new talent.

George Johnson was waiting for Alfie at the entrance to the yard, clutching a wrench as long as his arm. Alfie explained about Robbie Ruane and his interest in Morph's graffiti. 'Those two, or two just like them, were hanging around outside that party I went to. I think Robbie Ruane hopes I'll lead him to this kid.'

'If I see 'em hanging around again, I'll call up a couple of the lads and show 'em what's what,' George said, and swung the wrench like a baseball bat to demonstrate what he meant.

Alfie called Toby and told him what had happened.

'It shouldn't be a problem,' Toby said. 'Those two were on foot, right?'

'Right.'

'So we'll borrow your friend's van again. We'll drive around until we're sure no one is following us, and then we'll head for the place where we're supposed to meet Shareef.'

'No sweat,' George said, when Alfie asked if he could use the Transit van. 'As long as it isn't anything to do with sheep.'

'Cross my heart. I was also wondering,' Alfie said, producing the shard of stone, 'if you've ever seen anything like this before.'

George polished his bifocal glasses on the lapel of his cardigan, hooked them around his ears, and peered at the scrap of blackened stone, its cage of silver wire, the incised pattern.

Alfie explained that it had belonged to his father. 'Did he ever talk to you about anything like this? About old stones or pots, or cave paintings, anything at all like that?'

'What, like archaeology? Get out of it, Alfie. We mostly talked about the horses or the dogs. He had a soft spot for the greyhounds, did your father. We went up to Walthamstow together a good few times, back when it still had the old glamour.' George, fists plunged into the sagging pockets of his oil-stained cardigan, was looking beyond Alfie, into the past. Saying, 'Of course, he liked the horses even more. He always had a tip for me. Half of them were good tips, too. Trouble was, as he said himself, you never knew which half.'

Alfie jiggled the piece of stone on the end of its chain. 'You didn't see anything like this in the caravan? After he . . . disappeared.'

George shook his head. 'Is that where you found it?'

'A friend of his gave it to me a while ago. Quite a few years ago, actually.'

'A woman, I bet. He had someone mount it up in that filigree, and gave it to her to wear.'

'Something like that.'

'He was like catnip to the ladies, your father,' George said, with a fond smile. 'Sometimes they'd be waiting in his car, his girlfriends, while he talked with me and collected the rent. Very nice they were, too. Models and such. Anyway, the police turned his caravan over, didn't they? After he disappeared.'

'They did?'

It was the first time that Alfie had heard about it, but he'd never really talked to George about Mick Flowers before. He and George rubbed along in their odd relationship, talking about the weather and the government, the latest outrages perpetrated by traffic wardens on honest workmen and the latest scandals concerning the local council (George followed the ins and outs of local government as if it was a soap opera), but they'd never really talked about the past. They'd never talked about what had happened when Alfie's father had disappeared.

George said, 'Couple of 'em came poking around. Plain clothes. Probably from Scotland Yard, although I don't remember if they ever told me.'

'They searched the caravan?'

'I suppose they looked in it. They looked in everything else. Then your grandmother had me put a padlock on it, and that was that until you pitched up some years later.'

'Did they say what they were looking for?'

George shrugged. 'I suppose they were looking for clues about where your father had been and what he'd been up to. A bad business, Alfie.'

'I know.'

'If your father kept anything like that in his caravan,' George said, 'I expect the police took it away, as evidence and such. If you're lucky, they might still have it. When someone disappears the way your father did, the police like to keep anything that might be evidence. It's been more than twenty years, but you might be lucky.'

Alfie told George that it was definitely worth a try, but he was certain that the two men who had searched the caravan hadn't been policemen. Policemen would have taken away the love letters that Alfie had found years later in the sugar tin. No, the two men George had mistaken for plain-clothes police had been something else. Perhaps they had been working for the Nomads. Or perhaps they had been Russian agents, or members of the British secret service. In any case, Alfie knew that they would have been interested in only one thing.

The glyphs.

13

A little after three o'clock on Friday afternoon, Graham Taylor, the owner of the private detective agency that was helping Harriet surveil both Alfie Flowers and Rölf Most's little crew of maniacs, knocked on the door of her hotel room.

'I come bearing gifts,' he said, following her into the room and holding up a Starbucks bag. 'Coffee and doughnuts. I bet they cost me a tenth of what this place charges.'

'I'll have to pass,' Harriet said, as she put on her jacket. She was wearing a cream silk blouse and her good trouser suit. Her mobile phone was attached to her belt, its microphone was clipped to the collar of her blouse, and its earpiece was plugged into her left ear. 'Alfie Flowers and Toby Brown are supposed to be meeting Benjamin Barrett at four, I've been stuck here ever since Larry Macpherson went for a stroll, and if I don't leave right now I'm going to be late. Thanks for helping out, by the way. You've saved my life.'

Larry Macpherson was Carver Soborin's and Rölf Most's bodyguard, and it was likely that he was also working for the CIA. Following the hint dropped by Jack Nicholl, Harriet had discovered that he was a former American soldier who had served in the Marines and special forces before resigning his commission a couple of years after the first Gulf War (there was plenty of gossip about this part of his career, most of it derogatory, on internet sites used by ex-members of the US special forces) and becoming a freelance security consultant, advising companies about counter-terrorism measures. He'd served a brief prison term for credit-card fraud, and in 2001 had turned up in Afghanistan, where he had supposedly fought with Northern Alliance soldiers against the Taliban, and claimed to have located an al-Qaeda arms dump. Last year he had been arrested in Peshawar by the Pakistani intelligence service and accused of torturing Afghani refugees for information about the whereabouts of senior members of al-Qaeda,

presumably in the hope of collecting the rewards offered by the
US government for their capture. There were rumours that he'd
been working clandestinely for the CIA when he'd been arrested;
in any event, he'd been expelled from the country after just three
weeks in jail, and had immediately gone to work for Universal
Risk Management, a private company with strong links to the
CIA, which was supplying mercenaries and security personnel to
Iraq, so-called civilian contractors who guarded provincial outposts
of the Iraqi provisional authority and provided perimeter security for oil installations and power stations. And now he was in
London, riding shotgun on Carver Soborin and Rölf Most, and
possibly handling them on behalf of the CIA. The only consola-
tion was that if the CIA was using a rogue like Larry Macpherson
to manage the two psychiatrists, then it probably believed that
the hunt for Morph wouldn't yield anything useful and its commit-
ment was minimal, which meant that Harriet still had a chance
to get to Morph first.

'I shouldn't tell you this, but being paid to hang out in a luxury
hotel is money for old rope.' Graham Taylor was looking around
at the room, which was decorated in Hollywood Baroque: fake
antique furniture and a ton of gilt and brocade. 'Talking of which,
you must be coining it to be able to afford this place *and* the hire
of everyone in the firm bar the secretary.'

'I'm not going to stiff you, Graham.'

But the cost of employing everyone in Graham's agency, not
to mention the cool five hundred pounds a night for the hotel
room, was depleting Harriet's finances at an alarming rate; a couple
of weeks of this, and she would be flat broke. Luckily, her search
for Morph almost certainly wouldn't last as long as that. One of
Graham's operatives had intercepted mobile-phone calls between
Alfie Flowers and his journalist friend in which they had discussed
meeting Benjamin Barrett, Morph's accomplice, this very afternoon. Harriet had been planning to get as close to this meeting
as she could, but an hour ago, just as she was getting ready to
leave, Larry Macpherson had decided to go for a stroll. Two of
Graham Taylor's operatives were tag-teaming him, while Harriet
had been keeping watch on Rölf Most and Carver Soborin, and
waiting for Graham Taylor to take over.

Graham was a genial, unflappable ex-copper, neatly anonymous in an off-the-peg suit. Harriet had worked for him for three years, her very first job after she'd left university. His agency specialized in industrial-injury claims – interviewing claimants and their workmates, videoing people with alleged back injuries humping dustbins, washing windows, or playing football or squash, following people who'd sworn they were too badly injured to ever work again to their new places of employment. Although it had been fairly mundane work, Harriet had learned enough streetcraft and people-handling skills to be able to set up her own one-woman agency, and she and Graham had remained friends, passing bits of business back and forth. Now she was employing him.

'If you do have money problems, I reckon we can sort something out,' Graham said, biting into a doughnut and dropping powdered sugar on his tie. 'You could come back and work for me, for instance.'

Harriet smiled. 'I'll think about it.'

Graham took another bite of his doughnut, and asked her to explain the set-up. 'It's been a while since I was at the sharp end.'

Harriet showed him the Sony laptop that sat on the gilt side table. Graham put on a pair of bifocals and studied its screen, which was cycling between views of two different hotel corridors, while she told him about the video camera that was watching the door of the suite where Carver Soborin and Rölf Most were staying, and about the camera watching the door of Larry Macpherson's room.

'They're across the corridor from each other and three floors above us, which gives us just enough time to use the stairs to beat them to the lobby whenever we see them leave their rooms.'

It had been the work of moments to emplace the two tiny, stick-on video cameras. Their tilted viewpoints and the flattening effect of their pinhole lenses made the two different views of the same hotel corridor look like stills from a German Expressionist movie.

Graham looked at Harriet over the top of his bifocals. 'Is that it?'

'That's it, unless you can work out how to get into the rooms to plant something, or how to hack into the hotel's switchboard.

Janice and I were taking turns to watch the camera feeds, and Alan was watching the front of the hotel.'

Janice chain-smoked and was given to bitter monologues about her ex-husband, but her company had definitely been preferable to that of spaniel-eyed, wet-lipped Alan.

Graham said, 'Alan give you any trouble?'

'Apart from his tendency to stare at my breasts when he talks to me?'

'He doesn't mean any harm by it. Thirty-five years old, and the poor lad is still living with his parents – I don't deny he's got what they call personal issues. But he's a sly one with a video camera.'

'I bet he is. Anyway, he and Janice are tailing Larry Macpherson, and I have to be somewhere else, which is why I really appreciate it that you've come out to give me a hand.'

'I hope they know not to mix it up,' Graham said. 'That file you gave me suggests that Mr Macpherson is a very tasty geezer.'

'I told them that if they have the faintest suspicion that Larry Macpherson has spotted them, they should drop the tail at once.'

'How about your other targets? Are they at home?'

'Rölf Most and Carver Soborin went down to the dining room to have breakfast, and came back an hour later. They haven't stirred out of their suite since. They had their lunch sent up.'

'Do they ever leave the hotel?'

'Rölf Most went jogging in the park yesterday, just after we set up. Other than that, they've stayed inside.'

'No visitors.'

'Not one. Of course, they could be doing all kinds of business by phone, and we'd never know. And they were in London for at least two days before I found out, and I don't have the faintest idea what they got up to then.' Harriet glanced at her watch. It was twenty past three. 'I really have to go.'

'You're going to sit in the street, sucking up traffic fumes outside some gym in Hackney, hoping to follow Mr Barrett to the pot of gold at the end of the rainbow, while I sit here in the lap of luxury and watch the world's most boring movie on your laptop. Like I said, my part of this deal is money for old rope.'

'If anything happens, anything at all, call me.'

Graham sat on the edge of the big, square bed, took a sip of his coffee, and studied Harriet over the rim of the cardboard beaker. 'Are you sure you're up for a sustained bout of fieldwork? Janice told me you've been here ever since you first set up the cameras. If you don't mind me saying so, you look a trifle frayed around the edges.'

'I'll be fine. And I have your best operative to back me up.'

'Michelle's the best, all right. Almost as good as I used to be, way back when. Looks like you've got some movement, by the way.'

Rölf Most was leaving his room, wearing the electric-blue warm-ups he'd worn yesterday when he'd puffed slowly around the Serpentine.

'It looks like he's going jogging,' Harriet said, grabbing her little rucksack and heading for the door. 'I'll follow him down and make sure you keep watch here.'

'What if the other guy takes it into his head to go for a constitutional too?'

'I seriously doubt that Carver Soborin will go anywhere on his own,' Harriet said, and banged out of the room, buoyed up by an anticipatory jolt of adrenalin, mapping out possible moves in anticipation of tailing Benjamin Barrett. But as she went down the stairs towards the lobby, her mobile began to vibrate at her waist, and when she answered, Janice told her that she and Alan had lost Larry Macpherson.

'He went into a pub. Alan followed him inside, but he must have dodged straight through and left by the back door.'

'When was this?'

'About ten minutes ago. We did a quick trawl around the area, but no luck.'

'Do you think he spotted you?'

'I don't know. It's possible,' Janice said, 'but we were keeping well back. I mean, we do know how to tail someone.'

'Larry Macpherson is a professional. He might have pulled the trick with the pub out of habit,' Harriet said. But she had a feeling that things were beginning to spin out of control, was already wondering if the man might have pulled a diversionary move, drawing surveillance away from Rölf Most.

Janice said, 'What do you want us to do?'

'Head straight back to the hotel. Dr Most is going for a jog, and I'd like you to keep an eye on him, just in case he's planning to meet someone.'

Harriet phoned Michelle, the operative following Alfie Flowers, and told her that she might be late. She reached the lobby just in time to see the psychiatrist exit the lift and head towards the doors: a short, portly man wearing tinted glasses and with his white hair fluffed bouffant-style, looking a little like Santa Claus's younger brother in his blue designer warm-ups and box-fresh trainers, walking past the plate-glass window of the shop where guests could buy expensive souvenirs of their stay. Harriet waited for thirty seconds before following, hanging back as the psychiatrist walked along Park Lane towards a pedestrian crossing. They were heading south, moving in the same direction as the traffic. She was concentrating on her target and didn't see the white Volkswagen people-carrier that came sharking up behind her until it swerved onto the pavement. Its side door slid back and there was Larry Macpherson, smiling over the automatic pistol that he was pointing at her, saying, 'Are you going to cooperate, Ms Crowley, or am I going to have to fuck you up?'

14

Elliot Johnson said, 'If he's supposed to be meeting you right now, how come he's still chatting on the radio?'

Toby said, 'Because he's yanking our chain. Because he wants us to arrive way before he does, and sweat it out in the presence of his intimidating muscle-building pals until he decides to grace us with his company.'

Alfie said, 'That's why there's no point going inside until he goes off the air.'

'Learn from us, young man,' Toby said. 'We have the wisdom of the ages, and know that patience is the first and greatest virtue.'

It was five past four in the afternoon. The three of them, Alfie Flowers, Toby Brown, and Elliot Johnson, were sitting in the Transit van, which was illegally parked across the road from the entrance to the Majestic gymnasium. Elliot sat behind the wheel; Toby leaned at the window; Alfie was wedged between them. The radio was tuned to Mister Fantastic FM, 94.7 on the dial. Shareef's phone-in show had just finished, there'd been a string of ads for Red Stripe beer and club nights in pubs and community centres, and now Shareef was handing over to the next DJ, a woman who called herself Sugar Silk, chatting with her about his own show, asking her what was coming up on hers.

'Maybe he's already inside,' Elliot said. 'Maybe he's broadcasting from the gym. Pirates can set up anywhere. I mean, that's the point. It's do-it-yourself radio.'

Elliot was a tall, lanky, sweet-natured kid, long wheat-coloured hair tied back in a loose ponytail, wearing combat trousers and a Libertines T-shirt, and sitting on the base of his spine with his frayed Converse All-Stars up on the dash next to the steering wheel, his knees tucked against his chest. It had been Alfie's idea to involve him. At the yard, Elliot had backed the van into the garage and Alfie had climbed in through the rear doors, so that anyone who might be watching wouldn't be able to see him;

then they'd picked up Toby at a café on Upper Street, and had taken a circuitous route to Kingsland Road. They'd been parked opposite the Majestic gymnasium for half an hour now, Elliot growing more and more fidgety while Toby smoked with a kind of absent-minded fury and leafed through a fat biography of George Savile (1633–95), first Marquess of Halifax, essayist and sedulously anti-Catholic member of Charles II's court, and Alfie watched the gym and thought about the enhanced versions of two of his grandfather's photographs that Elliot had given him.

One was of the four Nomads and the anomalous stone; the other of Alfie's grandfather standing next to the stone in the cave. Digital enhancement had revealed that the complex patterns incised into both stones appeared to be identical. Alfie had made Elliot swear that he wouldn't tell Toby about them, and Elliot had promised that he wouldn't. Asking was he right in thinking that the patterns on the stones were like the pattern Morph used in his graffiti?

'This has nothing to do with Morph,' Alfie had lied. 'This is strictly family business, so not a word, okay?'

Now Elliot said, 'Don't you think one of you guys should at least go in, check the place out?'

'Shareef wants to meet us just as much as we want to meet him,' Alfie said. He'd taken half a Valium before setting out, just enough to take the edges off the world and maintain a Buddha-like equilibrium.

'He wants us to make his protégé famous,' Toby said, turning a page of his book. He was wearing his black linen jacket over a black T-shirt, faded black 501s. The front of the T-shirt and the lapels of the jacket were liberally dusted with cigarette ash. 'If it comes to it, he'll wait for us. And besides, if you haven't noticed, he's still talking on the radio. Cultivate patience, young grasshopper.'

Shareef and Sugar Silk's banter cut off in mid-sentence, and there was only the hiss of dead air on the Transit's radio.

When Toby reached across to fiddle with it, Elliot caught his wrist, saying, 'They're switching transmitters again. They switch around all the time, which is why the signal keeps cutting out. Don't you old guys know that?'

Sugar Silk came back on air, telling her listeners that after Shareef had stirred everyone up, it was time to chill out with two hours of lovers' rock. 'Don't forget: please leave your guns at home, don't get caught up in that evil zone,' she said, and segued into a block of ads.

Elliot said, 'They switch around from transmitter to transmitter. They have themselves a studio at a central location, and a bunch of low-power transmitters on top of high-rises. That way the feds can only track down and seize the transmitters, they can't work out where the pirates keep their studio equipment, their decks and mixers, all their expensive shit.'

Toby looked at him. 'The feds? Who are these feds?'

'The authorities. The law,' Elliot said.

'He's pulling your leg,' Alfie said.

'Kid's been watching too much American TV,' Toby said, closing his book and stuffing it into his khaki satchel. 'He does have a point, though. Shareef has finished his show, and he could be mere moments away from this place. Remember what we agreed, Alfie. I do the talking. You take the pictures and keep your mouth shut.'

'As long as you ask all the right questions,' Alfie said.

'I looked at your list, didn't I?'

'Which I thought we were going to discuss.'

'What's to discuss? Elliot, are you clear about what you have to do?'

Elliot stretched in his seat, smiled his goofy smile. 'I keep watch, see who goes in and who goes out. And when your meeting's over, you'll come out with the guy and shake his hand so I'll know who he is, and I do my best follow him.'

'In the van if he gets in a car, on foot if not,' Toby said. 'Once he gets where he's going, you phone us, and we come and find you.'

Elliot said, 'What if he uses a back door to leave? Or suppose he decides to stay put when you're done?'

Toby said, 'If he goes out the back, we'll sprint out the front, pile into the van, and away we go. And if he doesn't go anywhere when the meeting is over, we'll all sit tight right here until he does.'

Alfie said, 'It sounds like we're making it up as we go along, doesn't it?'

Toby said, 'That's only because we *are* making it up as we go along.'

'You two old guys should take care in there,' Elliot said.

'He wants to talk to us,' Alfie said. 'What's to worry about?'

But he felt a definite tingle of apprehension as he and Toby crossed the busy road. The entrance of the Majestic Gymnasium was squeezed between a nail parlour and a fast-food joint selling jerk chicken: a red door with a short passageway behind it that led into a big, windowless space cheerlessly illuminated by racks of buzzing fluorescent lights slung under a low, water-stained ceiling. The smell of its stale warm air, compounded from old sweat, floor matting and rubbing alcohol, reminded Alfie of the gym at his boarding school. This wasn't the kind of gymnasium that called itself a fitness centre, the kind of place where young urban professionals used expensive running machines, rowing machines and fixed bicycles in front of banks of TVs, with a sauna and a lap pool, fresh flowers, lots of blond wood and pretty receptionists in tracksuits. This was a muscle factory, a place where men came to carry out the serious work of rebuilding their bodies. One man lay flat on his back on a padded bench, raising with quivering arms and tensed face a bar bent by the weight of the metal discs attached to either end. Other men worked the levers and push-bars of machines that looked as if they had been ripped out of a car plant and only very slightly modified. Heavy springs tensing and relaxing, bars working back and forth, stacks of metal discs rising and falling inside steel columns. A man planted solid roundhouse blows on a canvas punchbag criss-crossed with black tape that another man held steady by clasping it to his body. A man facing a big, age-spotted mirror danced inside the whirling cradle of a skipping rope. Green carpet tiles were dotted with blackened circles of discarded chewing gum. Hip-hop blasted from speakers hung near the ceiling, competing with the clanking machines and the effortful grunts of men toiling with the grim joyless effort of competitors in a masturbation contest.

There was a kind of concession stand near the door, a counter faced with peeling wood-effect Formica, display shelves crammed with plastic jars of vitamin pills and amino-acid pills and protein mixes. The big man behind the counter, dicing bananas and mangos on a chopping board, pointed his knife at Alfie and Toby and said that they must be Shareef's four o'clock.

'And you must be Watty,' Toby said.

The man's smile dropped a notch. He was in his twenties, wearing white Adidas tracksuit bottoms and a black mesh T-shirt. Gold chains tangled on the smooth keg of his chest. His muscular arms gleamed with oil. His shaved head was wrapped in a red scarf tied with a big knot at the back. 'So you know me, huh?'

'You have a certain fame in sheep-rustling circles,' Toby said.

'I heard you took them back. Good for you. I told Shareef we should do something about it, but before he could get his shit together, you guys stepped in.'

'How about Morph?' Toby said. 'Did he have anything to do with that little stunt?'

Watty looked at Alfie and said, 'What do you press?'

'Press?'

'Press. Bench press,' Watty said. He lifted the chopping board and with the blade of the knife swept the chopped fruit into an industrial-sized blender.

'You mean weights?'

'What else we talk about? Of course weights.' Watty spooned white powder from a big plastic jar over the chopped fruit, added a pint of milk. Looking at Alfie as he screwed on the lid of the blender, saying, 'I go up to three hundred and twenty. You think you can do that?'

'I don't know. I've never tried.'

Watty's smile broadened. 'You're all right,' he said, and flipped the switch of the blender.

Toby said, raising his voice to be heard over the sturdy roar of the machine, 'Is your friend Shareef going to show?'

Watty switched off the blender, studied the frothy yellow goo inside, flipped the switch again. Saying to Alfie, 'You a big man, but you look soft. I bet you can't even lift your own weight. Which is what? One hundred seventy, one hundred eighty? What you think?'

Alfie smiled. 'I think you're hustling me.'

Toby took out his packet of cigarettes. 'We can't wait long. We're busy journalists: the news doesn't write itself. If Shareef doesn't show soon, we'll have to move on to the next story.'

'No smoking in here,' Watty said. He unscrewed the top of the blender, lifted it from its base, and offered it to Alfie.

'I have my own,' Alfie said, and showed him his bottle of banana milk shake.

Watty shrugged and said to Toby, 'You want some of this?'

Toby looked up at him through his unruly fringe. 'If it doesn't have nicotine in it, I'm not interested.'

'This is all natural,' Watty said. He lifted the blender to his lips and drank about a pint of yellow goo straight down.

'So is nicotine. One of those little miracles of Nature that make you think that maybe there is a god after all. Unlike this stuff,' Toby said, picking up the plastic jar of white powder and studying the label. 'Creatine. Don't tell me that comes from some rain-forest tree.'

'It's good for the muscles,' Watty said placidly. 'I bet I could build you up in a month. Have you working out, have you drinking my special mix here, have you eat a pound of egg white each day – that's the easiest protein to digest – and plenty of boiled chicken and baked potatoes.'

'Sounds dreadful,' Toby said. 'I think I'll stick to my own special diet of coffee, cigarettes, and shredded nerves. By the way, maybe you can settle a little bet between me and my friend. Did Morph help out with those sheep, or was that just you and Shareef?'

'Man, I need to forget about that. The way those fucking sheep stank? And one of the fuckers bit me. No one told me sheep could bite.' Watty took another swig of his special mix, wiped his lips on the back of his forearm, and said to Alfie, 'A month of my undivided attention, you'll be bench-pressing your own weight, which is something every right-thinking man should be able to do.'

The big man was definitely stonewalling, Alfie thought. Every time Toby confronted him with a direct question about Morph, he veered off at an acute angle. And if he was stonewalling, it meant that he knew something, and was doing his best to hide it. Alfie decided to try a little spur-of-the-moment amateur psychology and took out his Nikon, saying casually, 'Mind if I take a few pictures while we're waiting?'

'Of what? This place?'

'Of you, actually.' Alfie fitted the flash attachment to the camera, switched it on and said, as its mosquito-whine rose in pitch, 'I'm a photographer. I take pictures of London characters in their natural setting. Doing what they do where they do it.'

'You think I'm a character, uh?'

'A strong one,' Alfie said. 'No pun intended.'

Watty made no attempt to hide his interest. 'So what you do with these pictures? You sell them?'

'When I can.' The flash was charged. Alfie casually raised the Nikon, focused, and took a picture of the big man.

Watty blinked and said, 'Shouldn't I pose or something?'

'I want a candid look. Why don't you make up some more of your special mix? Toby, would you mind stepping out of the way? I want a nice clear shot of our friend behind his counter.'

'Maybe you should have me doing weights,' Watty said.

'Anyone can lift weights,' Alfie said. 'Even a couple of flabby white guys like us. No, what looked good to me was the way you had with that big knife and the fruit. Casual but smooth, like you've been doing it all your life.'

Watty picked up his big knife and struck a pose, giving Alfie a big shit-eating grin. 'So what, you want something like this?'

'Don't look at the camera,' Alfie said. 'Just do your thing. Behave as if I wasn't here. That's what I mean by the candid look.'

While the big man halved a mango and sliced out chunks of its flesh, Alfie took several shots and made encouraging noises. He'd switched off the flash – he'd only used it to get Watty's attention – and was working now with the glare of the fluorescent lights. The two guys using the punchbag had stopped to watch and the man dancing around the whirling loop of his skipping rope was looking at them in the mirror, but the other men continued to work their machines and lift their weights, oblivious to everything but their own efforts.

Alfie said, 'I guess you must drink a lot of that stuff.'

Watty diced a banana, his knife flashing, rat-a-tat-tat. 'About a gallon each and every day.'

Toby, who had guessed at once what Alfie was up to, stood off to one side in a kind of slouch. Watching quietly as Alfie framed another shot and said to Watty, 'Do you always make it up the same way?'

'Depends what I can get in the market. I buy in bulk, whatever is going cheap on the day. The skill is in the mix. Getting the right balance. See, some fruits are acid, and some are alkali. You got to be careful not to go too far in either direction, or else your stomach react and it doesn't take up the good stuff.' Watty glanced up after Alfie took the picture, saying shyly, 'Do I get to see these when you're done?'

Alfie had started to use his camera to get Watty to relax and loosen up, so that he might just possibly let out an indiscretion or two. But he was getting into the shoot now, thinking that there was something nice going on between the gleaming contours of the big man's muscular arms, the wet sheen of the knife blade, and the shine on the greasy wood-effect Formica that faced the counter. He could print it up on high-contrast paper, flash it before printing to emphasize the bleached look of the fluorescent lights . . .

He said, 'I'll send over a bunch of prints. If you put one up on the wall, let me know, I'll come back and sign it. I'm getting some good shots, so just keep doing what you do. You make that stuff up just for yourself, or for whoever wants it?'

'Anyone puts three pound in the box can drink as much as they want.'

'Sounds like a good deal.' Alfie got a nice close-up shot of Watty's hands and the knife, said, 'So, do you own this place?'

'Me?' Watty grinned. 'No way. I manage it is all.'

'For who? For Shareef?'

'For Shareef's old man, innit. Shareef just use the place where he can meet people. Always do business in a place of business. He's smart that way.'

'I heard his radio show. He's smart all right. He does all kinds of business, I bet. He's got the pirate radio, he's got Morph . . .'

'That's his big thing right now. Or it was.'

'It was?'

But Watty was looking at something behind Alfie now. Saying, 'Hey, Shareef. What do you say?'

A slender black teenager was coming towards them, wearing a tracksuit of some shimmering violet-hued futuristic material, wraparound sunglasses and a white skullcap, carrying a briefcase and walking with a kind of wincing, sway-hipped swagger, as if his suede loafers were pinching his feet. He reached across the counter and gave Watty a complicated handshake that involved slapping palms and bumping knuckles, saying, 'My man Watty. Have these guys been troubling you?'

'I been having my picture taken. It's cool.'

Shareef looked at Alfie and Toby through his sunglasses and said that he hoped he hadn't kept them waiting too long, he'd had to attend to some other business first.

'We've been learning all about the goodness of fruit,' Toby said.

Shareef took off his sunglasses. He had high cheekbones and large lustrous eyes, a frowning air of solemn innocence. Looking at Toby as if disappointed in what he saw, saying, 'First off, I have to see a press card, something like that.'

Toby got out his wallet, flipped it open, held it up to Shareef's face. 'That's my NUJ card – the National Union of Journalists. I can also show you my donor card if you want proof that I'm a caring, sharing sort of guy.'

Shareef studied him, then said, 'We can talk in my office.'

This was a small room where stacks of cardboard boxes loomed over a small table and a few plastic stacking chairs. As he sat down, Toby said, 'So I hear you're an entrepreneur.'

Shareef placed his briefcase on the table, took out the smallest mobile phone Alfie had ever seen, and set it on top of the brief-case. He wore a gold ring that yoked his forefinger and middle finger like a cut-down knuckleduster. He said, 'I have various interests. What's that?'

'My notebook,' Toby said, flipping it open. 'I wouldn't want to misquote you. How about starting things off by explaining how you and Morph got together?'

Shareef put up his hands, palms out, as if pushing something away. 'Slow down.'

'I thought we were going to talk about Morph. I thought I was going to get the full story. How you met him, how you two got together—'

'First thing, before we get into that, I have to decide if I can trust you.'

'I thought we were past that,' Toby said. 'My friend Alfie and me, we've given Morph plenty of coverage. The first story about his work — that was ours. So was the coverage of what he did to those vans, and the piece in the museum. We wrote that up and got it published in a national newspaper, and all we want in return is to talk to your talented friend.'

Shareef nodded, serious, unsmiling. 'I appreciate what you did, which is why I allowed you to come here. But now I need to know if you can help me take this thing to the next level.'

'The next level?'

'I need to establish Morph as a presence. He has to grow. He has to become a personality. He has to become more than a curiosity, good for fifteen minutes in the news. You understand?'

'Why don't you explain it to me?' Toby said.

'He has to plug into the media at every level. He has to become a brand. Like when people talk about reggae, they talk about Bob Marley, yeah? The man has been dead a long time, since before I was born, but that who people think of first, when they think of reggae. Especially white people, who don't know from Black Twang or Vybz Kartel or Tipper Irie.'

Toby said, 'When people talk about taggers, especially taggers who are against what's happening in Iraq, you want them to talk about Morph.'

'Exactly. That's why I need to know how you gonna help me. That's why I need to know who you are, who you know, where you at, what you can do.'

'You already know what we can do,' Toby said. 'You know we're interested, and you know we can help you. What we need from you, if we're going to take this to the next level, is to arrange a meeting with Morph. We need to interview him. We need to find out about him, put a human face to the famous and contro-versial tagger, let people know who he is, where he's from, why he does what he does—'

'I don't think so.' Shareef was smiling for the first time, smiling and shaking his head. 'Morph doesn't do interviews in person. You want to ask him something, you ask me. But before you start asking your questions, I need to know where this profile is going to be placed.'

Toby gave Alfie a can-you-believe-this-guy? look, said, 'How this works, the better the material, the better the story. And if you want a good story, you have to give us something interesting or controversial. Something we can use as a hook to hang the story from, something that's going to catch the public's eye.'

Shareef considered this, then said, 'I see that. And because you already published those very useful articles, I'll cut you some slack. I'll assume you'll be able to place the piece somewhere like *GQ* or *Vogue*.'

Toby gave Alfie another look and said, 'Why not?'

Shareef leaned back in his chair, regarding Toby and Alfie, his fingers steepled together. They were long and slender, with neatly trimmed nails. He said, 'The tagging, that's just part of it. That's just what they call a means of expression. Like the thing with the sheep, and the thing in the museum. A way of getting attention. But he isn't just a tagger. He's more than that.'

'What you're saying is, don't mistake the medium for the message,' Toby said. Alfie noticed that so far he hadn't written anything in his notebook.

Shareef said, 'What I'm saying, he's an artist.'

Toby said, 'Is he genuinely against what's happening in Iraq, or is that just a pose?'

Shareef looked at him.

Toby said, 'That's what his cartoons are all about. Not to mention the sheep and the thing in the Imperial War Museum.'

'Oh, he believe in what he say, one hundred per cent.'

'Is that because he comes from Iraq?'

Shareef paused, then smiled again. 'Sure. Why not?'

Alfie leaned forward, wanting to ask Shareef where exactly in Iraq did Morph come from – was it from the north, the mountains there? But Toby was already saying, 'Why is he living in London? Is he a refugee? Did he come here legally or illegally?'

Shareef shrugged. 'What does it matter how he came here? He's here, he's making his statement about how he feels about his homeland.'

Toby said, 'You feel that you have to protect your friend. I understand that. But I'm not going to turn him in to the authorities. The reason I ask so many questions is that I want to find that hook I told you about. If he came here because he felt that he was in danger in Iraq or, even better, if he'd done something to make him a political refugee, that makes his story more interesting, more saleable.'

Shareef said, 'As a matter of fact he *is* a political refugee. Or his father is.'

'What did his father do?'

'He got himself arrested, thrown into prison.'

'Do you know the details?'

'I know it wasn't in Iraq, it was somewhere in Turkey. See, they fled from Iraq to Turkey, and then they got into trouble there, and they come here.'

'Morph's father was arrested in Turkey,' Toby said, writing in his notebook.

'Morph say that it was a mistake, the police thought he was someone else. But maybe you can put down it was for political agitation of some kind.'

'Let's stick to the facts. Why did they leave Iraq?'

Shareef shrugged. 'Because of the situation there, why else?'

'No specific reason?'

Shareef shrugged again. 'They settled in Turkey, and then Morph's father was arrested.'

'Because the Turkish police mistook him for someone else. Do you know who it was they mistook him for?'

'I suppose someone they wanted to arrest.'

'He was in prison how long?'

'About a year, maybe a little less. Then the Turks realized their mistake and let him go.'

'And he came here, with his son. Can I talk to him?'

'No, and not because I don't want you to. The man is dead. Had himself a heart attack a few weeks ago, and died of it. So you see now why Morph does what he does, and I think that all you need to know.'

Alfie could no longer keep quiet. He didn't have any more time for this young hustler, with his expensive tracksuit and his briefcase, his attitude and his evasions. He said, 'We're not the only people looking for Morph.'

'Forgive my friend,' Toby said, giving Alfie a hard look. 'He's a photographer. He sees things in Morph's work that I don't. He's grown very passionate about it.'

'A gallery owner by the name of Robbie Ruane is paying men to follow me,' Alfie told Shareef. 'I bet he has men following you, too.'

Shareef didn't say anything, but from the way he looked at Alfie, Alfie knew that he'd hit a nerve.

'He wanted me to find Morph for him,' Alfie said, 'and when I refused, he put his men onto me. Maybe he came to talk to you, too. If he did, don't make the mistake of trusting him. He's looking for Morph because he wants to make a deal with him, behind your back.'

'I know all about that guy, and he needs me more than I need him,' Shareef said. He was trying to brazen it out, but there was a wariness in his gaze now. 'He knows that if he wants to make a deal with Morph, he has to come to me. Just like you guys come to me.'

Alfie dug into the pocket of his camera bag, pulled out the digitally enhanced photograph of the anomalous stone and the four Nomads, and thrust it towards Shareef.

'Hey, Alfie,' Toby said. 'Knock it off.'

Alfie ignored him, told Shareef, 'Take a good look.'

Shareef glanced at the photograph, shrugged.

Alfie said, 'The pattern on the stone – it's like the pattern Morph uses to frame his cartoons.'

Shareef looked at the photograph again, bending close. 'What's this about?'

'The photograph is of something my grandfather found in Iraq about seventy years ago. So you see,' Alfie said, 'Morph and I, we have something in common. Something, I bet, he would really like to talk about.'

'He don't talk to anyone but me. And even then he don't talk a whole lot. Ask him why he does what he does? He just smile and shrug. That's why he a true genius,' Shareef said. 'Because he is what he is. He is what he does. It comes out of his life, and it *is* his life.'

'My life and his life seem to be mixed together,' Alfie said. 'That's why we need to talk.'

Shareef shook his head. 'You can talk to me, but only when you think of how you can help him get what he deserves. When you do, give me a call. But now, if you two gentlemen don't mind, I got some other business I need to attend to. Can you find your own way out, or do you want me to call Watty, ask him to help you?'

15

Dr Rölf Most climbed into the back of the people-carrier, out of breath and happy, smiling at Harriet and saying, 'Like catching fish from a barrel.'

Harriet was sitting with her hands in her lap, white plastic looped tightly around her wrists. Larry Macpherson had pushed her into the rear seat and fastened the plasticuffs in one fluid movement, had ripped her mobile phone from her waist and its earpiece from her ear, removed its SIM card and snapped it between finger and thumb. He'd been going through her rucksack, carefully inspecting each item – her change of underwear, toothbrush, toothpaste and lipstick, two paperback novels, the keys for her car and the keys for her flat, lock pick, notebook, pepper spray – when Rölf Most had opened the door of the people-carrier. Now he slid sideways to make room for his employer, and pulled his automatic pistol from the waistband of his cargo pants.

'That will not be necessary,' Rölf Most said calmly, settling opposite Harriet.

'Let's hope not,' Larry Macpherson said, resting the butt of the pistol on his thigh, aiming it at Harriet's midsection. He wasn't tall, but had a definite physical presence, deep-chested and broad-shouldered in a blue denim jacket over a black T-shirt, black cargo pants, black boots polished to a mirror finish. Black hair sleeked back from a widow's peak, cheeks raddled by ancient acne, eyes masked by close-fitting mirrorshades. He wore a Breitling Navitimer on his left wrist, a large skull ring on the middle finger of his right hand, a small gold ring in his left ear.

The driver, a wiry, sandy-haired man with a hard-core Scottish accent, wanted to know where he was supposed to go.

'When I am finished with Ms Crowley we will need to go first to the river and then to where the target tries to hide from us,' Rölf Most said. 'Meanwhile, we will drive around.'

As the people-carrier pulled into the stream of traffic, the psychiatrist started to introduce himself, and Harriet said, 'I know who you are.' Her mouth was very dry and her heart was beating quickly and lightly, but she felt surprisingly calm. 'Shouldn't you be looking after your patient?'

'Dr Soborin has room service and his jigsaw puzzles, and most of all his Ganzfeld Stimulation. He is as happy as a puppy. Would you please tell me, Ms Crowley, what you have done with the boy who calls himself Morph? Where are you hiding him?'

Harriet shrugged. As long as she didn't give anything away, she thought, they would keep her alive. There would be a chance, no matter how small, of escape. Sunshades were pulled down across the side windows of the people-carrier. They were the kind that parents buy to protect their children from sunburn, tinted pale blue and printed with happy cartoon faces. She sat with her wrists cuffed, watched by a killer armed with an automatic pistol, a man who was almost certainly crazy, and an audience of insanely cheerful anthropomorphic dogs and cats.

Rölf Most smiled. He had a white goatee and rosebud lips and rosy cheeks. 'I know that you know who I am talking about.'

Harriet shrugged again.

'Or perhaps you are still looking for him,' Rölf Most said. 'That is why you come to my hotel yesterday, and begin watching me.'

'I don't know what you mean.'

'You will not deny you planted those video cameras. Mr Macpherson found them almost at once, of course.'

'All I know is that I was walking along Park Lane when your man ordered me into this vehicle at gunpoint and put these on me,' Harriet said, lifting her wrists to display the plasticuffs to Rölf Most. 'Which I think is rather rude, don't you? I assume you want a friendly chat, so why don't you take them off?'

Trying to keep the mood light, trying to show that she was not scared, that she believed him to be a reasonable man.

'They're for your own protection,' Larry Macpherson said, his voice even and unhurried, yet creepily menacing. 'If you weren't under restraint, you might be tempted to try something silly, and I'd have to hurt you.'

Harriet looked at Rölf Most and said, 'I was hoping we could have a friendly discussion about our mutual interests.'

The psychiatrist studied her, stroking his goatee with finger and thumb. His pale blue gaze was sharp and bright but also unfocused, as if he was distracted by an internal dialogue. At last, he said, 'How is the Nomads' Club, by the way? Were you ever made a member, or does it cling still to that silly rule about excluding women?'

'You know very well that the Nomads' Club disbanded years ago.'

'Officially, yes, after the unfortunate and very mistaken action it took in Lebanon rebounded on it. But unofficially, I believe, it is still very much in bed with the secret services. And even if you are not a member, you pursue its interests. Even though your contact at MI6, Mr Jonathon Nicholl, told you to desist.' Rölf Most paused, and when Harriet didn't comment, said, 'Perhaps it is because you wish to make amends for what your father did.'

'I never really knew my father,' Harriet said.

'No, of course not. Your father ran away and your mother took custody of you. I believe she committed suicide while you were still a teenager, no? A few years later, you discovered that your father had committed criminal acts for which he was arrested and sectioned, and shortly afterwards, he also killed himself.'

Both Harriet and Rölf Most swayed sideways when the people-carrier turned a corner. Larry Macpherson didn't move at all, his pistol aimed unwaveringly at Harriet, his mirror-masked gaze unfathomable.

Harriet said, 'You're making connections that aren't there, Dr Most. The sins of the parents setting their children's teeth on edge, it isn't even kindergarten Freud. It's worse than phrenology. It's the kind of cheap insight a fortune-teller with a crystal ball and a fake gypsy accent gives you after you cross her palm with your Visa card.'

'But I believe I have touched on something, have I not?' Rölf Most said, with a kindly, engaging smile. His tone was soft and pleasant, his accent mid-Atlantic. 'Your father misuses the glyphs and makes such a terrible mess of his life and the lives of his followers, and you are worried – no, you are *frightened* – that you have inherited the same weakness. You are worried that you might be as crazy as he is. It is that which drives you to prove yourself better than the circumstances of your birth.'

'You don't know anything about me.'

'I know a great deal about your father,' Rölf Most said. 'And I look at you, Harriet, and I see that you are the child of the man. You project an image of calm and resolution, but underneath that I see fear and desperation. I see someone afraid that she might have inherited the tendencies of her poor crazy father and her suicidal mother. I see someone so desperate to make amends that she disobeys a direct order from her MI6 handler.'

'My father wasn't crazy because of a flaw in his genes, Dr Most. He was crazy because he spent too much time exposed to the glyphs. As you should know, because your patient, Dr Soborin, was also psychologically damaged by exposure to glyphs, as were most of the people who worked for him at mind's i. And how about you? You've been working on them too, haven't you? That's why you're here. Before you attempt to diagnose me, Doctor, I suggest you take a good hard look at yourself.'

Rölf Most ignored this, saying with saccharine sympathy, 'I quite understand why you disobeyed Mr Nicholl. You have a very strong sense of duty, and also a strong moral imperative. That is why you feel you must make the world right any way you can, even if it means disobeying a direct order. That is why you have not told Mr Nicholl everything you found out about the graffiti artist who calls himself Morph. You told him what you had to, just enough to prove that you were doing a good job, but you kept a lot of it to yourself, didn't you? Because you believe that you are serving a higher cause than the interests of the British government.'

'If you get rid of these plasticuffs, I'll be happy to discuss the cause I'm serving.'

'You are not in a position to make any kind of deal,' Rölf Most said. 'But if you do tell me all you know, freely and honestly, it will save you and those close to you considerable pain. Which reminds me to ask, how are Julius Ward and Clarence Ashburton? Are they still living in that house in South London? Perhaps I should pay them a visit, to find out whether or not they are entertaining a young guest, and to find out what they know about this affair.'

Harriet met his pale blue gaze and said, 'They don't have anything to do with this.'

'But that *is* where you are keeping Morph, is it not? It must be, because we have already checked your flat in the Barbican and found no trace of him there. So sad, by the way, to find that an attractive young woman like you is living on her own.'

'That's a cheap remark, Doctor.'

'Perhaps you live alone because it is part of your ideal of purity. To save the world, you must rise above ordinary life.'

The people-carrier turned another corner. Sun flared behind the cartoon cats and dogs printed on the blinds. Harriet could see taxis and cars and a red single-decker bus through its windscreen, people moving past offices, a pub, life just an inch away from her, impossibly out of reach.

'You're wasting time,' Larry Macpherson said. 'She isn't going to answer any of your questions and it doesn't matter anyway, because she doesn't know anything we don't. We should do her and dump her.' He shifted the pistol that rested on his thigh, angling it so that its muzzle pointed between Harriet's eyes.

Harriet felt a cold electric spark snap inside her head. She was looking at the man's face, not the gun, but there was nothing she could read there.

'No, no, no,' Rölf Most said. 'We must do it my way. There will be no unpleasant questions from the secret services or the police, and besides, we may very well learn something.'

For a moment, Larry Macpherson looked as if he wanted to argue the point. Then he tucked his pistol into his cargo pants, reached under his seat and lifted out an aluminium briefcase. He rested it on his knees and snapped it open, took out a pair of fat black Sennheiser headphones, the kind that club DJs wear, reached across the narrow space, and fitted them over Harriet's ears. He plugged the lead into a cheap CD player and set it beside her, then took out a roll of grey gaffer tape, ripped off two short lengths, and pressed his thumb and forefinger against Harriet's right eye, peeling back her upper eyelid and applying a strip of tape, fixing it open. He taped her left eye too, then sat back and watched her go cross-eyed as she tried and failed to blink. The noise of the people-carrier's engine and of the traffic around it were muffled but not completely shut out by the headphones.

Now Rölf Most took something from the briefcase, a small

black cylinder with a spray nozzle at one end. He took out a surgeon's vinyl glove and worked it over his right hand, saying, 'Hold her still.'

Larry Macpherson caught Harriet's chin in a tight grip as the psychiatrist leaned forward and spritzed cold mist up her nostrils.

'I am sure you know what that is,' he said, sitting back, carefully stripping off the glove and dropping it and the black cylinder into the briefcase.

Harriet's nostrils were numbed by the spray, but she could taste it at the back of her throat. A nauseating oily bitterness spreading over her tongue, crawling down her throat. She knew what it was, all right.

'That is Dr Soborin's invention,' Rölf Most said, reaching once more into the briefcase. 'And this is mine.'

It looked like an old-fashioned sci-fi ray gun, with a pistol grip and a flared, hooded lens.

'I call this a glyph gun,' Rölf Most said, pointing it at Harriet, smiling when he saw her almost imperceptible flinch. 'It is a much faster way of delivering the goods. More powerful and more intense.'

Larry Macpherson's iron grip turned her head, so that she was facing Rölf Most. The psychiatrist set the lens of the glyph gun about a foot from her eyes. 'I cannot promise this will not hurt,' he said, and pressed the trigger.

16

As they walked out of the Majestic Gymnasium, Toby said to Alfie, 'And what was *that* all about?'

'I think he has a better offer. Probably from Robbie Ruane.'

'I think so too. The little shit has clearly been using us to raise his friend's market price. What I meant was, where did you get that photo? I thought your grandfather's stuff had been taken away by his colleagues.'

Alfie chose his words carefully. This wasn't the time or place to tell Toby about the journals and diaries he'd found in the safe deposit box. 'It turns out that my grandmother held on to a few photographs. One of them was the photograph from Antareus's pamphlet – the photograph of the four Nomads. They uncovered a stone with a pattern cut into it, and I thought that the pattern looked like the one Morph uses to frame his graffiti. But I couldn't be sure of it until Elliot had digitally enhanced the print.'

'And you think that it helps prove that there's some kind of link between your grandfather's work and Morph.'

'I thought it might interest Shareef,' Alfie said, as they pushed through the door at the end of the short passageway into sunlight and the rush of traffic along the Kingsland Road.

'Shareef is a teenage hustler who wants to be the black Malcolm McLaren,' Toby said, pausing to light a cigarette. 'He isn't interested in the glyphs for themselves. He's only interested in how much he can sell them for. Where's Elliot?'

The white van was gone. Alfie and Toby crossed to where it had been parked, looked up and down the road. It was gone, all right.

'I had to move,' Elliot said, when Alfie called him on his mobile. 'A gang of traffic wardens started working the street, so I thought the best thing to do would be to circle around the block and wait for you to come out.'

'Well, we're out now,' Alfie said.

'Ask him why he didn't call us,' Toby said.

'Why didn't you call us?'

'You were in a meeting,' Elliot said. 'Tell Toby to stay cool. I'll be right there.'

'Stay cool?' Toby said, after Alfie had relayed this message. 'Jesus. How can I *stay cool* when I've just realized that I trusted a hippy to do a man's job?'

On the other side of the busy road, Shareef came out of the entrance of the Majestic Gymnasium, stopped at the kerb, set his briefcase between his feet and stood there looking north, his tiny phone held against his ear. A battered blue Mercedes swerved out of the traffic and screeched to a halt beside him. It was driven by the manager of the gymnasium, Watty. Shareef climbed into the Mercedes and said something to the big man, who gave Alfie and Toby a big smile before accelerating away, heading south towards the City.

Two minutes later, the white Transit van pulled up. After Alfie and Toby piled in, Elliot began to explain again about the traffic wardens, but Toby cut him short and told him to turn this rust heap around, head south and keep a lookout for a blue Mercedes. Elliot waited for a gap in the traffic and made a three-point turn, acknowledging with a cheerful wave the horn and flashing lights of a truck that braked sharply with an explosive sneeze.

'I can't believe this,' Toby said. He was working his shock of hair with both hands, staring through the dusty windscreen at the traffic ahead.

'What was I going to tell the wardens?' Elliot said. '"I know I'm parked on a double yellow but please don't give me a ticket because I'm a private detective on an important case"?'

Toby said, 'Why not?'

'They would have given me a ticket anyway.'

'And Flowers would have paid it.'

Alfie said, 'I would?'

Toby said, 'You're on an important quest. The price of a parking ticket is a small price to pay for the knowledge you seek, blah blah blah.'

Elliot said, 'You guys should have told me that, when you made me park on a double yellow.'

Alfie said, 'You have to remember that we're making it up as we go along.'

Elliot said, 'What about this Mercedes?'

Toby said, 'It's dark blue, four doors, two Jamaican guys in it, one little, one large.'

'It's that one,' Alfie said, pointing at the Mercedes as they went past it.

It was parked outside the new mosque, just beyond the bridge over the Grand Union Canal. Watty sat behind the wheel, head tipped back, a baseball hat pulled low over his eyes, listening to some kind of hard-core beat that was making the big car tremble on its shocks. There was no sign of Shareef.

Elliot found a parking space a hundred yards down the road, and said, 'If your friend has gone into the mosque, how long do you think he's going to be?'

Toby adjusted the side mirror so that he could see the blue Mercedes. 'Why don't you go ask him?'

'I was sort of hoping this wouldn't take too long,' Elliot said. 'Cassie and me are supposed to be going out tonight. Nothing special, y'know, just hanging in Camden with some friends, maybe catching a band. But she's going to cook something before we go out, and I promised I'd be over at her place by seven.'

'If you want to abandon us in our hour of need, you'll have to leave the van,' Toby said.

'As if I could trust you old guys with it. I mean, I heard about the sheep.'

'The sheep were Alfie's idea,' Toby said.

'I promise that this won't involve any sheep,' Alfie said.

Elliot looked at his watch. 'I guess I can stick around for another hour or so . . . What do you think he's doing in there?'

'Given that it's a mosque,' Toby said, 'I doubt that he's playing bingo.'

Elliot said, 'I thought this guy was Jamaican.'

Toby said, 'Which means what? He has to be a Rastafarian? Shame on you, young grasshopper.'

Elliot shrugged. 'I just didn't expect him to be a Muslim.'

'Maybe he converted, like the guy who tried to blow up a plane with his shoe,' Toby said, lighting a fresh cigarette. 'We could be mixed up in something really clandestine. Think about it, Flowers. This Shareef is a Muslim convert who hangs out with a mysterious Iraqi who's painting anti-American cartoons on every flat surface in London. They probably met in this very mosque. They could be meeting in there right now.'

Alfie said, 'Just because he's a Muslim doesn't mean he has to be a terrorist.'

Toby said, 'Morph's graffiti is definitely no ordinary graffiti. It could be the tip of some kind of insidious plot to undermine the War Against Terrorism.'

'He's kidding,' Alfie told Elliot.

Toby said, sucking with relish on his cigarette, 'Even if I'm half-right, it's a hell of a story. Boys, I'm rich. I think I've just struck the mother-lode. When I write this up, I'll be able to name my price.'

Alfie leaned in close and said quietly, 'Are you really going to write about this?'

'I've *already* written about this – that's why Shareef wanted to talk to us. And you can stop making spaniel eyes at me, I promise that I won't write one word about you.'

'You better not.'

'Cross my cold black journalist's heart.'

'Anyway, I don't think he's meeting Morph in there.'

'Again with this Shareef-is-really-Morph bullshit.'

'The more I think about it, the more I'm certain that Morph put up the original graffiti, but he didn't have anything to do with the stunt with the sheep or the fake exhibit at the Imperial War Museum. Watty said that Morph *was* Shareef's big thing. Not is, *was*. I don't think that Morph wanted to become famous, or make money from his work. I think that was entirely Shareef's idea, and Morph walked away from it.'

Elliot said, 'This Shareef? Is he a small guy, wearing a purple tracksuit? If he is, he just now came out of the mosque and got into the Mercedes.'

17

There was a stuttering burst of light so powerful that it seemed to burn clean through Harriet's brain; then it was over, and Larry Macpherson let go of her chin and sat back. She was blinded by layers of brilliant white after-images, but felt a peculiar singing calm. She knew exactly what Rölf Most's strange gun had done to her. Her visual cortex had been put into an excitable state by the drug she'd absorbed through the mucous membranes in her nose, and then it had been blasted by glyphs designed to hyperstimulate a specific neural configuration and force her consciousness to adopt a particular state. She was certain that it was some kind of fascination glyph, probably a variant of the fascination glyph that Carver Soborin had used in Nigeria. At their most potent, fascination glyphs induced a kind of uncritical awe or wonder akin to a mystical experience; more usually, they were no more than visual velcro. They made the things they framed or underlay seem to be more interesting and attractive than they really were. The Nomads' Club had used them in the Second World War to sex up propaganda dropped behind Nazi lines; Carver Soborin had used them in the experimental advertising campaign which had gone so badly wrong; Morph had used one to attract attention to his cartoons. Several years of biofeedback training had made Harriet immune to the static patterns of ordinary fascination glyphs; now she hoped but couldn't be certain that her training had also made her immune to the glyphs blasted into her brain by Rölf Most's gun.

The psychiatrist leaned forward and plucked off the strips of tape that held open her eyelids, doing it so quickly that she didn't even have time to flinch. Two sharp winces of pain, and then she could blink again. The complex after-images were shredding into discreet, lively shapes. The cartoon dogs and cats on the blinds seemed to lean in and turn towards her.

'Do not worry,' Rölf Most said. 'I do not give you enough gun to make you low. Only enough to make you suggestible.'

Bright shapes swam in front of his smile as he explained that the glyph gun contained an array of ten thousand small, powerful light-emitting diodes controlled by a hard drive. It fired a glyph that locked the subject's attention, and then delivered whatever had been programmed into it, flashing its complex images at seventy-two cycles per second so that they were detected by the brain without conscious perception.

'I find subliminal bursts to be very effective. No doubt because there is no distortion caused by an attempt by the consciousness to make sense of what it sees.'

Larry Macpherson's mobile phone rang. The mercenary listened to it for a moment, then said, 'The meeting is over and my man is following the target.'

'What about Mr Flowers?' Rölf Most said.

Larry Macpherson repeated the question into the phone, said, 'Last my man saw of him, he was talking to his journalist friend, Toby Brown, outside the gymnasium. The guy who drove them to the rendezvous took off before the meeting ended. Looks like we lucked out after all. We have the target all to ourselves again.'

The after-images were everywhere Harriet looked. It was as if she was watching the world through an exotic aquarium inhabited by prickly crowns and grids, dots swarming like flies and slow snaky curves rippling in impalpable currents . . .

Entoptics. Form constants. Phosphenes. Visual percepts.

Harriet was familiar with the entire bestiary, knew that they were caused by clusters of neurons in her visual cortex firing at random, an after-effect of exposure to the drug and the glyphs. Even so, they seemed to have a life of their own, jiggling and wriggling and crawling out there in the world, beginning to form shapes, glimpses of faces and animals as her brain struggled to decode the patterns, make sense of the random input. When she'd been very young, she'd had a recurring dream . . . or not really a dream, but a hypnagogic vision that had preceded the surrender to true sleep, when entoptics had bloomed and burst in the swarming dark behind her eyelids, taking on shapes and forms, becoming faces that grinned and gaped and faded away as if people were stepping up to a window one by one, each looking in at her for a moment and then stepping past to make way for the next in line. The faces becoming increasingly grotesque until one more horrible than the rest would fly straight at her, and she'd wake up with a start, as if she'd fallen from some great height into her own bed.

Her grandfather had first taught her how to control that dream; much later, Clarence Ashburton's biofeedback training had built upon those early lessons. Now, drugged and blasted in the people-carrier, Harriet used that discipline to shape her totem animal from drifting swarms of entoptics. It took only a little effort of concentration to find him, a familiar little mouse with oversized ears, large human eyes, and a cheerful smile, peeking out at her from behind Rölf Most's snowy bouffant as the psychiatrist leaned forward to switch on the CD player connected to the headphones clamped over her ears.

A voice began to whisper in her ears, telling her how bad she was, how bad the world was, how much worse it was going to get . . .

'This won't do anything to me,' she heard herself say, but Rölf Most smiled and shook an admonitory finger, told her that if she couldn't keep quiet he'd have to let Larry Macpherson have his way with her.

Harriet kept quiet. The voice whispered on inside her head, sly and insinuating, telling her that she was worthless, her whole life was worthless, there was nothing left to her but grinding grey misery with no joy or hope . . . She thought that it was laughably cheesy, a self-help tape from hell, and her friendly little mouse seemed to agree, winking and smiling at her as he popped up in the different places that her wandering gaze fell upon, now sitting on the end of Larry Macpherson's automatic pistol, now dangling from the rear-view mirror by his elastic tail. Although she tried to stay focused on his antics, cartoon cats and dogs were leaning in at the edges of her vision, becoming grotesque as gargoyles, and she couldn't help worrying that the wheedling voice was sliding beneath her defences like a snake slithering beneath the sill of a door, sinking in through the fresh wounds that the glyph gun had burned into her brain, fucking up her head beneath the level of conscious thought.

And now her hallucinatory state was moving into the third stage. The people-carrier seemed to stretch, becoming an endless corridor; the centre of her vision brightened and everything at the edges swirled and smeared, a swirling vortex lined with flickering grids like racks of television screens where gargoyles leered and screamed, a tunnel of living light like the one through which the astronaut plunged at the end of that Kubrick movie. Her totem was hiding somewhere in the flickering lattices – she caught a glimpse of him now and then – but she knew that she shouldn't look too closely because of the other things that lived there, things worse than cartoon gargoyles, and she tried instead to concentrate on the patch of reality at the end of the tunnel, the world of ordinary streets beyond the windscreen of the people-carrier, a clear, bright patch no bigger than the palm of her hand . . .

After Harriet's grandfather had died, she and her mother had moved out of London to a rambling farmhouse in Suffolk. Her mother had wanted to escape everything that reminded her of her husband, and believed that Harriet would be happier growing up in the countryside than in London. In one corner of the farmhouse's walled garden, hidden in a patch of rough grass, nettles and Queen Anne's Lace, were the remains of an old well, a circle of crumbling brickwork a yard high, its round mouth protected by a square concrete slab that Harriet would push to one side whenever she wanted to commune with the strangely fascinating darkness at the bottom of the shaft. Ferns and mosses grew in the rotten courses between the old bricks; once, she found a small toad in a crevice, its eyes like black stones, its skin mottled gold and brown. There was always water at the bottom of the well; even at the height of the hottest, driest summer, she could feel its cool damp breath when she leaned over the low wall. And when the sun was directly overhead it was possible to see, nine or ten feet below, her head silhouetted at the edge of a little circle of reflected light where clouds moved like stately ships across the sky, everything mirrored precisely in the dark, still water, yet somehow different, as if she was looking through a magical gateway into the sky of another world.

It was a little like that now, as the voice dripped its poison inside her head and she fixed her gaze with a kind of hopeless desperation on the little patch of sunlit reality at the far end of a tunnel of whirling lattices that threatened at any moment to topple inwards and squeeze her shut like an eye. She didn't know how long this lasted. Later, she worked out that it could have been no more than fifteen or twenty minutes, but at the time it seemed like hours: the combined effect of the drug and the glyphs stretched time as well as space.

Despite her best efforts, Harriet might have lost all sense of herself and the real world if Larry Macpherson's mobile phone hadn't rung again, its perky rendition of the opening bars of 'Born in the USA' disrupting her trance. The mercenary told Rölf Most, 'It seems Flowers and his two friends are following the target after all.'

'You said just now they parted ways after their meeting.'

Harriet tried to focus on Rölf Most's face. For the first time, the psychiatrist sounded worried.

'They did. My man followed the target to a mosque, and then Flowers and his two friends turned up. My man wasn't sure what was going on, so he hung back. The target exited the mosque and moved on, and Flowers and his friends stayed right on his tail. The target made another stop a little way up the road, and now my man is wondering what to do: should he go with the flow or step in?'

Harriet watched Rölf Most consider this. It was like looking at someone on a TV at the far end of a railway carriage. The psychiatrist tugging at his goatee, saying, 'No doubt Mr Flowers hopes that the target will lead him to the boy, just as we do. This is very inconvenient.'

'Should we be talking about this in front of her?'

'She is by now in another place. And I think we must decide what to do straight away.'

'Until we know whether or not the target is going to meet the boy we can't do anything that would risk blowing the tail.'

'Nevertheless, now that he has talked to Mr Flowers we must talk to him as soon as possible. They may have made some kind of deal.'

'If that's what you want, let's wait until he goes back to that flat where he's been hiding out. If Mr Flowers and his buddies are still on his tail, we'll move in and secure them, and you can pay a visit to the target and do your thing.'

'And if he meets with the boy somewhere public, and Mr Flowers decides to move in?'

Larry Macpherson shrugged. 'Then we hang back, see what gives, wait until the boy goes someplace we can snatch him with minimum fuss. If he happens to be with Flowers at the time, what the hell, it isn't like he or his friends are going to give us a problem.'

'All this is, as you say, "doable"?'

'Trust me, we're dealing with amateurs. What about her?'

'Ms Crowley is an amateur too. Also, I believe she is about primed. We will go to the nearest bridge now, and drop her off.' Rölf Most's face loomed over Harriet like a falling moon as he lifted the headphones from her head and said softly, 'I need to know just two things, and then we are done here. Will you help me?'

Harriet nodded. She knew who he was and knew what he had done to her, knew that she didn't have to say one word, but she was floating free of all anxiety and fear and it seemed easier to agree with him . . .

The psychiatrist patted her hand reassuringly. His white hair like the swirl of ice cream in a cone from the ice-cream van, his look one of fatherly concern. His rosebud lips moving inside the nest of his goatee.

'We know all about Morph's friend, Harriet. We know all about Benjamin Barrett. He tried to hide from us, but we found him again, and we have been following him for some little time now, waiting for him to lead us to Morph. That's why we know that Mr Flowers had a meeting with him just now. Tell me: why did you send Mr Flowers to talk to Mr Barrett? And what did they talk about?'

Harriet was confused. She knew that Alfie Flowers and his journalist friend were supposed to be meeting with Benjamin Barrett – she'd been on her way to catch up with them – but she didn't know why.

Rölf Most said, 'What kind of deal were you thinking of offering Mr Barrett? Or should I say, what kind of deal was the Nomads' Club thinking of offering him?'

Harriet heard herself say, 'There isn't any deal.'

'Really? Then why did Mr Flowers meet with Mr Barrett?'

She shook her head.

Larry Macpherson said, 'I think you gave her too much gun, turned her brains to mush. Even if she does know something she'll never give it up now.'

Rölf Most slapped Harriet's face twice, palm and backhand, saying, 'Look at me, Harriet. Only at me.'

She looked at him. He seemed much closer now, and the lattices flickering and whirling around her were expanding into thin air, growing fainter . . .

'Will you swear on the memory of your dear departed father that Mr Flowers has nothing to do with you or with the Nomads' Club?'

Harriet shrugged. She didn't know where to begin to explain Alfie Flowers's connection with the Nomads.

'Yes or no?'

'In a way . . .'

'Mush,' Larry Macpherson said dispassionately. 'The state she's in, I could do her right now and it would take her ten minutes to realize she's dead.'

Rölf Most ignored him, saying to Harriet, 'So Mr Flowers does not work for you directly. He pursues a parallel investigation.'

Harriet nodded.

'You look for Morph, and so does he.'

She nodded again.

'Where is Morph? Do you know where he is?'

She shook her head.

'Have you met with him?'

'No.'

'Have you talked to him?'

'No.'

'Have you talked to his friend, Benjamin Barrett?'

Harriet shook her head again.

'Is he a guest of Julius Ward and Clarence Ashburton?'

Harriet shook her head once more.

Larry Macpherson said, 'She doesn't know shit, Doc. Let's do her and dump her and move in on the target before these other guys screw things up.'

'We will let her go,' Rölf Most said, and turned his head to talk to the driver. 'Pull over on the bridge itself. We let her go there.'

Larry Macpherson said, 'You really think she'll do herself?'

'If not now, then soon.'

'Easier if I do her right now.'

'But this way, it is more fitting. Besides, she really is no problem to us, and nor are the others. The Nomads' Club is a spent force. Her death will force its last two members to realize that.' Rölf Most leaned in, looking at Harriet, saying softly, 'We are taking you to a place where you can put an end to all your pain. All you need to do is take a single step into the air. One step, and then you do not have to do anything else ever again. One step, and all your pain will be taken away. Do you understand me, Harriet?'

She nodded. She was definitely coming down. The swirling lattices were receding to the edges of her vision. The cartoon cats and dogs on the blinds were more or less cartoon cats and dogs again. She caught a last glimpse of her totem from the corner of her eye, but the small brown mouse with his innocently cheerful human smile slid out of sight when she tried to look at him directly. Vanished like a burst soap bubble. She felt a pang of regret at his going. She owed him so much. He had helped her to centre herself, had stopped her being overwhelmed by the monsters and boojums that inhabited the flickering entoptics.

The people-carrier pulled up at the kerb. Larry Macpherson produced a butterfly knife and sliced through the plastic loop that bound Harriet's wrists, then in one smooth movement grabbed hold of the collar of her jacket with one hand, slid back the side door with the other, and pushed her out.

Harriet fell to her hands and knees, but managed by careful stages to get to her feet, paving stones see-sawing beneath her as she staggered just a few feet from a glittering rush of traffic, all sharp edges and malice. It was a little like being drunk, she thought, when the body grows stubborn and clumsily self-conscious and you have to take control of it and maintain your dignity by sheer force of will. She knew that the tilting whirl of everything around her was an illusion caused by her jangling, blasted senses, knew that if she could only get it together she could straighten up and walk away, but that didn't stop her lurching forward like a sailor on a storm-tossed boat; when she fetched up against a low wall, she grabbed hold of its gritty stone and leaned gratefully against it.

The wall was at the edge of a high place, the sky pressing as close as a cellar ceiling, the river sliding away below, tilting into a vast gulf that seemed to be tumbling away into the bright centre of the world. It would be so easy to lean out just a little more, to follow the slow tilt of the world and swoon softly into the strong sure embrace of the river. Just like sinking into a feather bed. But that wasn't her idea; that was the voice, slithering into her thoughts like a snake under a door.

The hell with that, Harriet thought. Or perhaps she said it aloud, because a man walking past gave her a startled glance. She took a breath, took another. Tried to focus. She was standing on Blackfriars Bridge, looking downriver towards the slender span of the Millennium Bridge, St Paul's Cathedral on one side and the industrial bulk of Tate Modern on the other. The white people-carrier was parked a little way behind her in the bus lane, its hazard lights flashing. Larry Macpherson was standing beside its door, holding his automatic pistol by his thigh. The hell with him too, Harriet thought, and turned and walked away. Someone else might have thought that voice was their own voice. Someone else might have surrendered to it. Someone else might have jumped, or walked home and swallowed the contents of their medicine cabinet, or drawn a warm bath and lain down in it and slashed their wrists. But she knew what was real and what wasn't.

She kept up this monologue as she walked along the bridge towards the south bank, telling herself that she was doing fine, that all she had to do was put one foot in front of the other and keep walking. Her back was a single clenched muscle waiting for the impact of a bullet or Larry Macpherson's implacable grip, but when she reached the end of the bridge and looked back, the white people-carrier had gone.

They really had let her go. Either they believed that the glyph and the drug and the tape had worked, that she was so feeble and defenceless that she'd let that snaky voice slide in and take control, or they simply didn't care what happened to her. I'll make the arrogant sons-of-bitches care, she thought, and searched for her mobile phone, going through the pockets of her jacket twice over before remembering that Larry Macpherson had taken it from her. The man watching her unsmilingly as he snapped the SIM card between finger and thumb. He'd taken her rucksack too, but that didn't matter, she had a twenty-pound note tucked inside one of the cups of her bra. She'd get it changed in the pub next to the bridge, use a payphone to call Graham Taylor, ask him to come and pick her up. Meanwhile, Alfie Flowers must have led Graham's operative to Shareef, they'd had their meeting . . .

Harriet was pushing through the glass doors of the pub when she realized with freezing clarity what Larry Macpherson's phone call and that weird conversation with Rölf Most had been about. Realized that while Graham Taylor's operative had been following Alfie Flowers, Larry Macpherson had had someone following Shareef – and now they were all on a collision course.

18

'Stay three cars behind,' Toby advised as Elliot followed the blue Mercedes, both vehicles driving south down Kingsland Road.

Elliot said, 'This is more old-geezer wisdom.'

Toby said, 'I believe I learned it from *Miami Vice*. Possibly the finest cop show of the 1980s, although I don't suppose you'll have ever heard of it, young grasshopper.'

'Actually, I think my dad has some episodes on DVD.'

'Ouch,' Toby said, and plucked an imaginary arrow from his chest.

The Transit van followed the Mercedes as it turned left down Commercial Street, left again down Fashion Street, and right into Brick Lane's one-way system.

'Look out for a place called Urban Graphics,' Alfie said, peering through the van's windscreen, feeling an electric spurt of excitement.

It was just past the old brewery, in the middle of a short row of shops. Alfie and Toby spilled out of the van as soon as Elliot found a place to park, just in time to see Watty follow Shareef into the gallery.

Toby looked at Alfie and said, 'Is this something else you haven't told me about?'

'Robbie Ruane gave me his business card, that time he stopped by my yard.'

'And this is his place. Classy.'

Alfie said, 'I have to admit that it looks like you were right about Shareef. He used us to make Morph famous, and now he's going to try to get a better deal with Robbie Ruane.'

'You should also admit that you were wrong about Shareef and Morph falling out. Shareef wouldn't waste his time making a deal if he knows that Morph isn't going to cooperate.'

Alfie shook his head. 'If he can convince Robbie Ruane that Morph is a recluse who doesn't like to talk about his art, Shareef can keep making and selling fakes as long as the market will bear it.'

'If you're right, why are we wasting our time following him? Elliot has a hot date, and I have my book to finish. Old George Savile Halifax is just about to come down really hard on the Catholics.'

'I'm hoping that I'm wrong,' Alfie said. 'Perhaps Morph really is a recluse. Or perhaps Shareef is hoping to make a deal with Robbie Ruane so he'll have a fat wad of banknotes to wave in front of Morph's face and convince him to do the right thing.'

Toby studied Alfie, his dark, close-set gaze suddenly serious. 'You really want to find him, don't you?'

'I want to know what he knows about the glyphs,' Alfie said.

They climbed back in the van, used the wing mirror to watch the gallery. When Elliot checked his watch and yawned and stretched with luxurious unselfconsciousness, Toby looked up from his book and said, 'I hope we're not keeping you up beyond your bedtime.'

'I didn't get much sleep last night. There were these three helicopters making like strafing runs. Not police helicopters, but the big Army helicopters, the ones with two sets of rotors. Flying way lower than police or civilian helicopters are allowed to fly.'

Toby said, 'Chinooks. Fuckers woke me up too. It's probably something to do with the big terrorist strike they keep telling us to expect. I heard that they've reactivated the emergency communications centre under Holborn, and they're refurbishing the deep bunkers under Whitehall and Bethnal Green. Also, there are plans to mobilize troops within an hour of any major incident to key locations where they can control the movement of traffic, or block it altogether. You have a dirty bomb going off in the centre of London, you don't want millions of radioactive people spilling into the shires. Better to let them die of radiation poisoning right in their homes. Ditto for any kind of bioweapon. Try to get out of London after one of those goes off, and a sniper or an attack helicopter will take you down.'

'Something is seriously wrong with my life,' Alfie said. 'I'm only thirty-two, I should be out in the world, having fun. Instead, I have to listen to your bullshit conspiracy theories.'

'This is one hundred per cent bullshit-free fact,' Toby said. 'I have a friend who works in the Home Office. He says everyone there is tremendously spooked. He says they all keep survival packs in their homes. Bottled water, freeze-dried food, a flashlight, a medicine kit. Right by the front door, so they can grab it and run when the shit hits the fan.'

Alfie said, 'And you believe him?'

'Why wouldn't I believe him?'

'I notice that *you* aren't carrying a survival kit.'

'I have something far better than that,' Toby said. He speared two fingers inside the breast pocket of his jacket and took out a plastic tube, showed Alfie and Elliot the two white tablets inside. 'Sodium cyanide. Check it out.'

'You're kidding,' Elliot said.

Toby displayed his bad dental work. 'One is more than enough to kill a horse. If things get bad, I'm off to the pub for the longest lock-in session in history. And if they get *really* bad, I'm going to dissolve these in the most expensive whisky I can afford, and anyone who wants to go out with me is welcome to take a sip.'

'Jesus,' Elliot said.

'He's kidding,' Alfie said. 'They're probably aspirin.'

Toby shook the tube and said, 'A friend who works in the School of Tropical Medicine gave them to me. He told me that if you drop one of these babies in a jam jar of vinegar, it'll kill off an entire wasp nest in ten minutes flat.'

'What, aspirin?' Elliot said.

'He means cyanide,' Alfie said. 'And he's still kidding.'

Toby was watching something in the wing mirror. 'Shareef just came out of the gallery,' he said.

Elliot started the Transit van as the blue Mercedes went past. 'You shouldn't kid around about stuff like that,' he said.

Toby lit a fresh cigarette. 'Why not?'

'Because sooner or later it's going to happen,' Elliot said, with killing simplicity.

They followed the Mercedes north through Shoreditch to a council estate of deck-access housing and tower blocks bordering the Grand Union Canal, not far from Franks House. The Mercedes pulled up in a car park sandwiched between two tower blocks;

Elliot parked the Transit a couple of hundred yards away, next to a short row of lock-up garages. As Shareef and Watty walked towards one of the tower blocks, he said, 'Leave this to me,' and started to get out of the van.

Toby said, 'Leave what to you?'

'You want to know where those guys are going, right? You can't follow them because they know who you are, but they don't know me.'

Toby, watching Elliot walk away across the car park, said to Alfie, 'The kid fucks up, he doesn't get any pocket money.'

Alfie said, 'That stuff – is it really cyanide?'

'When the balloon goes up, you're welcome to join me. You can break with teetotalism for the first and last time in your life.'

'Elliot's right. It isn't funny. What are you doing?'

Toby had opened the door. 'Since you can't drive, I'm going to have to be the one who sits behind the wheel in case we have to make a quick getaway.'

After Toby had walked around the front of the van and climbed up into the driver's seat, Alfie said, 'Why would we want to make a quick getaway?'

Toby lit another cigarette. 'I have a funny feeling that we're entering the Twilight Zone.'

'You're nervous.'

'This is a little edgier than book reviewing. I mean, at any given book launch you're almost certain to run into an author you've displeased with your less than fulsome praise, but usually he'll be content to give you a dirty look or turn his back on you. A friend of mine once had a glass of white wine thrown in his face, but that's about as far as it goes. What are you doing?'

Alfie washed down half a Valium with a mouthful of banana milk shake. 'Maintaining my equilibrium.'

'This gets any more intense, I'm going to ask you for some of that.'

Elliot came back about ten minutes later, excited and out of breath, leaning in at Alfie's window and saying, 'Well, I did it.'

Toby said, 'I hope you mean you found out where they went.'

'It was a lot easier than I thought it would be,' Elliot said. 'I rode up in the lift with him and his friend, and this old lady with one of those wheeled shopping baskets who got off on the tenth floor. Shareef and his friend and me rode the rest of the way to the top, the fifteenth. That's where they have their flat, 1509, right on the corner looking out over the canal.'

Alfie said, 'They didn't suspect anything?'

'They started giving off this hostile vibe when they realized I wasn't getting off before they did. But when we got out, they went one way and I went the other, and then I doubled back after they went through the fire door. Which had a window in it, so I could watch them through it and see where they went. I think they're squatting. The whole top floor is being fixed up or torn down or whatever. There were fresh nail-marks in the frame of the door of their flat, like it had been boarded over, plus someone had fitted a new lock. So what do we do now?' Elliot said. 'Are we finished for the day?'

'You have a nice evening with Cassie,' Alfie said. 'We'll hang out here a while.'

'I promised George I'd bring the van back.'

'We'll take good care of it,' Alfie said, and asked Elliot if he needed taxi fare.

Elliot said it was okay, he had just enough time to walk to the Angel and get the Tube. 'Also, I nearly forgot. When I was in the lift with Shareef and his friend, I noticed a piece of graffiti that could be by your guy.'

Alfie said, 'Are you sure?'

'I could only look at it out of the corner of my eye, because I didn't want them to know that I'd spotted it, if you see what I mean. But yeah, pretty much.'

After Elliot had gone, Toby said, 'So now I guess we sit here, eat pistachio nuts, and shoot the shit, like real detectives on a stake-out.'

Alfie said, 'I think we should go up there.'

'We already tried to talk to Shareef, and it ended up with him threatening us with Watty.'

'We can tell him that we know he's been trying to cut a deal with Robbie Ruane even though Morph doesn't want anything to do with it. We can tell him that we know he and Morph have fallen out and he's trying to cover it up, that we know the stunt with the sheep and the stunt at the museum were his work, not Morph's, which is why he gave us the run-around instead of doing the right thing after we put Morph's name in the papers.'

Alfie had thought it through while waiting for Elliot to come back. He'd tried to work out what had gone wrong the first time he'd talked to Shareef, and decided that he wasn't going to get anywhere by explaining why he needed to talk to Morph. What he had to do was work out what he thought was going on, make a story out of what he knew and what he thought he knew, and then confront Shareef with it, and give him a choice.

He said, 'We'll say that either he tells us about Morph – how he met him, where Morph comes from, his real name – or we'll go to Robbie Ruane and tell him everything we know. We'll tell him that either he helps us, or we'll help Robbie Ruane.'

'And then Watty throws us out of the window.'

'Perhaps you should stay here. I'll tell Shareef you're waiting for me, that you'll give Robbie Ruane a call if I don't come back with all my bones unbroken.'

'Would you do that? Help Robbie Ruane, I mean.'

Alfie shook his head. 'Of course not. My agent says that Robbie Ruane is basically a crook, and you and I have met the man, we know that he isn't to be trusted. But if Shareef believes that we'll go to Robbie Ruane, that we'll tell him what we know and offer to help him find Morph . . .'

'He'll be scared that he'll lose his deal, that Robbie Ruane will step in and take Morph away from him.' Toby smiled and said, 'It's a not a bad plan, but you know it probably won't get you anywhere.'

'Following him around hasn't done us any good, has it? Maybe Shareef knows where Morph is, maybe he doesn't, but in any case I don't think he's going to lead us to him.'

'Elliot saw that graffiti. Maybe Morph is up there with Shareef right now. They've stuck a pizza in the oven and are sitting down to watch the six o'clock news.'

'And that's another reason why I should pay Shareef a visit. But even if that piece of graffiti Elliot saw in the lift is the real thing, it only proves that Morph was here at some point. It doesn't mean he's coming back,' Alfie said.

That was when the black Range Rover roared up, braking hard as it cut in front of the van. Headlights flared in the rear-view mirror – another vehicle drawing up behind them – as the driver of the Range Rover got out, reaching the van in two strides, jerking open the door beside Toby and sticking a gun right in his face.

As Graham Taylor drove Harriet away from Blackfriars Bridge, he talked into the headset of his hands-free mobile phone, staying in touch with Michelle, the operative who had followed Alfie Flowers and Benjamin Barrett from the gymnasium on Kingsland Road, telling Harriet that Alfie Flowers and his friends had followed Benjamin Barrett from an address in Brick Lane to a council estate in Hackney, and that someone else had definitely been following them, an unidentified white male, blond, driving a black Range Rover. Telling her that the driver of Alfie Flowers's Transit van had followed Benjamin Barrett and his friend into one of the tower blocks and come out again ten minutes later, talked briefly to Alfie Flowers and the journalist, Toby Brown, and then walked off.

'Michelle thinks that he probably discovered where Benjamin Barrett is hiding out,' Graham said.

Harriet was slumped in the passenger seat of her battered Peugeot 205, dirty warm air blowing over her face through the window that Graham had broken when he'd hot-wired the car – the keys were in her purse, her purse was in her rucksack, and her rucksack had been taken by Larry Macpherson. She was coming down hard from Rölf Most's drug, shivering and sweating by turns, a dull headache throbbing behind her eyes, and she was still haunted by ghostly flickers of the glyphs. Floaters faintly falling across her vision, shapes pulsing in the corners of her eyes, vanishing when she tried to look at them directly.

She said, 'Where's the Range Rover? Is it in sight of Alfie Flowers and his friend?'

'It pulled over just outside the council estate. Michelle left it behind when she followed Mr Flowers and Mr Barrett to the tower block.'

'He's waiting for Larry Macpherson and Rölf Most. Graham, we can't leave Alfie Flowers sitting there. Michelle will have to blow her cover. She's going to have to move in and warn him—'

Graham was listening to his headset.

Harriet saw his expression change, and said, 'What's wrong?'

'Bad news,' he said, and told her that the Range Rover and a white Volkswagen people-carrier had just boxed in Alfie Flowers's Transit van, that Alfie Flowers and Toby Brown were being forced into the people-carrier at gunpoint, that it was driving right up to the entrance of the tower block. Pausing, then saying, 'Rölf Most and the blond man who was driving the Range Rover have gone into the tower block. There's a third man behind the wheel of the people-carrier, presumably looking after the prisoners.'

'Is it Larry Macpherson? Blue denim jacket, black hair?'

Graham asked Michelle, then said, 'She says the driver has red hair, a camouflage T-shirt.'

'There's no one else in the people-carrier? Just the driver and Alfie Flowers and Toby Brown?'

'She thinks so. She can't be sure.'

'Get us there as fast as you can.'

Graham was a skilful driver, police-trained, but in the stop-and-go rush-hour traffic that clogged Clerkenwell and Shoreditch it took twenty minutes to reach the council estate. Michelle was waiting for them at the far end of a row of lock-up garages that stood at right angles to the tower block. A slim young black woman in motorcycle leathers, reassuringly calm and competent, she told Harriet that the situation hadn't changed: Mr Flowers and Mr Brown were being held prisoner in the people-carrier, and as far as she knew Dr Most and the blond man were still inside the tower block.

Harriet peeked around the corner at the people-carrier, but she couldn't make out who was inside because it was parked with its rear towards her and the blinds were drawn over its side windows. She said to Michelle, 'Any sign of a fourth man? He's hard to miss. Well built, blue denim jacket and black cargo pants, mirrorshades. He should have been in the people-carrier too.'

'I saw only Dr Most and the driver. The driver's still sitting right there in his vehicle with Mr Flowers and Mr Brown,' Michelle said, pointing to the people-carrier parked in front of the entrance to the tower block. 'If anyone else is involved, I haven't spotted them.'

Graham said, 'Mr Macpherson may be watching the rear of the tower block. In case Benjamin Barrett tried to slip away.'

Harriet allowed that it was possible, but she had a vague feeling that something wasn't right. She was sweating in the warm sunlight, trying to force her thoughts through the dull pulse of her headache. She asked Michelle if she was certain that the man who had been following Benjamin Barrett hadn't spotted her.

'That's why I ride a motorcycle,' Michelle said. 'When you're following someone in a car, if they suspect something, they look out for other cars. They don't see me.'

'She knows what she's doing,' Graham told Harriet.

'Saying that, I'm surprised Mr Flowers and his friend didn't spot the Range Rover on their tail,' Michelle said.

Harriet said, 'They're complete innocents. They don't have the faintest idea about what they've stumbled into, and they didn't expect to be followed.'

Graham said, 'This Dr Most, does he mean them harm?'

'Almost certainly.'

'And Benjamin Barrett?'

'Definitely. I know what you're thinking, Graham, but calling in the police won't do any good. It could turn into a siege. Someone could get hurt.'

'People are going to get hurt if we *don't* bring in the police.'

Harriet looked up at the face of the tower block, a grid of beige panels and windows blankly reflecting the late-afternoon sunlight. Fifteen floors, no point even thinking of trying to find where Benjamin Barrett was hiding out; it would take at least an hour to do a floor-by-floor search . . .

She said, 'If the police do manage to arrest Rölf Most, they won't be able to hold him. He has immunity – the people who matter know that he's looking for Morph and have given him free rein. The police will have to let him go, and then, if he hasn't already told Larry Macpherson or someone else where to look for Morph, he'll go to ground. He'll make sure he shakes off any tail we try to put on him, and then he'll go looking for Morph himself. But if we wait for him to come out, we can follow him to wherever Morph is hiding out. *Then* we can call the police.'

Graham shook his head. 'Even if the police have to let Rölf Most go, we'll have saved Alfie Flowers and his friend, not to mention Benjamin Barrett and *his* friend.'

Harriet said, 'It's too late to help Benjamin Barrett. By now, Rölf Most will have zapped him, made him spill everything he knows about Morph. If we hang back, we can follow him—'

'Calling the police is the right thing to do,' Graham said, taking out his mobile phone. 'You can't see that because you're too close to this thing, you've lost all sense of perspective. But later—'

Michelle cried out.

Harriet turned, looked up, saw a dark shape tumble away from the edge of the tower block's roof, a man-shaped shadow plunging headlong past windows full of sunlight. Something, a shoe, spun away as the man rolled in the air and smashed into the roof of the people-carrier. The vehicle bounced on its shocks, its windscreen and side windows exploding as the sound of the impact, like someone stamping a dustbin flat, echoed off the looming face of the tower block. Pigeons were shocked into the air from every roof all around, and Harriet started to run across the car park.

It was like being in a car crash – a tremendous jolting noise, glass shattering and falling, and then a dazed silence. Alfie and Toby had been lying on the bench seats in the back of the people-carrier, their hands bound behind their backs. Now they managed to sit up, snowfalls of broken safety glass dropping from their shoulders and hips, saw that the roof was buckled and bowed, saw the driver, his head covered in blood, blood running from a deep gash in his scalp, feebly trying to push away a deflating air bag.

Then someone, a blonde woman, was wrenching at the door beside Alfie, and a man pulled open the door beside the driver and rapped him smartly on the head with a length of black rubber tubing. The impact made a loud, hollow sound and the driver fell sideways and lay still. The man leaned in and quickly patted him down, opening his denim jacket and removing the gun with which he had menaced Toby a few minutes before, when Toby had tried to talk to him.

The side door squealed open; Alfie and Toby staggered out. A man's body lay face down on the people-carrier's roof, cradled in a deep indentation. It was Watty, his face turned towards Alfie, congested and swollen, one eye half-closed in a ghastly wink. One of his arms was bent in half a dozen places. His white tracksuit bottoms were rapidly darkening as blood soaked into them.

Alfie looked away, and the grey-haired man who'd coshed the driver told him to turn around, sliced through the plastic tape that bound his wrists. The blonde woman pulled a small black rucksack from one of the seats of the people-carrier, briefly inspected its contents. As Alfie retrieved his camera bag, she said, 'Where's Benjamin Barrett?'

Toby said, as the grey-haired man cut his bonds, 'Who are you guys?'

The woman stepped up to Alfie. Tall and slim in a dark trouser suit, just a couple of inches shorter than him, saying, 'Benjamin Barrett. Where is he?'

There was a compelling intensity in her gaze.

For just one moment, Alfie was tempted to give it up, but then caution won out over fear. 'Why do you want to find him?'

'Because I want to save him if I can. Where is he?'

The grey-haired man told the woman that they should wait for the police, but she shook her head, said that by the time the police arrived it would be too late. 'They made this poor guy kill himself and they've probably finished with Benjamin Barrett too, but if we move in right now there's the slimmest chance we might be able to save him from himself.'

Toby brushed crumbs of safety glass from his hair. 'If you're not the police, who are you working for? Maybe we could see some ID.'

'I'm Harriet Crowley; he's Graham Taylor. Graham and his people are working for me, and I work for the Nomads' Club,' the woman said, looking straight at Alfie.

The shock blew clean through him, like winter's coldest wind. He said, 'I think we can help each other.'

Harriet Crowley said, 'You don't have the faintest idea what you've blundered into. Just tell me where Benjamin Barrett is hiding out, I'll do the rest.'

Alfie took a breath. He said, 'Maybe I don't know everything, but I do know that we both have an interest in this. We'll go up there together.'

Harriet studied him for a moment, then said, 'After this, we're going to have a long talk.'

'Absolutely.'

In the lobby, Harriet hammered at the call buttons of the pair of lifts, stepping back when one of the sets of doors slid open. The grey-haired man, Graham Taylor, raised the gun he'd taken from the driver of the people-carrier, lowered it again as an entire family stepped out – father, mother, and three daughters in descending size, the women all in black chadors that left only their eyes visible, the husband in a natty houndstooth jacket. In the lift, after Alfie had punched the button for the fifteenth floor, Harriet asked if Rölf Most had said anything to them after they'd been pulled out of their van.

Toby had to hold his lighter with both hands when he lit his cigarette. 'If you mean the guy with the white hair, he asked us where he could find Benjamin Barrett. And because his man was pointing a gun at us we told him.'

'Did he say what he was going to do?'

Alfie said, 'He said that he was looking forward to talking to me.'

That wasn't quite it. It had been something like, 'I am very much looking forward to an intimate chat.' Alfie felt a chill, remembering the way the man had looked at him. He was leaning in a corner of the lift, fumbling in his camera bag for his pills. There was a dark pressure behind his eyes and a parched metallic taste at the back of his throat, warning signs that if he wasn't careful, if he didn't maintain his equilibrium, he was going to be struck down by a seizure. He washed down a whole phenobarbitone tablet with a mouthful of banana-flavoured milk shake while Toby said, 'They made Watty jump, didn't they? I mean, I've never worked for the Samaritans, but when we talked to him a couple of hours ago he didn't strike me as the suicidal type. They made him jump and told Shareef he'd be next if he didn't tell them what they wanted to know.'

Harriet said, 'Rölf Most has other methods of persuasion. He probably made that poor man jump because he could.'

She was looking at the graffiti on the walls of the lift. *Rhoda did Kwame 31/5/04.* Names in pneumatic lettering written with black or red or silver felt-tip. Elaborately indecipherable swirls and curlicues that might as well be the tags of Martian invaders. After a moment, Alfie saw what Harriet had spotted – one of Morph's cartoons. Just the cartoon, no glyphs framing it, a silhouette taken from the photograph that had been on the front pages of every newspaper in April: a man, robed and hooded, teetering on a box with his arms outstretched, the Christ figure of Abu Ghraib prison.

Harriet saw that Alfie had seen it too. For a moment their gazes met; then she looked away. Alfie said, 'You want to find him too.'

She nodded tightly. 'Before Rölf Most does.'

Graham's mobile phone began to ring as soon as they came out of the lift onto the fifteenth floor. He answered it, listened for a moment, then told Harriet that Michelle had just seen Rölf Most and the blond man leave the building. 'They must have taken the stairs, or used the other lift. They're checking out the people-carrier.'

Harriet rounded on Alfie. 'Where is he?'

'Flat 1509, in the corner—'

She was running, crashing through a fire door. Alfie followed Graham and Toby as they chased after her down a corridor lit by unshielded fluorescent tubes. Most of the doors were boarded up. There were puddles of water on the bare concrete floor. Harriet was banging on the door of flat 1509 with the heel of her hand, saying loudly, 'Benjamin? Benjamin Barrett? Don't be scared. We're here to help you.' Pausing, listening for a reply that didn't come, then telling Graham, 'It's locked, and I can hear someone crying on the other side.'

'He calls himself Shareef,' Alfie said.

Harriet said, 'Shareef? I know what they did to you. They drugged you, they shone a light into your eyes. I know you're feeling pretty bad right now, but I can help you.' She paused, waiting for a reply, then said, 'I really can help you, Shareef. All you have to do is open the door.'·

Someone cried out inside the flat, a wordless wail that raised the hairs on the back of Alfie's neck.

He said, 'Shareef? This is Alfie Flowers. It's safe to come out now. We can talk, anything you want.'

There was a violent crash from somewhere behind the door.

Harriet said, 'Shareef, don't listen to the voice. Do you understand me? Don't listen to it.'

There was another crash. The fluorescent lights down the length of the corridor went out.

Graham pushed Harriet out of the way and started to kick the door at the point where the lock was mounted. When it snapped open, he said, 'Wait there,' and stepped into the hallway beyond, the gun held up by his face.

When he came out, just a minute later, he had a grim look on his face.

Harriet said, 'Shit,' and pushed past him into the flat.

Graham looked at Alfie and Toby. 'Do you know what this kid – Benjamin Barrett, Shareef, whatever – do you know what he looks like?'

'I'll do it,' Alfie said.

Floating above his fear on a cushion of Valium, he followed Graham into the hot, dim hallway. There was a smell of burnt meat, as if someone had left a roast too long in the oven; it grew stronger when Graham opened a door and said, 'He's in here.'

Alfie didn't want to look but knew that he had to. Shareef lay on the floor of the bare little bedroom beside a low table cluttered with electronic equipment. His body in its natty tracksuit bent like a bow, resting on its heels and the back of its head. Alfie saw a fat orange electrical cable clamped between white teeth, saw wisps of grey smoke. He stepped back from the doorway and said, 'That's him.'

'He ate the cable from what looks like a radio transmitter,' Graham said.

As Toby explained that Shareef had been a DJ for a pirate radio station, Alfie noticed something twinkling darkly at the end of the hallway. He walked towards it, past the door to the kitchen into an L-shaped living room lit by a bare bulb hung from the ceiling. There was a sofa with a sleeping bag crumpled on it like a shed cocoon, a TV and a boom box side by side on upturned milk crates, a cheap pine table littered with pizza boxes and styrofoam clamshells, felt-tip pens and uncapped cans of spray paint, sheets of plastic and razor blades and surgical scalpels. An uncurtained window looked across the canal towards derelict factories and other tower blocks. But Alfie barely noticed any of this, because everywhere over the walls were cartoons framed in swirling glyphs, dense and agitated as swarming bees.

Harriet said, 'After all these years, they still give you trouble, don't they?'

Alfie wrenched his gaze from the swarming glyphs, turned to look at her.

She said, with a faint quick smile, there and gone, 'Obviously the treatment didn't work as well as it could.'

Alfie made a connection. 'You're Mr Prentiss's granddaughter.'

Remembering how the little girl had sneaked up behind him in the bleak winter garden, calling him a spy, jumping about with mischievous glee.

Slouched in the doorway, Toby said, 'Which would mean that you're the daughter of Christopher Prentiss, otherwise known as Antareus.'

Alfie said, 'We found out about the pamphlet that your father published.'

Harriet's expression didn't change, but something hardened in her gaze. 'My father abandoned my mother and me just after I was born. And if you know anything at all about him, you'll know why I use my mother's maiden name.'

Toby said, 'It's a bit like a family reunion for you two, isn't it? How do the bad guys fit into this? Do they have anything to do with this Nomads' Club?'

Harriet said, 'Rölf Most is a psychiatrist who is treating a man called Carver Soborin. And Carver Soborin was my father's psychiatrist.'

Toby said, 'Rölf Most learned about the glyphs from Carver Soborin, and Carver Soborin learned about them from your father. And your father stole them from your grandfather.'

He picked up a sheet of plastic from the dining table and held it up to the light that fell through the uncurtained window. Alfie saw the shape cut out from it, realized that it was the stencil for one of Morph's cartoons, a cowboy riding a cruise missile rodeo-style, the edges smudged with black spray-paint.

'We can talk about this later,' Harriet said. 'Right now, we have to catch up with Rölf Most before he catches up with Morph.'

Alfie said, 'He did something to Shareef. Something that made him kill himself.'

Harriet nodded. 'After he made him tell everything he knew about Morph.'

'And Watty – the man who jumped off the roof. Rölf Most did that too.'

'He used the glyphs,' Harriet said. 'He injected them with a drug and zapped them with what's called a fascination glyph to put them in a highly suggestive state. He questioned them, and when they had nothing more to tell him, he told them to kill themselves.'

Toby whistled a couple of bars of the theme music of *The Twilight Zone* as he shuffled through sheets of plastic on the table.

Harriet ignored him, telling Alfie, 'That's what this is all about. Rölf Most wants to know everything that Morph knows about the glyphs, and that's why we have to find Morph before he does.'

Toby said, 'What's with this "we", paleface?'

Alfie shot him a look and told Harriet, 'What he means is we'll be glad to help.'

Graham was waiting outside the flat. 'They're in the black Range Rover,' he said. 'Currently heading south down Shoreditch High Street. Michelle is right on their tail.'

'You don't have to come with me, Graham,' Harriet said. 'You've already done more than enough. If you want to stay here, wait for the police . . .'

Graham smiled. 'I wouldn't know how to begin explaining this. And besides, I think I had better drive. You're in no fit state.'

19

Graham's mobile phone rang again as they came out of the entrance of the tower block. Harriet led the way through the small crowd gathered around the people-carrier. Kids had climbed onto the roofs of nearby cars to get a better view; people stood at their windows on different floors of the tower block on the other side of the car park. Sirens wailed in the distance. All the way down in the lift, the three men standing silently around her, thinking about what they'd seen in the flat, she had been trying to work out her next move. She was angry and anxious, believed that the deaths of Benjamin Barrett and his friend were her fault, was certain that Benjamin Barrett had told Rölf Most where he could find Morph and knew that she had to catch up with the psychiatrist right away, figure out some way of taking him down . . .

Her ace in the hole was that Michelle was on his tail, but now Graham was saying into the microphone of his headset, 'It isn't your fault.' Telling Harriet, 'They abandoned the Range Rover on double yellows outside Liverpool Street Station. Michelle followed them inside, and Larry Macpherson ambushed her when she reached the bottom of the stairs. Tapped her on the shoulder, and when she looked around, made a gun-shape with his fingers and pointed it right in her face.'

A splinter of ice pricked Harriet's heart. 'Is she all right?'

'She's shaken up but basically okay. She says the bastard winked at her and walked off into the crowd. She went straight back outside, circled around in case they came out of the other entrance, but they probably used the Tube to get away.'

'Shit. They must have been on the alert ever since they realized that these two were trying to follow Shareef.'

The journalist, Toby Brown, pointed at Harriet with the roll of plastic sheet he'd taken from the flat, and said, 'Don't go blaming us.'

Harriet lost it for a moment and rounded on him. 'Of course you're not to blame. You're just an idiot who doesn't have a clue about what he's stumbled into.'

After a brief silence, Graham said, 'The driver of that people-carrier probably told them about us. It isn't anyone's fault. It's one of those things.'

Trying to pick up Rölf Most's trail at Liverpool Street would be a waste of time, Harriet thought, but there was still one angle left. She said to Graham, 'Tell Michelle to head for the Dorchester Hotel. If they are going to ground, they'll have to send someone to collect Carver Soborin. We can use him to find them.'

'And meanwhile,' Graham said, 'they could be picking up Morph. Or anyone else Benjamin Barrett told them about.'

Alfie said, 'Robbie Ruane. Someone should warn Robbie Ruane.'

Harriet said, 'Who is Robbie Ruane?'

Alfie said, 'After he left the Majestic Gymnasium, before he came here, Shareef – Benjamin Barrett – visited an art dealer called Robbie Ruane.'

Graham said, 'He owns that place on Brick Lane?'

Alfie nodded. 'Urban Graphics. He came to me after he saw the photograph of Morph's graffiti in the *Independent*. He wanted me to help him find Morph.'

Harriet said, 'This art dealer is looking for Morph too?'

'He thinks Morph could be the next Damien Hirst.' Alfie was fishing for something in his camera bag, a business card. 'He stuck this in my letter box,' he said, and handed it to Harriet.

She borrowed Graham's phone, punched in the number for the gallery. The phone at the other end of the connection rang; an answering machine picked up. When she dialled Robbie Ruane's mobile, she got the answering service.

Graham said, 'Are you thinking what I'm thinking?'

Harriet said, 'After Rölf Most zapped me, he dropped off Larry Macpherson at Brick Lane. He questioned Robbie Ruane, Rölf Most came here and questioned Benjamin Barrett, they met up again at the station . . .'

They ran for her car. Alfie Flowers and Toby Brown squashed themselves into the narrow back seat; Harriet rode shotgun;

Graham took the wheel. As they sped out of the council estate, Toby unrolled the sheet of plastic he'd taken from Shareef's flat and handed it to Alfie, saying, 'It looks like someone was trying to make up a stencil for the pattern that frames those cartoons.' He and Harriet watched as Alfie studied it. Toby said, 'Is it the real thing?'

Alfie shook his head. 'It isn't finished. But it doesn't look right either.'

Harriet looked at the two of them, the journalist all in black, black hair falling forward over his clever, pale face, Alfie twisted sideways, staring at the sheet of plastic he'd laid against the window, a big, round-shouldered man who'd sweated through a Hawaiian shirt decorated with guitars and palm trees and hula dancers. She said, 'If you think this means something, you had better tell me.'

Toby said, 'Flowers thinks that Shareef had taken to faking Morph's work because he and Morph had a falling-out, and he didn't want to blow the chance of a juicy deal with Robbie Ruane.'

'The glyphs on the walls of the flat were genuine,' Alfie said.

Toby shrugged. 'So Morph was staying with Shareef once upon a time, but he moved out.'

Harriet said, getting into it, 'That wasn't Benjamin Barrett's flat – it was where he was hiding out. I found out where he really lives. Rölf Most was having it watched.'

Toby said, 'Remember what Elliot said about pirate radio stations, Flowers? They have their studio in one place, and transmitters in several different locations. Maybe Morph needed a place to stay, and Shareef let him use the squat where Mister Fantastic FM had put up one of their transmitters. But he and Morph had their falling out, Morph upped and left—'

'And then Shareef needed a place to hide, so he used the same flat,' Harriet said.

'And took Watty along with him as protection,' Toby said. 'A lot of good that did.'

Graham slowed to a crawl as he drove past the Urban Graphics gallery, looking around at the street and the passersby, pulling over and leaving the engine running.

Harriet said, 'I'll check it out. Everyone else stay in the car.'

Graham said, 'I should come with you. At least one of them is armed.'

'That's why you're going to give me the gun you took off Rölf Most's driver.'

It was a Mark III 9mm Browning High Power, the military version with the metal grip, just like the one that Harriet had learned to use on the Army range outside Reading before she'd gone to Nigeria. She checked that there was a round in the chamber, held the gun down by the side of her leg as she walked up to the gallery.

The place was fronted by a large plate-glass window, *urban graphics* in a big red spray-paint swirl across it, no lights showing inside. Harriet's reflection swam up to meet her in the glass door. She looked like her own ghost. The door was unlocked. Her heels ticked loudly on the white concrete floor when she stepped inside, looking left and right, seeing something slide away from her. She raised the gun, but what she'd seen was only an echo of the glyph with which she'd been zapped, a scatter of dots that for a moment hung sharp and clear in the air, and then began to drift and fade. A man-sized sculpture in rusting scrap metal stood in the middle of the stark white floor; paving slabs decorated with random dots of colour were fixed in a neat row along one wall. The dots were chewing-gum, Harriet realized, which someone had meticulously painted in bright primary colours. To the rear was a desk – a slab of sandblasted steel on concrete blocks, and a chair that looked like it had been stolen from the deck of the Starship *Enterprise* – and a spiral staircase leading to the first floor.

A pair of yellow household gloves lay at the foot of the stairs, giving off a strong chemical smell that tickled Harriet's memory. She stood there for a full minute, listening to the quiet still air, before daring to call out Robbie Ruane's name. Her voice echoed in the gallery space. No one replied.

As she climbed the staircase, leading with the gun, the smell grew stronger, sweetly pungent, thick in her nose and mouth, bringing the dull pulse of her headache right into her eyes. A moment from the past rose up inside her, a memory of dissecting a white rat in biology class in school, and she knew that what she could smell was formaldehyde.

The whole of the first floor had been knocked through. On one side, tucked under a gallery bedroom, was a compact kitchen that looked like the cockpit of a jet airliner; on the other was the living space, a black leather couch facing a widescreen TV across a glass coffee table that stood on a cowhide rug, a bookshelf stuffed with art books, jagged paintings on the walls, the biggest lava lamp she'd ever seen, shaped like a rocketship, and a large, free-standing fish tank beyond it, where a man knelt as if in prayer.

Something gripped Harriet from the nape of her neck to the small of her back. She found herself sitting on the floor, the gun dangling in her lap, things swarming as busily as ants across her sight. She'd blanked out for a second. Shock. She stood up carefully, tried to blink away tangles of dots and wavy lines. Her scalp felt cold and tight. The silence in the flat had taken on a dense quality, as if compressed at the bottom of a couple of miles of ocean; she jumped when the motor of the big fridge in the kitchen kicked in, but it helped bring her back to herself.

'Mr Ruane?'

She stepped forward, watching the kneeling man over the front sight of the Browning, saw that he was bent over at a painful angle and his arms were tied behind his back with electrical cord, saw that his head was submerged beneath the surface of the liquid that half-filled the glass tank. A black lamb, its eyes milky, its wool sodden and stinking of formaldehyde, lay stiffly on the birchwood floor in front of the tank and the dead man. There was a vivid puddle of fresh blood too, maggoty white shapes lying in it. Human fingers. One was still wearing a gold ring.

Robbie Ruane had been tortured, and when he'd given up what he knew about Morph, or when it had become clear that he didn't know anything useful, he'd been killed. Drowned in formaldehyde. It had been quick and brutal, and Harriet was certain that it had been the work of Larry Macpherson; according to one of the newspaper stories about his arrest in Peshawar, two of his Afghani prisoners had lost their little fingers while in his custody.

Downstairs, she found nothing on the desk but a tangerine iMac and a large leather-bound diary stuck with invitations to parties, gallery openings and book launches that Robbie Ruane wouldn't be going to. She briefly thought about ransacking the computer, but she was fairly certain that the art dealer hadn't known anything useful. Larry Macpherson had just been tidying up a loose end. She stuck the Browning in her jacket pocket, used a handkerchief to pick up the phone and call the police, and then got out of there.

'Head for the Nomads',' she told Graham, after she'd explained what she'd found.

Alfie said, 'It really exists?'

'Just barely.'

'And you belong to it.'

Harriet shook her head. 'It's a very old-fashioned club. Men only.'

Toby said, 'Why are we going there?'

Harriet said, 'It's for your own protection. If Rölf Most didn't find out from Benjamin Barrett where to find Morph, he'll definitely want to pay both of you a visit.'

Alfie started to ask her about the Nomads' Club. The poor guy hunched over his camera bag on the back seat, trying to make sense of everything. He said, 'My father was working for them, wasn't he? When he disappeared, I mean.'

'You can ask them all about it,' Harriet said. Her head ached and entoptics were flashing in and out of the corners of her vision.

'My grandfather's friends – are they still alive?'

'Two of them.'

'Who else?'

'That's it.'

Toby said, 'That's it? These two guys – they must be in their eighties. They can protect us?'

'The men I hired to protect them will protect you,' Harriet said. 'No more questions, okay? I need to think.'

She needed to rest, to give up the struggle and slip into calm, warm oblivion. Rölf Most had won – what was the point of trying to carry on? She shook her head, knowing that the thought was an echo of the voice, the snake sliding under the door, but she really did need to rest . . .

They were stuck in the usual traffic jam around the Elephant and Castle when Graham's mobile phone rang. He handed it to Harriet. It was Janice. She told Harriet that there had been a fire alarm at the hotel and the whole place had been evacuated.

'Where's Carver Soborin?'

Harriet felt surprisingly calm. As if the worst thing had already happened, and everything else was mere detail.

'We're looking for him right now,' Janice said.

'Don't bother. He's gone.' Harriet switched off the phone and told Graham what had happened. Leaning back in her seat, closing her eyes to the garish rush of the world, saying ruefully, 'They've been one step ahead of us all the time.'

20

The Nomads' Club was an ordinary red-brick detached house near Tooting Common, looming behind a low wall and an unkempt privet hedge. No lights showed in its windows. A small truck was parked in front of the gate, its load-bed piled with sand to increase its effectiveness as a makeshift barrier. The truck moved forward as the Peugeot approached, then laboriously backed into position again as Graham Taylor parked the little car in front of a pair of flaking garage doors.

As everyone climbed out of the car, a man wearing black trousers, a black bulletproof vest and a black watch cap materialized out of the shadows by the Gothic porch. Harriet Crowley shook his hand and they walked to the gate, talking in low voices. Toby said to Alfie, 'What do you think?'

Alfie was looking up at the house, its silhouette against the darkening evening sky. 'I think it could do with a tower or two, some mist, bats . . .'

'Or a drawbridge over a moat filled with sharks.' Toby's face was briefly illuminated as he lit a cigarette. 'How about our new friends? Do you think we can trust them?'

The Valium that Alfie had taken earlier was blunting the various shocks of the past couple of hours – being held at gunpoint, Watty smashing into the people-carrier, seeing Shareef's body. He felt calm, his thoughts moving slowly and easily through a comfortable fog, no edges anywhere. He hadn't found Morph, but he had found the Nomads' Club, and believed that was even better. He said, 'I think they want what we want. I think that, basically, we're all on the same side.'

Toby shook his head. 'Maybe they want what we want, but I'm not so sure that they're on our side. I mean, you haven't heard from them in all these years, they didn't even bother to warn you about this bad guy, Rölf Most—'

'Well, they came to our rescue, and that excuses a lot.'

'Only after Watty decided to use the people-carrier as a target for his swan dive. And what were they doing there in the first place?'

'I suppose they were following Shareef and hoping he'd lead them to Morph, just like we were.'

'Or they were following us.'

'Why don't you ask them?'

'Actually,' Toby said, 'I think you should do most of the talking. I know, I know, it's out of character for me to keep quiet, but your grandfather and your father were both part of this thing of theirs, and that must count for something.'

'You want me to ask them if they were using us to find Morph. What else?'

'I think you should ask them about everything,' Toby said.

Alfie smiled. 'So do I.'

The man in black took Graham Taylor around the side of the house; Harriet led Alfie and Toby through the front door and along a wood-panelled hall to a large, dimly lit room where the members of the Nomads' Club were waiting for them. There were glass-fronted bookcases along two walls, black oak floorboards partly covered with oriental rugs, heavy red velvet curtains drawn across a bay window. A grandfather clock with an elaborate face that told not only the time but the phase of the moon and the positions of several major constellations ticked in one corner. A laptop computer on a heavy desk cycled a star-field screensaver beneath a huge, sooty oil painting of a European man in some kind of tribal dress, one hand on the pommel of his curved sword, the other holding the bridle of a lugubrious camel.

Two old men sat in wing armchairs on either side of a large fireplace with green tiles and a mahogany mantelpiece. As Harriet led Alfie and Toby towards them, one of the men slowly got up, using both hands to lever himself out of his chair. Wearing an old-fashioned pinstriped suit, standing as straight-backed as a soldier at a memorial service, he had a shock of white hair that stood up as if he had been electrocuted, and dark glasses with small round lenses and wire rims.

Alfie had last seen him more than twenty years ago, when he had helped to clear out Maurice Flowers's papers and artefacts.

After Harriet had introduced Alfie and Toby, the old man stuck out his right hand, and said, 'M'name's Ashburton, Mr Flowers. Clarence Ashburton. I must apologize for the circumstances, but I'm glad to meet you at last.'

'You knew my grandfather,' Alfie said.

'Indeed I did,' Clarence Ashburton said, still holding out his hand, looking at nothing in particular. Alfie realized that the old man was blind, and stepped up and shook his hand. Clarence Ashburton responded with surprising vigour, then turned to his companion and said loudly, 'Do wake up, Julian. He's here.'

The other man was a bald, shrunken gnome with a patch strapped over his left eye and a tartan shawl wrapped around his shoulders. An inverted bag half-full of clear liquid hung on a hospital stand, connected by a long loop of plastic tubing to a shunt under a sticking plaster on his stick-thin forearm. He stirred and without opening his good eye said with some force, 'You know very well that I never sleep. Is that the boy?'

'And Mr Brown, the journalist.' Clarence Ashburton turned back to Alfie and Toby and said, 'Allow me to introduce you to Dr Julius Ward. He and I are, I am very much afraid to say, the last of the Nomads.'

'Tell them to sit down,' Julius Ward said, 'and offer them all a shot of brandy. I'm an old-fashioned doctor,' he explained, looking up at Alfie and Toby, 'and still believe in the restorative powers of a good stiff drink.'

When they were all seated, and Harriet Crowley had set a silver tray with a crystal decanter and balloon glasses on a leather hassock and splashed brandy into five glasses (Alfie refused his), Clarence Ashburton said that he hoped that they could rise above these unfortunate circumstances, and asked Harriet to bring him and Julius up to date.

She gave a quick, lucid account of what had happened at the tower block, her discovery of Robbie Ruane's body, and how Rölf Most and the others had escaped their tail and extracted Carver Soborin from the hotel. When she had finished, Julius Ward said, 'It sounds like a comprehensive shambles. No offence, my dear, but you do seem to have made rather a hash of things.'

'You can fire me any time you want,' Harriet said calmly.

'She has done her best in an increasingly difficult situation,' Clarence Ashburton said. 'It's clear that while our adversary may well be insane, he has more control over matters than we had previously believed.'

'He has Larry Macpherson's help,' Harriet said. 'That doesn't excuse what happened, but it goes some way towards explaining it.'

Julius Ward opened his good eye, looked at Alfie, and closed it again. He was clutching his brandy glass in both hands, like a sugar-starved child holding a lollipop. 'Let's hear what Mr Flowers has to say for himself. That's why we brought him here, isn't it? Perhaps he knows something that we do not.'

'I very much doubt it,' Harriet said. 'I brought him and his friend here because I was worried that they were going to get themselves killed.'

Alfie chose his words carefully. Valium muffled the excitement of having found the Nomads' Club, made it seem like a telephone ringing in a distant room. 'I admit that Toby and I don't know half of what you seem to know. So why don't you tell us your story? If there are any gaps, perhaps we can help you out.'

Clarence Ashburton turned this around at once. 'Since you admit that you have rather less to bring to the table than we do, I rather think that before we consider your offer of *quid pro quo*, you should tell us how you found out about the relationship between Morph and Mr Barrett.'

Alfie looked at Toby, who shrugged and took a big swallow of brandy. 'It's very simple,' Alfie said. 'I saw one of Morph's cartoons, and knew that the glyph which he used to frame it was the real thing. Toby and I found out about a party where he was supposed to be making an appearance, but Benjamin Barrett pulled a stunt with some sheep instead. We traced the sheep, got hold of Benjamin Barrett's mobile phone number, and managed to convince him to meet us. When he didn't tell us anything useful, we followed him. We hoped that he would lead us to Morph. What we didn't know was that you were following him too – or you were following us, it isn't quite clear.'

'You didn't know about Rölf Most, either,' Harriet said. 'Which is why I had to get you out of trouble.'

Alfie said, 'The other thing we know – we think we know – is that Shareef and Morph had a falling-out. We think that the stunt with the sheep was all Shareef's work, and so was the other stunt he pulled off at the Imperial War Museum. And just now we found stencils in the flat where he was hiding. It looks like he was trying to work out how to fake Morph's cartoons. If it wasn't for the fact that I started out on this whole thing because I saw a piece of graffiti containing a genuine glyph, I could easily believe that Shareef staged the whole thing. That Morph never existed.'

'He exists,' Harriet said. 'I talked to someone who knows him, and saw his immigration records. His real name is Musa Karsu. He came here with his father, seeking political asylum.'

Alfie said, 'Have you talked to his father? Does he know anything about the glyphs?'

Harriet shook her head. 'He died six weeks ago. A heart attack.'

Julius Ward said, 'How did you know that the glyph Morph used in his graffiti was genuine, Mr Flowers? And conversely, how did you know that the ones created by Benjamin Barrett were not genuine?'

Alfie said, 'I think you know why.'

Julius Ward said, 'Do you still suffer from epileptic seizures?'

'Not often.'

'When you do, are they serious?'

'They're absence seizures that last only a few seconds. Sometimes I get an aura or premonition before one hits, sometimes not.'

'What have your doctors prescribed to control them?'

'Phenobarbitone.'

'And does it help?'

'More or less. I also use Valium, sometimes other sedatives.'

'Would I be right in thinking that the reason that you have been looking for Morph is that you hoped to learn more about your condition? That the reason you agreed to come here is that you're hoping for a cure?'

The old man was sharper than he looked.

Alfie admitted, 'It's one reason.'

Julius Ward said flatly, 'We can't cure you, Mr Flowers. I'm afraid that there is no cure for what happened to you. The damage is permanent.'

He was watching Alfie with his one good eye. Everyone else around the fireplace was watching him too. Alfie took a breath, and said, 'Do you know what happened to me?'

'You found something that your grandfather had hidden away: a copy of a very powerful glyph and a small supply of a powdered extract from a certain plant,' Clarence Ashburton said. 'We believe that you tasted the extract and were under the influence of the psychotropic drug it contains when you looked at the glyph. You suffered a severe epileptic seizure. Worse than that, the combination of the drug and the glyph caused a permanent change to your visual cortex.'

'He's nodding,' Julius Ward said. 'He already knows this much.'

'I guessed that it was something like that,' Alfie said. 'But I didn't know for sure until now.'

His disappointment twisted deep inside him, a hook planted in his heart. He had hoped that Morph could not only have helped him understand what had happened to him, but might also have known how to reverse it, or at least might have been able to lead him to someone who could help him. And in a way that was how it had turned out; he'd gone looking for Morph, and had discovered his family's history instead, had found the Nomads' Club. But now they were telling him that nothing could help him, that there was no undoing what the glyphs had done to him . . .

Julius Ward said, 'We cannot cure you. No one can. But we may be able to help you, as David Prentiss once helped you. We have a small supply of the necessary drug.'

'Haka.'

'Some call it that. If you wish, we could wean you off your dependence on phenobarbitone and replace it with David Prentiss's treatment.'

Clarence Ashburton said, 'Your grandmother preferred to put her trust in medical science. After your father died, she wanted nothing more to do with us, and made us promise that we would have nothing to do with you. Until now, we have respected her wishes, but if you would like us to help you we will be glad to do so.'

'This treatment – is it any better than phenobarbitone?'

Julius Ward said, 'I believe there would be fewer side effects.'

'But it wouldn't cure me.'

'I'm sorry, Mr Flowers. I am no miracle worker, and haka is no miracle plant.'

'I remember that my grandfather once said that haka was supposed to have grown in the footprints of Adam and Eve, after they were expelled from the Garden of Eden – which was somewhere north of Baghdad.'

'Your grandfather was a good man and a fine scholar, but he was also something of a romantic,' Clarence Ashburton said, with a dry smile.

The light of a nearby table lamp was doubly reflected in the round lenses of the blind man's dark glasses; photographs in silver or leather frames crowded around the lamp's beaten copper base. When he'd first sat down, Alfie's gaze had been immediately drawn to one of these: four men standing in front of a large stone. Now, pressing forward, he said, 'I know that my grandfather found the glyphs when he was working in Iraq in the 1930s, and I know that haka was used in the religious ceremonies of a semi-nomadic tribe, the Kefidis. Are Morph and his father members of that tribe? Did they come here from Iraq?'

Harriet said, 'I don't think we should get into that right now.'

She was sitting stiffly in her chair, one hand cupped to her face, shielding it from the glare of the lamp. She hadn't touched her brandy.

Clarence Ashburton said, 'What did your grandfather tell you about his work?'

'Very little, and I remember even less,' Alfie said. 'But I do recognize one of the photographs on the table there, the one of the four men and what my grandfather called the anomalous stone. It was taken during an archaeological expedition he led in the 1930s. He's one of the men in the picture, David Prentiss is another, and I believe you two make up the rest of the party. You were excavating the remains of a religious community from the fifth century, and discovered a large stone much older than the church into which it had been incorporated and marked with strange patterns – with a glyph. My grandfather found out about

another site associated with the glyphs, and while he was excavating that, he discovered a system of caves. He found rock art
inside them, and also a twin of the anomalous stone.'

Toby drained his brandy glass and set it down, picked up the
one that Alfie hadn't touched, and said, 'I suppose you got all this
from the same mysterious place you got that photograph you
showed Shareef.'

'I found a photocopy of my grandfather's journal that my grandmother had made,' Alfie admitted.

'You found out where your grandfather had got hold of the
glyphs that fucked up your head, and you didn't quite get around
to telling me.'

'It was family business.'

'The whole thing turns out to be family business,' Toby said,
his close-set gaze fixed on Alfie.

'It's the business of the Nomads' Club,' Clarence Ashburton
said mildly, 'and we are grateful for your help. Would you like to
hear our side of the story?'

'I'd like nothing better,' Toby said, 'even though I have a strong
feeling that I'm not going to be able to write about any of this.'

Harriet said, 'Not one word.'

Julius Ward said, 'Are you all right, my dear?'

She flapped a hand. 'Just a little tired. It's been a very long day.'

'If you would like to rest—'

'We have to decide what to do. Carry on, Clarence. Now
they're here, they may as well know the whole sorry story.'

Clarence Ashburton said, 'Your grandfather, Mr Flowers, was
helping to develop oilfields in the north of Iraq, around the city
of Mosul. He was a keen amateur archaeologist, and in the 1930s
Iraq was an archaeologist's paradise. It has been home to a succession of early civilizations. The Sumerians, the Babylonian and
Assyrian Empires, a succession of Persian dynasties . . . It is a place
where history is everywhere underfoot. Time runs deep there.
While the inhabitants of Britain were running around in animal
furs and daubing themselves with plant juices, Mesopotamia was
controlled by a vast bureaucracy that bequeathed us the calendar
and the basis of our mathematics. Writing was invented there;
agriculture was invented nearby; some of the first cities in the

world were built there. At any rate, your grandfather mounted a number of small archaeological expeditions, and in 1936 invited several of the youngest members of the Nomads' Club to join him in an excavation of the church of a fifth-century Christian sect.'

Alfie said, 'Then you aren't the original Nomads.'

'As a matter of fact,' Clarence Ashburton said, 'the Nomads' Club predated the discovery of the glyphs by more than a century. It was founded in 1818 by seven gentlemen explorers who resolved to hold meetings once every two years to discuss their travels. And so they did, in an upper room of a coffee shop on the Strand. The meetings continued there until 1842, when one of the founding members – my great-great-grandfather, as a matter of fact – died of malaria in Borneo. He left a considerable portion of his fortune to the Nomads, and they bought a property in Soho, a small house where they could hold their meetings and maintain a library and map room.'

'Which doesn't mean that his great-great-grandson is in charge now,' Julius Ward said.

'No more than I was then,' Clarence Ashburton said, 'when we were young and foolish and carefree.'

'When we were young, at any rate,' Julius Ward said. 'The three of us – David Prentiss, Clarence and myself – were just out of school, adventuring in the summer before we went up to university. We thought your grandfather was the most tremendous hero, and quite the athlete for an old man of thirty-two. Despite the appalling heat, the abominable food, and a raid by armed bandits, we had a wonderful time, and we signed up again without a moment's thought two years later, when your grandfather proposed a second expedition to a site in the Zagros Mountains. But if you have read your grandfather's journal, you will already know this.'

Alfie said, 'Toby doesn't know about it, and he's caught up in this too.'

And hearing the story in chronological order would help him get it straight in his head, give him time to work out what he needed to ask the two old men, the last of the Nomads' Club. Most of all, of course, he wanted to ask them about what had happened to his father, how his disappearance figured in all this.

Clarence Ashburton said, 'After your grandfather discovered the anomalous stone, and dispatched it to England as a gift to the British Museum—'

Alfie said, 'I talked to someone in the museum about the glyphs. He told me that my grandfather's donations had been removed at some point.'

Julius Ward said, 'Once we realized its significance, the stone and Clarence's other gifts were removed from the museum by the secret service. I would imagine that MI6 still has them somewhere – probably in the Welsh slate quarry where it stores souvenirs of past campaigns.'

Clarence Ashburton said, 'We are getting ahead of ourselves. To return to your grandfather, Mr Flowers, if I may . . .'

Julius Ward said, 'Of course you may. Just answering the boy's question.'

Clarence Ashburton said, 'After your grandfather found the anomalous stone, he searched the archaeological records pertaining to the immediate region and discovered a brief description of a stele – a decorated standing stone – that a Catholic missionary, Father Tomas Anselm, had found in the Zagros Mountains. The pattern on Anselm's stele, although much weathered, was clearly identical to the pattern on the anomalous stone, and your grandfather organized a second expedition at once, planning to excavate the area around the stele.'

Julius Ward said, 'This was in a blind draw overlooking a river valley in the mountains, very hot during the day and freezing at night. The site was nothing much to look at, no more than a few low mounds on a flat apron of rock, the remains of a simple church within a small compound. Well, we were young and enthusiastic, we set to with a will, and after a couple of weeks we discovered the old church's secret – a shaft that led into a network of caves running back into the hillside. And at the bottom of this shaft was a stone engraved with a pattern identical to that on the anomalous stone and on Anselm's stele. This stone was larger, clearly had been shaped and carved *in situ*, and, so your grandfather believed, might have been the original. But more importantly, beyond this stone, deeper in the cave system, were wall paintings and carvings that were clearly much older than the church.'

'They were thousands of years older,' Clarence Ashburton said. 'There were marvellously vivid paintings and engravings of horses and gazelles. And there were numerous examples of abstract art, and several of those were potent glyphs.'

Julius Ward said, 'Of course, we didn't really understand the significance of what we'd found until much later.'

For a few moments, the two old men contemplated their memories. The grandfather clock dropped a handful of ticks into the silence, echoed by drops of liquid dripping from the base of Julius Ward's inverted plastic bag into its transparent regulator.

Toby jackknifed forward in his chair, holding his brandy glass in both hands, lamplight glowing on one side of his pale face. 'So the sect that built the two churches got the glyphs from the caves? Why? I mean, if they were Christians, what use did they have for what were obviously pagan symbols?'

Clarence Ashburton said, 'My own research established that the sect believed that speaking in tongues – glossolalia – was an integral part of Christian worship. It was not an uncommon belief in the early days of Christianity. The descent of the Holy Spirit upon the Apostles after the Resurrection is the most famous instance, of course. And members of the church which St Paul founded in Corinth most certainly spoke in tongues, while verses in the Acts of the Apostles suggest that other churches experienced it too. These practices may have been prefigured by certain prophetical experiences of the ancient Israelites – Samuel gives us an example in his first book, chapter 19, verses 20 to 24. And of course there are numerous instances of shamanistic rituals in which the participants achieve states of ecstasy similar to those which accompany glossolalia, while glossolalia remains part of the experience of worship in modern Protestant groups such as the Pentecostalists and the Adventists. We think that the Christian sect which built the churches discovered by your grandfather made use of glyphs and the drug, haka, to achieve what they believed was a spiritual union with God. They flourished for less than a century before the Byzantine Empire conquered the area; after that, they were persecuted as idolaters and their communities were destroyed or dispersed.'

'So they got high on drugs and zapped themselves with these

glyphs,' Toby said. He was caught up in the story and had forgotten that he had asked Alfie to do all the talking. 'But where did the original glyphs come from? Who carved the stones and painted the paintings in the caves? Was it this tribe, the Kefidis?'

'The Kefidis certainly used glyphs in their religious ceremonies,' Julius Ward said, 'and they claimed to have been using them long before the arrival of the Christian sect. But they also said that they had nothing to do with the cave art we found, and I believe that they were telling the truth. The glyphs we found in the caves almost certainly dated from the Late Palaeolithic. They are at least ten thousand years old, made by a people who vanished long before the Kefidis settled the area.'

'Abstract patterns similar to those which make up the glyphs are found almost everywhere Palaeolithic cave art has been found,' Clarence Ashburton said. 'But the complex patterns we discovered are, as far as we know, unique. Of course, here I must invoke the law of taphonomy, or grave law. And the law of the grave is one of the most important and intractable problems with which archaeologists must deal. All archaeological specimens are merely the lucky survivors of a much larger sample. The further back in time one looks, the greater the taphonomic distortion of the record. And so with prehistoric art. Some did not survive because it was temporary, in the form of unbaked clay or charcoal drawings. Or because it was in the form of carvings in the landscape – geoglyphs, like the White Horse at Uffington, a rare example which survived only by chance. And then there are dendroglyphs – carvings on trees – and drawings on wood and on leaves, and drawings and tattoos on the body. All of these were ephemeral, and very few have ever been found. Art made on the walls of caves is more permanent, but even so not all rock art can be expected to survive. Or, if it does survive, can be expected to be found.'

Julius Ward said, 'Which is to say that after all these years we still do not have the faintest notion why glyphs have not been found at any other Palaeolithic site.'

Clarence Ashburton said, 'When we discovered the glyphs, we did not have any idea what they were for, or what they could do. At the time, we believed that the representational paintings of animals were far more important than mere abstract patterns. Fortunately, we were sensible enough to keep our power dry. We did not rush into print, and we did not tell anyone outside the Nomads' Club about our discoveries. I say fortunately, because the very next year, David Prentiss, Harriet's grandfather, discovered that the semi-nomadic people who lived in the same part of the Zagros Mountains, the Kefidis, still made use of the glyphs.

'David was the brightest of us, a scholar of anthropology, and at the tender age of twenty-one was already fluent in Arabic and Kurdish. He heard about the Kefidis when he visited a local market to buy fresh food and fell into conversation with the village elders, who told him that the Kefidis worshipped the Devil and performed what they called "filthy dances" before graven idols. David was intrigued, and resolved to find out more. After we returned home, he discovered a description of one of the "filthy dances" by the same Catholic missionary, Father Anselm, who had discovered the stele that had led us to the site of the church, and to the caves beneath. Early next spring, he returned to Iraq—'

'And I went with him,' Julius Ward said

'Quite right,' Clarence Ashburton said. 'Perhaps you should tell this part of the story.'

Julius Ward looked at Alfie and Toby, surveying them from the shelter of his armchair like a wise, wrinkled, one-eyed turtle. 'Perhaps these young men are tiring of our stories.'

Alfie told him that they weren't. Toby poured a finger of brandy into his glass and said gloomily, 'I suppose this is all off the record too.'

Clarence Ashburton said, 'Every bit of it, I'm afraid.'

Harriet said, her voice peevish, pinched, 'You've already told them far too much.' ·

Clarence Ashburton said, 'It's ancient history now. Tall tales from another age.'

Julius Ward said, 'I should think Mr Flowers deserves to hear about his family history.'

'*He* isn't family,' Harriet said, meaning Toby.

'I promise not to reveal a thing,' Toby said. 'Cross my heart and hope to die if I do. Go ahead with your story, Dr Ward – don't pay any attention to me.'

'David Prentiss and I returned to Iraq early in the spring of 1939,' Julius Ward said. 'I had some Arabic and a smattering of Kurdish, but David spoke both languages like a native. He dressed like a native too, and politely turned down the Administrative Officer's offer of three policemen to escort us. He believed that we would learn more if we did not have armed guards, and so we rode alone into the Zagros Mountains, to the village where the Kefidis spent each winter, not far from the site where we had discovered the caves.

'The Kefidis were a proud but peaceful people, cheerful, friendly and welcoming. The men wore long white shirts and white coats over baggy trousers, but unlike their neighbours did not routinely go about armed. Although they did not enjoy good relations with their neighbours, who as David had learned the previous year despised and feared them, their long-barrelled rifles were used only against wolves that attacked their sheep in the mountain pastures. We stayed with them for three weeks, and quickly learned that they knew about the old church. They were intensely curious about what we had found there. They had visited the caves after we had left the previous year, but claimed that their own pictures were more holy, and promised that we would see them by and by. David spent much of the time in conversation with their elders, while I spent much of *my* time in a makeshift surgery. The Kefidis had never been visited by a doctor and were terrified of hospitals. Most of my patients had only minor ailments – colds and minor fevers and infected cuts or insect bites and so on – and were easily treated with aspirin and sulphonamide powder and bandages. But even those for whom I could do nothing, a young girl with tuberculosis and an old man with liver cancer, thanked me for my attention.

'When we had arrived at their village, the Kefidis were preparing to move to summer pastures high in the mountains, where they lived in tents until the autumn when the migration was reversed. The whole tribe went, from the smallest baby to the oldest woman, with everything loaded on ponies, which the women led, while the men drove their herds of sheep with the help of fierce dogs. We travelled with them, six or seven miles each day. I remember how hot and dusty the days were, and how cold and clear the nights, the stars bright and looking so close that you felt you could reach up and prick your finger on them.'

Julius Ward paused, looking at something far beyond the dim, overheated room. Then he said, 'On the night the Kefidis arrived at the place where they made their summer camp, while the women and children were setting up the tents and unpacking everything, the men slipped away, walking silently in single file, carrying musical instruments and other things in leather sacks, and faggots of wood on their backs. We were allowed to go with them, climbing above the snowline to a natural basin or arena set among steep bare rocks. At one end, a small grove of gnarled holly oaks grew around a flat shelf of rock as big as this room. That was where the men built their fire after they had scraped away the snow and ice. When they had lit it, they stripped off their sheepskin coats and their shirts, and on each other's bare chests and backs they painted in ochre and charcoal the various kinds of geometric design which made up the glyphs. Several of them took from their bags long strips of birch bark into which intricate patterns had been burnt, and hung them from the bare branches of the oaks. When they were done, the patriarch of the tribe stepped forward, unfolded a sheepskin, and with the help of two young men hung it from a branch of the largest oak and stretched it out with cords pegged to the ground, revealing the intricate pattern painted on it in red and black. All this was done with as much reverence as a priest setting a chalice of consecrated wine upon the altar. A brazier was set up in front of the sheepskin, and a fire lit in it. Then the men sat facing it, and David and I sat with them, stripped to the waist but not painted, shivering in the crisp cold of the mountain air – shivering with excitement, too. Pipes were lit and passed around, and that was where I tasted for the first time the drug from the plant that the Kefidis called haka.

'The patriarch recited a long story in the language of his tribe, and at some point I saw that the pattern on the sheepskin stretched above our congregation, lit by the flickering fire in the brazier, had come alive. It is the only way I can describe it. I looked away, and it was with me still. It was inside my head. David was smiling blissfully while tears ran down his cheeks, and so were the men around us. And then the music and the dancing began.

'If you have ever seen the dances of the Mevlevî dervishes, or the ritual flagellations of the Shi'ite Muslims on the day that celebrates the martyrdom of their saint, you will have some idea of those dances. The mountain people did not flagellate themselves, but when they danced around the fire that burned on the rock shelf, tossing flames higher than the tops of the oaks, there was the same wild abandon, as if every man had given himself utterly to the dance. Until it seemed, as T.S. Eliot once put it, that they were nothing more nor less than the still point of the turning world. Or as in Yeats's poem about the leaves of a chestnut tree fluttering in summer wind and sunlight, it was no longer possible to tell the dancer from the dance. It was a ritual that seemed as old as the human species. It took us outside of time. We were in neither the past nor the present nor the future . . .'

After a moment, Alfie said, 'These people, the Kefidis – do you think that Morph is one of them?'

Julius Ward focused on him. 'The Kefidis no longer exist. I returned to Iraq after the Second World War, but as a saboteur rather than an archaeologist. At the time, there was considerable unrest in the north-east of Iraq. The Kurds were threatening to start a war of independence, and they had the support of the Soviet Union. Britain sent in troops to make sure that the oilfields were secure. David Prentiss and I went too, to destroy the source of the glyphs in case they fell into the hands of the Soviets. We brought down a section of the cliff, and we blocked up the outlet of a stream that ran through part of the cave system. The whole place was buried and flooded. We dug up Father Anselm's stele too, and brought it back to the Nomads' Club.'

Alfie wondered if they still had it, if he could see it.

'Alas, it was destroyed when the Nomads' Club was burned down,' Clarence Ashburton said. 'The stones fell through into the basement when the floor gave way, and the fall and the heat of the fire shattered them. The original of your grandfather's journal was lost too, and so much else . . .'

Julius Ward said, 'After we had flooded the caves and sealed the entrance, we went to look for the Kefidis. But there had been outbreaks of partisan fighting throughout the region, and it seemed that the neighbours of the Kefidis had taken the opportunity to massacre them. I suppose it is possible that this graffiti artist of yours is a descendant of someone who escaped the massacre and kept the old traditions alive, but until I meet him I cannot say for certain that he is.'

Clarence Ashburton said, 'All these years, we have believed that only the Nomads' Club knew the secret of the glyphs. In 1939, Julius and David returned from Iraq with the story of their adventures among the Kefidis, and they also brought back seeds and dried leaves of haka. Soon we had all been educated in the true nature of the glyphs, and that was the beginning of our downfall.'

'We experimented with haka, and we experimented with the glyphs,' Julius Ward said. 'Fortunately, most of the glyphs we had discovered were not particularly potent, but we were young, yes, and foolish, and full of curiosity. We saw too much.'

'And at one time we were working for the war effort,' Clarence Ashburton said. 'It wasn't all foolishness. It had a point to it then.'

'Not a very effective one,' Julius Ward said.

'We agree to disagree,' Clarence Ashburton said.

Alfie, remembering that his grandmother had met his grandfather while he had been working for SOE during the war, said, 'You were spies.'

'Officially, we have never worked for any government agency, except in an advisory capacity,' Clarence Ashburton said. He was gently patting the air beside his chair, and when he found the edge of the tray on top of the hassock he leaned over and carefully set down his empty brandy glass.

'Unofficially,' Julius Ward said, 'the glyphs made a significant contribution to the war effort. That's why the anomalous stone was removed from the British Museum, you see. They were especially useful during interrogation sessions of captured spies – use of haka and the fascination glyph helped to smash the Nazi spy ring in Britain, and helped to turn many of those spies into double agents who fed false or misleading information back to their controllers.'

Clarence Ashburton said, 'There was a glyph that cast what your grandfather, Mr Flowers, liked to call "glamour" on documents in which it was embedded. Just as fairy glamour in the old stories could make glass seem to be jewels or stones gold, this glyph helped made fake documents seem authentic. Another caused distraction, preventing those affected by it from concentrating on a single thread of thought; a third affected the deep part of our brain that generates fear, just as the markings of a poisonous snake automatically make us step away from it, even though we may not know why. But although their effects were statistically significant in the mass, the glyphs had only a very mild effect on any individual exposed to them without the benefit of haka. After the Second World War, their use was abandoned. The Nomads' Club continued to have links with the secret service, but we were considered to be old school, gentlemen spies, eccentric relics of an earlier age.'

Julius Ward said, '"Eccentric" is a kind way of putting it. To be blunt, we have spent altogether too much time studying the glyphs, and over the years our work has exacted its toll. I can no longer eat solids, and must subsist on broth and this blasted drip. Clarence is blind, although it's a peculiar kind of blindness, what the psychiatrists call blindsight. If you make to slap him in the face, for instance, he'll flinch from the blow, but he won't do it consciously. His eyes work perfectly well, but his mind doesn't register what they see. Your grandfather, Mr Flowers, and Harriet's grandfather, they weren't so badly affected. Perhaps they were obsessive about the glyphs, but nothing beyond that. And your father mostly kept away from 'em. By the time he was old enough to join the Nomads, we knew what they could do to a man.'

Alfie said, 'It didn't end after the Second World War, did it? When my father disappeared he was on some kind of business or mission to do with the glyphs.'

'He already knows half of it,' Toby said, splashing more brandy into his glass. 'You'd better tell him the rest.'

'It was a bad business,' Julius Ward said. 'Almost as bad as this.'

'We really should not talk about it,' Clarence Ashburton said.

'Oh, I rather think that the statute of limitations has run out by now,' Julius Ward said.

'It never runs out where affairs like that are concerned,' Clarence Ashburton said.

Julius Ward dipped most of his face into his balloon of brandy, like a hummingbird feeding at a flower, took a sip, and said, 'The boy deserves to know.'

'Nevertheless, this is a matter of national security.'

'It may have been a matter of national security during the Cold War, but the Cold War is over,' Julius Ward said. 'In fact, as we now know, it was over before it began. The Russians were a threat only because we made them a threat. Most of their so-called deterrence was no more than hollow posturing. It took us forty years to discover that, and the lives of many of my friends. And the life of my son, too. Mr Flowers, would you promise not to mention any of what you learn here outside this room? And you too, Mr Brown.'

'Of course,' Alfie said.

Toby Brown said cheerfully, 'Imagine I'm not here.'

Julius Ward said, in that steady voice that seemed so at odds with his shrunken body, 'Unless you have a copy of the Official Secrets Act to hand, Clarence, I believe that will suffice. When your father disappeared, Mr Flowers, he was indeed engaged on a vital mission. He was working with my son, who was also a member of the Nomads. A dealer in black-market antiquities was offering what he called a unique carved stone for sale, and we discovered that the pattern with which it was engraved was identical to that on your grandfather's anomalous stone, Anselm's stele, and the original that was by now buried in the caves in the Zagros Mountains. Our first thought was that someone had found those caves. But according to the dealer it had been discovered at the site of an ancient monastery in eastern Syria, close to the border with Turkey.'

Clarence Ashburton said, 'It seems that the sect did not have two places of worship, as we had supposed, but at least three.'

Julius Ward said, 'In any case, the stone had made its way to Lebanon. My son and your father posed as potential buyers and made a bid for it, but were trumped by a man they believed to be working for the Soviets. After they were unsuccessful in their attempts to interest the British secret services, my son and your father decided to take matters into their own hands, and blew up the stone and the place where it was being stored. But the Soviets had their revenge. My son and your father were lured across the border into Syria with the promise that they would be taken to the place where the stone was found. Then they disappeared. After *perestroika* I learned from a colonel in the KGB that they had been ambushed and shot dead, and their bodies burned in the desert. I'm sorry, Mr Flowers, but there it is.'

'It was over twenty years ago,' Alfie said, but he felt the hook in his heart twist again.

Julius Ward said, 'As soon as they learned about us, the Soviets moved against the Nomads' Club itself. They ransacked and set fire to my son's home and your father's flat, and did the same to our premises in Soho. It was a very bad time . . .'

He paused, looking at something inside his head.

Alfie was thinking about the blackened piece of stone that his father had given Miriam Luttwak, that she had then given to him, and wondered if it was a fragment of the much larger stone that his father had destroyed. 'Some people will tell you that when you're in the middle of the shit, you don't have time to be afraid,' Mick Flowers had once told Alfie, during one of their rare father-son talks about his photojournalism. 'It isn't true. But if you fix on what you have to do, you can deal with your fear. You can put it to one side and get on with what you have to do.' Alfie thought now of his father, racing across the desert with his friend towards the Syrian border in an open-top car, not the Morgan but definitely some kind of sports car, a white scarf around his neck, his blond hair blown back by a hot wind, doing what he had to do without hesitation.

'It was a very bad time,' Clarence Ashburton said again. 'It was the end of the last vestige of any influence the Nomads' Club had with the government and the secret services. That was when we decided that we should withdraw from the sphere in which we had once been active, and allow ourselves, as it were, to wither on the vine.'

Alfie said, 'But here we are. It's still going on. You discovered the glyphs, my father died because you wanted to keep them secret, but now someone else knows about them.'

Toby said, 'This guy, the one who tried to kidnap us. Christ, who *did* kidnap us, at gunpoint. He's the psychiatrist who's treating Harriet's father's psychiatrist. And Harriet's father was using the glyphs in the cult he founded after he moved to America and started to call himself Antareus.' Toby was on his fourth or fifth glass of brandy, speaking carefully but lucidly. Looking at the two old men, saying, 'All that's part of your history too, right? What I'd like to know is, what does this guy want? What does he want with Morph, with the glyphs? What does he want with us? So let's cut to the chase and talk about him. Talk about what we're going to do about him. I mean, you brought us here to protect us, but we can't stay here for ever.'

Julius Ward said, 'Harriet?' Turning his head to look at her and saying her name again, more urgently.

At first sight, she seemed to have fallen asleep. Slumped stiffly in the wing armchair, her blonde hair loose around her slack face. But her eyes were wide open, staring at nothing at all, a strong regular tremor was passing through her body, and her hands – when Alfie saw this, he started to his feet, realizing that she wasn't asleep at all – were fluttering in her lap like panicked birds.

21

Afterwards, when Harriet's seizure had passed from rigid tremors to lax sleepy confusion and she had been put to bed (Julius Ward had unhooked himself from his drip and had gone upstairs to tend to her, the tartan shawl still wrapped around his shoulders as he laboriously climbed the staircase step by step), Alfie sat with Graham Taylor at one end of a long refectory table in the big, old-fashioned kitchen. Toby sat at the other end with one of the men who were guarding the house, sharing a takeaway pizza with him, sipping brandy and Coke. Definitely drunk now, but holding up his end of the conversation as he talked with the burly man about his recent spell in Iraq where he'd worked as a bodyguard for oil company executives. An automatic pistol, a big Mag-Lite flashlight and a walkie-talkie lay on scarred pine next to a stack of pizza boxes and a laptop whose screen flipped through different views of the exterior of the house and its garden in fuzzy whites and greys. Now and then the walkie-talkie emitted little staticky bursts, the men on watch outside talking to each other.

Alfie told Graham that Harriet would be fine. 'All I ever wanted to do after one of my major seizures was sleep. And after a few hours' sleep I would be back to normal.'

'She pushed herself too hard,' Graham said, and told Alfie that when he'd picked Harriet up at Blackfriars Bridge after Rölf Most had let her go, she'd been weaving on her feet and muttering to herself like a punch-drunk boxer. 'She refused to talk about it, but I know that this Dr Most did something bad to her. I think he injected her with some sort of drug, something to make her talk. She managed to pull herself together, but the effort just about finished her off — you saw how she was after she came out of the gallery, after she'd discovered that Larry Macpherson had killed the owner. I shouldn't have let her go in. I should have checked it out myself, but she's too bloody headstrong for her own good,' the private detective said. He blew on his mug of coffee before taking a sip. His suit jacket was hung on the back of his chair and his shirtsleeves were rolled up above his elbows, showing the blurred blue tattoo of a swallow on his forearm.

Alfie liked the man. His amiable, creased face reminded him of the comedian who'd been in just about every *Carry On* movie, and he seemed dependable, straightforward, and pretty much bombproof. Graham studied Alfie over the rim of his coffee mug, his eyes, pouched under brows like black brush strokes, weary but alert, and said, 'You should get some rest. You're safe enough here. These lads are all ex-special forces. I bet they cost an arm and a leg, but they seem to know what they're doing.'

'I'm a little too agitated to be able to sleep right now,' Alfie said. He felt fragile, ghostly, in the bright light of the kitchen. Things had gone badly, hopelessly wrong: he'd taken a wrong turning and there seemed to be no way out. He'd learned everything he'd ever wanted to know about the glyphs, but nothing he'd learned was in any way useful, and he'd been told that what they'd done to him was irreversible. And while he sat here, while Harriet Crowley lay in a post-seizure stupor, Rölf Most was chasing down Morph . . .

Alfie asked Graham what he knew about the glyphs, but the private detective shook his head and said that all he knew was that Harriet had hired him to run a surveillance operation on some bad guys.

'Very bad guys too,' he said, and told Alfie about Larry Macpherson's colourful history.

Alfie asked him about Rölf Most and the other psychiatrist, Carver Soborin.

'I never laid eyes on Dr Soborin,' Graham said, 'and Harriet didn't tell me much about him. I got the idea that he was sort of helpless, that he was more or less dependent on Dr Most. As for Dr Most, you met the guy, you probably know as much about him as I do.'

Alfie remembered the white-haired man peering in at him after he'd been tied up and ordered at gunpoint to lie on one of the bench seats inside the people-carrier. The way he'd cocked his head while he studied Alfie, his bright, birdlike stare, the little lopsided smile when he'd said, 'I am very much looking forward to an intimate chat.' Presumably, Alfie thought, the same kind of chat he'd had with Shareef and Watty, one which would have ended with a command to kill himself.

He told Graham Taylor, 'One of Harriet's friends said that the man is insane. I can believe it.'

They got to talking about Harriet Crowley. Graham Taylor told Alfie that she had worked for him before she'd set up on her own, that she'd been the best operative he'd ever had.

'She was a quick learner, and absolutely fearless. She'd stand up to anyone. My firm deals with fairly routine stuff, mostly surveilling people trying to claim for permanent damage caused by work-related injury – you'd be surprised how many people try it on with insurance firms or their employers – but she gave it everything she had. After she'd learned all she could from me, she went into business for herself. She specializes in skip-tracing – looking for people who don't want to be found. People who do a moonlight flit, leaving the rent unpaid, running out on credit-card and utility bills . . . People who use false addresses to set up credit-card and store-card accounts – there's more and more of that happening, enough to keep anyone in full-time employment. And she takes on heartbreakers, too, the kind of cases most of us won't touch. Husbands who've disappeared after popping out for a packet of cigarettes. People who can't stand their lives for whatever reason, and go out to work one day and don't come back. And the worst of all the heartbreakers: missing kids. Runaways. She spends a lot of time around King's Cross, places I wouldn't go near after dark. You know about her father?'

'A little.'

'Did you know that he walked out on her when she was very young? And later on he killed himself?'

Alfie nodded.

'Any psychologist would probably tell you that she's been looking for him ever since. That all these missing husbands and missing kids are surrogates. That by mending other broken families she's trying to fix what she can't ever fix for herself, and so on. Anyone who spends five minutes with her would know it was bullshit. What it is, Alfie, is that she has this absolute sense of right and wrong,' Graham said. 'Which means that sometimes she can be a real pain in the neck, because most people slip a little, especially when doing the right thing is the hardest thing to do. She gets a look, maybe you've seen it.'

'Sort of full on.'

'Exactly. When she makes up her mind, that's it, don't waste your time trying to change it. But the other side of it is that she'll give you her full attention, she'll listen to whatever you have to say. Plus, once she commits, she commits. She brought you here, maybe she told you things you didn't especially want to hear, but she did it because she thought that it was necessary.'

Graham was telling Alfie a story about a marathon investigation involving work-dodging employees in the mail room of British Telecoms headquarters who were using their employer's facilities to run a fan club for the Kray twins, when Alfie's mobile phone rang.

It was George Johnson. He was at the yard. Alfie's caravans had been burgled.

Alfie insisted on going there at once. Although George had told him that it didn't look like his safe had been touched, he was afraid that the photocopy of his grandfather's journal had been taken; from the little he'd learned about Larry Macpherson, it seemed quite possible that the man could have cracked the safe, taken everything in it, and locked it again. Toby Brown was too crocked, Harriet Crowley had been knocked out by the powerful sedative that Julius Ward had given her, and none of the men guarding the house could be spared, so Graham Taylor volunteered to drive him to Islington.

Graham reckoned that Larry Macpherson or Rölf Most or whoever else might have broken into Alfie's place would be long gone, but he circled around the block anyway, the gun he'd taken from the driver of the people-carrier lying in his lap. When Graham was satisfied that it was safe, Alfie got out of the Peugeot and unlocked the chain around the gates, followed the car into the yard, shut the gates and padlocked the chain. It was well after midnight. The lights of a few insomniacs burned here and there in the houses that backed onto the yard, a police siren twisted somewhere in the distance, but otherwise the city was as dark and quiet as it ever got. When Graham Taylor climbed out of the Peugeot and shut the door, it seemed as loud as a gunshot.

The noise woke George Johnson, who had fallen asleep in one of the plastic chairs outside the big garage. After Alfie had introduced him to Graham Taylor, George said that whoever had broken into the caravans had tried to break into his workshop too, and had set off the burglar alarm.

'The police have been and gone,' he said. His fists were shoved into the sagging pockets of his cardigan. He looked belligerent and sleepy. 'A couple of kiddie cops who gave me the usual bollocks. Took them all of five minutes to look around, then they gave me a crime number, told me to tell you to make a list of what had been taken and get in touch with the cop shop. I said what about DNA or even good old-fashioned fingerprinting, and they said it was hardly the crime of the century, probably a junkie looking for something he could unload in a hurry to buy his next fix.'

Alfie took a crowbar and an inspection lamp from the tool locker, pried up the manhole, and in the light of the lamp spun the safe's tumbler back and forth. George helped him heave the safe's heavy door back on its hinges, and his heart lifted on a flood of relief when he saw the Marks and Spencer carrier bag which contained his grandfather's diaries and journal. He pulled the bag out, kicked the safe's door shut, the solid noise echoing off the girders of the pitched roof, and levered the manhole cover back into place.

The lock of the door of the caravan which housed his darkroom had been forced. Its floor was covered in papers, negatives and contact sheets pulled from the drawers of his filing cabinets, but none of the equipment had been touched, which Alfie thought was highly significant. A junkie would have taken at least one of the cameras, or the little stereo system and Alfie's collection of CDs. The box in which he'd stored the prints of Morph's graffiti that he'd made was lying among the litter of papers on the floor, but a brief search failed to turn up the prints, and he was certain that they and the negatives had been taken. The caravan in which he had his living quarters was in a similar state: every cupboard and storage crate had been opened and everything in them had been tipped onto the floor, including a cardboard box full of stuff that his last girlfriend still hadn't collected.

He dumped his grandfather's journal and diaries into a holdall, threw in a couple of shirts and a random assortment of underwear, his razor and toothbrush, and told George he might be away for a few days.

'Are you in trouble?'

'It's nothing to do with the police.'

'That's not what I asked,' George said patiently.

'Old family business, partly.'

'What can I do to help?'

'Could you keep an eye on the yard for me? I don't think there'll be any more trouble – they found what they were looking for. But if you spot anyone shady, anyone you think is watching the place, anything like that, call the police. Don't try to deal with them yourself.'

'I take it you don't think this was an ordinary break-in.'

'I'll explain everything when I get back,' Alfie said.

Graham Taylor called softly. He was standing in the deep shadow of the ragged line of bushes and trees that bordered the yard, and pointed across the railway cutting when Alfie stepped up beside him. Alfie saw two, three, four shadows slip over the fence at the edge of the park on the other side of the cutting and begin to make their way down the steep slope. One lost his footing and rolled all the way to the bottom, got up and started straight across the railway lines. A moment later, someone began to rattle the gates at the entrance to the yard.

George said, sounding remarkably calm, 'Whoever they are, it looks like they came mob-handed.'

Graham said, 'I suggest we take our leave, gentlemen. The question is, how can we unlock those gates without letting in the unfriendlies?'

Alfie said, 'Can't you drive the car straight through them?'

'If I had a bigger car, and if you hadn't wrapped an anchor chain around them.'

'I'll deal with it,' Alfie said.

He tossed his camera bag and holdall into the back seat of the Peugeot, dashed back to the garage, unhooked the weed-burner, slung it over his shoulder and ran out, following the car as it moved forward across the concrete apron. Two figures were pulling at the gates, hands hooked through the mesh strung across their metal frames, swinging them back and forth in the short arc allowed by the padlocked chain. When Graham switched on the Peugeot's headlights, the men screwed up their eyes against the glare and redoubled their efforts.

Alfie saw ragged, layered clothes, lank hair tangled around faces blackened by ingrained dirt. Hands clutching at the wire mesh like starfish. Mouths opening and closing without a sound. Their friends were rattling the tall boundary fence along the top of the railway cutting now. The trees and bushes bordering it were shaking and rustling as if caught in a high wind. Alfie snatched up the cigarette lighter that dangled at the end of a yard of string tied to the strap of the weed-burner, cracked the fuel valve. The propane lit with a solid thump and Alfie opened the fuel valve as far as it would go, swept the yard-long spear of blue flame across the hands that clutched at the gates. The two men howled like dogs and staggered backwards, trying to shake off the flames that clung to their sleeves. Alfie managed to jab the key into the padlock that fastened the loop of heavy chain, but had to let go when one of the men lurched forward and tried to grab him. George stepped up and swung the big wrench he'd taken from the garage, pivoting from his hips to deliver a solid roundhouse blow. The gates shuddered from top to bottom and the man fell flat on his behind, howling.

Alfie grabbed the padlock, twisted the key and kicked the gates open, then turned tail and ran for the Peugeot. A black Range Rover roared down the street, braking hard and blocking the gates, and a man burst out of the bushes at the edge of the yard and ran at Alfie, arms held stiffly by his sides, head lunging forward, running so fast that he couldn't stop when Graham reversed the Peugeot into his path. The running man slammed into the side of the car and fell on his back, but other men were emerging from the bushes now, converging on George as he jogged towards the fire engine. He swung his wrench at the nearest, missed. As momentum swung him halfway around, the man closed in and wrapped his arms around him. George head-butted him and broke

free, chopped the wrench in a short arc that connected with the
back of his assailant's head. The man dropped in a heap. George
swung the wrench back and forth, stepping forward as the other
men retreated, asking them breathlessly if they wanted a piece of
this, then threw it at them and made a dash for the fire engine,
pulled himself into its cab, slammed the door, and started it up.

Two men climbed out of the Range Rover which blocked the
entrance to the yard. One was the blond man who'd pulled a gun
on Alfie and Toby in the car park of the council estate; his
companion smiled at Alfie and shook his finger in front of his
face like a teacher admonishing a recalcitrant child, then raised
an arm to shield his eyes as the bright beams of the fire engine's
headlights caught him.

The fire engine was moving forward, gathering speed, swerving
past the little Peugeot, and the two men threw themselves left
and right as it smashed through the gate and hit the Range Rover
square in the side with a tremendous bang. It backed up a few
yards, then moved forward again, shoving the Range Rover out
of the way.

Alfie wrenched open the door of the Peugeot and fell inside.
Graham stamped down on the accelerator and the little car shot
through the narrow gap between the gatepost and the rear of the
fire engine, swinging through a hundred and eighty degrees as
Graham hauled on the handbrake, slamming over a speed bump
so hard that Alfie levitated off his seat, hit his head on the roof
and bit his tongue and saw a bright flash of white light. He
grabbed the handle above the door, saw that a ragged gang of
men were chasing headlong after the Peugeot. Graham took the
corner in third gear and said calmly, 'You better put on your seat
belt.'

The car rattled over two more speed bumps, flew across a mini-
roundabout.

As he tried to marry his seat belt's clip with its buckle, Alfie
said breathlessly, 'They're mopping up loose ends.'

Graham said, 'If they came here for you . . .'

Alfie said, 'They probably went after the Nomads' Club, too.'

Light flared – a bright glare overflowing the rear-view mirror.
Graham swore, and the Peugeot surged forward, all four wheels

off the ground for an airy moment when it shot over another speed bump, its engine howling as Graham changed down from fifth to third and swerved out onto Caledonian Road.

Caledonian Road, half-past midnight: cars and vans parked on either side under the orange glow of streetlamps, rows of dark shopfronts, a group of men outside a Turkish social club turning to watch as the Peugeot screamed past with the battered black Range Rover in hot pursuit. Graham drove at sixty miles an hour towards King's Cross, swerving onto the wrong side of the road again and again as he overtook slower vehicles. Alfie saw a queue of cars ahead, waiting at a set of traffic lights. Graham told him to brace himself and swerved out and drove straight across the junction, right in front of a bus that filled the window on Alfie's side with the glare of its headlights and the enraged howl of its horn. Then they were past, hurtling over the canal bridge. Alfie saw in his side mirror that the bus had stalled, blocking the junction, and told Graham that he could slow down.

'Are you kidding?'

The Peugeot blasted straight through green traffic lights at the junction with Pentonville Road, triggering the flash of a speed camera, and Graham barely slowed at the sharp right turn into the one-way system of the northern end of Gray's Inn Road, changing down to third again, using the handbrake to make a long sliding turn. That was when the Peugeot's offside tyre blew with a sharp explosion that Alfie thought for a moment was a gunshot. The nose of the little car dipped as it slewed sideways across four lanes, jolted over the kerb, thumped onto the pavement, and took out a telecom junction box with a flat bang that sounded exactly like the noise Watty had made when he'd struck the roof of the people-carrier. The doorpost beside Alfie buckled; the window exploded in a shower of sharp granules that stung his face and hands. Graham hauled hard on the steering wheel, dropped to second. The engine screamed and the cabin filled with the smell of burning oil. The blown tyre made a flapping noise as it shed strips of smoking rubber; the bare wheel rim sounded like an angle grinder, shooting a comet-tail of sparks.

Graham fought the steering wheel, but as he turned onto Euston Road the tyreless wheel locked up completely. The rear end of the Peugeot spun out and slammed into the dividing rail; the engine died and wouldn't start again; Graham shouted at Alfie, told him to run for it.

Alfie had to put all his weight against the buckled door to force it open. He clambered out awkwardly, his bruised knees aching stiffly. As he reached inside the car to grab his holdall and camera bag, the black Range Rover braked hard a dozen yards away, headlights blazing under the sharp orange light of the street-lamps. The doors opened on either side and the two men got out, taking their time. Graham, bracing himself against the roof of the Peugeot, shouted a warning, then fired a single shot into the air. Alfie ducked down, trying to make himself as small as possible. Graham shouted again, telling the men that if they took one more step he'd shoot to kill.

The black-haired man in the denim jacket smiled, reached behind himself and took out a chromed automatic pistol. Taking his time, letting Graham get off one more shot before he extended his arm and fired. Alfie saw Graham's head snap back, saw him collapse behind the Peugeot. On the far side of the road, under the canopy in front of King's Cross Station, people watched as the man in the denim jacket walked up to the Peugeot and stepped around its snub-nosed bonnet. Alfie shouted, a wordless denial, as the flash of the *coup de grâce* shot lit up the man's face.

22

Harriet woke in the musty guest-bedroom of Clarence Ashburton's house with a splitting headache, a sore tongue which she'd bitten during the seizure she didn't remember having, and a feeling of ineradicable dread. As she dressed by the light filtering through the dusty curtains, her fingers fumbling at buttons and snaps, she tried to remember going to bed. The two old men had been telling Alfie Flowers and Toby Brown about the discovery of the glyphs, and then . . . Then there was a blank, a gap. She went downstairs and found Toby Brown, Julius Ward and Clarence Ashburton in the study. Toby was kneeling between the armchairs in which the two old men sat, bent over a large-scale map of northern Iraq spread on the floor. Julius Ward was using his walking stick to point to something on the map.

'No way,' Harriet said.

Toby smiled up at her. 'Sleeping Beauty awakes.'

Julius Ward said, 'How are you feeling, my dear?'

Harriet told Toby, 'There's no way you're going anywhere near Iraq or the source of the glyphs. Don't even think about it. And where's Alfie Flowers?'

Toby said, 'I think you need to be brought up to speed,' and told her that last night Graham Taylor had driven Alfie to his yard after his tenant had called and told him that his caravans had been burgled, that Graham and Alfie had been ambushed by Rölf Most's men, and Alfie had been kidnapped. He paused, then said, 'I'm afraid that it gets worse. There's no easy way of saying this, so I'll say it straight, no chaser. Your friend Graham Taylor was shot dead.'

For a few moments it was quiet in the room, the three men waiting for Harriet to speak. Only Clarence Ashburton's blind, benevolent gaze was fixed anywhere near her face.

She said, squeezing the words past a dryness in her throat, 'Graham has a wife – an ex-wife. Also two teenage daughters. Do they know?'

Toby said that the police would have contacted them. Harriet found her way to a chair and listened numbly while he explained that Graham and Alfie had borrowed her Peugeot to drive over to Islington. The police had traced its ownership, and when they had discovered she wasn't at home, they'd called her mobile phone – the number was in the memory of Graham's mobile – and Julius Ward had answered.

'They had all kinds of questions for you,' Toby said, 'but Julius insisted that you were in no condition to speak to anyone.'

'Which was quite true,' Julius Ward said.

'They came around anyway,' Toby said, 'but the guy in charge of security convinced them to hold off.'

'You should have woken me up,' Harriet said.

'You were out cold,' Toby said. 'You slept right through everything.'

Julius Ward asked again how she was feeling. Did she have a headache, did she feel strange in any way, was she seeing any flashing lights?

That was when she learned that she'd had a full-blown epileptic seizure.

Clarence Ashburton cleared his throat and started to say that unfortunately that was not the end of the night's excitement, but Harriet couldn't take any more bad news, couldn't sit still for a moment longer. She felt that the walls were closing in around her, she needed to clear her head, and went for a long walk on Tooting Common, trailed at a discreet distance by Mark Mallett, the owner of the private security firm that was keeping watch on Clarence Ashburton's house. She walked very quickly, the hollow scraped in her chest by the news of Graham's death slowly filling with guilt and self-disgust, as a hole dug in wet ground will fill with muddy water.

It was a perfectly ordinary Saturday, the air balmy, big-bellied clouds sailing the sky, people walking their dogs, children running about, men playing a pick-up game of football. A dry ache swelled in Harriet's throat and she cried a little, hot angry tears that she wiped away with her sleeve as she walked. The small part of her mind not taken up with trying to comprehend the enormity of what had happened knew that the tears were only a symptom of her grief, not the real thing. The real thing would come later . . .

She walked back to the house, waited for Mark Mallett to catch up with her at the gate. He was a trim, middle-aged ex-SAS officer, his hands jammed in the pockets of his leather jacket as he walked up, his face a study of neutrality. She asked him what he'd told the police, and he said that she needn't worry, he'd played a dead bat.

'I told them that my men were providing security for Mr Ward and Mr Ashburton because a threat had been made on their lives. They wanted to know who had made it and why it hadn't been reported; I told them that the nature of the threat wasn't very clear, which was why, presumably, it hadn't been reported. They weren't very happy about it, especially when they had to come back an hour later. The detective inspector in charge rather got in my face, emphasized that he wanted to talk to you sooner rather than later.'

'Why did they come back?'

'Hasn't anybody told you what happened here?'

'What happened here? I thought it was at King's Cross.'

'They hit Mr Flowers's place, and a couple of hours later they hit this place too. Or tried to.'

Mark showed Harriet a sooty place on the concrete of the driveway, a patch of shrivelled grass. There had been two of them, he said. Two men who had set themselves on fire while running past the truck that blocked the drive, running straight at the front door.

'My man in the truck shot and wounded both of them, and by the time the other guys got to the scene he'd put both of them out with a fire extinguisher. Outstanding work in my opinion – if you want to pay him a bonus I'll happily pass it right along. Any idea why they tried to suicide-bomb this place?'

Harriet knew at once that they must have been low men, no doubt turned by Rölf Most's glyph gun, but she couldn't tell Mark that. She didn't tell the police, either. She spent most of Sunday afternoon in an interview room at Paddington Green police station, going over Friday night's events with two Special Branch officers, and didn't say a word about Rölf Most and Larry

Macpherson, the glyphs and the low men. The Special Branch officers showed her photographs of the corpses of the two men who had turned themselves into firebombs, trying to shock or shame her with close-ups of swollen faces, cracked charred skin. Telling her that one had been an Irish labourer of no fixed abode, the other a vagrant who hadn't been carrying any kind of identification.

Before the interview began, Harriet had secreted a pin between the second and third finger of her left hand, its point resting against the heel of her palm. When she felt herself beginning to be overcome by the horrors that the two Special Branch officers laid in front of her, she closed her hand and jabbed herself with the pin. The sharp little stabs of pain helped to keep her mind clear and focused. She thought of Larry Macpherson luring men to the Range Rover with the promise of drink or drugs, or simply snatching them off the street at gunpoint. Spraying the drug up their nostrils, taping back their eyelids. And Rölf Most leaning forward, the glyph gun in his hand . . .

She jabbed herself with the pin, told the Special Branch officers that she'd never seen the men before, had no idea why they had set themselves on fire. They said that another man, a drug addict with a string of convictions for petty theft, had been badly injured at Mr Flowers's property, and was currently lying in a coma in the Royal Free Hospital. They showed her his photograph, asked her if she had seen him before. They showed her footage of Graham Taylor's murder culled from CCTV cameras around King's Cross, three short, grainy movies shot from different angles, all with the same horrible ending. They showed her photographs of Graham Taylor's body, crumpled between the flank of her car and a set of railings, his head turned sideways, his face resting in a glossy pool of blood. They laid photographs of Larry Macpherson and his blond accomplice in front of her and asked her if she knew anything about these men, asked her why they had shot and killed Graham Taylor, why they had snatched Alfie Flowers.

Harriet used the pin, held in her shock and grief and anger, gave non-committal answers. The Special Branch officers made it clear that they didn't believe that she was cooperating fully, and at the end of the interview told her that although they had no reason at present to detain her, they would like to talk to her again very soon. Waiting a whole minute for her to say something, both of them looking hard into her face, before they dismissed her.

That evening, her MI6 handler, Jack Nicholl, called. 'We need to talk. Same place as before, eight a.m. sharp.'

Harriet started to ask him if he knew where Rölf Most was, but he'd already cut the connection.

They met at the restaurant in St James's Park and took a leisurely stroll around the lake. Jack Nicholl listened carefully to Harriet's second-hand story about the siege of Alfie Flowers's yard, the car chase, Graham Taylor's execution. When she had finished, he said, 'The SB officers showed me the footage of your friend's murder. Very nasty.'

Larry Macpherson had paused before firing the shot that had killed Graham Taylor. Looking around, finding a camera pointed at him and smiling straight into it, a cold cruel feral smile that bared all his teeth. Harriet had no doubt that he wanted her to know that he'd shot and killed her friend. That he was taunting her, daring her to follow him. She was also certain that that was why the two low men had been dispatched against Clarence Ashburton's house.

She said, 'Are Rölf Most and Larry Macpherson still in the country?'

'They left two hours after your friend was shot, a private jet out of Biggin Hill. It stopped in Athens to refuel. The pilot signed the fuel bill on the apron, no one else got on or off. And then it flew on to south-east Turkey.'

'To Diyarbakir.'

Jack Nicholl looked at her. It was a sunny morning, and his eyes were masked with tinted sunglasses. A copy of the *Daily Telegraph* was tucked under one arm.

She said, 'That's where Musa Karsu and his father were living before they came here. They fled from Iraq to Turkey, Musa Karsu's father was arrested and spent time in prison, and when he was released they came to London.'

'The plane landed at Kaplaner airport in Diyarbakir at around eight-thirty in the morning local time, and left an hour later, heading south-east. And that's all we know. We don't have anyone who could get to the airport in time to see who got on or off after the plane arrived, and we didn't think it would be a good idea to involve the local police. And although we are fairly sure that the plane headed for Iraq after it left Diyarbakir, I'm afraid that we don't know exactly where it ended up. Flights into and out of Iraq are still under US military control, and we thought it prudent not to ask them, given Mr Macpherson's CIA connection.'

Harriet said, 'It probably went to Mosul. From there, it's just a short drive up into the mountains to the place where the Nomads' Club discovered the glyphs.'

After a beat, Jack Nicholl said, 'I think that's more than likely. Shall we sit down?'

They sat on a bench, looking towards the lake where a low jet of white water pulsed. Geese quarrelled over crusts of bread that someone had scattered on the grassy bank. Smartly dressed men and women walked past, carrying briefcases and attaché cases and laptops towards their offices. One man wore a bowler hat, a rare and notable sight these days, even in Whitehall.

Harriet said, 'Alfie Flowers was right. Benjamin Barrett and Musa Karsu had a falling-out, or perhaps Musa Karsu got frightened. Perhaps he saw the low men watching Benjamin Barrett's flat, and knew what they were, what they implied. So he fled. He went back to where he came from.'

Jack Nicholl nodded. 'The trouble is, there are a dozen ways he could have left the country. I'm running a check on the obvious places – airports and Eurostar and so on – but so far nothing has come up. He could have bought a foot-passenger ticket for a cross-Channel ferry, or taken one of those coaches that takes about five days to get to Istanbul if you're lucky enough to catch one that doesn't break down along the way. Or he could have hitched a ride on one of the fishing boats that make most of their money smuggling people in the opposite direction. That is, if he did go back. Which we still don't know for sure.'

'We don't know for sure, but Rölf Most knew,' Harriet said. 'He went to Diyarbakir because Benjamin Barrett must have told him that Musa Karsu had gone there.'

'I managed to extract a big favour from our friend in MI5. She's having her informant ask around on our behalf. If he finds anything, she can tell you this afternoon,' Jack Nicholl said, and patted the copy of the *Daily Telegraph* which he'd laid on the bench between them. 'You'll find something of interest in there. And if you decide to act on it, don't for Christ's sake tell me.'

'I understand.'

'As far as my people are concerned, the matter is over. Rölf Most and Larry Macpherson have left the country, they're someone else's problem. I don't happen to agree with that, but . . .'

'But your hands are tied.'

'It's a filthy business,' Jack Nicholl said, staring towards the lake. 'Three outright murders, not to mention the men they turned. The two poor bastards who set themselves alight, the man in a coma, and the others too. They're all going to die, aren't they?'

'Low men don't last very long. The metabolic changes are irreversible.'

Jack Nicholl shook his head, repeated, 'A filthy business. I really don't want to know what you plan to do, Harriet. But when it's all over, perhaps you'll let me buy you a drink, and we can talk about it off the record.'

'I'd like that,' Harriet said, and discovered that she meant it.

'Whatever you do, be careful,' Jack Nicholl said.

After he'd gone, Harriet picked up the copy of the *Daily Telegraph* and took a long, meandering stroll through the West End. When she was as certain as she could be that she wasn't being followed, she sat in a Starbucks and looked at the two pieces of paper that had been folded into the newspaper. One gave her the time and place for a meeting with Susan Blackmore, the MI5 agent who handled the Kurdish informant, Şivan Ergüner. The other was an infrared satellite photograph of mountainous terrain. A narrow valley was circled in red grease pencil. An arrow pointed to a cluster of tiny white lozenges labelled *Vehicles*.

On the other side of the photograph was a brief note in a firm clear hand.

Taken by Quick Bird satellite, 0620 GMT Monday 7 June. I think you know where this is, Harriet. I'm afraid that the bastards are knocking at the front door of your grandfather's old playground.

Susan Blackmore had some positive news. Harriet met her at one of MI5's semi-clandestine offices, a warren of dismal rooms in what had once been a business that supplied cheeses to restaurants, close to Holborn Viaduct. She told Harriet that Şivan Ergüner had found someone who was looking after Musa Karsu's meagre possessions. 'Musa Karsu left them with his friend last Tuesday. He said that he had to go back home.'

Harriet said, 'Did he say where, exactly?'

'He thinks somewhere in Turkey.'

'Did he say anything about Diyarbakir? It's a city in south-eastern Turkey.'

'He didn't mention any place in particular.'

'Does this friend know how Musa Karsu planned to get there?'

Susan Blackmore shook her head. 'Apparently, Musa was in something of a state. He dumped his stuff, told his friend to look after it until he got back, and took off.'

'What did he leave behind?'

Susan Blackmore consulted her notebook. 'Some clothes, a portable TV, a box full of pens and spray-paint cans, comic books. Nothing of any significance, according to Şivan.'

Harriet spent a little time with a travel agent and discovered that there were half a dozen ways to get to Turkey. By road or by rail, by ferry from Venice, Brindisi or Trieste, by ferry or hydrofoil from Greece. If someone couldn't afford or didn't dare to use a direct flight from London, it would take them several days to reach Turkey, and at least another day to cross the country to reach Diyarbakir, perhaps much longer than that if they hitched. Which meant that there was an outside chance that Musa Karsu was still travelling, that she could reach Diyarbakir before he did . . .

When Harriet returned to Clarence Ashburton's house, Toby Brown was waiting for her, eager to share some news. He'd leaned on his ex-wife, who worked for Amnesty International, and she had discovered that not only had the charity organized a letter-writing campaign on behalf of Musa Karsu's father and a dozen other men after they had been arrested by the Turkish police on the same trumped-up charge, but that a prominent community leader in Diyarbakir had also been trying to help them.

'Musa Karsu must know this guy,' Toby said, after Harriet had told him what she had learned from Susan Blackmore. 'If he really has gone back to Diyarbakir, he might have turned to him for help. And even if he didn't, I bet this guy knows his friends, and will have some idea about where he might be staying.'

Harriet admitted that it was a good lead, that it gave her a chance to find the boy before Rölf Most and Larry Macpherson did.

'You mean that it gives *us* a good chance,' Toby said, and with a flourish produced two airline tickets to Diyarbakir. He told her that Clarence Ashburton had contacted an old friend of his who could help them out, an archaeologist who'd lived and worked in Turkey for more than thirty years. 'We'll find Musa Karsu, and figure out some way of dealing with the bad guys who are looking for him. Use the kid as bait to flush them out if we have to, go to the local police, anything to find out where they've stashed poor old Alfie.'

As far as Toby was concerned, it was a done deal. Harriet decided to go along with it, but she didn't tell him that his friend was by now almost certainly dead, murdered after Rölf Most had mined him for everything he knew. She didn't tell him about the satellite photograph either, didn't tell him that it was very likely that Rölf Most was even now excavating the system of caves beneath the ruined church where the glyphs had been discovered. She'd help the journalist look for Musa Karsu in Diyarbakir – two days should be long enough to find out if the boy had returned home – and then she would ditch him and head for Iraq, the Zagros Mountains, and the source of the glyphs. She wasn't certain what she'd do when she got there, but she was fairly sure that she wouldn't be coming back. She cashed out her savings account, and changed most of it into US dollars. According to one of Mark Mallett's security men, an ex-SAS soldier who had spent several months working in post-invasion Iraq as a bodyguard, it would be easy to get hold of weapons and explosives in Iraq. The place was littered with them.

Harriet knew that she was doing this because Larry Macpherson had goaded her.

She knew that she was doing this to avenge Graham Taylor's murder.

She knew that she was doing this as some kind of atonement for her father's betrayal of the Nomads' Club.

She didn't care.

PART TWO
THE SOURCE

23

Harriet and Toby were more than seven hours in the air, with a two-hour layover at Istanbul because there were no direct flights between London and Diyarbakir. For much of the time, Toby frowned his way through a fat biography of Sir Henry Wotton (1568–1639), a gentleman poet famously sent abroad to lie for the good of his country, making cryptic jottings in a small spiral-bound notebook, topping up his complimentary orange juice with vodka that he'd bought in Heathrow's duty-free shop. Beside him, Harriet rehearsed over and again their cover story and her plans, looking for flaws, trying to work out all the angles, trying to convince herself that they wouldn't be ambushed as soon as they arrived, trying to work out what to do if they *were* ambushed. By the time they landed at Diyarbakir, her stomach was an acid knot, the headache which had never quite gone away after Rölf Most had zapped her with the glyph gun was thumping relentlessly in her temples, and she was seeing little flashes of internal lightning from the corners of her eyes and worrying that they were the early-warning signs of another full-blown seizure, that the glyphs had finally done permanent damage to her, just as they'd permanently damaged Clarence Ashburton and Julius Ward and Alfie Flowers. Just as they'd permanently damaged her father.

Their contact, Richard Elfingham, was waiting outside the arrivals gate. He was a couple of dozen years older than in the photograph of Clarence Ashburton's dear friend and former colleague that Harriet was carrying in the pocket of her jacket. A tall, stooped man in a safari suit, with an unruly corona of white hair and a lined and deeply tanned face, he was holding under his chin a piece of paper with Harriet's name printed on it in wobbly capitals for all the world to see.

Harriet's self-control evaporated in a quick flare of temper. She snatched the sheet of paper from the archaeologist, ripped it in half, crumpled the halves into the smallest possible ball, and flung it away from her as far as she could, as if she was trying to get rid of every petty annoyance that had distracted her ever since she'd woken up and found out that Graham Taylor had been shot and killed, and Alfie Flowers had been kidnapped.

Toby couldn't resist making a smart comment. 'Good move. We don't want to draw any attention to ourselves, do we?' he said, and introduced himself to the archaeologist, shaking his hand and thanking him for interrupting his work to come all the way out here to help a couple of strangers.

Richard Elfingham assured them that doing a favour for two colleagues of Clarence Ashburton was no problem at all. 'Any friend of Clarence is a friend of mine, and besides, I'm repaying a very large favour he did for me a few years ago. He scratches my back, I scratch yours, and round and round the world goes, hmm?'

Harriet shook his hand too, and apologized for her rudeness. Her anger had burnt itself out quickly, leaving only a sticky residue of embarrassment. 'You're not at fault: I am. I should have made it clear to you that there could be other people looking for the boy, people who mean him harm,' she said, then told Toby that she needed a private word with Dr Elfingham, and steered the archaeologist to one side.

'The other favour I asked of you,' she said. 'We need to talk about that later. Meanwhile, don't say anything about it to Mr Brown.'

Richard Elfingham laid a finger next to his nose. It was a noble, twice-broken nose that hooked to the left and gave him the profile of a Roman emperor. 'Don't worry. I haven't forgotten how we used to operate in the old days – wheels within wheels, need to know and all the rest. Everything's in order,' he said, in a hoarse whisper, 'and I won't say another word about it until we have a little privacy.'

The archaeologist led Harriet and Toby out of the small terminal building to a car park simmering in the late-afternoon heat, telling them that he'd found the fellow they wanted to talk to. 'It wasn't too hard. Mehmet Celik is a community leader, well known and well liked. If anyone can help you find this boy, he can. I arranged for you to meet him this evening, after prayers. Thought you'd want to do it sooner rather than later.'

Toby said to Harriet, grinning around a freshly lit cigarette, 'What did I tell you? Everything is going to be all right.'

Harriet said to Richard Elfingham, 'Did you tell Mehmet Celik why we want to talk to him?'

'Thought it best not to. If he does know where the boy is, he might well warn him that a couple of people from London are looking for him.'

Toby said, 'But we're the good guys. We're here to save the kid's life.'

Harriet said, 'He can't know that. You did the right thing, Dr Elfingham.'

Toby said, 'He'll want to help us after we've talked to him. The first part of our mission, it's a done deal.'

'Let's not count eggs and call them chickens,' Harriet said, but for the first time in four days she felt something relax inside her, a kinked nerve unkinking, a cramped muscle loosening. Perhaps Toby Brown was right. Perhaps everything was going to work out after all. Perhaps Mehmet Celik would roll over and introduce them to Musa Karsu, and Musa Karsu would agree to come back to London; or perhaps he wouldn't need to come back because he didn't really know anything about the glyphs, he'd simply reproduced the fascination glyph because he'd seen it somewhere and thought it looked good . . .

Richard Elfingham unlocked a filthy, battered Jeep Cherokee and drove them to their hotel. He was a terrifying driver, tailgating shamelessly and changing lanes on a whim, paying more attention to his passengers than to the road. Harriet hardly noticed. She spent most of her time checking the cracked wing-mirror: to see that they weren't being followed.

'Of course, if this fellow Mehmet Celik can't help you,' Richard Elfingham said, raising his voice to be heard against the flapping rush of muggy air at the open windows, 'you two are going to have a very interesting time of it, looking for a young refugee in Diyarbakir. Did you know that it's the fastest-growing city in Turkey?'

From the back seat, Toby said, 'I know it's where many of the Kurdish refugees from Iraq ended up.'

Richard Elfingham said, 'It's not only refugees from Iraq that have swollen the city's population. There are plenty of internal refugees too, from villages razed to the ground by the Turkish army during the Kurdish insurrection of the 80's and 90's.'

Toby said, 'The guerrilla war with the PKK.'

The two men showing off their knowledge of the world to each other, as men do.

Richard Elfingham said, 'They call themselves Kongra-Gel now, and the whole sorry business seems to be starting up again. Anyway, Diyarbakir is at the edge of the Tigris Basin, and the Tigris Basin is the heartland of the Kurdish separatist movement. After the Turkish army destroyed villages in an attempt to cut off the PKK's supply lines in the mountains, most of their inhabitants fled here, to the *gecekondü*, the shanty towns. And there are Palestinian and Iranian refugees too, not to mention refugees from Iraq. During the first Gulf War, a million Kurds just like this boy you're looking for crossed over the mountains from Iraq. I can't believe that he chose to come back here from London, by the way. To most of the people living here, London seems like paradise — so you can imagine how badly off they are, the poor sods.'

'As you know, people wanted to kill him, in London,' Toby said. 'That's why he came back here. That's why we came here, to help him out.'

When Harriet had talked to Richard Elfingham on the telephone, she'd told him that she and Toby Brown were coming to Diyarbakir to look for a young Kurdish refugee who had achieved a certain fame with his graffiti art. The boy had left London for some reason, she'd said, and she and Toby had been hired by the owner of an art gallery who wanted them to find the young artist and persuade him to return. Even though it borrowed promiscuously from the truth, she'd thought this cover story was threadbare when she and Toby had put it together, so full of holes that any moderately bright child would have had a hard time deciding which one to pick on first; fortunately, Richard Elfingham had chosen not to question it.

'If this boy is in some kind of trouble, this city is a good place to hide,' the archaeologist said. 'Two million people live here, and most of them are under twenty-five.'

The Cherokee had slowed to a crawl by now, caught up in

nose-to-tail traffic that with much flashing of headlights and horn music crept along a wide avenue. People crowded the pavements in front of shops plastered with advertisements for soft drinks and shampoo and baby food. Neon signs simmered in the soupy air. Graffiti looped across walls. Richard Elfingham translated some of the slogans. They wished long life to Apo. They claimed that Apo would soon be free. Apo was Abdullah Öcalan, the former leader of the PKK, imprisoned on the maximum-security prison island of Imrah under a sentence of death ('Not that the government will dare to carry it out,' Richard Elfingham said, 'now that they're so close to joining the European Union') while his name continued to spread out into the world.

The ancient city wall, partly shrouded in scaffolding, loomed in the distance against a setting sun that simmered balefully behind the layers of pollution. Richard Elfingham said that the wall had been built of black basalt by the Byzantines on top of the remains of the original Roman wall, and that it had inspired the city's lovely, sinister nickname, the Dark.

'So tell me, what do you think of this wonderful old city, hmm?'

Harriet had been with Toby Brown long enough to know that this was the perfect opening for one of his smart-arse quips. She turned to give him a warning look and he smiled at her, plucking the front of his black linen shirt from his pigeon chest, saying, 'What do I think? I think it's too damned hot; I'm sweating like a kiddie-fiddler in a Santa suit. This hotel we're going to – does it have air-conditioning?'

After checking in at the hotel, they ate an early supper in a tiny restaurant in a square at the edge of the city's clothes bazaar, lingering over tooth-piercingly sweet pastries and tiny cups of muddy coffee, killing time until their appointment with Mehmet Celik. Richard Elfingham kept the conversation flowing, reminiscing about archaeological work that he'd done with Clarence Ashburton in the 1960s, talking about his own work at Çatal Höyük. He was part of an international team that took up residence there each summer, working on complexes of Neolithic houses up to 9,000 years old that were crammed together like

the cells of a beehive because they had been built before streets
had been invented, and were entered through holes in their roofs.
There were burial chambers, animal-head trophies, wall paintings
of men being eaten by vultures, and the earliest known landscape
painting, which, anticipating the cliché of B-movies about
cavemen, depicted the eruption of a nearby volcano. Hundreds
of other smaller but no less crucial finds had helped to build up
a picture of one of the world's oldest civilizations.

Harriet wondered if the inhabitants of this fabulously ancient
settlement had known anything about the glyphs.

At last Toby announced that he had to go use the facilities, the
hole in the ground or whatever they had here, and Harriet could
talk with Richard Elfingham about the other subject they'd
discussed on the phone: her one-way trip to Iraq.

He told her that the actual arrangements had been made by
the fixer who had helped him organize an excavation in Diyarbakir
two years ago, when restoration work on the city wall had exposed
the foundations of a Roman gatehouse. 'He's a very sound man,
completely trustworthy. Expensive, of course, but these things are
relative. A hundred American dollars will do the trick as far as
he is concerned, and you'll need another two hundred to pay his
uncle, who can get you as far as a town called Zakho. That's only
a few kilometres inside Iraq, but apparently this uncle knows of
people in Zakho, taxi drivers and truck drivers and such, who
should be able to take you further. My friend says that there will
be no difficulty getting you across the border, but his uncle can't
guarantee your safety after that.'

'I can look after myself,' Harriet said.

Richard Elfingham studied her for a moment, then said, 'This
boy you're looking for must be very desperate indeed if he's
chosen to go back to Iraq. Let's hope that you find him here
instead, hmm?'

'Even if we do find him, I have other business to attend to in
Iraq. No matter what happens, the man who can get me across
the border has to pick me up the day after tomorrow.'

'At six a.m., as agreed.'

'And please, not a word of this to Mr Brown. He insisted on
coming here to help me find the boy, but for his own sake I don't

want him to go any further. After I'm gone, I'd be really grateful if you could do your best to make sure that he returns to England in one piece, but don't do anything that will put yourself in harm's way.'

Toby came back to the table, sitting down, sniffing his fingers, saying that he'd just taken a prizewinning dump and there was no bloody toilet paper in the place – he'd had to follow local custom and use his hand. He was more or less sober now. He'd taken a long cold shower at the hotel and was wearing brand-new tan Caterpillar boots, black Paul Smith jeans and a fresh black T-shirt under his crumpled black linen jacket. He had passed on the chance to sample the local beer during the meal, sticking to Pepsi-Cola instead. Harriet knew that he'd been wisecracking ever since they'd left Heathrow because he was trying to cover up his nerves with noise. But she also knew that, despite his smart mouth, he was clever and resourceful, and as determined as she was to find Musa Karsu, track down Rölf Most's people, and find out what had happened to his friend Alfie Flowers.

Maybe he'll get his chance. Harriet thought. But only here in Diyarbakir. There was no way he was coming with her to Iraq. She had enough deaths on her conscience already.

24

Richard Elfingham insisted that Mehmet Celik was a good man, a public figure famous for his work with the poor, but Harriet felt her stomach begin to knot up as they drove through one of Diyarbakir's shanty towns towards the community leader's office. The poverty was a shock: third-world, brutally squalid. The stink of woodsmoke and sewage infiltrated the Cherokee's air-conditioning as it moved slowly through narrow streets of open-fronted shops and shacks built of corrugated iron and breeze-blocks. It was close to nine in the evening, but everyone seemed to be out and about. Gangs of little boys chased alongside, knocking on the windows and calling out for *para*, calling out for *stilo*. For money, for pens. Boys in hand-me-down clothing were selling fruit and sweets and single cigarettes at street corners. Boys were cooking snacks on grills improvised from oil drums. Boys were serving tea from aluminium pots to passers-by. So far Harriet hadn't seen a single little girl, and most of the women wore headscarves or were wrapped from head to foot in black chadors. With her bare head, a long, loose man's shirt and an ankle-length skirt, she was beginning to feel as exposed as if she'd walked straight off the beach in a clinging swimsuit.

Richard Elfingham rapped sharply on his horn, and a boy in a ragged black robe dragged a donkey out of the way. The animal was almost completely hidden beneath a load of swollen white nylon sacks – only its muzzle and spindly legs were visible. The Cherokee surged past it and pulled up outside a row of shabby one-storey shops. A small boy wearing, of all things, a red Arsenal shirt that hung off his narrow shoulders and came down to his knees, trotted up and spoke to Richard Elfingham, who told Harriet and Toby that this was the right place. The boy led them through a shopfront that had been turned into an internet café, past teenagers and men hunched in front of old computers on rickety tables, most of them wearing headphones and playing shoot-'em-up video games, into the back room.

Mehmet Celik was a studious-looking man in his thirties, wearing blue jeans and a clean white shirt, the sleeves neatly rolled above his elbows. Standing up behind his bare metal desk, reaching across it to shake hands with Richard Elfingham and Toby, inclining his head to Harriet, then indicating the plastic stacking chairs in front of the desk and saying something in what Harriet supposed was Kurdish.

'I think he's saying that he's happy to see us,' Richard Elfingham said.

The man who had remained seated to one side of the desk, an older man with a stocky, wrestler's build and a brush of greying hair, said, 'Mehmet Celik says he is pleased to welcome you. He asks you to sit down. So please, sit down.'

A third man, a slender youth in a brand-new Adidas tracksuit, blue with a red stripe, leaned against a wall, his arms folded across his chest. The room was small and square and very hot, built of roughly mortared concrete blocks and lit by a single unshielded bulb that, dive-bombed by moths and beetles, dangled from the end of a cable stapled to one of the beams of rough wood that supported the corrugated iron roof. There were cardboard boxes stamped with Arabic writing stacked along one wall. There was a filing cabinet with piles of paper on top, weighted with stones. An unglazed window overlooked a small yard where, in the glare of a string of light bulbs, small boys sat on the ground, cross-legged and straight-backed, their arms folded across their chests while an old man with a ragged white beard talked to them.

Mehmet Celik saw Harriet looking at the children, and made a short speech.

The seated man said, 'He says there are very many children in the *geceköndü*. Families with eight or ten children, they are not uncommon. Without school, the children have no future. They become beggars, they become thieves. With school, they have the chance to become something. They know this. They are eager to learn. We teach them in shifts. We begin in the morning and finish late at night.'

Mehmet Celik said something and sat down. His interpreter said, 'He tells you our people are very poor in all things but faith and their children.'

Harriet, Toby, and Richard Elfingham sat down too, and the young boy in the oversized Arsenal shirt carried in a tray laden with small curved glasses on red or white saucers, an aluminium teapot, and a fretted metal bowl piled high with lumps of sugar. The boy stared at Harriet until the interpreter said something sharply and made to cuff at him, then giggled and trotted out of the room. Mehmet Celik filled the glasses with black tea, set them in front of his guests, and offered the bowl of sugar lumps to each of them in turn.

The interpreter said, 'We have only a little time for you, but we listen carefully to what you have to say.'

Mehmet Celik nodded.

Toby looked at Harriet, said, 'May I?' and gave Mehmet Celik the cover story. Musa Karsu's graffiti art; the fictitious gallery owner who wanted him to return to London. He did a good job, speaking simply and plainly, pausing at the end of each sentence to let the interpreter retell it in Kurdish. He explained how they had found out that Mehmet Celik had helped Musa Karsu's father and said, 'We're hoping that you'll help us. And, of course, allow us to help Musa Karsu.'

Mehmet Celik said something, and the interpreter said, 'You say you come all this way to help the boy. How do we know this?'

Toby extracted an envelope from the inside pocket of his black linen jacket, took out the photocopies folded inside, and laid them out on the desk. The photograph of the cartoon which had first alerted Harriet to Musa Karsu. The story about graffiti sprayed on the sides of the vans of a delivery company. The story about the fake exhibit in the Imperial War Museum.

Mehmet Celik inspected the photocopies one by one, picking them up and looking at them, handing them to the interpreter. The young man in the tracksuit unpeeled himself from the wall and stepped up behind Mehmet Celik, jabbed his forefinger at the photograph of the cartoon of President Bush riding a bomb cowboy-style, staring hard at Harriet and Toby as he spoke, making sure that they took in the smouldering contempt that tightened every muscle of his face.

'He say this artist is not a Kurd,' the interpreter said. His smile showed a gold tooth. 'He say that Kurds love America.'

'*Amrika, Kurdi dost!*' the young man in the tracksuit said, staring fiercely at Harriet and Toby.

'He say there is a great friendship between Americans and Kurds,' the interpreter said, and picked up his glass of tea and drained it with a lip-smacking slurp.

The young man began to speak again. Mehmet Celik interrupted him, but the young man shook his head angrily and spoke with some force. The interpreter said, 'He wants you to know that because of the Americans, Saddam is gone and for more than ten years the Kurds have a democratic government in the north of Iraq. Soon we will have a real homeland. Soon we will have money from oil. There is plenty of oil in the north. The Kurds will be rich, they will be strong. That's why they love Americans, he says, and says why should we help you find this boy, this troublemaker who does not love the Americans? That is what he asks you.'

Harriet said, ignoring the young man, looking at Mehmet Celik, 'You helped Musa Karsu's father. He was arrested and put in prison unjustly, and you worked hard to get him released. You helped the father. Why not help the son?'

The interpreter translated this, and Mehmet Celik said in English, 'Maybe I help the boy. But why do I help you?'

'He means, he helps his people, but you aren't his people,' the interpreter said,

Harriet said, 'Your friend in the tracksuit is right. Musa Karsu and his father aren't Kurds. But you helped them all the same.'

Mehmet Celik and the interpreter seemed taken aback by this. The interpreter talked at length in Kurdish. Mehmet Celik replied, and the young man started to say something too. He seemed to be disagreeing with the other men; when Mehmet Celik held up a hand, he spat a single word and returned to his position by the wall, arms folded across the breast of his blue tracksuit, glaring at Harriet and Toby while Mehmet Celik opened a drawer of his desk, took out two photographs and set them over Toby's photocopies with the air of a gambler revealing an unbeatable hand.

The interpreter said, 'He wants to know if you ever see these men. He wants to know if perhaps they are your friends.'

One was the man who had driven the people-carrier when

Harriet had been abducted; the other was the blond man who had held up Alfie Flowers and Toby at gunpoint, who had been with Larry Macpherson when Graham Taylor had been executed. Both men were staring into the camera with sullen defiance. The driver had a black eye, and a bandage strapped with adhesive tape to his newly shaven skull, above his ear. Harriet remembered that he'd been hurt when Benjamin Barrett's bodyguard had smashed into the roof of the people-carrier, and then Graham had coshed him, taken his gun . . . The other man had a black eye too, more recent than his friend's, still puffing up, and there was blood under his nostril and a raw scrape along one cheekbone.

Harriet felt a widening dismay, felt her skin turn cold, a prickling along her arms as the fine hairs there stirred and lifted. What should have been a simple request for help and information had turned a sudden corner. It was as if, while paddling in sunlit shadows, a wave had lifted her up and swept her out into the open ocean, a vertical mile of water yawning beneath her where unknown monsters patrolled.

She met Mehmet Celik's calm gaze and said, 'They're definitely not my friends. I know them, yes, but only by sight – I don't know their names. They work for a man who wants to harm Musa Karsu.'

The interpreter said, 'You are rivals. You both want this boy.'

Harriet felt that Mehmet Celik was trying to X-ray her. She said, 'We want to help him. They don't.'

Toby said, 'Where did you get these photographs?'

The interpreter smiled and said, 'We take them after we arrest them.'

Harriet and Toby looked at him. Richard Elfingham sat up a little straighter.

The interpreter said, 'They come here to Diyarbakir, start to ask questions. They look for Musa Karsu, just like you do now. They cause trouble – they threaten people. When we hear of this, we have them arrested.'

Harriet said, 'The police arrested them? Where are they now?'

Toby said, 'Was there another man with them? Tall, blond, a little overweight?'

The interpreter shook his head and said, 'Not the police. We arrest them ourselves.'

Toby said, 'His name is Alfie Flowers. One of those men helped to kidnap him a few days ago, in London.'

The interpreter indicated the man in the tracksuit and said, 'His people keep the peace here, so the *jandarma*, the police? So the police do not come into the *geceköndü* and cause trouble. What happen, his people arrest those two men and bring them here. Mehmet Celik asks them why they threaten the people. They say that this boy is a terrorist. They tell Mehmet Celik that if he knows where the boy is he must tell them, otherwise he is a terrorist too. They say that if he does not tell them it will be very bad for him. They say that it will be very bad for anyone who hides the boy.'

Mehmet Celik said, 'They are British, like you, yes?'

Harriet was beginning to get a very bad feeling about what they'd walked into, with their laughable cover story and their naive idea that the community leader would roll over and help them, just like that. She said carefully, 'Would you let me talk with these men? I might be able to help you find out more about them, and what they want.'

Mehmet Celik made a short speech, all the while staring at Harriet. The interpreter said, 'We are not fanatics and criminals like Kongra-Gel. We do not kidnap and kill foreigners, or assassinate policemen and politicians. We are ordinary men, peaceful men, trying to do our best for our people by democratic means. So we do not ransom these men, we do not cut off their heads in front of a video camera and dump their bodies by the side of a road. But they are a problem to us. We could hand them over to the police, but maybe the police let them go. Maybe the police take their side, and accuse us of kidnapping them. So we give them to friends who take them to the mountains near the border with Iraq. They are very beautiful, the mountains, very wild. Our friends take them there and free them, tell them that if Allah wishes them to live they will live.'

Richard Elfingham said, 'My friends did not come here to cause trouble. They came to you in good faith, to ask for your help.'

'For you, Dr Elfingham, it is no problem,' Mehmet Celik said, adding something in Kurdish.

The man in the tracksuit shrugged in a way that suggested that although he didn't agree with Mehmet Celik, he wasn't going to argue the point.

The interpreter told Richard Elfingham, 'He says we know who you are. We know you are a man of his word. But these friends of yours, we do not know them.'

Richard Elfingham said, 'They have not come here to cause trouble. I can absolutely vouch for that.'

Mehmet Celik prodded one of Toby's photocopies and said, 'Why you come here? It is nothing to do with art.'

The interpreter said, 'He wants you now to tell the truth.'

There was a silence in the hot, brightly lit room. Outside, the sweet treble voices of the boys rose and fell in unison, chanting the lines of text to which their teacher was pointing on a blackboard. Harriet was sweating beneath her loose shirt. Her pulse thumped painfully in her forehead. Toby was sweating too; wet saddles of perspiration were growing under the arms of his black linen jacket. He looked at the man in the tracksuit, looked at Mehmet Celik, said, 'Can I ask something? Are we under arrest here?'

Richard Elfingham said, beginning to sound ruffled, 'I don't know who those two men are, but they don't have anything at all to do with my friends.'

Harriet said, 'Musa Karsu's people are nomads, just as the Kurds were once nomads, but they lived in the mountains long before the Kurds came to live there. They kept sheep – like many Kurds, they were shepherds who moved their flocks to pasture high in the mountains in the summer, and moved them back down before the snow began to fall.'

She waited while the interpreter translated this.

She said, 'My grandfather visited them before the Second World War. After the war, he came back to the same place, but they were gone. We thought that they had been killed, or that they had moved away. And then we saw this.' She pointed to the photocopies of Alfie Flowers's photographs of Morph's cartoons. 'And we knew that the people my grandfather befriended more than fifty years ago – their descendants – were still alive. Not because of the cartoons, but because of the pattern around them.'

★   ★   ★

Harriet did not tell Mehmet Celik everything. She didn't tell him about the source of the glyphs, didn't explain how Carver Soborin and Rölf Most had perverted them. Instead, she described how her grandfather and Julius Ward had visited the Kefidis more than sixty years ago, described the ceremony they had witnessed – the drug, the sheepskin painted with a pattern like the pattern that Musa Karsu had used to frame his cartoons, the wild, ecstatic dance – and told him about her search for Musa Karsu in London after she had spotted his graffiti.

When she had finished, Mehmet Celik smiled and said, 'At last we hear the truth. At last we hear the same story that Musa tells me.'

Harriet said, 'If Musa Karsu is here, if he has returned to Diyarbakir, if we could talk to him—'

Mehmet Celik shook his head.

The interpreter said, 'That will not be possible.'

Mehmet Celik said, 'I think you tell the truth, so I will tell you that I am sorry, but this boy you are looking for, he is not here.'

Harriet decided to believe him – at least for the moment. She said, 'But you know him. He lived here, with his father, before his father got into trouble with the police.'

'After his father was arrested, Musa work for me. Always he makes drawings,' Mehmet Celik said, and lapsed into Kurdish.

The interpreter said, 'He tells you that the boy makes many drawings. If he did not have paper he drew on the wall. If he did not have a pen, or charcoal, he drew with a stick in the earth. He says that he believes the boy would have drawn on his body in his own blood if he had nothing else. He was like this ever since he came to Diyarbakir. He did not stop making drawings, although his father grew very angry and punished him when he found him doing it. I have seen his drawings myself. Not pictures, but the patterns. The patterns around the pictures.'

Mehmet Celik touched one of the photocopies, tracing with his forefinger the glyph around one of the cartoons. He said in English, 'They are in my head. Sometimes I have dreams about them.'

With the help of the interpreter, he told Harriet and Toby the story that Musa Karsu had told him, a story of persecution, massacre and exile that, Mehmet Celik said, was the lot of Kurds everywhere. According to Musa Karsu, the village of the Kefidis had been attacked by its neighbours some sixty years ago, and most of the Kefidis had been killed. Musa Karsu's grandfather and several others had escaped and settled in a small village near the town of Dohuk, where they had lived quietly, occasionally returning in secret to the mountains where they had once lived. Then, during the Anfal campaign in 1988, the culmination of Saddam Hussein's plans to eradicate the Kurds from his country by any means necessary, many members of Musa Karsu's family had been murdered and the survivors had fled to Turkey, where Musa Karsu had been born. They returned home after the first Gulf War, when America and its allies established a safe haven for the Kurds in the north-east of Iraq. Not to the village near Dohuk, but to their original home in the Zagros Mountains; the neighbouring villages, whose inhabitants had massacred the Kefidis all those years ago, had, like so many others, been bombed and gassed during the Anfal campaign, and the survivors had been executed or relocated. Musa Karsu's family had lived there peacefully until just over a year ago, just after the American invasion of Iraq, when American soldiers had come to the little village. They had taken away Musa Karsu's family, but Musa Karsu and his father had escaped because they had been hunting in the mountains, and had fled across the border into Turkey.

It seemed that Morph's father had drunk heavily, a vice Mehmet Celik disapproved of, but forgave because he felt sorry for the man. Through the interpreter, he said, 'The Americans took his family. He lost his wife and three daughters. He was very sad, very bitter. He worked for a shoemaker here, and his son helped him. They made a good living here for a little while, but then Musa Karsu's father was arrested because he bought his brandy from a smuggler, and this smuggler also brought in weapons from Iraq. Many people were arrested at this time because the government wanted to prove to the Americans that they were against terrorism. I was able to get some of them released, and meanwhile I looked after Musa Karsu, who was too young to know how to carry out his father's trade by himself. When Musa Karsu's father was freed, they both went to London. The rest of the story, I think you know it.'

Harriet started to ask about the village in Iraq where Musa Karsu's family had lived, but Mehmet Celik help up a hand and said, 'I help you. Now you help us.'

He spoke in Kurdish to the interpreter, and then to the man in the tracksuit, who gave another sulky shrug. The interpreter pointed to Toby and Harriet, and said, 'You will come with me. There is a question – a mystery. Perhaps you can help us understand it. Dr Elfingham, you have my word they will be safe with us. You have the word of Mehmet Celik. When we are finished, we bring them back to their hotel.'

Richard Elfingham protested, saying that he was responsible for Harriet and Toby's safety. 'If you want to take them somewhere, I think that I should come along too.'

The interpreter looked at Toby and said, 'Does this man know everything that you know?'

'Well, not exactly—'

The interpreter said, 'Then I am sorry, Dr Elfingham. You cannot come.'

Harriet said, 'We'll be fine.'

Toby said, 'We're going with these guys?'

Harriet said, 'Why not? They helped us, we're simply returning the favour.'

All she had to do was get through this, and then she would be on her way to Iraq. Musa Karsu had told his friend that he was going home, and Harriet was certain now that he hadn't meant Diyarbakir.

'I'll wait for you,' Richard Elfingham said, glaring at the interpreter. 'I'll be outside, in my Jeep. And if you don't come back in an hour, I will call the police.'

'You had better make it two hours,' the interpreter said. 'Where we have to go, it is a little way from here.'

The man in the tracksuit and the interpreter, whose name was Emre Karin, led Toby and Harriet to a battered Toyota saloon parked a little way down the street. Emre Karin squeezed into the back with Toby and Harriet, the man in the tracksuit took

the seat next to the Toyota's driver, and the car set off, the driver
beating a smart tattoo on his horn to clear a way through the
throngs of pedestrians.

Toby lit a cigarette, offered the pack to Emre Karin, and casually asked where they were going.

'That would spoil the surprise,' the interpreter said. He took
three cigarettes and handed two of them to the men in the front
of the car.

After fifteen minutes of crawling through crowded streets, the
car crossed onto a belt of wasteground and picked up speed,
rushing up a steep track. Bushes and scrubby trees surprised in
its headlights whipped past; ahead, a cliff – no, Harriet thought,
it was the city wall, but it looked as big and solid as a cliff –
loomed against a clear, starry sky. The car stopped beside a lesser
stone wall that skirted an outcrop of rock. Emre Karin switched
on a small flashlight and led Toby and Harriet along a narrow
footpath that climbed uphill between one- and two-storey houses,
with the man in the tracksuit bringing up the rear. None of the
houses had windows facing onto the path and it was very dark;
the only light came from the dancing beam of Emre Karin's flashlight and the cold stars spread above.

'Just the spot for an execution,' Toby said quietly.

Harriet slipped her arm through his to steady herself. 'Let's
think happy thoughts.'

'I'm thinking about what they said they did to those two guys
who work for Rölf Most.'

'They're the bad guys. We're the good guys.'

'Right. And what are *these* guys?'

'They're concerned citizens.'

'They may be on our side, but they still scare the shit out of
me.'

'They told us what they know about Musa Karsu. That's helpful,
isn't it?'

'If we can believe them.'

Emre Karin knocked on a low wooden door set in the wall
of a square brick building. It was opened by an old man wearing
a baseball cap and a long black robe done up the front with small
wooden pegs. A rifle was cradled in his right arm, an ancient Lee

Enfield that looked as if it might last have been fired during the Second World War. He talked briefly with Emre Karin and then stepped aside, and Harriet and Toby followed the interpreter into what had once been some kind of light industrial factory. Emre Karin picked up an oil lantern and led them across a floor of packed earth, past a cluster of blue plastic drums and two long work tables to the far corner, where a cage of steel mesh was set against a bare brick wall. When the interpreter lifted the oil lantern above his head, the man squatting on a pile of straw inside the cage raised his head to look up at it.

His face was slack and expressionless, and there was something wrong with his eyes – the pupils were so fully dilated that not even a rim of iris showed around them. His shirt and trousers were filthy and ragged, and the right leg of his trousers was stiff with dried material – mud or blood – from thigh to ankle. There was an iron bracelet around his left ankle, and the end of the bracelet's short chain was fastened to a bolt driven into the brick wall behind him. He stank of urine and old sweat, and of something else, a sharp, sweet smell like nail polish or rotten pears. His head swivelled like an owl's, following the movement of the lantern as Emre Karin turned to Harriet and Toby.

'You tell me,' the interpreter said, his voice choked with anger. 'You tell me what it is they did to him.'

Harriet asked Emre Karin if the two men who had been arrested had been carrying something that looked like a cross between a gun and a flashlight. Emre Karin said sure, they had been carrying guns, automatics.

Harriet said, 'Just ordinary guns?'

'Good ones. Sig-Sauer.'

Harriet said, 'They weren't carrying any other kind of weapon?'

Emre Karin spoke in Kurdish to the man in the tracksuit, then told Harriet, 'My friend says he searched the car they hire at the airport. He didn't find anything. All they were carrying were the Sig-Sauers, knives, and flexible sticks. Sticks with little lead balls inside them, for knocking people out.'

'Saps,' Harriet said.

'Yes, and also grenades that do the same thing. Flash-bangs, the Americans call them. Also handcuffs.'

Everything the dedicated kidnapper needs, Harriet thought. She supposed that Rölf Most wouldn't have entrusted his precious glyph gun to his sidekicks. He would have turned the low man himself, then got back on his plane and flown on to Iraq. To the source of the glyphs.

Emre Karin told her that the man had been found on the street where Musa Karsu and his father had lived and worked. 'A street of shoemakers. Children were making fun of him and his friend—'

Harriet said, 'There were two of them? Wait, of course there were. Low men usually work in pairs, or packs.'

They were standing around the oil lantern, which Emre Karin had set on the packed-earth floor a little way from the cage in which the low man squatted. The low man's chain made a soft sliding rattle whenever he moved. His breathing was effortful and thick, as if his mouth was full of wet sponge.

Emre Karin said, 'You have a name for what he has become. So I must believe you know what happened to him.'

Harriet said, 'The higher functions of his brain have been destroyed. His memories and his personality, everything that makes us human. Everything that distinguishes one person from another.'

Toby laughed. It had a harsh, high edge to it. With his face half in shadow and his disordered mop of black hair, he looked a little like a mad scientist from a cheap horror movie. He said, 'You're telling us he's a zombie? He's a fucking zombie?'

'He definitely isn't a corpse brought back to life by a voodoo sorcerer. But essentially, yes, I suppose that's what he is. Low men don't have any free will. They do what they've been told to do during the short latent period after they've been . . . treated. That's all they know.'

'A zombie,' Toby said. 'That's great. Really. That's absolutely great. I'm as much a part of this as you are. I'm in it up to my fucking neck, just like poor Alfie Flowers. And you wait until we're lost in the middle of some slum in a city in the asshole of Turkey before you bother to tell me that the people we're up against can turn ordinary human beings into *zombies*. I guess I must have "sucker" written on my forehead. I didn't see it the last time I looked in the mirror, but it has to be there, because that's exactly what I am.' He was staring at Harriet, breathing hard, the muscles in his face working. He looked like he might burst into tears or hysterical laughter or both at once. He said, 'Is there anything else you haven't told me? Werewolves? Vampires? The Beast from Twenty Thousand Fathoms?'

Harriet said, 'I suppose that if a low man was told that he was a wolf or a vampire, he'd try to behave like one. But he wouldn't *be* one.'

Toby looked at her, and for a moment she thought that he was going to try to hit her. Her heart quickened, she felt a tickle of adrenalin. If he tried it, she knew that she would have to take him down, she'd have to kick him in the knee or stamp on his instep. And after that, everything would be changed. It was one of those moments where everything is balanced on a knife-edge, and a breath or a look can make it fall the wrong way.

After a moment, Toby shook his head and said, 'Oh boy. I'm hearing this, but I can't believe it.' Looking at Emre Karin, saying, 'Do *you* believe it?'

Harriet said, 'I'm telling you the truth. If you can't handle it, that's your problem.'

'Really? Zombies and werewolves and vampires? And here I am without my stake and holy water and silver bullets.'

'You have your razor-sharp wit. Maybe that'll do it.'

Toby smiled. 'A zombie walks into a bar, says, "Why is this place so dead?"'

Harriet smiled too; then they were both laughing.

Toby ran his fingers through his hair. 'This isn't bullshit. They really can do this.'

'Remember the two men who set themselves on fire and attacked Clarence's house? They were low men too. So were some of the men who attacked Alfie Flowers's yard.'

Toby said, 'Alfie said that he saw a couple of men watching his place. They ran away when he challenged them. He said they ran very fast, with this weird Groucho Marx gait.'

Harriet said, 'They were probably low men too. Rölf Most had at least one low man watching Benjamin Barrett's flat, so why not Alfie Flowers's place as well? They're good at watching, if that's what they're told to do. Their free will is gone, but their intelligence isn't.'

'You didn't think to tell me any of this. It sort of slipped your mind.'

Harriet said, 'I told you what you needed to know. I didn't think we'd run into any more of them.'

'But we have. Is there anything else I should know about?'

'I don't think so. The low men are about the worst thing the glyphs can do. And they're nowhere near as dangerous as someone like Larry Macpherson.'

'Of course. We mustn't forget the trigger-happy maniac.'

Now the moment had passed, Harriet felt sorry for Toby. After her mother had died, she had discovered a small cache of her grandfather's letters, had tracked down Clarence Ashburton and Julius Ward and discovered the truth about her father's cult, his madness and his suicide. Before she'd been pitched headlong into the nightmare of mind's i's botched experiment in Lagos, she'd had several years to get up to speed with the matter of the glyphs. But Toby Brown had had to pick things up along the way amidst murder, kidnap, and now this: his first stand-up encounter with a low man. The poor fellow was like a punch-drunk boxer reeling on his feet, the crowd screaming and flashbulbs blinding him while he waited for the knockout blow.

The young man in the tracksuit asked a question. Emre Karin replied, then told Harriet and Toby, 'I say to him that you are discussing this poor man. This low man.'

Toby said, looking at Harriet, 'Absolutely right. A discussion about policy.'

Harriet asked Emre Karin about the other low man. 'What happened to him?'

'What happened, he died. It was this morning. This other one will die soon, I think. He will not eat.'

Harriet said, 'He can't digest solid food any more.'

When a low man was turned, his higher brain functions were destroyed and his limbic system, the part of the brain that controls emotions, was altered. Like an experimental rat whose pleasure centre had been wired up to a lever which it would keep pressing until it dropped dead of thirst or sheer exhaustion, all a low man wanted to do was what he had been told to do during the latent period after he'd been zapped.

'Most of his physiological functions have been messed up. His heart rate, his blood pressure, his digestive system . . . That's why he smells of rotten pears − it's actually acetone. His blood is full of acetone and organic acids, and he gives them off when he breathes. Just about all he can handle is sugar. Give him sugar and he'll suck it right up. It's instant energy.'

Emre Karin said, 'Sugar will keep him alive?'

'For a little while. Where did you find him and his friend?'

'They were watching the place where Musa Karsu used to live. Children were teasing them, to throw things at them, stones, rubbish. It is what children do to madmen sometimes. The two men run off but they come back, and the children start teasing them again, so somebody ask my friend's people—' Emre Karin nodded towards the man in the tracksuit '− to help. They chase the two men, who run very fast, but only for a little while. Very soon they are caught. And my friend sees that they are not ordinary madmen. He finds a picture of Musa Karsu in one of their pockets, and that's when he remembers the other two men, the British men he arrested.'

Harriet realized that Rölf Most must have seen Musa Karsu's immigration file. It was pure luck that he hadn't had access to Amnesty International's files, that he hadn't found out about Mehmet Celik.

Emre Karin said, 'My friend also finds out this man's name. He is Mohamed Jalan. He works at the airport, as a cleaner of aeroplanes. He was still carrying his identity card and his airport pass. Mohamed Jalan has a wife, and six children. If we knew, when we arrested them, what those men did to him, I do not think we would have given them the chance to live.'

The man in the tracksuit asked a question. Emre Karin said, 'He wants to know if we can cure this poor fellow.'

Harriet said, 'I'm sorry, but no.'

'You are sure of this.'

'The damage to the brain is permanent, and so is the damage

to his body. You'll be able to keep him alive on sugar and water for a while, but in a few days, a week at the most, he'll die.'

After Emre Karin had translated this, the man in the tracksuit nodded once and walked away across the floor of the little factory. Emre Karin said to Harriet, 'Now we are being so honest with each other, I have one question I must ask you. Musa Karsu told Mehmet Celik that the men of his people would dance like dervishes after they smoke the leaves of a certain plant and stare at a certain pattern, something like the patterns Musa Karsu draws. Not the same, but similar. Musa Karsu said that this pattern affects the minds of the dancers. They would feel the spirit of Allah descend upon them, closer than their skin, as close as their thoughts. You told us a similar story. I must ask you now: when an ordinary man is turned into what you call a low man, do they use on him a pattern that is also like the patterns that Musa Karsu draws?'

This sturdily built grey-haired man in his tweed jacket with leather patches on the elbows and shapeless cord trousers, his gaze serious and steady as he waited for her answer.

'Yes,' Harriet said, because there was clearly no point in dissembling.

'This is why those men want to find Musa Karsu. Because they think he knows other patterns, perhaps more powerful.'

'They want to use him,' Harriet said. 'We want to help him.'

The man in the tracksuit came back. He was carrying the old man's Lee Enfield.

Harriet felt a tingle of alarm and Toby took a step backwards, his hand raised to his chest as if pushing something away, but the man in the tracksuit walked straight past them. Maybe he was planning to put them up against a wall and maybe he wasn't, but right now his mind was set on another task, a necessary but unpleasant one. He looked grim and determined, stepping up to the makeshift cage, raising his face to the darkness above him and saying something in a low tone, a prayer or a blessing or perhaps a plea for forgiveness, then working the bolt of the rifle, fitting its butt to his shoulder, and squinting down its length at the low man.

The low man looked up at him with vacant interest, his eyes shining blankly in the yellow lamplight.

Harriet turned away. The flat hard noise of the mercy shot echoed off the flat roof.

Toby said, 'Jesus *Christ*.'

Emre Karin said, 'Your friend, Dr Elfingham, does he have a mobile phone?'

Harriet said, 'A satellite phone.'

Emre Karin took a mobile phone from the pocket of his tweed jacket and held it out to her. 'You must call him now. You must thank him for his help. You must tell him that you are happy to go with us.'

Toby said, 'Wait a minute. Where are we going?'

Emre Karin smiled. 'Do not be afraid. We have much to talk about, so we will not shoot you just yet.'

25

Rölf Most stashed Alfie in an outhouse or storeroom in a quiet, remote area at the end of a rough track, a long drive from the private jet's final destination. For four days, Alfie sat on a mattress with a hood over his head and his hands fastened behind his back with steel handcuffs, the handcuffs fixed with plastic wire to an iron ring bolted to the wall. The ring was about a yard off the ground and the plastic wire didn't have much free play in it, so he was forced to sit up with his back against the wall, his elbows bent like the wings of a plucked chicken.

The hood was a loose, roughly stitched double layer of black cloth which Larry Macpherson had pulled over Alfie's head just before the private jet had landed. Alfie had worn it when he'd been escorted off the plane, had worn it during the long car ride, squashed between two men who'd barely exchanged a dozen words on the entire journey. Alfie didn't dare to take a peek at his surroundings until he'd been dumped on the mattress and he was certain that he'd been left alone, rubbing his head against the rough wall at his back, pulling up the hem of the hood until he could catch a glimpse of the bare dirt floor around the stained ticking of the mattress, and three walls of roughly mortared cinder blocks. The wall on his right had a narrow window let into it, covered by a piece of flattened tin pierced with dozens of tiny holes. There was a low door made of unpainted planks in the middle of the wall straight ahead, a couple of yards beyond his bare feet, and the covered bucket of a chemical toilet to his left. It was very hot in the bare little room during the day, hotter than it ever was in London, and unpleasantly cold at night. He wasn't sure what country he was in, but believed that it must be Iraq. That was where the glyphs had come from; that was what Rölf Most had questioned him about after speed-reading the photo-copied pages of his grandfather's journal.

Alfie had been brought onto Rölf Most's small private jet

hooded and handcuffed much as he was now and more than half scared to death, convinced that he would be tortured, questioned, and killed. After Larry Macpherson had shot Graham Taylor dead, he'd shoved Alfie around the Peugeot and made sure that he'd seen Graham's body before marching him to the battered Range Rover at gunpoint. While the blond man drove them away from the scene at speed, heading into Bloomsbury, Larry Macpherson rifled the contents of Alfie's holdall and camera bag, pulling out the sheaf of photocopied pages, flicking through them, asking Alfie if it was what he thought it was.

'I don't know. What do you think it is?'

Larry Macpherson slapped Alfie's face with the rolled sheaf of paper, hard enough to make his nose bleed, and repeated the question. His cool, watchful expression might have been carved in stone. Alfie sniffed back a glob of bloody mucus and swallowed it, told the mercenary that it was a copy of a journal his grandfather had made.

'Where was it hidden?'

'In a safe.'

'You made a mistake when you came back for this stuff. Bad for you, good for me,' Larry Macpherson said, and told the blond man to stop, they needed to switch vehicles.

After the blond man had broken into and hot-wired a car, Alfie was handcuffed and hooded and thrown into its back seat. Larry Macpherson made a brief phone call, telling someone that he had acquired Mr Flowers and a bunch of very useful documents, and then caressed Alfie's hooded face with the muzzle of his gun, jabbing Alfie's tender nose, telling him that since he was already a dead man he should set his mind on cooperating with Dr Most so that when the time came it would be quick and painless. 'Otherwise it'll be slow and painful, I personally guarantee it.'

As it turned out, cooperating wasn't an option. After a drive at speed out of London, Alfie was marched onto a small plane and, still hooded, buckled into a seat. After the plane had taken off, Larry Macpherson ripped off Alfie's hood, grabbed his hair and pulled his head back. Alfie had enough time to notice the white leather everywhere – quilting the curved walls of the cabin, upholstering the single row of fat armchairs that could be set to face in any direction. And then Rölf Most sat down right in front of him, looking as pleased as a cat in a creamery as he leaned forward and stuck the nozzle of a little black cylinder under Alfie's nose and squirted something cold up both nostrils. Larry Macpherson used his thumbs to hold Alfie's eyelids open while Rölf Most took aim with the weirdest-looking gun Alfie had ever seen, and shot his head full of light.

Alfie hadn't had a major seizure for years, but he hadn't forgotten what it had been like. It would start with a feeling that the world wasn't quite right, as if he'd been transplanted into a parallel universe where everything looked the same yet was weirdly and obviously fake, and then, when there was no turning back, an unscratchable itch would begin to grow inside his skull. That was the focal onset of the seizure, suddenly opening up like one of those Japanese paper flowers that bloom from a pellet into a rose or chrysanthemum when they are dropped into a glass of water, sweeping across both hemispheres of his brain in a Jacksonian march, a swelling unstoppable tidal wave that scattered his thoughts like flotsam. But when Rölf Most fired his weird gun into Alfie's face, there was no warning, no focal onset. He watched the psychiatrist raise his gun, he was blinded by a flash of white light, complex and filthily alive, and he jerked awake some time later with no idea of where he was or who he was, as helplessly blank as if he had just been born. All he knew was that this kind of thing had happened before, that it would pass. And with the thought came a sudden rush of memory, and he opened his eyes and saw Rölf Most studying him, looking happier than ever.

The psychiatrist asked every kind of question about Alfie's grand-father, the excavations in Iraq and the source of the glyphs, about the Kefidis and their ceremony, and Alfie told him everything he knew. It wasn't as if he had a choice, and besides, Rölf Most had the photocopy of the journal in his lap, consulting it now and then before asking more questions. He asked Alfie about his epilepsy, and after Alfie told him about his accidental exposure to the glyph that his grandfather had kept hidden in his desk, the psychiatrist seemed to go inside his head for a little while, muttering to himself and alternately nodding and shaking his head as if conducting some kind of internal argument. At last, he told Larry

Macpherson to kindly hold Mr Flowers still, he wanted to try something else, and jammed the cylinder under Alfie's nose again, gave him a freezing burst of the drug-laden spray.

'Better tape his eyelids open,' Rölf Most told Larry Macpherson, and called to the blond man, who was sitting in the front of the cabin, told him that he wanted a video record of this little experiment. The psychiatrist fired up a laptop, leaning to one side so that the blond man could video what was on the laptop's screen and then turning the laptop around to show Alfie the glyph pulsing on the screen, an intricate thorny black circle pulsing out into the air, into Alfie's head, a black pulse expanding across his vision, obscuring Rölf Most's eager smile. The last thing Alfie saw was the blond man aiming his little digital video camera over the psychiatrist's shoulder. Then the second seizure smashed into him like an express train.

After being held in more or less one position for four days, Alfie's shoulders had fused into a bar of iron and his spine was a chain of stiffly swollen knots that ground against each other whenever he made the slightest movement. He felt like he'd been beaten up, forced to run the London Marathon, and beaten up all over again. He was filthy too, his trousers stiff with dried urine, his best Hawaiian shirt soaked through with sweat, but thankfully he could no longer smell himself except when he slowly and painfully changed position; when he did, he was reminded of lifting the lid of one of his dustbins after it had been cooking all day in the summer sun.

The days were marginally better than the nights. The cloth of the hood wasn't completely opaque, and enough light leaked through the planks of the door and the pinholes in the tin over the window to bleach out the shapes that swam in the darkness beneath the hood, behind his eyes. As night fell, these shapes became more vivid, and Alfie had to try his best to ignore them, scared that they might resolve into a pattern or shape that would trigger another seizure. After the two major fits he'd suffered at the hands of Rölf Most, he felt permanently primed, ready to go off at any moment. He believed that the fierce, filthy light of the psychiatrist's weird gun had done him permanent damage, that some residue of the glyphs driven into his brain was generating strange thoughts. The kind of thoughts that might have driven Watty to make his dive off the top of the block of flats, a perfect six all the way down to the roof of the people-carrier; the kind of thoughts that might have driven Shareef to swallow the live cable.

Alfie was visited each morning and evening by the two men who took care of his needs with resentful efficiency. The routine was the same each time. The hem of the hood was rolled up above his mouth, a plastic cup was tipped to his lips. It was refilled as many times as he wanted, and then one of the men fed him by hand, shovelling cold rice and beans into his mouth with a metal spoon that kept ticking his teeth, and several times cut his tongue and drew blood. After an arbitrary number of spoonfuls the hood was rolled back down, Alfie's handcuffs were uncoupled from the ring bolted to the wall, and he was led to the chemical toilet. When he was finished and had hitched up his greasy trousers, his arms were grabbed and he was more or less thrown onto the mattress and made to sit with his back against the wall, and his handcuffs were reattached to the ring.

All this was accomplished in a monastic silence. When Alfie had first been fed by his guards, he'd asked for his phenobarbitone tablets, tried to explain why he needed them, and one of the men had told him to shut the fuck up and cuffed him so hard that stars had burst in the semi-darkness inside the hood. Alfie's nose had started to bleed again, and his ears had rung for hours afterwards. He hadn't said another word.

When he'd been left alone on that first night, he'd spent some time fantasizing about escape. He'd twist from his captor's grasp as he was led to the chemical toilet, trip the man up and fall on him and pound him senseless with his forehead. Or when he was finished on the toilet he'd rear up, ram his head into the man's solar plexus and render him breathless before taking him down . . . But even if he could overpower the man who led him to the toilet, a snatched glimpse from beneath the edge of his hood had shown Alfie that his other guard had been standing in the doorway, no doubt ready to shoot if he showed the slightest sign of cutting up rough. Another fantasy slowly replaced the fantasies of escape.

Wherever this place was, it was eerily quiet; he might have been the last survivor of some catastrophe which had wiped mankind from the face of the earth. Alfie, who had spent almost all of his adult life in London, found the silence horribly unnerving, and began to wonder if his guards had walked away and left him to shrivel and die of thirst in this squalid little room. He slept fitfully, and when at last he heard the door creak open and pinpricks of sunlight flared through the material over his face, he felt a pang of hopeless gratitude. All thoughts of escape gone, he meekly allowed himself to be fed and watered, and led to the toilet, allowed himself to be pushed onto the mattress and fastened to the iron ring in the wall. As good as gold, as his grandmother used to say.

After that first night of captivity, Alfie gave up all ideas of escape. His captors weren't going to kill him, or at least they weren't going to kill him right away. All he had to do was sit tight and endure this. But time passed so very slowly, the way it had passed during his several childhood illnesses. He remembered lying in bed all one summer day, weak and feverish, watching sunlight dance in the leaves outside the open window, watching clouds move across the sky. The clouds making shapes for their own amusement as they travelled, remote and utterly indifferent to his plight.

Alfie's memory was his only resource. When he was not dozing in the drowsy heat of the day or trying to shiver himself to sleep at night, he returned over and over again to his most comforting memories. Memories of his childhood. Of his father. He remembered the last time he'd seen his father: the beach, the kite, the driftwood fire, the session with the laced joint. He remembered his birthday treat from the previous year – before his grandfather's death, before his accident. His father had driven him up to London and they'd seen a film, *Herbie Goes Bananas*, in a screening theatre in Soho. Alfie, at nine years old already too sophisticated for talking cars, had thought that the film was no more than all right, but had loved the privilege of having the ten rows of plush seats to himself. It was like being a prince or a millionaire, and he'd decided that when he became rich and famous and built his mansion, with its helipad, waterfall-fed swimming pool, and funfair, he would have a private cinema just like this one. He remembered that after the screening he'd been taken to the treasure cave of Hamley's, where he'd chosen the Airfix kit of HMS *Ark Royal* for his birthday present (but really the whole wonderful magical day had been a birthday present); remembered that he and his father had had an early supper in a restaurant in Chinatown, where his father had spoken Chinese with the old woman who served them, and had showed Alfie that when you ran out of tea, you tipped up the lid of the aluminium teapot to let the waitress know that you wanted more.

Mick Flowers, with his leather jacket and rock star's hair, his worldly sophistication, returning from his adventures in far-flung wars with little warning, exhausted and dishevelled, sleeping twelve hours a day, his rock music making the old house tingle, taking Alfie on a trip to Aldeburgh to eat fish and chips on the stony beach, the best fish and chips in the world, taking him to London for lunch with his agent, in the Chelsea Arts Club, staying overnight in the little flat and driving back to the house in Cambridge, racing through back roads in the little red Morgan . . . On another trip they'd stopped at a village pub where Alfie ate a packet of crisps and drank lemonade from a heavy, dimpled glass while his father drank two pints of beer and smoked cigarettes that he rolled one-handed. His favourite camera, the Nikon, hung around his neck. Alfie remembered that his father had unfolded a copy of the *Racing Times*, told Alfie he could choose any horse he wanted.

'I'll put five quid down to win, Chief, and if it collects, you can keep the winnings. How does that sound?'

Mick Flowers had phoned up his bookmaker using the public phone next to the toilets, five pounds either way on Alfie's horse, and fifty on a certainty on the three o'clock at Wincanton. The next day he'd slipped Alfie his winnings, told him to keep quiet about it because his grandmother wouldn't approve.

That was Mick Flowers, with his swashbuckling charm and spur-of-the-moment whims, his casual attitude to his work (always true to the ethos of photojournalists, he called his photographs snaps, never showed any pride over his most memorable pictures), the unpredictable way of life that meant he couldn't take responsibility for his own son. After his father had disappeared in Lebanon,

Alfie had refused to believe that he was dead, a stubborn denial that had survived the delivery of Mick Flowers's bloodstained passport to the British embassy in Beirut, that had been sustained by every kind of comic-book scenario. His father had to pretend that he was dead because he was working under deep cover against fiendish enemies. He'd been wounded in an explosion or by a bullet that had grazed his head, had lost his memory and his possessions, and was being cared for by a friendly tribe of Bedouin. Or he'd been kidnapped (but only after a terrific struggle that had left every one of the many men who had finally subdued him bloody and bruised), and was incarcerated in some deep dungeon, chained on straw, his face turned up to the sunlight that fell through a small high window as he plotted his escape.

Perhaps Alfie's thoughts turned to his father because he himself was trapped now in a version of one of his childish fantasies. Because the glyphs had been the cause of his father's death, and they would be the cause of his death, too.

Best not to think of that.

Best not to think that somewhere in the Foreign Office in London, in a shadowy, high-ceilinged room with wood-panelled walls hung with heavy gilt-framed oil portraits, Toby Brown was talking to men in chalk-stripe suits and club ties, telling them everything he knew about the kidnapping of his friend. Best not to think that helicopters loaded with grim SAS troops were at this very moment beating towards him. Best not to think about Harriet Crowley, about what she might be doing to secure his freedom . . .

Larry Macpherson came for Alfie early in the morning of his fifth day of captivity.

Alfie jerked awake when the door opened, saw a vague glimmer of light through the close black weave of the hood, heard the door rattle in its frame when it was kicked shut, heard someone cross the room in half a dozen quick steps. Something small and hard, the muzzle of a gun, was screwed against the top of his head, and Larry Macpherson's unnervingly calm voice said, 'Ease forward, nice and slow. You even think about playing up, your brains will be decorating this wall.'

Alfie did as he was told, shivering in the early-morning chill, his pulse beating in his throat. The wire that secured his handcuffs to the iron ring was cut; the hood was ripped from his head.

Larry Macpherson squatted on his heels beside the mattress, black hair sleek as a cemetery rat's brushed back from his widow's peak, his face still and watchful and devoid of any human emotion, his eyes masked by mirrorshades, his pockmarked cheeks darkened by several days' stubble. He wore polished combat boots, brown and green camo trousers, and a green flak jacket. His hands dangled between his thighs, enveloping an automatic pistol.

He studied Alfie for a few moments, then said, 'Man, but you stink. You know that? I'm gonna have to get you into a shower and give you some clean clothes before you're fit for civilized company. But before I take you out of here, you and me are going to have a little talk. Are you up for that?'

Alfie nodded, feeling a freezing caution.

Larry Macpherson took off his mirrorshades, hooked them in the neck of the T-shirt he wore under his flak jacket, fixed his gaze on Alfie's face. It was the first time that Alfie had seen the man's eyes. They were deep-set and very dark, almost black, twin sparks of liquid light glinting in their centres. 'I want it to be clear that what we say is between the two of us. I have to know that you won't go running your mouth off to my crazy boss or his even crazier friend. Do you promise you won't repeat what we're about to talk about?'

Alfie nodded again.

Larry Macpherson cocked his head slightly, said, 'I need to hear it.'

Alfie had to work up some spit and swallow it before he could speak. His throat felt as if it had turned to wood, and the two words, the first he'd spoken since his guard had told him to shut the fuck up, came out in a croak. 'I promise.'

'When my boss shot you with that glyph gun of his, you seemed to have some kind of fit. What I want to know is, were you faking?'

'It isn't the kind of thing you can fake.'

'That's what my boss thinks, which is why you're still alive. He believes that accident you told him about gave you some kind of brain damage that makes you sensitive to the glyphs. That's why, when he used his gun on you to make you answer his questions truthfully, you had a fit instead. That's why you had another fit when he showed you a different glyph, on his laptop. He says that when you're drugged up and shown what he calls a potent glyph, before the glyph can do whatever it's supposed to do to you, your brain has some kind of electrical storm and shuts you down. Does that sound about right?'

Alfie nodded, waiting to see where this was leading.

Larry Macpherson said, 'He also believes that even if you aren't drugged up when you're shown a glyph, you can still tell whether or not it's potent.'

'That's how I got into this in the first place,' Alfie said. 'When I first saw one of Morph's graffiti, I knew that the pattern he used to frame it was potent.'

'I remember the story you told my boss.'

'It's a true story.'

Larry Macpherson spent fifteen minutes going over the old familiar ground. Alfie's childhood accident, his search for Morph, his discovery of his grandfather's journals. At the end he said, 'Luckily for you, the man believes all this. It intrigues him, and he thinks it makes you useful, which is why he's just taken delivery of a special piece of kit that he thinks will show him exactly what happens in that brain of yours when you're exposed to a glyph. That's why he sent me down to fetch you. See, back in London, we were hoping to find that kid, Morph, Musa Karsu. We were going to make him tell us where he got that glyph he used in his graffiti. But we found you instead, and my boss reckons you're an even better catch. He thinks your grand-daddy's journal has led him to a place where he can find many more glyphs in that cave, thinks that some of them may be very powerful, very strong. He also thinks that he can use you to figure out which ones are potent and which aren't. He's going to wire you up, expose you to any glyphs he finds, see if they change the way you think. And you better pray it works, because it's the only reason you're still alive.'

'What will he do afterwards? After he's used me to test these glyphs?'

'He plans to kill you.'

Although Alfie had more or less expected this answer, it still shot a chill straight through him, from the top of his head to the soles of his bare feet.

Larry Macpherson showed his teeth in a mirthless grin, like an animal getting ready to bite. There was no way it could be mistaken for a smile. He said, 'That's *his* plan, but it isn't mine.'

Pausing, letting Alfie think about that.

Alfie said, 'You have your own plans for the glyphs.'

'I've seen what he can do with that glyph gun of his. I know it can make someone sing like a canary or kill themselves, I know it can turn men into zombies. That's something of value right there, but now the man reckons he's about to lay his hands on a whole bunch of really powerful glyphs. To be frank with you, he's as crazy as a jailhouse bedbug, and I don't think these things should be entrusted to a crazy man, do you?'

'Not at all.'

Alfie thought that the glyphs shouldn't be entrusted to *anyone*.

Larry Macpherson said, 'So we're agreed on that much at least. Which is good, because right now I'm your only hope. Want to know why?'

'I have a feeling you're going to tell me.'

'I guess you have a right to be pissed, what with being chained up here after my boss treated you like a lab rat. But right now, if I were you, I'd listen very carefully to what I have to say, because it's your only chance of getting through this.'

'Why do you want to help me?'

'We're going to help each other. How it's going to work, I'll take you up the hill and you'll do your thing for him, you'll let yourself be wired up, you'll tell him the truth about whatever he finds. And then, when I know what's what, I'll make my move. I'll step in and take charge. You understand?'

'You'll kill him.'

Larry Macpherson shrugged, his face watchful but otherwise expressionless.

Alfie said, 'How do I know that you won't kill *me*?'

'Because I need you to show to certain people what the glyphs can do. I need you to verify that they're potent. So how about it? Do we have a deal?'

'How do I know I can trust you?'

'You don't. But on the other hand, you don't have any choice. Either you cooperate with me or you die.'

'Then I suppose I'll have to cooperate with you.'

'Good man. Think you can stand up?'

Alfie's arms were still cuffed behind him and his legs felt like wooden posts, but he managed to get to his feet on his own. Larry Macpherson told him to turn around, stick his hands out as far as they would go, and Alfie did what he was told, thinking that the man was going to undo his handcuffs. Instead, the mercenary grabbed hold of the little finger of Alfie's right hand and twisted hard. An incredible bolt of pain shot up Alfie's arm and exploded inside his head. He'd once been so close to a lightning strike that he'd seen the flash and heard the thunderclap in the same instant. The pain was as shocking as that. White light went off behind his eyes and he cried out and fell to his knees.

Larry Macpherson squatted beside him, grasped a handful of his hair, pulled his head sideways, and said into his ear, 'Don't worry, it isn't broken, just dislocated. Pop it back in, it'll be stiff and sore for a couple of days, but it'll heal.' Pushing Alfie's head away, running the muzzle of his gun up Alfie's thigh, jabbing him in the balls and saying, his voice as calm as ever, 'Do I have your full attention?'

Alfie nodded once, blinking away tears.

Larry Macpherson said, 'Don't even think of telling my boss about our little agreement. It won't do you any good because I'll deny it and he won't believe you, plus it'll piss me off, and you don't want that. And if I think for one second that you're trying to play me, if I think you're lying about the glyphs when the man shows them to you, I'll do something far worse than dislocate a finger. Back in Afghanistan, a couple of the men I paid to guide me through the mountains had the idea of selling me out to one of the local warlords. They crept up on me one night when we were staying in some pissant village, but I took away the gun one of them stuck in my face, wounded him, and killed his friend. Next day, to make sure the others knew not to try to mess with me, I hung the fucker, but I took my time. Hauled him up, let him choke and dance a little, let him down again. Up and down, up and down . . . It took him a long hour to die. Would have taken him even longer if I hadn't had some other place I had to be.' He ran the muzzle of the pistol up Alfie's belly, jabbed him again, turning the gun's barrel so that the foresight caught a twist of cloth and skin. 'You understand?'

Alfie understood that whatever he did, it wasn't very likely that he'd get out of this alive. Still, he nodded. If Larry Macpherson wanted to kill Rölf Most, that was all right with him.

Larry Macpherson stood up. 'Now we've got that clear, let's get going. The man can't wait to see you do your stuff. He's so excited he's about to shit his pants. No lie.'

26

Harriet had a vivid moment of déjà vu when she walked into the narrow living room of the apartment where she and Toby Brown had spent the night, and saw the journalist and Emre Karin perched on the edge of a leather sofa, leaning over the map spread at their feet. Remembering Toby consulting a similar map in Clarence Ashburton's study while Julius Ward pointed to something with his walking stick, hoping now that Toby hadn't gone and spilled what she'd managed to keep back from Mehmet Celik and Emre Karin. She'd managed to snatch a moment with Toby last night, had made him promise that he wouldn't say so much as a word about the source of the glyphs. But now she wondered all over again if he could be trusted to keep his mouth shut, if he really understood that there was a lot more at stake than the lives of Musa Karsu and Alfie Flowers.

Toby greeted her cheerfully, a cigarette stuck in a corner of his grin, told her that if she wanted breakfast she'd better get to it: there were tea and rolls, cheese and slices of melon. 'Emre tells me they have the best melons in the world here.'

The interpreter was smoking too. The ceiling fan stirred eddies of grey smoke beneath the ceiling.

Harriet stared hard at Toby and said, 'Look at the two of you, all cosy together. Are you going to tell me what you've been plotting?'

Toby had been almost hysterical after the low man was shot and killed, convinced that he and Harriet would be next. Now, just a few hours later, he was on first-name terms with their kidnappers and believed that they were more or less on the same side. Harriet wasn't so sure. Last night there had been all kinds of loose talk about rescuing Musa Karsu and Alfie Flowers, of reclaiming the glyphs from the infidels – as if the patterns were no more than some kind of archaeological relic, or a folk tradition as harmless as bagpipes or basket weaving. But Harriet didn't want simply to stop Rölf Most from getting his hands on the glyphs: she wanted to destroy them. She believed that allowing them to fall into the hands of people who had no real idea what they could do would be as dangerously irresponsible as giving a couple of pounds of warm, shiny plutonium to a toddler.

She had slept badly, alone in the only bedroom of the apartment, up on the seventh floor of one of the modern blocks outside the ancient walls of the city. Trying and failing to work out how she could possibly escape from the Kurds and find Richard Elfingham and his fixer, dozing off and waking dry-mouthed and sweating from claustrophobic dreams that, thankfully, she didn't remember. At last giving up on sleep and watching the sky brighten beyond the neighbouring apartment blocks, feeling both an immense, oceanic weariness and a jangling anxiety, like a cross between jet lag and stage fright. When Toby had knocked on the door and asked if she was awake, it had taken a major effort of will to walk out of the bedroom and start dealing with the situation.

Emre Karin had exchanged his tweed jacket for a green canvas windbreaker. He sat back on the sofa and looked up at her, saying, 'There is a problem I must tell you about.'

Beside him, Toby said, 'A slight change of plan. Nothing serious.'

Emre Karin said, 'It seems that your good friend Dr Richard Elfingham was not convinced by your telephone conversation with him last night. He has unfortunately involved the police. Right now, they question Mehmet Celik, but it is okay, he will not tell them anything about this thing of ours, and they must soon release him, of course, because he is an important man.'

Toby squashed the stub of his cigarette in the big marble ashtray that anchored one corner of the map. 'The police aren't a big problem. Really. Emre has worked out how to get around it.'

Harriet sat on a leather hassock. The room was cluttered with furniture that seemed too large for it. The picture window, opening onto a sliver of a balcony, gave a view of the neighbouring apartment block and a strip of sky white as a headache. She said, 'Wouldn't it be easier to go to the police and straighten this out? I could tell them that Richard Elfingham was concerned for us, and made a mistake.'

She could tell them she'd been kidnapped and, after that had been straightened out, have Richard Elfingham's fixer smuggle her out of Diyarbakir and across the border into Iraq.

Emre Karin said, 'Perhaps your police have a sense of humour, but I assure you that *our* police do not. They will not say, "Oh, it is a mistake, that's fine, now you go." They will want to question you about this mistake, one day, two days, as long as it takes until they are satisfied. Then, almost certainly, they will deport you. And, of course, they will make much more trouble for us.'

Toby said, 'This means we can't go through the Habur Gate into Iraq as planned. But Emre says there's another way.'

'Slightly more uncomfortable, slightly more expensive,' Emre Karin said. 'But don't worry. It's okay. We have made all the arrangements. We will still make our rendezvous with our friends in Iraq.'

Last night, Mehmet Celik and Emre Karin had told Harriet and Toby that they would travel south to the Habur Gate, the main border crossing between Turkey and Iraq, and after crossing into Iraq they would meet up with a group of *peshmerga* soldiers who would take them to the Kefidis's old village, where they hoped to find Musa Karsu. Apart from the rendezvous with the soldiers, it wasn't so very different from the route that Harriet had planned to take with the help of Richard Elfingham's fixer. But now Emre Karin and Toby Brown seemed to be talking about something more complicated and probably much more dangerous. Harriet knew that it was a done deal, but she was reluctant to abandon the chance of getting back on course, of somehow getting away from these well-meaning amateurs. She said, 'If I could meet with Dr Elfingham, if I could talk to him face to face, I'm sure that I could convince him to tell the police that a mistake had been made.'

She'd suggest meeting Richard Elfingham somewhere public, and escape before the archaeologist arrived – tell her minders that she needed to use the toilet, jump onto a bus, order tea at a café and throw it into their faces, cause a scene . . .

Emre Karin was shaking his head, saying, 'We have no time for that, and no need – because we go now.' He raised his voice and said something in Kurdish.

The two teenagers who'd been guarding Harriet and Toby

came into the room. One had an automatic pistol shoved down the front of his jeans. Harriet said, 'At least let me change into clean clothes.'

'Actually, that's another problem,' Toby said. 'These guys couldn't pick up our stuff. The hotel is being watched by the police.'

Emre Karin said to Harriet, 'You have money? American dollars?'

Harriet said warily, 'A little.'

She had ten thousand dollars in a money belt under her skirt, and a wedge of Turkish lira wrapped in a spare change of underwear in her little leather rucksack.

Emre Karin said cheerfully, 'Then you can buy new clothes in Iraq. No problem.'

As they went down the stairs, the teenage guards fore and aft, Toby and Emre Karin tried their best to convince Harriet that although the arrangements had been made in a hurry, everything was going to be fine, they would be looked after by men who made their living smuggling people across the border. But it did nothing to diminish Harriet's sense of foreboding, of things unravelling. When they came out of the service entrance into a wide alley that separated their apartment block from its neighbour, and she saw the slat-sided truck parked beside a row of tall steel rubbish bins, saw the sacks of onions piled up on its load-bed, she said, 'You have got to be joking.'

And said it again when the driver and his mate, two young men in jeans and leather jackets, climbed onto the back of the truck and pulled aside sacks to reveal a large wooden packing case snug against the wall of the cab, saying to Emre Karin, 'You seriously think I'm crossing the border in that?'

The interpreter laughed. So did Toby Brown, in on the joke.

Emre Karin said, 'This would not of course be a safe way to get through the Habur Gate. There are long queues, and the security there, they use dogs, they use machines that can detect a man's heat, which is why we cross elsewhere. No, this is necessary to get you *to* the border, because since the Kongra-Gel ends the ceasefire there are police checkpoints on the road, and also the police will be looking for British tourists kidnapped by Kurdish criminals.'

'It'll be an adventure,' Toby said.

'That's what I'm afraid of,' Harriet said.

The packing case was padded with blankets, with just enough space inside for Harriet and Toby to sit facing each other. The driver gave them a plastic carrier bag containing oranges and bottles of water before fastening the lid and covering it with sacks of onions.

'I don't suppose I could smoke the odd cigarette,' Toby said, as the truck started up.

'I don't suppose you could,' Harriet said and asked why he and Emre Karin had been studying the map.

'I know exactly what you're thinking, but don't worry. All it was, he was showing me the route we are going to take. He said that as we were about to set off on our grand adventure we had to trust each other and share everything we knew. Words to that effect, anyway.'

Harriet braced herself as the truck made a sharp right turn, and said, 'You didn't say anything about the caves to your new friend?'

'Not a word. Cross my heart and hope to die.'

'When he pointed out the village, he didn't drop any hints, ask you any leading questions?'

'He was very matter-of-fact. Here is where we are going, this is the route we are going to take, that kind of thing. No trick questions, nothing like that.'

'So he thinks we're going to the village to look for Musa Karsu and save him from Rölf Most.'

'Isn't that what we're doing?'

'Not exactly.'

There was just enough light filtering through the slats of the crate's lid and the onion sacks piled over it for Harriet to see Toby Brown's expression change. He said warily, 'What do you mean? Isn't the point of this to find the poor kid before Rölf Most does?'

Harriet said, 'I really thought that Musa Karsu had gone back to Diyarbakir. Otherwise, I wouldn't have wasted time looking for him here. But there was something else I planned to do, whether or not we found him.'

She told him about the satellite photograph that Jack Nicholl had passed to her, told him that someone, almost certainly Rölf Most, seemed to be digging out the entrance to the caves, told him about the arrangement she had made with Richard Elfingham. On the whole, he took it rather well.

'So this has been about the glyphs all along.'

Harriet said, 'You came here because you hoped to find Alfie Flowers. I came here because I want to find Musa Karsu, but more than that, because I want to protect the source of the glyphs. We didn't find Musa Karsu in Diyarbakir, but if I'm lucky I might still be able to do something about the glyphs.'

'You think that Alfie is dead, don't you?'

'I can't be certain, but I think it's likely that Rölf Most probably used the glyph gun to make him talk, and then had him murdered. I'm sorry.'

After a short silence, Toby said, 'When Alfie asked me to help him find Morph – Musa Karsu – he was lit up like a Christmas tree, and if you knew anything about Alfie Flowers you'd know that isn't normal. He's the kind of guy who sort of sidles through life, always on the margins, or in a kind of parallel universe that only occasionally intersects with our own. I mean, he doesn't live in a house or a flat like any normal human being, he has that yard, his caravan . . . He's probably the only person in Islington who lives in a fucking *caravan*. And he likes to maintain what he calls his equilibrium. He likes his habits, he likes things the way he likes them because he thinks it helps keep his epilepsy under control. The poor guy,' Toby said, dry-eyed and calm as he eulogized his friend, 'I don't think he realizes how often he zones out. Anyone who met him for the first time would think that he was at best a Great British Eccentric, at worst a deserving target for a mob of peasants with torches and scythes or the kind of people who want to burn down the houses of paediatricians. Well, he may be a few straws short of the full thatch, but he's always been there for me. He was there when I got married, wearing a white tux and gloves if you can believe that, and he was there for me when my wife and I split up. We're good friends. I suppose I'm his best friend, when it comes down to it. And then he sees one of Morph's cartoons and asks me to help him, comes out with these outrageous stories about his childhood, his family. Who would have known? *I* didn't fucking know – I didn't have clue one. One minute he's so deeply stuck in his habits it would take a case of dynamite to shift him, the next he's raving about patterns that can seriously change your mind. The funniest thing? He really thought that Morph could help him. His epilepsy had been caused by looking at the wrong kind of glyph, and he thought that there might be another glyph that would cure him. The poor guy. When Julius Ward told him that there was no way to fix what had happened to him, he looked so pale you could have sliced him up and sold him as paper.'

There was a silence. The truck slowed, made a sharp turn that pressed Harriet against the side of the packing case, started to speed up.

Toby said, 'The weirdest thing of all? His crazy story turned out to be true. At first, I went along with it because he was my friend, and also, I freely admit it, because it was a great story. I thought, God help me, I could make some decent money from it. And now . . . Well, here we are. Who'd have thunk? If I haven't said it before, by the way, I'm grateful that you let me come along with you. I mean, I know you have a low opinion of me, all that, you could have easily said no, but you didn't.'

'You would have come here anyway.'

Toby said, 'A week ago, if you'd told me that I would be chasing after a crazy scientist who'd kidnapped my friend, I would have told you that you were as mad as a bag of frogs in a microwave. Now it seems like it was the right thing to do.'

Harriet said, 'It *was* the right thing to do.'

They smiled at each other, knee to knee in the dim, cramped, rattling space.

Toby said, 'You don't want Emre or Mehmet Celik to know about the caves. You don't want these *peshmergas* to know about them either. But unless you have some kind of cunning plan to deal with Rölf Most and his hired guns, we could probably use their help.'

Harriet shook her head. 'They don't know everything about the glyphs. They don't know how dangerous they are, to begin with.'

As the truck rattled its way out of the city, she told Toby about her African adventure, sparing no details. Now that there was a possibility he would be riding all the way to the source of the glyphs, she wanted to horrify him, wanted to make sure that he knew just how high the stakes were, wanted to make sure that he understood why she couldn't allow Mehmet Celik's people to get hold of the glyphs.

She told him about the plan to field-test the effects of the fascination glyph by incorporating it in poster ads plastered all over Lagos, advertising a chocolate milk drink that, laced with Carver Soborin's patent mix of psychotropic drugs, was given away in schools. The idea was that the spiked chocolate milk would make the fascination glyph work on the minds of the children who drank it, proving its effectiveness by causing them to crave more and more of it; in effect, turning them into chocolate-milk junkies. Instead, the combination of drug and glyph had driven many of them insane. She told him about the clinics full of crazy children, dying children, children lying comatose on mats with flies crawling over their open eyes. She told him about the attempt to arrest Carver Soborin at his compound in the exclusive neighbourhood in Lagos where foreign oil executives and high-ranking government officials lived – an operation that had gone badly wrong after dozens of low men had swarmed out of the darkness, attacking police and soldiers with machetes and clubs, fists and teeth and fingernails. The running battle in which every low man had been slaughtered, and dozens of police and soldiers and civilian bystanders had been killed or wounded. Carver Soborin's escape to America, the convenient fast-track diagnosis of paranoid schizophrenia and his committal to a private clinic and the care of a very good friend of his wife's, Dr Rölf Most. No trial, no investigation, a government whitewash that hadn't caught the attention of a press that wasn't much interested, just after 9/11, in a scandal that had occurred in far-off Africa, that had involved only African children.

Toby Brown listened carefully, and at the end asked several astute questions. But he missed the point of the story, saying, 'Rölf Most is as crazy as Carver Soborin. That's why we have to stop him before something like that happens again.'

Harriet shook her head. 'It's why we have to make sure that the glyphs don't fall into the hands of your new friends.'

'They aren't terrorists, Harriet.'

'Perhaps not. But how good are they at keeping a secret?'

'That's what this is about, keeping your precious glyphs secret?'

'Carver Soborin didn't have access to haka, so he used a mix of psychotropic drugs he'd devised himself, chiefly an extract from the seeds of Syrian rue, *Peganum harmala*. It wasn't a bad choice, actually, because the seeds of Syrian rue contain beta-carbolines, harma alkaloids, that are similar to those in haka. But they're only *similar*, not identical, which is one reason why his little field test failed.'

Toby said, 'Those poor kids drank the drink, saw the glyphs and, essentially, got a bad trip.'

'There's a rumour that the work mind's i did in Lagos was for the CIA—'

Toby said, 'I knew it.'

Harriet said, 'It's only a rumour. If there ever was a connection between mind's i and the Agency, it was obscured by the usual smoke and mirrors. But I think that even without the sponsorship of the Agency or anyone else, Carver Soborin would have ended up carrying out something like the Lagos project anyway. Because he could. Because he's crazy – psychologically damaged by exposure to the glyphs. Most of the employees of mind's i were affected in some way. They suffered from a whole range of mental illnesses. Monomania, hypermania, paranoia, obsessive-compulsive behaviour, virulent phobias . . . More than half of them have either committed suicide or have attempted it more than once.'

Toby said, 'I remember that Julius Ward said that the glyphs had made him ill, and made Clarence Ashburton blind in some kind of weird way—'

The truck slowed, stopped. Harriet heard voices outside – Emre Karin's voice, the voices of other men.

Toby whispered, 'A police checkpoint.'

Harriet nodded. It would be easy to kick the sides of the crate, shout, get the attention of the police, but she'd already decided that Emre Karin had been telling the truth about them, that escaping into their tender care would be like jumping out of the frying pan into the fire, and now that she knew that she was being taken to within five miles of the source of the glyphs it was a lot easier to reconcile herself to the situation. She'd ride all the way with Emre Karin and his *peshmerga* friends if she had to, and then she'd work out some way of getting away, finding the source of the glyphs . . .

At last, the truck moved off. Harriet told Toby, 'The glyphs contaminate the minds of everyone who uses them. They're the psychological equivalent of plutonium. There's no good use for them, which is why I'm willing to do anything I can to get rid of them.'

Toby said, 'What would you have done, if we had found Musa Karsu back in Diyarbakir?'

'I would have tried to persuade him to come back with me to Britain.'

'And then you would have handed him over to the government.'

'For his own protection. The Nomads' Club definitely isn't in a position to keep him safe from people like Rölf Most.'

'Poor little sod,' Toby said. 'He's like an atomic scientist – everyone chasing him because his head is full of deadly secrets, nowhere to hide . . .'

Half an hour after passing through the police checkpoint, the truck turned off the main road, jolted down a steep rough track, and stopped. The sacks of onions were pulled away from the packing case and Harriet and Toby climbed out, blinking in the sunlight. Toby immediately lit a cigarette. Emre Karin told them they still had some way to go – they could stretch their legs before they set off again.

The truck was parked beside a small house with stone walls and a flat roof at the edge of the remains of a tiny hamlet. Fields grown wild and ragged ran down to a river that wound away down a narrow valley towards a distant prospect of mountains hung like smoke against the fierce blue sky. The driver and his mate were talking with an apple-cheeked old woman in a black dress and black headscarf, a cigarette dangling from her lips while she poured an amber stream of diesel fuel from a jerrycan into the truck's tank.

Emre Karin explained that black-market fuel was cheaper than the fuel in service stations – and besides, no Kurd liked to pay tax to the government which had oppressed his people for so long.

'Turkey takes crude oil from Iraq, and exchanges it for refined gasoline and liquefied gas. It used to be illegal, because of the UN sanctions against Saddam, but the government allowed it because there was money to be made. It stopped during the invasion, but now it continues again, and now it is legal. The tankers travel through the Harbur Gate because it is the safest way in and out of Iraq. And some of the fuel finds its way onto the black market. A little spillage here, a little wastage there . . .'

Harriet used the stinking outhouse, then caught up with Toby Brown and Emre Karin as they wandered through the ruins of the hamlet. Most of the houses had been bulldozed or set on fire, leaving little more than stark walls and heaps of rubble. Broken furniture rotted among weeds. The warm breeze pushed a creaking door to and fro on its single hinge. A pink plastic doll lay where a child had dropped it. A well was filled to the brim with rubbish.

Emre explained that this was one of the villages that the Turkish army had cleared at the height of the PKK's guerilla campaign. He slashed at the heads of weeds with a stick he had picked up, saying that the Kurds had a word, *hawar*, that was difficult to translate.

'It means something like hopelessness, something like sorrow. A feeling that there is no longer any home, no place of safety. You feel it in places like this.'

Toby said, 'Because of what happened.'

Emre shook his head. 'Because this could be our future. In some places, the people come back. But many sold off their herds when the army banned access to summer pastures, and they can't afford to buy new animals. And the young people who grow up in the *gecekóndü* forget their past, forget their roots with the land. That is what the Turks would like, of course. For us to forget our roots, forget that we are Kurds.'

The truck's horn tooted on the far side of the abandoned hamlet. It was time to go.

There were two more police checkpoints, the first delaying

them for only a few minutes, the second preceded by a long
queue of stop-go traffic. At last, eight hours after setting off from
Diyarbakir, they reached an isolated house that stood above a
rough meadow carpeted with a galaxy of alpine flowers, stretching
away towards a stunning view of steep brown foothills and snow-
capped mountains. Emre introduced Harriet and Toby to the men
who would be escorting them across the border. Two cousins,
Dilovan and Azat Tokmat. Azat was young and skinny, a red handkerchief knotted under his prominent Adam's apple. Dilovan, a
burly, competent man in his forties, with the deadpan face of a
nightclub compère, said that it would be a very easy journey,
there was nothing to worry about.

'We go across the river, we walk an hour, two hours, to a place
where a pick-up waits. The pick-up takes you into Zakho.'

Harriet said, 'Just like that?'

Dilovan shrugged and said why not, he'd done it many times,
it was no problem.

'Zakho is the nearest Iraqi town to the border,' Emre said. 'We
meet *peshmerga* soldiers there. Kurdish soldiers. They will take us
to their friends, and then we will do what we must do.'

It turned out that Harriet was supposed to pay five hundred
dollars for the services of the two cousins. Emre told her to give
Dilovan half right away; the rest would be paid when they were
safely across the border.

'I find a way for you to get to Musa Karsu's village, and you
pay the expenses. It's a good deal.'

Harriet and Toby were given army-surplus camo jackets and
trousers to wear. After shaking his head over Harriet's sensible
flat-heeled pumps, Dilovan produced a pair of Nikes that, padded
out with two pairs of socks, weren't a bad fit. They were given
plates of rice and tomatoes and cucumber, and thick flat bread
to eat it with. Harriet managed to clean her plate, but Toby only
picked at his food, his face pinched and pale. He'd been smoking
steadily ever since they had climbed out of the packing case,
lighting each fresh cigarette from the stub of the last. He'd smoked
or given away the cigarettes he'd bought duty-free at Heathrow,
and had bought a dozen packs of a cheap Turkish brand, Samsun,
from one of the men who hung around the house.

By now, they were sitting with Emre Karin and a couple of men wearing leather jackets in a stuffy, smoke-filled room where a television played some kind of interminable quiz show. Harriet dozed off, and Toby shook her awake when at last, around midnight, Dilovan announced that they were ready to leave. He and his cousin were wearing camo jackets and woollen caps, carrying heavy rucksacks and Kalashnikov rifles. Emre Karin and Harriet and Toby were given smaller packs (when Harriet fitted her little rucksack inside her pack, she discovered that it was lined with several plastic bags), and they all piled into a van that drove at speed along a rough track, headlights off, navigating by the cold, scant light of the stars and a crescent moon, stopping at the junction with a brand new tarmacadam road that snaked above a river that ran noisily in the darkness.

Emre said that this was the Hecil River, the official border with Iraq. He sounded nervous. Harriet asked him if he had done this before.

'This will be the first time I have left Turkey.'

'Oh, that's just marvellous,' Toby said. He was smoking his fiftieth or sixtieth cigarette of the evening. When he spoke, its red coal wobbled up and down in the darkness. 'I thought you were supposed to be our guide. How can you be our guide if you've never been where we're going?'

'These men are our guides,' Emre said. 'I am a teacher, but when I am asked to help the cause, I do it proudly.'

'Marvellous,' Toby said again.

The van did a noisy three-point turn and sped off, its tail lights sinking away into darkness. The two cousins led Harriet, Toby and Emre Karin straight across the road into a scrubby wood that pitched down towards the river. A small constellation of lights twinkled several miles downstream, an army camp on a bluff overlooking the river.

'They build a new bridge there, only for the army,' Dilovan said. 'Just before America invades Iraq, we see American troops cross in Humvees. Also many trucks. We know then what will happen.'

In the near-dark, Azat knelt at the edge of the river and pulled hard on something – a rope that rose from the water in a long dripping arc. Dilovan switched on a flashlight masked so that it showed only a spot of light the size of a fingernail, and from his pack took out the inner tube of a tyre and a foot pump that he used to inflate it. It took a while; the inner tube was a yard across. Azat went across first, lying on his back across the inflated tube with his pack on his stomach, pulling himself hand over hand. When his cousin had reached the far bank, Dilovan pulled the tube back across the river. It came quickly, glistening in the moonlight as it bobbed on the black water, attached to the rope by a loop of steel wire and a canvas collar so that it wouldn't be swept away. Then it was Harriet's turn.

'Don't fall out,' Dilovan said, just before he gave her a push to launch her. 'You will probably drown, but if you float, the current carry you away. If the guards on the bridge see you, they use you as target practice.'

The river was only twenty yards across, but the current was fast and the water was icy cold. Harriet was soaked through, her teeth chattering and her hands numb and cramped, when at last Azat grabbed her and hauled her up onto the bank, saying softly, 'Welcome to Iraqi Kurdistan.'

They cut across country, climbing a steep ridge, scrambling down into a valley, climbing up again. Dilovan took the lead and Azat the rear, the two cousins setting a furious pace and smoking more or less continuously as they followed narrow paths that looked like they had been made by animals, stopping around three in the morning on a dry shelf of rock beside a stream that burbled noisily over boulders. The pack which Toby was carrying turned out to contain a primus stove and a tea kettle, a plastic bag of sugar cubes, and tea glasses carefully wrapped in layers of newspaper. There was food, too, flat bread and cucumbers and a spicy sauce. Harriet thought that they had hiked at least twenty kilometres; Dilovan said that it was only ten, and they had a little way to go yet – they had to escape the buffer zone guarded by Turkish troops. When Harriet asked just how far 'a little way' actually was, he shrugged and said one kilometre, maybe two.

'I thought we only had to travel one or two kilometres before we got a ride,' Harriet said.

Dilovan shrugged again and said straight-faced that if he told the truth many people would not choose to cross into Iraq this way.

The five of them sat around the faint blue light of the primus stove. The night was cold and immense and very dark. The moon had set, and the sky was mostly covered by cloud. Azat, with Emre Karin translating, asked Toby about English football. He was an Arsenal fan, and was amazed that although Toby lived in North London, less than a mile from the team's stadium at Highbury, he had never once seen them play. Dilovan let Harriet examine his Kalashnikov, showed her how to field-strip it, told her that before the invasion he had driven trucks carrying potatoes and onions and flour into Iraq, returning with diesel oil in fibreglass tanks – 'doing fibre'. After the fall of Saddam, he'd spent a few months working for an Iraqi businessman who imported air-conditioners from Western Turkey to Baghdad. He'd earned good money, he said, but each round trip had taken three weeks, and now it was too dangerous.

'Even in Mosul, the Iraqis stone trucks, they shoot at them, and there are many bandits on the road. Also, the Turks some-times mortar the road. They get much money at Customs for every truck that passes through the Habur Gate, but they see Kurds making a profit, so sometimes their true nature show itself.'

They dozed for a couple of hours and then, with the sky beginning to lighten in the east, struck camp, waded across the stream and climbed the steep side of the valley. The bright point of the sun lifted into a gap between the interlocking hills. Harriet's knees and ankles ached; Toby Brown sounded like a steam engine, and he'd finally given up trying to smoke and walk at the same time. Emre Karin slogged grimly behind him, head down, as they followed a narrow, deeply rutted track past scrubby fields and the shells of burnt-out farmhouses. At last, Dilovan told them to stop, and took out a chunky radio and talked into it for a few moments. Harriet saw a quick blink of light straight ahead, shining for a moment inside a clump of trees at the bottom of the track. For a moment, she thought that the light of the rising sun had caught a window of some lonely house. But then it blinked again, and she realized that it was the headlights of a vehicle, realized that they had made the rendezvous with the *peshmerga* soldiers who were supposed to take them the rest of the way.

27

Alfie was relieved to discover that Rölf Most's special piece of kit was no more than a portable electroencephalograph. He was familiar with the way EEGs worked, knew they were harmless; several times after his childhood accident, he'd spent a night or two hooked up to one in Addenbrooke's Hospital, so that the doctors could capture the activity of his brain during a seizure. And after he learned that all Rölf Most wanted to do was use an EEG to measure changes in the electrical activity of his brain when he was confronted with potent glyphs, he felt a faint spark of hope, felt for the first time since he'd been snatched from the street outside King's Cross Station that he might survive this.

'You are sensitized to the glyphs, Mr Flowers,' the psychiatrist said. 'When we break through to the rest of the caves, your reaction to what we find there will be most instructive. You are my ideal guinea pig. Or more accurately, given where we search, a canary of the kind that miners once took with them, to give them early warning of lethal concentrations of poisonous or unbreathable gases.'

Rölf Most was as happy as a child whose every birthday has come at once, talking non-stop as he glued dozens of tiny electrodes to Alfie's scalp, saying that he was doing this for America, that the glyphs would make a significant contribution to the war against terror. Saying that if America didn't take command of the glyphs, America's enemies would, and asking Alfie to imagine what a dictator or a terrorist would do with them.

'I suppose they'd use them to try to change people's minds. Just like you.'

Larry Macpherson gave Alfie a hard look; Alfie did his best to ignore it. He was sitting in a white plastic chair while Rölf Most leaned over him, in one of the Airstream caravans of the camp at the site of the ancient church. Like the cabin of the little jet plane, the caravan's interior was all in white. White carpet, white walls and ceiling, bench seats covered in white fabric, white plastic furniture, white blinds covering whitewashed windows. Alfie was wearing a white bathrobe, Rölf Most and Larry Macpherson were both wearing white doctors' coats, and the fourth man in the caravan, Carver Soborin, the psychologist who had treated Christopher Prentiss, wore white trousers and a white shirt-cuffs folded back to the elbows, displaying the silvery scars of an old suicide attempt on his forearms. Carver Soborin was in his sixties, with a pale face like a clenched fist, white hair in a crew-cut, colourless eyes that swam behind slab-like lenses with a frosty tint, the kind of eyes that look up from a fishmonger's ice tray. When Alfie had been brought into the caravan, the old man had stared at him for about five seconds before losing interest and turning back to his half-completed jigsaw, an amorphous blob of white, like spilled milk, set on a white fold-down table. He was still working at it more than an hour later, while Rölf Most fixed the last of the EEG's electrodes to Alfie's scalp.

Every one of his muscles ached and he wasn't sure that he'd ever be able to stand up straight again, but otherwise Alfie was feeling pretty good. He'd been fed a stack of microwaved blueberry pancakes with so much syrup that he was still riding the sugar high, and had been allowed two minutes in a hot shower. He'd managed to get himself more or less clean in the allotted time, and then Rölf Most had treated the finger that Larry Macpherson had dislocated, numbing it with local anaesthetic and splinting it neatly. It throbbed pleasantly and distantly now, like the socket of a freshly extracted tooth, as Rölf Most parted Alfie's hair, applied a spot of surgical glue to his scalp and attached another electrode, saying cheerfully, 'When confronted with extremists, you must sometimes use extreme methods to defend yourself. To defend democracy. In the end, it is what you are fighting for that makes the difference.'

Alfie said, 'That's true. I don't suppose terrorists would try to use the glyphs to turn a profit.'

Larry Macpherson shot him another warning look.

Rölf Most said, 'There is nothing wrong with profiting from knowledge. I have made a significant investment in this research. I have taken a large risk in the hope that I will win a large reward.

In that respect, I'm no different from any other entrepreneur. But I am also loyal to my adopted country, which is why I will first offer to sell what I find here to the government.'

The psychiatrist believed that he alone understood the true significance of the glyphs. Neither the Nomads' Club nor Morph's people figured in his balance sheets. Their traditions were a resource to be extracted, refined and sold on, like oil. As he carefully attached the electrodes, he told Alfie that it had cost him more than ten thousand dollars to buy the EEG and have it express-shipped to Mosul. But that was nothing, it was a mere bagatelle compared to the cost of the whole venture: searching for Musa Karsu in London, shipping vehicles and other equipment to Iraq in anticipation of discovering the source of the glyphs, paying the wages of mercenaries . . . He was flying high on glyph-hunger, could talk the hind leg off a barber. Actually, sitting in the chair while Rölf Most fixed electrodes to his scalp was very much like being at the barber's, Alfie thought, with Larry Macpherson glowering at him like a customer impatient for his turn.

Rölf Most was confessing now that, until a couple of weeks ago, his research on the glyphs had reached something of a cul-de-sac. Generations of shamans had developed a small number of potent glyphs by trial and error over the course of thousands of years; he had attempted to develop many more by renting time on a cluster of supercomputers, producing in only a few weeks millions of complex combinations of the entoptic elements that made up the glyphs. But without extensive testing on human subjects, there was no way of discovering which, if any, of these patterns were potent, and there were trillions of possible combinations of the entoptic elements to explore, a figure incomprehensibly large to the human mind. What he needed, Rölf Most told Alfie, was a set of rules that could be used to filter the few potent combinations from the vast number which had little or no effect on the minds of human observers. Analysis of the handful of glyphs that Christopher Prentiss had stolen from the Nomads' Club hadn't given him enough common elements to construct a workable rule-set, but soon he would add many more to his collection. These would not only be useful in the war against terror, but would also enable him to use the supercomputer cluster to discover entirely new classes of glyph.

'I knew all along that the source of the glyphs was somewhere in northern Iraq. I had read Christopher Prentiss's pamphlet, of course, and before he committed suicide the man had amused himself during his sessions with Dr Soborin by dropping hints about the Kefidis and the source of the glyphs. But these hints had been short on hard fact, and the only copies of the journal, maps, and drawings which your grandfather had made during the excavation of the source of the glyphs had been lost when the Soho premises of the Nomads' Club had burned down. Some years ago, professional thieves hired by Dr Soborin burgled the house where the last two members of the Nomads' Club lived, but they found nothing useful. And although I was able to discover from the records of missionaries the location of the village where the Kefidis had once lived, I soon learned that they had been massacred by neighbouring tribes some sixty years ago, and a search for survivors turned up nothing useful.

'I had been considering the extreme option of kidnapping Clarence Ashburton and Julius Ward and forcing them to reveal everything they knew, even though they were under the protection of the British secret services for whom they had once worked. Then I learned that not only was some graffiti artist spraying a version of the fascination glyph all over London, but that you, Mr Flowers, the grandson of the man who had discovered the source of the glyphs, had published a photograph of one of these very graffiti in a newspaper. I was employing a computer geek to maintain a set of bots, programmes that tirelessly search the internet for glyphs and glyph-like patterns, and your photograph won their interest at once.'

Rölf Most had been so convinced that the graffiti artist, Musa Karsu, could lead him to the source of the glyphs, the caves mentioned in Christopher Prentiss's pamphlet, that when he'd headed for London with Larry Macpherson and his team, he had also sent a small team of mercenaries, several of whom had experience of working deep drifts in the coalfields of Kentucky and Virginia, to wait for him in northern Iraq. But Musa Karsu had proven to be unexpectedly elusive, and Rölf Most had turned his attention to Alfie instead.

'Imagine my surprise when I discovered that you owned a copy of your grandfather's journal. And imagine by how much that surprise was compounded when I found out that exposure to a glyph in your childhood had made you hypersensitive to them, turned you into the ideal test subject. It is no coincidence, I think. It can only be the working of manifest destiny.'

'I'd prefer to call it bad luck,' Alfie said.

'What you call bad luck is in fact the glory of sacrificing your-self for the greater good,' Rölf Most said. He fixed the last of the electrodes to Alfie's scalp, clipped its wire into the thick braid that ran down Alfie's back, and plugged it into a digital recorder the size of a pack of cigarettes. He switched on the recorder and checked its self-diagnostic program, humming happily to himself, saying, 'Now we are good to go.'

Larry Macpherson said, 'Shouldn't you test it out first?'

Rölf Most's smile was full of sly delight. 'That is exactly what I intend to do. Find Mr Flowers some suitable clothes. I wish to introduce him to the destiny in which he does not believe.'

As soon as he had arrived, handcuffed in the passenger seat of Larry Macpherson's black Range Rover, at the place where Rölf Most and his mercenaries had set up camp, Alfie had recognized it from the old photographs tipped-in to the photocopy of his grandfather's journal. It was a triangular wedge of rough ground as big as a couple of soccer pitches, set into cliffs that overlooked a river gorge, and unchanged after sixty years apart from a fan of rubble that had fallen from the bluff that reared above it, the work of David Prentiss and Julius Ward when they'd revisited the site after the Second World War. The ruins of the church and other buildings were no more than a regular pattern of humps in the stony ground, dotted with thorny bushes, scarred by exploratory trenches made by a neat little yellow backhoe during the search for the entrance to the caves. That had been discovered beneath the rockfall, a shaft dropping to an antechamber that was connected by a short passage to the system of caves that ran under the cliffs. The passage had been blocked by slabs of rock blasted from its ceiling, damming the outflow of an underground stream and flooding much of the cave system, but the blockage had been removed, two galleries had been pumped out, and now Rölf Most's men were opening up another passage that might lead to other caves beyond the second gallery.

Alfie, dressed in black overalls, heavy boots that pinched his toes, and a hard hat, was lowered down the narrow shaft in the bucket hoist which had been used to remove spoil during the excavation of the passage. The antechamber at the bottom of the shaft was smaller than he had expected, a roughly circular space with naked rock walls starkly lit by floodlights on scaffold stands.

'I want you to see this,' Rölf Most said, steering Alfie towards a recess where a floodlight shone on a shattered stone stump.

It was the remains of the twin of the anomalous stone. Sixty-six years ago, Alfie's grandfather had posed next to it; ten years later, David Prentiss and Julius Ward had blown it up. The markings incised into what was left of its face looked a little like the lines on the pad of a thumb, magnified enormously. Rows of short straight lines. Rows of hooked lines curving off towards the top corners. Nested arcs. Three nests of spiral lines off-centre, with riverine lines running in parallel towards the base. Rölf Most jogged the floodlight and the lines seemed to swirl and flow as shadows danced across the carved surface.

Alfie said, 'If you're hoping to ring my bell, I'm sorry to disappoint.'

He had a strange feeling, though, standing where his grandfather had once stood. As if the brightly lit chamber was full of ghosts, and he was only a step away from becoming a ghost himself.

Rölf Most showed his upper teeth, whinnied through his nose. 'We will see from the EEG if it "rang your bell". There are more interesting patterns further in. You are perhaps familiar with the drawings your grandfather made of them. Think of it, Mr Flowers! Some ten or twenty thousand years ago, during the last Ice Age, this complex would have been a very holy place. Initiates would have made a special journey to reach it, and before they went any further, they would have entered a trance state induced by drugs and dancing and drumming, or perhaps by solitary meditation – perhaps in front of this very stone. Only then could they begin their initiation. Guided by shamans through passages that were narrow and winding, deliberately difficult to access, they would have encountered patterns that became increasingly complex, and increasingly potent. As will you. As will all of us.'

'You want me to see the rest of the caves?'

'Now you are down here, you may as well have the whole tour,' Rölf Most said.

Alfie knew that he was being set up, but he also knew that he didn't have any choice. If he resisted, Larry Macpherson would drag him through by his hair or by his heels. With his whole skin coldly tingling, aware of the electrodes glued to his scalp, he followed the psychiatrist into the low mouth of the passage that led deeper underground. The passage was very narrow and switch-backed gently, the water on its floor a foot or more deep in places. There was a scramble through a hole less than three feet high and about eighteen inches across at its widest point ('I hope the symbolism of this entrance is not lost on you, Mr Flowers,' Rölf Most said jauntily), and then the passage opened out onto a long, high-ceilinged gallery where a slope of loose cobbles spilled in a narrow arc down to a black wedge of water.

The floodlights here were battery-operated, dimmer. It was as cool as a meat locker and held time the way a vase holds water. The slow drip from a glistening stalactite into the black pool was like the tick of a clock counting the same second over and over. Alfie's pulse seemed as loud as a jackhammer in his ears; when Larry Macpherson dislodged a pebble as he squeezed through the crevice, the rattle of its fall was like machine-gun fire.

Rölf Most used a powerful flashlight to point out several places high up on the belly of rock that loomed above the narrow entrance. Charcoal sketches of two horses, one above the other. A larger painting of a horse on a flat panel of stone, executed in exquisitely shaded blacks and reds, with an arched tail, pricked ears and a rolling eye. A flexing cross of red and yellow ochre dots. Several gazelles done in red ochre, seeming to emerge from the shadows of a crevice near the ceiling.

'Perhaps there were more once upon a time, but this is the lowest part of the system and it has partly flooded, as you can see. If there was any cave art at the level at which we now stand, it has long since been washed away, and that which survives is not in good condition. The best is up there,' Rölf Most said, pointing the beam of his flashlight at a crevice tucked under the rock ceiling. 'You would crawl in there, with a burning brand, or perhaps a lamp made of grass and animal fat, lie on your back, and look at a pattern about a foot from your face. Don't worry, I won't insist that you look at it – it is a fascination glyph, something I already know. Fortunately, the second gallery is in much better condition, and contains some very interesting items. I insist that you see it,' Rölf Most said as he turned to Larry Macpherson and handed him a small black cylinder. 'Dose him up.'

After Larry Macpherson had squirted what felt like half a gallon of freezing, drug-laden spray up Alfie's nostrils, Rölf Most led the way up the gentle pitch of a ladder that had been laid on a slope of loose rubble. Tingling with anticipatory fear, with Larry Macpherson right behind him, Alfie followed the psychiatrist through a ragged opening into a cramped space like a side-chapel in a church. A light came on behind him, one of the battery-powered floodlights. It cast his shadow across a flat sheet of rock just two yards away. A great bison stretched at full gallop, outlined in charcoal and shaded with red ochre, vibrant, alive. Its shaggy head was haloed with a dense crowd of curving lines and zigzags, swirls and dots, stark black pigment against pale stone, so fresh that they might have been applied just hours before. Alfie shut his eyes at once, but the glyph had already burned itself into his eyes, expanding and contracting with his heartbeat.

He tasted burning metal, felt that he was falling through a crowd of fireflies. He heard someone cry out, a horrible cry of despair echoing off hard stone, and then the seizure took him.

28

The half-dozen *peshmerga* soldiers waiting in the dusty little grove were commanded by a tall, grave man with a bony face and black, brush-cut hair who called himself Terminator. He shook hands with Toby, then took hold of Harriet's hand, his gaze lingering and sincere as he thanked her for her courage and the great gift that she was making to the cause, turning away before she could reply, shouting at his soldiers, kicking at a man who was slow to get to his feet. Harriet paid Dilovan and Azat the rest of their fee, and followed Toby Brown and Emre Karin to Terminator's Toyota 4x4. The other soldiers climbed into a battered pick-up, and they set off at once, taking a road that skirted Zakho, crossing a river at an arched stone bridge and driving past a small township of brown tents which Terminator said was Camp Redeye, set up by the American army to house refugees after the first Gulf War.

Emre and the *peshmerga* commander talked politics as they drove south. The two men stuck to English out of politeness to Harriet and Toby, but Toby was uncharacteristically quiet, sucking on his cigarette as he gazed out of the window, and Harriet didn't feel like contributing to the conversation either. The hike across country had taken more out of her than she liked to admit; she found it hard to stay focused as she tried to work out how to escape from the soldiers, constructing and rejecting scenarios in her head while Emre and Terminator prattled on and heavy metal thumped and screeched on the stereo – an Iraqi band, Acrassicauda. Toby fell asleep beside her, and she reached over and plucked the cigarette that dangled from his fingers and squashed it on the heel of one of her trainers.

From Terminator's conversation with Emre, Harriet gathered that the *peshmergas* were members of the moderate, pro-Western Kurdish Democratic Party which controlled this part of northern Iraq and profited from the cross-border trade with Turkey.

Terminator's take on Iraqi politics seemed to be entirely prag-
matic. Anyone who helped the Kurds was good; everyone else,
whether neutral or actively hostile, was bad. George Bush One
was okay. John Major was okay. George Bush Two and Tony Blair
were okay too. So were Condaleeza Rice and Donald Rumsfeld
and Colin Powell. The Japanese and Italians and Poles were okay.
The French and the Germans were definitely not okay. The
Spanish had been okay, but now they had withdrawn their troops
from Iraq they were not so good. Turkey was sometimes okay,
Terminator said, waggling his hand from side to side, sometimes
not. In short, like the young tracksuited vigilante who had executed
the low man, Terminator was an enthusiastic supporter of the
invasion. Now that Saddam was gone and they had the support
of the Americans, he said, the Kurds would have plenty of influence in the reconstruction of Iraq. They already had ministers in
the interim government; for the first time, they had political legit-
imacy.

'We reclaim our land at last,' he said, looking at Harriet in the
rear-view mirror. He wore aviator-style glasses, tinted gold. 'And
it is thanks to your courage we also reclaim an important part of
our heritage.'

Terminator drove at a steady speed, beating time on the steering
wheel to the heavy metal's bludgeoning beat. The little finger and
ring finger of his left hand were missing, the edge of the palm
sealed with white scar tissue. They slowed at a *peshmerga* checkpoint, lines of stones and oil drums laid along the road to mark
lanes, a crude hut not much bigger than an old-fashioned outdoor
lavatory. The soldiers manning it waved them straight through.
They overtook tankers and freight trucks. They overtook a long
string of army trucks grinding uphill in low gear. Several of the
vehicles were towing field guns that wouldn't have looked out of
place in the Second World War. Terminator sounded his horn and
flashed his headlights as he drove past. A convoy of low-loaders
went by in the other direction, carrying Iraqi tanks stripped of
their treads and gun turrets. Destined for some Turkish foundry,
Emre said. There were only a few civilian vehicles, mostly people-
carriers and minibuses, and white taxis with orange body panels
front and rear. The countryside seemed emptier on this side of

the border, drier and bleaker, worn out by thousands of years of habitation. Trees scattered among dry scrub. Gullied hills. Mountains in the distance, floating at the rim of the bleached sky. A few villages of square houses with roof-support poles sticking out of their whitewashed walls. A landscape out of the mythic West of cowboy movies. Harriet, exhausted and half-asleep, wouldn't have been surprised to have seen a wagon train snaking away across a rocky slope, or a band of Red Indians strung along a ridge, silhouetted against the white sky.

Just before noon, Terminator swung the 4x4 off the road. The pick-up truck crammed with soldiers followed, the two vehicles bumping up a steep track to an old *peshmerga* encampment on a hilltop. A few lean-to tents camouflaged with brush, shallow trenches scraped into the stony ground, the blackened circles of old cooking fires, a three-hundred-and-sixty-degree view of bare ridges and stony slopes. While Harriet and Toby sat with their backs against an outcrop of sun-warmed rock, Emre Karin and the soldiers took turns to wash their faces and hands with water poured from a jerrycan before lining up for midday prayers. Moving with habitual grace while reciting brief passages from the Qur'an, raising their hands as if to cover their ears, folding their hands right over left upon their chests, bowing low, hands on knees, straightening up, prostrating themselves on the dusty ground.

While the soldiers proclaimed the greatness of God and dutifully submitted to His will, Toby said to Harriet, 'I've been thinking. Emre and his friends seem pretty sincere, so shouldn't we think about telling them the whole story? I mean, we could probably use their help to deal with Rölf Most, and in a way the glyphs sort of belong to them.'

Harriet wasn't in the mood to discuss this, was too tired to hide her exasperation. 'Do you really not get it? If the glyphs belong to anyone, they belong to the Kefidis, but apart from Musa Karsu, who might well be dead by now, the Kefidis no longer exist. They were massacred by their neighbours sixty years ago – by Kurds like Terminator and his little gang. And in any case, the glyphs are horribly dangerous. The low men and all the rest of Rölf Most's little party tricks are just the beginning, if we don't stop him. And that's why we're here. To stop him. To stop him and anyone else, no matter how sincere they might be, from using the glyphs.'

She was out of breath and the headache she'd been suffering more or less continuously since her seizure was thumping forcefully behind her eyes. But her angry little speech didn't seem to have made an impression on Toby, who said with maddening reasonableness, 'The main thing is to stop Rölf Most using the glyphs. Absolutely. But I don't think that you should treat these guys like children. This is their country, after all, and they've already done a lot for us—'

'I didn't ask for their help, if that's what it is, and frankly I don't need it either. Let them go look for Musa Karsu – as far as I'm concerned he's a side issue now. What we have to do is get to the source of the glyphs and find out what Rölf Most is up to. If we can get there in time, we have to try to stop him. If we don't, well, I suppose I'll have to chase after him. And if you don't want to follow me, whatever you do afterwards for God's sake don't tell these people about the source of the glyphs. Not that it will matter, because I intend to make sure that no one will be able to get into those caves ever again. But the fewer people who know about them the better,' Harriet said, staring at Toby, feeling at that moment, because she was angry and frustrated and headachy and so very tired, that it wouldn't be any great loss if he didn't come back from this.

Toby returned her stare. His pale face had grown a heavy stubble. His eyes were bruised from lack of sleep. 'So all we have to do is get away from Emre and his friends, trek across country, deal with Rölf Most and *his* friends, and blow up the caves. I hadn't realized that it was so simple.'

'I have plenty of cash. Once we get away from the *peshmergas*, we can buy what we need.'

'Oh good, because I was beginning to think you didn't have any kind of plan.'

'You don't have to come with me.'

'Even if we do manage to stop Rölf Most getting his hands on the glyphs, that won't be an end to it, will it? The CIA knows about the glyphs, our own spooks know about them . . .'

'It draws a line,' Harriet said.

'For the Nomads' Club, or for you?'

'That's a cheap shot.'

Toby shrugged. 'I came here to find out what happened to Alfie, and now I seem to be caught up in some kind of personal vendetta. I mean, your father stole the glyphs, Carver Soborin learned about them from him, Rölf Most learned about them from Carver Soborin—'

'Do I feel some kind of responsibility for what my father did? No, I don't. I hardly remember the man. But the Nomads' Club unearthed the glyphs in the first place and my grandfather was part of that: it's family business and it's the business of the Nomads' Club, the two things are woven together. It's only right and proper that the Nomads' Club helps to bury the glyphs before they can do any more harm, and because our secret services have been told to back off there's no one else to do the job.'

The men sat up on their haunches and recited the closing prayer. *As-salaamu alaykum wa rahmatullah.* Peace on you and the mercy of Allah.

Toby got to his feet as they did, dropping his cigarette and crushing it under the sole of his boot. Telling Harriet, 'The Nomads' Club is just a couple of old guys and their memories. You've cast yourself as their champion, but do you really think you can do this on your own?'

Harriet stood up too and said, 'Don't do anything rash.'

'Or what? You'll knock me off with a ricin-tipped needle, or some kind of deadly karate move?'

'If you lead the *peshmergas* to the source of the glyphs, I won't need to "knock you off". Do you really think they'll just thank you and let you walk away?'

'If I was going to tell them about those caves, I wouldn't be discussing it with you. I would have already done it. I'm on your side, Harriet, but you're not the Lone Ranger, and I'm definitely not Tonto. Think about it.'

As it turned out, the *peshmergas* had their own plans. While his soldiers brewed tea and broke out US army ready-to-eat rations, Terminator used an old, briefcase-sized satellite phone to talk to someone, then walked over to Harriet and Toby, trailed by Emre

Karin, and squatted in front of them. Studying them through the tinted lenses of his glasses before saying, 'My commandant sent a patrol to look for the people who you say are looking for this boy. They just now report back.'

Harriet's alarm cleanly pierced the pulse of her headache. 'You have people at the village?'

Terminator smiled. 'Of course. You think my commandant sits around, waiting for you? He sent a small group, good men, very experienced. They approach the village on foot, study it a long time. They see no one. This is not a surprise. Most of it is ruined, and already Americans took away the family of the boy we look for, the only people who lived there.'

Harriet said, 'Are your people still in the village?'

She was thinking that if the *peshmergas* ran into Rölf Most's mercenaries, it was going to make her job very much harder.

'Don't worry,' Terminator said. 'They know what they are doing. They are professionals. They watch the place from a distance, and when they see no movement they go in and check it out. Now they pull back, set up an observation post, watch the road in and out. If anyone comes, they will see them.'

Toby said, 'The people looking for Musa Karsu, they aren't figments of our imagination. Right, Emre?'

Terminator said, 'My good friend Emre tells me all about what happened in Diyarbakir, the two Americans and the rest. I also know that the others fly into Mosul and then drive east, towards the mountains. This was four days ago. My commandant checks it out with the airport people. The question is, if they are not at this village, where are they?'

Harriet gave Toby a hard look, trying to convince him by sheer force of will to keep quiet, to say nothing about the source of the glyphs. She said, 'Perhaps they have already found Musa Karsu.'

Emre said, 'It is possible.'

'It is possible,' Terminator said, studying Harriet. 'But their plane, it is still at the airport. So it is also possible they look for the boy elsewhere. What do you think?'.

Harriet said, 'I think we must do everything necessary to stop these guys getting hold of this boy.'

'That's good, because my commandant asks me to tell you that he looks forward to talking with you about everything you know,' Terminator said, and got to his feet and walked off.

Toby said, 'Was that some kind of threat?'

Emre said, 'His commandant is anxious to find Musa Karsu, and so he is anxious too, because he wants to do his duty. We all want the same thing, we are on the same side, so everything will be okay.'

'Of course it will,' Harriet said.

But she felt that everything was slipping away from her. If she and Toby didn't get away from Terminator and his soldiers before they reached Mosul, they would be forced to give up everything they knew about Musa Karsu, the glyphs, the source. Meanwhile, Rölf Most and his men were probably still excavating the caves, only five miles from the village where Musa Karsu had grown up. If they didn't run into the *peshmerga* soldiers there, they'd be caught when they returned to Mosul . . .

An hour later, shortly after driving through the town of Summel, they hit a traffic jam on a road that wound between steep, scrub-covered hills. The southbound lane was full of trucks and tankers crawling forward a few dozen yards and stopping again with hissing air brakes, and then the traffic was nose to tail, there were trucks pulled over at the side of the road, and men were setting out plastic chairs and lighting little stoves and brewing tea, clearly settling in for the day. Terminator drove down the middle of the road, using his horn, flashing his head-lights, the pick-up full of soldiers right behind. The road bent around a bluff of naked rock that bulged like a forehead, revealing a river and a steel bridge just a hundred yards away. Trucks, tankers, buses and cars were queuing two or three abreast, and the bridge was blocked by coils of razor-wire, a pair of sand-coloured Humvees, and an eight-wheeled Stryker armoured vehicle topped with an M2 .50-calibre machine gun. American soldiers were walking up and down between the vehicles, exam-ining papers, ordering people back into their vehicles. They didn't seem to be letting anyone through. There was a similar checkpoint at the far side of the bridge, a queue of traffic snaking away uphill. Black smoke, lots of it, rose into the blue sky beyond the straight edge of a ridge.

Terminator turned, resting his automatic pistol on the headrest of his seat, saying, 'You will not cause trouble.'

'What do you mean?' Harriet said.

'You will not tell these soldiers why we are here together, where we are going.'

Emre cleared his throat and said, 'Everything will be okay.'

'Those guys look like they mean business,' Toby said. A trio of American soldiers in desert camo, webbing belts hung with gear, assault rifles cradled in their arms, faces hidden by helmets and sunglasses, were walking towards the 4x4 and the pick-up.

Terminator said, 'You will tell them you are journalists. You travel with us, make a story about us. Okay?'

Harriet said, 'Of course.' Adding, because Terminator was still staring at her above the muzzle of his pistol, 'Think about it. We entered this country illegally. We're chasing Americans who are chasing Musa Karsu. The last thing I want to do is get involved with the US army.'

Terminator smiled and said, 'Maybe we don't need you to find this boy, or the Americans who are looking for him. Think about *that*. It's in your interest to come with us.'

Harriet said again, meeting his gaze, 'Of course.'

That was when Toby opened the door. Shouldering it open and scrambling out so quickly that he stumbled and almost fell to his knees. Emre made a grab for him, missed. Then Toby was jogging towards the three American soldiers, his hands raised in a gesture of supplication and surrender.

29

Rölf Most told Alfie, 'Here is your normal waking trace, and as you can see it consists of low-voltage, fast-activity patterns.'

On the screen of the laptop, the irregular yellow line wavered across a dark green grid laid over a light green background.

The psychiatrist pressed the space bar; the screen jumped. 'And here is the sleep state into which you lapsed after you had your seizure, and you see that the trace is very different, that it consists of slow waves of relatively high voltage.'

Now the line filled half the screen with the silhouette of a range of tall, steep mountains, different heights, different shapes.

'Burst-pause,' Carver Soborin said from his corner in the caravan's white space, where he was working on yet another white jigsaw.

Rölf Most said, 'You're with us today. Very good. *Very* good. Do your jigsaws, stay focused, there are great wonders ahead of us. He's quite right, Mr Flowers. This trace shows the burst-pause activity typical of non-REM sleep. Slow, oscillatory firing of clusters of neurons distributed across the entire brain, the signature of true unconsciousness. In the waking state, or during REM sleep, when you dream, groups of neurons fire in continuously changing patterns, representing the enormous variety of processes required to sustain those two types of consciousness. In non-REM sleep, however, their firing is synchronized. And something similar happened when you were confronted with the glyph.'

He scrolled backwards along the EEG trace. More mountains, these close-spaced, and as regular as teeth on a saw.

'In an ordinary person,' Rölf Most said, 'treatment with my drug mixture followed by exposure to a potent glyph forces the brain to adopt a particular state. It is not unlike the process that occurs when a person is presented with a single object — a red ball, for instance. In that case, specific groups of neurons in the visual system of the brain, those associated with spherical shape and the colour red, are induced to fire, and they in turn excite other neurons in other areas of the brain, such as for instance those associated with a particular memory of a red ball. Likewise, if a person in the hypnagogic state induced by my little cocktail is presented with a potent glyph, that glyph causes specific sets of neurons to fire in a particular sequence over and over, inducing a single repetitive brain state. Fascination, for instance, or fear. That single state dominates all others. It becomes the only thing the subject can think about, and if the period of exposure is long enough it induces a permanent change in the subject's consciousness.

'But when you, Mr Flowers, are exposed to a potent glyph, something very different happens. Your brain does not adopt the particular state which the glyph should induce. Instead, the electrical activity in your cortex lapses into this repetitive spike-and-wave activity at three Hertz on the EEG, typical of a petit mal seizure. It is like the trace of the non-REM sleep, but even more synchronized. Hypersynchronized, in fact. The cortical neurons are either all firing together, or they are all silent. In short, Mr Flowers, you suffered a seizure that rendered you insensible. And then that lapses into the true unconsciousness of non-REM sleep, as we have already seen,' the white-haired psychiatrist said, hammering the laptop's space bar, scrolling the trace forward, 'and at last we see the normal trace again, as you recover consciousness.'

'You never recover,' Carver Soborin said from his corner. 'Not really.'

Rölf Most said cheerfully, '*You* certainly never recovered, but that's your charm, of course. He has been exposed to too many glyphs, Mr Flowers. Without his jigsaws, he is liable to lapse into a fugue, or a babbling monologue, or some other form of mechanically repetitive behaviour. But as long as he has his jigsaws and his Ganzfeld Stimulation, he is, as they say, as right as rain. Do you know what it is, a Ganzfeld Stimulation? Of course you don't. It is a form of snow-blindness reported by Arctic explorers. If a person gazes for long enough at a featureless field of vision, such as the flat, snowy landscape of the North Pole, all colour drains from the field of vision, and then all visual experience fades too. Would you care to guess why?'

'Not enough brain states,' Carver Soborin said, without looking up.

Rölf Most clapped his hands together. He was entering one of his manic periods, smiling from ear to ear, his eyes glittering. 'An apple for the bright boy in the corner! He's right, Mr Flowers. A person requires a critical number of differentiated brain states for their conscious experience to be sustained. In Dr Soborin, we try to obtain a homogeneous brain state akin to non-REM sleep. A Ganzfeld nirvana that frees him from the unfortunate side effects caused by his pioneering work on the glyphs.'

'Sometime I think that you understand me,' Carver Soborin said, without looking up from his puzzle. 'But then you say something that proves that you really don't.'

'Oh, I understand you all too well, do not worry about that. He's my sounding board, Mr Flowers, my source of inspiration. I owe him an incalculable debt because I have learned so much from him about the glyphs. And now, with your help, I will surpass his pioneering work. You're a rare specimen. In an ordinary subject, a particular potent glyph forces the brain to adopt the particular state it encodes. But not you. Your brain reacts violently when you are exposed to a potent glyph. You have an epileptic seizure, and hey presto! The slate is wiped clean. It is a very effective defence mechanism.'

'But not ideal,' Alfie said. 'Not from my point of view.'

'Oh, but it makes you an ideal test subject. If you are exposed to potent glyphs, you have a full-scale seizure. And then you recover, and you are good to go once more. A miner's canary that can be used over and over,' Rölf Most said, turning to a second laptop. 'But I think I will now test you without the drug cocktail, and find out what differences there are in your reactions to potent glyphs and mere patterns. Don't be dismayed – from what you told me, without the drug I think you will react positively to potent glyphs, but I do not think you will have any seizures. I don't want to harm you, Mr Flowers. I want you to be part of this little family. What fun we're going to have together!'

30

Harriet and Toby were taken up the hill in a Jeep, climbing above the bridge and the river in its deep, rocky channel. Emre insisted on coming with them, telling the American soldiers that he was their interpreter, twice climbing back into the Jeep after they turfed him out, finally being allowed to stay despite Harriet's objections. Terminator and his soldiers were left behind on the road, arguing with the American soldiers guarding the bridge.

'Here's a familiar phrase,' Harriet said to Toby. They were jammed together in the back seat of the Jeep, speaking in fierce whispers with their heads almost touching. 'Frying pan and fire.'

Toby, still wired from the escape, said, 'Didn't you hear what our *peshmerga* friend said about how much his commandant was looking forward to talking to us about everything we know? *Everything*, Harriet. Not just the stuff you were willing to tell him, but all the rest, whether you wanted to or not. As soon as he said it, I knew you were right and I was wrong, and I decided that I was going to do my best to find a way of getting away from his tender care. And I did it, too – but that's okay, you don't have to thank me.'

'You are our guests,' Emre said, overhearing this. 'You tell these people it is all a mistake, we get back with the *peshmergas*, all will be fine.'

'No offence to you, Emre, but your *peshmerga* pals were treating us like prisoners,' Toby said. 'Maybe you didn't notice the big fucking gun Terminator pointed at us just now, but it definitely got *my* attention.'

'That was a mistake, yes. But don't worry, he will apologize for it.'

'Oh, I'm not worried about it now.'

Harriet nodded towards the two soldiers in the front of the Jeep. 'You really think these guys will help us?'

Toby said, 'I know you don't trust anyone, but I'd rather take my chances with them than with the *peshmergas*. If we're lucky, they'll take us to Mosul, and then we'll have a breathing space to work out what to do next.'

If the Americans did take them to Mosul, Harriet thought, she would definitely find a way of leaving Emre and Toby behind. Although she was relieved that they'd escaped from the *peshmerga* soldiers, the journalist's panicky recklessness could have got them killed, and she wasn't sure that they'd be any better off in the hands of the US army. She would have to find some way of talking herself out of this, leave Toby and Emre behind, and go on alone, as she had always planned.

The Lone Ranger – why not?

The Jeep roared over the top of the ridge and sped along a dusty, deeply rutted track to a wide, flat spot at the edge of a scarp where a Humvee was parked. Half a dozen American soldiers and a single civilian were standing like tourists at a beauty spot, looking out across the wide valley to a distant hillside and a pair of helicopters floating above it amongst curtains of smoke. They were Apaches, the US army's primary attack helicopter, moving backwards and forward like wasps at the entrance to their nest, continuously changing height and position, the beat of their rotors merging into a faint, sleepy drone. As Harriet climbed out of the Jeep, one of the Apaches dipped down and darted forward, emitting a puff of white vapour at either side of its fuselage as it launched a pair of rockets. The sound of the explosions came a few heartbeats after the double flash, two columns of black smoke boiling up as the helicopter beat backwards and its companion moved in and hosed the ground with streams of tracer-lit fire from its nose-mounted chain-gun.

The corporal who had taken charge of Harriet, Toby and Emre saluted an officer, handed over Harriet and Toby's passports, and explained that he'd found these two British nationals with a whole bunch of *peshmerga*, that one of them, the guy, claimed to be a reporter. He had some kind of union card, but no form of official accreditation.

The officer, a captain, was lean, deeply tanned and about Harriet's age, DAVIS printed in black ink on the name-tape sewn to his flak jacket. He glanced at the passports, handed them to the civilian, and asked the corporal about the other guy, the local.

'He claims to be their interpreter, sir,' the corporal said. He was holding Harriet's little rucksack in one hand.

'Who are you working for?' the civilian said, as he methodically thumbed through Harriet's passport. He was a stocky man in top-of-the-range hiking gear, an automatic pistol holstered at his hip, his mild face shaded by the bill of a black baseball cap. Harriet, sensing a fellow spook, took an instant dislike to him.

She said, 'We're freelance journalists, embedded with the *peshmergas*. Following them around, a day in the life, that sort of thing.'

Toby said, 'Actually, the soldiers – the Kurds? We were having a slight disagreement with them. Nothing serious, but we're sort of relieved that you took us off their hands.'

'If you guys are looking for a story,' Captain Davis said cheerfully, 'you've found a good one.'

Toby said, 'We're supposed to be in Mosul, and we were wondering, perhaps you could give us a lift?'

Captain Davis ignored him, telling Harriet, 'I reckon it's the kind of story that has universal appeal. We're the good guys. And over there are the bad guys, who are currently getting ten different shades of shit blown out of them.'

On the distant hillside, clumps of shattered pines and swathes of scrub were burning around the smashed ruin of a small building. The helicopters were hovering side by side above this, their prop wash driving complex arabesques through the veils and columns and reefs of rising smoke.

Harriet said, playing along, 'Who are the bad guys? Terrorists? Freedom fighters?'

'Same difference,' Captain Davis said, studying her. He had a wry, laconic manner, a laid-back charm. He said, 'These particular bad guys, though, they're truck thieves. Hijackers.'

'You're using attack helicopters to deal with truck thieves?'

'We're the army, ma'am. We're not trained in the finer points of justice. We're trained to kill people and blow things up. We're pretty good at it too, as those fellows are finding out. Why don't I tell you what happened? You'll love it – it has what I believe you might call a satisfying classical simplicity.'

'By which you mean that you're the good guys, you chased and caught and killed the bad guys, and made the world safer for democracy.'

'Damn right.'

'Just like in the movies.'

Harriet was trying not to watch as the civilian checked through the contents of her rucksack, examining her satellite phone, riffling through the pages of her Moleskine notebook, which contained details of the location of the source of the glyphs, set down in a simple substitution code. Luckily, she hadn't been stupid enough to have brought along a map, or the satellite photograph of the source of the glyphs that Jack Nicholl had given her.

Toby, no doubt feeling that he was safe now, lit a cigarette. Emre Karin stood behind him, taking care not to catch anyone's gaze. The invisible Kurd.

'It's even better than the movies,' Captain Davis said. 'How it started, a bunch of bandits stole a couple of truckloads of satellite dishes last night, just this side of Mosul. They shot and killed the truckers, and one of their own number was wounded in the crossfire and got left behind. Which pissed him off so much that when we arrived on the scene he'd already talked to the local police and informed on his friends. We chased after them, and cornered them at the roadblock we set up at the bridge. There was a firefight, and when we proved to have superior firepower, the bandits beat a retreat and holed up in a farmhouse. And now those Apaches are finishing them off. I know what you're thinking: this is the kind of shit we deal with daily, no big deal. But I happen to think it's one of the better actions we've had recently. Usually the bad guys shoot at us or lob an RPG or mortar round and fade, or they set up mines or IEDs – Improvised Explosive Devices – along one of our routes. This time we actually got to engage them face to face. For a minute or so, it was almost like a real war. If you want to write this up, I'll be happy to give you all the details,' Captain Davis said, pointing to the two helicopters that were harrying the far ridge. 'Maybe you should take a photograph – those guys look like they're about done.'

Harriet said, 'The problem is, we had a little trouble and we lost our kit. But if you can get us to Mosul you can be sure we'll write it up.'

Toby said, 'Absolutely. Perhaps one of your soldiers has pictures we could use.'

The civilian stepped forward and said, 'Mind telling me how you got into the country?'

Captain Davis said, 'Do we have a problem here?'

The civilian said, 'These people don't have accreditation, and they don't have stamps anywhere in their passports either.'

Harriet said, 'I don't think I caught your name.'

The civilian said, something hardening in his expression, 'I'm the guy you have to explain yourselves to. What was your point of entry? Turkey? Syria? Kuwait?'

Harriet said, with a sinking feeling, 'We came from Turkey.'

The civilian said, 'And how exactly did you cross the Turkish border?'

Harriet shot Toby a warning look and said, 'We came through the Habur Gate. I don't know why they didn't stamp our passports. Perhaps you should take it up with them.'

She knew that she'd been caught fair and square, but it was part of the game that you didn't give up your cover until it was entirely blown.

The civilian said, 'How did you link up with the KDP? Do you have an arrangement with them?'

'Of course,' Toby said. 'Although it's sort of unofficial, if you know what I mean.'

'Do you have a point of contact, someone we can talk to, to verify your story? How about the man in charge of those soldiers you were riding with? If we brought him up here, would he confirm your story?'

Toby said, 'As I mentioned, we were having a slight problem with our *peshmerga* friends. What you might call a difference of opinion.'

The civilian said, 'Your interpreter, is he with the *peshmergas*? Or did he come with you?'

After a moment of silence, Captain Davis said, 'Are you sure these people are up to no good, Bob?'

The civilian said, 'I don't know what they're up to, but I definitely think they entered the country illegally, probably with the help of the *peshmergas*, who have themselves a nice little racket smuggling people and luxury goods across the border. What I think I'd like to do is take them in for further questioning.'

Captain Davis shrugged. 'I'm more than happy for you to take them off our hands, Bob. After those Apaches finish up, we're going to be walking up that hill, doing sweeps. I don't have the inclination to deal with a couple of freelance journalists who are looking for some kind of an adventure. No disrespect intended, ma'am,' the soldier said, smiling at Harriet. 'But this is as much for your safety as my friend's satisfaction.'

The civilian said, 'Believe me, it has everything to do with my satisfaction. The easiest way would be if you called in one of those Apaches, have them give us a lift.'

Captain Davis shook his head. 'Those birds will be heading back to Dohuk after they've finished up here, for refuelling and rearming.'

The civilian said, 'It would take one of them about thirty minutes to fly us to Mosul.'

'They're not my birds, Bob. You can try talking to their CO, but you know he's going to say more or less the same thing. What I *can* do is loan you a Jeep and a couple of men. How does that sound?'

'To be frank, it sounds like you aren't backing me up.'

'If you don't think you can hack it, you'll have to wait here while we do the job we're paid to do, come back with us to Mosul when we're finished.'

The civilian stared at him for a moment, then said, 'You said you'd give me two men?'

'She's your catch, Twetten,' Captain Davis told the corporal. 'Take one volunteer from your squad and ride along with our friend.'

The civilian looked at Harriet. 'If you're working for some agency, now's the time to tell me. We can get this all straightened out, and you can be on your way.'

Harriet briefly thought of giving him Jack Nicholl's name. Of telling him, yes, she was working for Her Majesty's government, that Mr Nicholl could confirm that she had urgent and highly confidential business to attend to, and he would be of the most enormous help to her mission if he could arrange a lift to Mosul . . . But she knew that anything she told him would have to be checked out, and if MI6 discovered that Jack had helped her he'd be in deep shit, and she'd be flown home on the next plane. So she parried the offer, saying, 'And which agency are you working for, Bob? The CIA?'

He stared at her for a moment more, his face impassive, then took Captain Davis aside and talked to him for a few minutes, the two men glancing now and then at Harriet and Toby. Harriet ignored Toby when he asked her what would happen when they reached Mosul. She turned her back on him and watched the two helicopters make another strafing run. At last, they were ordered to climb back into the Jeep. The civilian rode up in front, squeezed between Corporal Twetten and the driver; Harriet sat on the rear bench with Toby and Emre. They drove back down the hill, past the *peshmerga* soldiers who sat by the side of the road, guarded by a couple of GIs, their weapons in a pile in front of them. Terminator watched them go past with a sour expression; Toby couldn't resist giving him a little wave, bye-bye.

They drove through the checkpoint and across the bridge, passing a blackened crater that had taken a big bite out of the road and two burnt-out trucks squatting on their wheel rims close by, passing the line of trucks and tankers and other vehicles that queued nose to tail on this steep straight section of road, waiting to cross the bridge. Men sat in their cabs and smoked and listened to their radios or gathered in small groups around fires or camp stoves, smoking and drinking tea. Harriet saw two men struggling to lift a large and obviously heavy cardboard box into the back of a slat-sided truck, and then the Jeep was passing pairs of men lugging big cardboard boxes downhill, men dragging boxes by themselves. Three men were boosting a box onto the load-bed of a pick-up. A man was lashing a box to the roof of a taxi.

The Jeep reached the crest of the slope and swerved to a halt beside an accident which half-blocked the road: a panel truck had run into the back of a flat-bed truck carrying two fat fibreglass tanks. One of the tanks was leaking a steady stream of black oil, spreading beneath the truck, running into the ditch by the side of the road. A body covered by a yellow tarpaulin lay beside the front wheel of the panel truck, and a small crowd of men were jostling around the rear, trying to climb inside, shouting and pushing at each other. A box lay on its side nearby, split open to reveal the air-conditioning unit inside.

The civilian told Corporal Twetten to keep driving. 'Radio for help if you want, but drive on.'

'Can't do that, sir,' Corporal Twetten said. 'If someone drops a cigarette in that oil it could light up the entire road. We're gonna have to police this until help turns up – it shouldn't take but five or ten minutes. Meantime, I suggest you look after your prisoners.'

Harriet watched as Corporal Twetten and the driver walked across the road, cradling their rifles. The corporal knelt to check the body under the tarpaulin and briefly used his radio, the driver walked towards the crowd of looters, shouting at them in English, and in the Jeep Emre startled Harriet by standing up and saying that he would help the soldiers. Saying, when the civilian told him to stay where he was, 'I speak Turkish and Kurdish. I will help the soldiers, tell these men to be calm, yes?'

'Sit down,' the civilian said, turning sideways in the front seat, his back to Harriet as he reached for the automatic pistol holstered at his hip.

Harriet saw her chance, surged up and locked her left arm around his neck and made a grab for his pistol. The man tried to pull away from her headlock and she went with him, still trying to pull the pistol from his grasp, sliding head first into the front seat with his weight across her upper body, her shoulders slamming against the steering wheel. He twisted free, and as she went after him his pistol went off and a hard noise and a searing pain in her shoulder knocked her down. The civilian started to get up, and Toby swung the Jeep's fire extinguisher in a wide arc that connected with the side of his head. The man lost his balance and made a grab for the top of the windshield. Toby hit him again and he went down.

As Toby and Emre dragged the unconscious man from the Jeep, Harriet groped in the footwell for his pistol. She felt something loose and jagged grate in her shoulder and for a moment thought that she would faint, but then her fingers closed around the grip of the pistol and she sat up, pointing it at Emre as he clambered into the back seat.

'Don't be fucking stupid,' Toby said, sliding in beside her and starting the Jeep.

A slow dark wave rolled through Harriet's head. Emre was watching her, his hands half-raised. She said, 'He isn't coming with us.'

'No time to argue,' Toby said, and stamped on the accelerator.

As the Jeep shot past the truck, Harriet saw that Corporal Twetten and the other soldier had climbed inside it and were wrestling with one of the men. They were on the point of dumping him into the little crowd of looters when the corporal saw the Jeep, did a perfect double take, and grabbed his companion's arm. Both soldiers jumped down and the crowd surged forward. Harriet heard a rattle of automatic fire, and then the Jeep sped around a bend.

31

Larry Macpherson said, 'Man, just look at you. You're still shaking.'

Alfie said, 'When he said that he would kill me – do you think he meant it?'

'Sure he meant it. He's crazy, but that doesn't mean he doesn't mean what he says. He'll calm down, maybe he'll even start talking about you being part of the family again, but don't you believe a word of it. When he said he was going to use you and lose you, that was the truth. See, you disappointed him. You took his ambitions and pissed all over them; your brain wouldn't do what he wanted it to do, and that got him so angry that his mask slipped, let the real man show through.'

Rölf Most's experiment hadn't gone well. Alfie had sat for more than an hour in front of the laptop, staring at a slide show of dozens of different arrangements of entoptic elements. Here and there, hidden at random intervals among the benign patterns, had been a potent glyph, seeming to stand out from the screen when it appeared, pulsing with ugly life. Fortunately, because he hadn't been dosed up with Rölf Most's cocktail of drugs, repeated exposure to this glyph hadn't triggered another seizure, but Alfie's headache and nausea had grown steadily stronger, and by the end of the experiment he was having trouble telling the patterns on the screen from those on the insides of his eyeballs.

While Alfie watched the slide show, Rölf Most measured his brain activity through the array of electrodes glued to his scalp, studying the EEG trace on a second laptop. Apparently, Alfie blanked out several times, although he had no memory of any of these little absence seizures, and according to Rölf Most only one of them corresponded to the presence of the potent glyph. At last, the psychiatrist called a halt to the experiment, saying that something was wrong – he hadn't been able to resolve a signature pattern in Alfie's brain activity whenever Alfie had been exposed to the glyph.

'There is too much noise in the system,' Rölf Most said. Pacing up and down in the confined, all-white space, slapping his fist into his open palm every time he turned. Three steps, turn, slap. 'Perhaps it is because you are still recovering from a major epileptic seizure, you are exhausted, and there is still a trace of the cocktail of psychotropic drugs in your system.' Turn, slap. 'Perhaps it is because you are undergoing withdrawal from your usual dosage of barbiturate.' Turn, slap. 'Perhaps, when you are fully rested, and I am able to test you in laboratory conditions using more sensitive equipment than a simple EEG, using for instance magneto-encephalography to resolve the fine detail of activity in your visual system – perhaps then I will be able to differentiate between your response to random patterns and to potent glyphs. What do you think?' he said, stopping right in front of Alfie's chair, staring down at him, punching his fist into his palm.

Alfie said truthfully that he didn't know what to think, but this somehow angered the psychiatrist. He thrust his face close to Alfie's and said, 'Perhaps you hold out on me. Perhaps without the drug you are able to play a trick, yes? You are able to hide or confuse your true reactions. Is that what you did? Tell me the truth!'

He slapped Alfie, quick and hard, catching hold of the lapels of Alfie's bathrobe when he tried to pull away, shouting right into his face, spraying him with spittle.

'You did something! I know you did something, some trick, some piece of low cunning. Maybe I should dose you up again, give you another seizure, yes, and another after that. Oh, I can make you jump like a pithed frog until you promise to co-operate.'

Rölf Most worked himself up into a fine fury, accusing Alfie of trying to fool him, of cheating, saying that it didn't matter, he was merely a small part of a much grander scheme. The psychiatrist was pacing up and down again, watched calmly by Larry Macpherson and more or less ignored by Carver Soborin, talking for fifteen minutes straight about how he would astound everyone with his discoveries and open the door on a new age of human consciousness, until at last he began to wind down, collapsing onto one of the white plastic chairs, saying that soon his men would break through the rockfall into the chambers beyond. Saying that he was certain that there was much to be discovered, more than enough to satisfy his backers.

'There will be more potent glyphs, no doubt about it, and you will help me prove their potency. You'll have to be drugged of course, and you'll have to suffer another fit, but it is all in a good cause. I will video your reaction to the glyphs, and then, well, then I am very much afraid, Mr Flowers, because of your stubborn refusal to cooperate, because you will not open up willingly to me, because you try to disguise your true nature, well, I must do with you what I would do with any laboratory animal that is no longer of any use. It is nothing personal, you understand . . .'

That was when Larry Macpherson had intervened, saying that they were all tired, it was time to take a break. Now he and Alfie were sitting side by side on a low strip of ancient wall near the edge of the gorge, Alfie in the white bathrobe and shower slippers, Larry Macpherson in his flak jacket and mirrored sunglasses. It was growing dark. Mist was creeping up the gorge, thickening the air, slowly erasing the view of the river and its rocky shoals and little islands where rough grasses or a few canted trees grew. Behind them, floodlights shone around the entrance shaft, and the diesel generator and water pumps made a low, steady thrum.

Alfie said, 'I was able to pick the potent glyph from all the others. You saw that. Just because he couldn't see any difference in the EEG traces whenever I did it doesn't mean that it wasn't real.'

Larry Macpherson said thoughtfully, 'That glyph he used – wasn't it the one he zapped you with back in the plane?'

'I wouldn't know. It knocked me out, remember?'

'I believe you,' Larry Macpherson said. 'As far as I'm concerned, it doesn't change a thing.'

But he was studying Alfie with cool surmise, and Alfie knew that he was thinking about Rölf Most's experiment, wondering if Alfie was any use to him after all.

Alfie said, 'Do you really think that you can bring this off by yourself?'

Larry Macpherson had let it slip that the two men who had

been helping him search for Musa Karsu in London should by now have arrived at the camp, after running a little errand over the border, in Turkey. Something must have gone wrong, and now he was going to have to do whatever he'd planned to do on his own.

The mercenary bared his teeth and said, 'There aren't more than a dozen of them. Plus a few low men wandering about the countryside, but they don't count for anything. The man couldn't resist turning this family who were living in the place where you were kept. He said they'd be useful as watchdogs, but by now they've probably all starved to death or fallen into ravines or been eaten by wolves . . . Frankly, I think he turned them because he could. Because he likes to play tricks, like that stunt he pulled in the cave. He's had you here all along, he could have experimented on you any time, but no, he waited until he could take you down into the cave, give his stupid speech, and knock you out with that picture. Anyhow, don't you worry about what I have to do. When it comes to it,' he said, lowering his voice and leaning close to Alfie, 'I'll do them all if I have to. Though I reckon that once I get rid of the man, I won't need to do more than one or two of them before they get the point and clear out. You going to let that good food go to waste?'

Alfie had set aside his TV dinner. Chicken and potatoes and sweetcorn and glutinous gravy, some kind of chocolate sponge pudding, it had been heated in the microwave of the field kitchen, a square tent open on three sides, where a couple of Rölf Most's men were sitting at a plastic picnic table in their muddy black overalls, forking up their own dinners.

'I'm not really hungry,' he said, and passed the plastic tray to Larry Macpherson.

Alfie felt as if two long thin needles had been pushed all the way through his eyeballs, and he was still seeing a swarm of luminescent floaters wherever he looked. He'd been scared that if he was exposed to another potent glyph while dosed with Rölf Most's cocktail it would do some kind of permanent damage to his brain, every bit as bad as the damage caused all those years ago when he'd snuck a look at the glyph his grandfather had hidden away. But now he knew that he was in greater danger from Rölf Most and Larry Macpherson. He knew that after he'd been dosed with the drug and exposed to any glyphs that might lie on the other side of the blocked passage, after he'd proved their potency by suffering a seizure, he would be murdered.

Sipping apple juice from a wax-paper carton while Larry Macpherson scooped up the food that he had rejected, Alfie felt immensely weary, eye-fucked, head-fucked, his dislocated finger throbbing inside its splint. He realized that if he was to have any chance of surviving this he would have to try his best to avoid being drugged again. If he was drugged he would almost certainly suffer a seizure, and if he had a seizure he'd be helpless . . .

He said, 'These backers that Rölf Most mentioned. Are they the CIA?'

'Why do you ask?'

'I heard the CIA was involved in something Carver Soborin did in Africa,' Alfie said, hoping that he could keep Larry Macpherson talking and work the conversation around to what he needed to ask.

'The man is a little too wild for the Agency,' Larry Macpherson said, around a mouthful of chicken and potato. 'And besides, after what his mentor got into in Africa, they're wary of the glyphs. By all accounts that was a real fucking mess . . . No, where he gets his money is a Delaware corporation that's funded by a bunch of extremely rich, extremely well connected and extremely patriotic businessmen. At least one of them has high-level contacts with the Agency, which is why we had a certain licence when we were operating in London. Maybe the Agency is planning to take a serious interest if this works out, but right now everything is completely deniable.'

'How about you?' Alfie was nurturing the small hope that if Larry Macpherson was working for a government agency there might be some kind of curb or control on his activities. But the man was shaking his head.

'I've worked for the Agency in an indirect way in the Stan, but right now . . .' Larry Macpherson forked food into his mouth and said, 'If you were hoping to be rescued by little black helicopters and Mulder and Scully, then I'm sorry, buddy. Unless my two pals turn up it's all down to me. My people are businessmen too: they're

very interested in the potential of these glyphs for internet advertising, and that's all I'm saying. But they'll see you right, don't you
worry about that. As long as you cooperate, that is.'

'As long as I'm a good little lab rat,' Alfie said. He had finished
his apple juice and was absent-mindedly shredding the carton.

'As long as can you do what you claim you can do,' Larry
Macpherson said.

'Those tests don't mean anything,' Alfie said.

'I told you it doesn't change a thing,' Larry Macpherson said,
scooping up the last of the chocolate pudding. He stuck the fork
deep in his mouth and made a loud sucking sound, then skimmed
both fork and tray out over the edge. The fork dropped straight
down, but an updraught caught the tray and for a moment it rose
high above their heads before tilting sideways and swooping down
towards the mist . . .

Alfie remembered a beach distant in both time and space, the
kite plummeting into the sea, his father kicking off his shoes and
dashing into the waves to rescue it. Just do it, he thought, and
said, 'Rölf Most says his men are going to break through soon.
Today, do you think? Tomorrow?'

Larry Macpherson shrugged.

Alfie said, 'When they do break through, Rölf Most will drug
me, make me look at whatever's in there, and video me while I
look, because if I have a seizure it will authenticate his discovery.'

'Uh-huh.'

'And then he'll want to kill me, because he won't have any
more use for me. He'll want to kill me, leave my body down
there. Which means that you'll have to kill *him*. In fact, you'll
probably have to kill everyone else down there,'

'I told you that you don't have to worry about that.'

'But if all this happens down there in the cave—'

'Hey. All you need to know is that when the time comes I'll
deal with everything, which is why I told you about it in the first
place. I don't want you getting in the way. I want you to drop to
the ground and fucking stay there until I tell you otherwise.'

Alfie said, 'I'll already be on the ground if I've had a seizure.
And then what?'

Larry Macpherson looked at him.

Alfie said, speaking quickly, knowing that he had only this one chance, 'If you have to kill him, if you have to kill everyone down there, how are you going to get me out? It took me three hours to recover from the last seizure, and I believe that four men had a lot of trouble getting me to the surface.'

'Maybe I won't have to kill everyone. I'll spare a few, and they can haul you out.'

'What if you *do* have to kill everyone?'

'If you're trying to make a point,' Larry Macpherson said, 'get to it.'

'I think there's a way of making sure that I don't have a seizure, even if there are potent glyphs down there. We can fool Dr Most into thinking he hasn't found anything and, more importantly, I'll be able to walk out of there. First of all, I need the medicine I was carrying when you kidnapped me. It'll help maintain my equilibrium.'

'What else?'

'When Rölf Most wants me jacked up on that cocktail of his, I'll make a fuss, so that he'll need you to step up and do it by force.'

'But I'll have emptied the little spray gadget,' Larry Macpherson said, catching on at once. 'So when I spray it up your nose, all you get is air. And without the drug you won't have a seizure, even if there's a hundred potent glyphs down there.'

'Exactly,' Alfie said, a freezing sweat prickling across his back while the mercenary considered this.

'I don't think so. For one thing, I need to know if any shit we find down there is the real deal. For another, I get the idea that you're planning some kind of dumb move.'

'Absolutely not. I know that if I'm going to get out of this in one piece I have to rely on you. I have to be your lab rat. But if I have a seizure—'

'It may not come to that. And if it does, let me worry about how I'll get you out of there. Okay?'

'Okay,' Alfie said.

Well, now he knew. Now he knew that Larry Macpherson was planning to leave him down there with Rölf Most. Now he knew that he'd better think – as soon as possible – of some other way of gaining an edge.

32

Half a mile down the road, barely a minute after they'd stolen the Jeep, Harriet saw a white minibus chugging up the long slope towards them, and ordered Toby Brown to pull over.

'We can't stop right now,' he said. He was hunched forward, strangling the steering wheel. 'But as soon as we're clear of this we'll break out the first-aid kit—'

Staring at her when she put the automatic pistol in his face. 'Pull over,' she said. 'We need another ride. This is far too conspicuous.'

Toby nodded, let the Jeep drift into the side of the road, a little way past the end of the long queue of vehicles waiting to cross the bridge. Harriet's broken collarbone was beginning to hurt like fury and an impressive amount of blood had soaked into the sleeve of her camouflage jacket, but as far as she could tell she'd been lucky: the bullet had exited cleanly, leaving a hole that wasn't much bigger than the entry wound. Once the bleeding was staunched and her arm was bound up she'd be as right as rain, she thought, but she had a bad moment when she climbed out of the Jeep, a wave of darkness rolling through her head, sweat popping out all over her body. She took a breath and told Emre Karin to come with her, pointing the pistol that she'd taken off the American civilian, a Heckler & Koch P7, at him when he started to protest, making him walk ahead of her as they marched into the middle of the road.

Harriet raised the Heckler & Koch into the air when it looked as though the minibus was going to try to swerve around her, fired a single round, and aimed the pistol straight at the driver, keeping it trained on him when the dusty little vehicle stopped and she walked up to it. After the driver had cranked down the window, Harriet told Emre Karin to explain to him that he was going to give them a lift. The driver, an impassive grey-haired man in a collarless white shirt, shrugged after Emre had relayed this to him, as if this was an everyday kind of occurrence, as if being hijacked at gunpoint was no worse than getting a traffic ticket.

Harriet, knowing that by now Captain Davis must know about the stolen Jeep, scared that at any moment the two Apache helicopters would come beating above the road and cut them to ribbons, shouted to Toby Brown, telling him to bring her rucksack and the Jeep's first-aid kit. She wanted to leave Emre behind, but Toby persuaded her that they needed the interpreter's help: they didn't know the country, and neither of them spoke Arabic or Kurdish.

'Also, I will treat your arm,' Emre said. 'Lucky for you that I know a little first aid.'

As the minibus turned around and drove towards Mosul, speeding past traffic heading all unawares towards the roadblocked bridge, the interpreter cut off the sleeve of Harriet's combat jacket, stuffed sterile cotton wool soaked in antiseptic in her wounds, fastened pads of cotton over them with adhesive bandages, and used a bandage roll to fashion a sling. Harriet swallowed a couple of military-strength painkillers and began to feel a little better. Just before they reached the little town of Girepan, she told the driver to stop and get out. While Toby took the wheel, she pulled a thousand dollars from her money belt and asked Emre to tell the driver that she was sorry they had to take his vehicle: she hoped this would go some way to reimbursing him. The grey-haired man stared at her after Emre Karin had translated this. He ignored the money that she held out to him through the window, then with slow, contemptuous deliberation, spat between his feet. Harriet threw the money at him and told Toby to get going, feeling dirty and ashamed.

They drove through Girepan and turned east, heading towards the mountains. Harriet, sitting in the shotgun seat next to Toby, using the GPS function of her Iridium satellite phone and a laminated map that Toby had taken from the Jeep to navigate, began to feel a cautious optimism. They were free of the *peshmergas*, they were heading in the right direction, and now that they had left the main road it was less likely that the American soldiers would be able to find them. The road threw snaky turns as it climbed above a river that foamed white over shoals of rocks. They cut through a pass and turned south and then east again, driving in a long straight run. Towards the end of the afternoon they reached a nameless settlement at a crossroads: a few single-storey houses and a gas station with a café next to it, a cinder-block shack and a few low tables and stools scattered beneath a flimsy lean-to constructed from corrugated iron sheeting and scaffold poles.

They sat in the minibus, drinking tea and picking through bowls of fatty lamb stew and rice, and talking about their options. Harriet showed Toby the route she'd plotted to the source of the glyphs. She told him that she didn't know what they would face when they arrived, she didn't know whether Rölf Most and his mercenaries would still be sitting there or whether they had found what they had been looking for and had packed up and left. And if they were still there, she didn't know how many there were, or how heavily they were armed. Pretty heavily, she suspected; after all, this was Iraq. Against that unknown number of highly experienced mercenaries, she had a single pistol with eleven nine-millimetre rounds left in its magazine, and a small element of surprise.

She had given up trying to pretend to Emre that this was anything to do with the boy, Musa Karsu. She was too tired, too weak from shock and loss of blood, to bother with all that now. The interpreter listened to Toby's brief explanation about the source of the glyphs, shrugged, and said, 'If you tell us this from the beginning, we could avoid much trouble.'

Harriet said, 'If we'd told you about this while you were holding us prisoner, your *peshmerga* friends would have gone there straight away, just as they did when they found out about Musa Karsu's village.'

Emre smiled. 'You still do not believe we are on the same side.'

The weaker Harriet got, the more confident he grew.

Toby said, 'Whether or not we were on the same side back in Diyarbakir, we sure as shit had better all be on the same side now.'

Emre Karin said, 'As far as I am concerned, nothing has changed. I am here to help you.'

Toby said, 'I don't suppose you know where we can stop off and buy guns and explosives.'

Emre shook his head. 'Was that your plan? It is a good thing you did not try it. You would have been cheated or robbed and killed, or turned over to a loyalist group who would have made political capital from your capture.'

Toby said, 'You're saying you can't help us.'

'I already help you,' Emre said, and attempted to persuade Harriet to allow him to use her satellite phone to call the commander of the *peshmergas*, telling her that she must see that she needed their help more than ever.

Toby, still badly shaken by the hijacking of the Jeep, backed him up, saying that as things stood they didn't stand a chance against Rölf Most and his merry band of mercenaries. Saying, 'Like it or not, we're all in this together. Either we come to an agreement about what to do, or I'm bailing out right here. And I don't think you'll be able to get very far on your own, seeing that this minibus has a stick-shift gear, and you only have the use of one arm.'

'In that case I think perhaps I will stay here too,' Emre said. 'I have no wish to commit suicide.'

Harriet said, 'Toby can stay here but you're coming with me. You can drive.'

'Alas, I do not know how.'

He returned Harriet's stare with a deadpan expression. It was impossible to tell if he was lying.

She said, 'You're coming with me. Otherwise you'll run to the nearest phone and tell your friends all about this.'

'You could always shoot me dead,' Emre said complacently.

'It's still an option,' Harriet said.

She felt that the two men were ganging up on her, forcing her into a corner. The painkillers were wearing off, her wound was aching badly, and it suddenly seemed very hot and close in the minibus. She got out and walked a little way down the road, trying to clear her head. A little group of children and women in headscarves were following a tractor and trailer across a newly ploughed field, picking up stones and throwing them in the trailer. A hot wind lofted veils of dust behind the tractor and winnowed the long grasses growing along the verge of the tarmac road. Snow-capped mountains stood in the distance.

Harriet felt ghostly, hollowed by shock and exhaustion. The ache in her shoulder was the only thing that felt real, the only thing anchoring her to the here and now. She knew that she had fucked up badly, all the way back to the beginning – when she'd decided to bring Toby with her, when she had decided that it was worth stopping off in Diyarbakir to try to find Musa Karsu. She also knew that she was not ready to give up, and that she wouldn't be able to do what she needed to do without the help of the two men, and, yes, of the *peshmergas* too.

Some Lone Ranger, Harriet thought. I probably knew all along that I'd need help, I just wouldn't admit it to myself. That's why I allowed Toby Brown to come with me, it's why I agreed to meet Mehmet Celik.

She sat by the side of the road until she had worked out exactly how to play the few cards she had. Then she got to her feet and walked back to the minibus, to tell the two men her terms.

The road ran east through a broad valley. Low reefs of cloud raced in from the north, skimming the hills ahead. By the time they reached a track that seemed to head in the right direction, they were driving through streaming mist, and the sun was no more than a vague red patch low on the horizon. Toby Brown switched on the minibus's headlights; Harriet told him to switch them off.

'We're in enemy territory now.'

They drove slowly in thickening mist and gathering darkness, wallowing along a rutted, potholed track that climbed and dipped and climbed again, squalls of white vapour blowing across their path, the windscreen wipers squeaking back and forth. When Harriet saw a small, low house appear off to the side of the track, her heart jolted and she lifted the pistol from her lap. She thought for a moment that either she had misread the map and her satellite phone's GPS, and had led them to Musa Karsu's village, or that Toby Brown and Emre Karin had somehow collaborated against her and had managed to deliver her into the hands of the *peshmergas*. But then the mist blew aside for a moment, and she saw that the flat-roofed, mud-walled house and its single, ramshackle outbuilding sat alone in a small grove of wind-stunted apple trees, with rough, rock-strewn pasture hummocking away on either side.

As the minibus lurched past, something gleamed in Harriet's sight, nagging at her like a shard of glass reflecting sunlight. Then she realized what she had seen and told Toby to jam on the brakes. When the minivan had stopped, she snatched the keys from the ignition and walked back down the track, her heart beating quickly and lightly, a hot needle jabbing at her wound with every step.

The fascination glyph was done in red paint, vivid against the badly mortared concrete blocks of the outbuilding, haloed around a stencilled cartoon – a grinning skull wearing a soldier's helmet decorated with a crude representation of the Stars and Stripes, the whole thing about a yard across. It seemed to Harriet that the glyph floated an inch away from the wall, burning through the mist and so completely capturing her attention that she almost jumped out of her skin when behind her Toby said, 'Is it real? I mean, is it one of Morph's?'

'I think so.'

Emre Karin said, 'I think so too. Musa Karsu drew things like this when he was working for us.'

Toby took a deep breath and let it out. 'We were right. He came home. He came all the way back here to protect the glyphs.'

Emre Karin said, 'Yes, but where is he now?'

The three of them stood with the mist blowing past, staring at the cartoon and the fascination glyph.

Harriet was the first to look away, turning with an effort, trying to blink away the after-image burnt into her retinas. The discovery of the glyph should have elated her, but instead she felt a smouldering dread. She was too late. Musa Karsu had already passed through here. By now he could be in the hands of Rölf Most, he could be dead . . .

Toby lit a cigarette and said, 'It looks fairly fresh. Maybe he's camping out here, or somewhere close by.'

Emre said, 'My friends are not very far from here. Perhaps he stopped here on his way to the village. Perhaps they have found him already. We should call them, I think.'

The two men were still staring at the bright red piece of graffiti. Harriet said, 'The road to the village is on the other side of this hill or mountain or whatever it is. I don't think he was on his way home when he did this; he was heading towards the same place we're heading, towards the source of the glyphs. That's a lot closer than the village, and that's where we'll find him, if he's anywhere to be found.'

'We should look around,' Toby said. 'He could be using this place as a hideout.'

Toby took charge of the flashlight that Harriet fetched from her rucksack; she aimed the pistol at shadows and dubious corners. The house contained two small bedrooms and a much larger room with a scorched hearthstone in its centre. Judging by the straw bundles that hung from a rafter and the dried cow flop and goat droppings on the pounded earth floor, it looked as if the people who had been living here shared their house with their animals. Someone else had been camping out – there were aluminium foil containers and half a dozen soft-drink cans scattered about, cigarette butts, a rumpled copy of a pornographic magazine – but Harriet didn't think that it had been Musa Karsu. There was a stained mattress and a chemical toilet in the little outbuilding, and Emre found a fresh grave to one side of the house, a mound of raw earth not much more than a yard long.

'Rölf Most's men came here,' Harriet said. 'They were looking for Musa Karsu, they asked questions, they killed someone to force the others to tell the truth . . .'

Emre nodded. He had a solemn look.

Toby said, 'What about the rest of the people who lived here?'

'They're probably dead,' Harriet said. 'At least, I hope so . . .'

As they walked back up the track towards the minibus, rough grass fading into mist on either side, Toby suddenly stopped, put his hands to his mouth, and called out Musa Karsu's name.

'Don't *ever* do *anything* like that again,' Harriet said. At that moment, she could have cheerfully shot Toby. Although his voice had been instantly swallowed by the misty twilight she felt a sudden prickling nervousness, felt that something was out there in the mist, watching them. She said, 'Didn't I tell you that we are in enemy territory? There could be patrols, or someone could be watching the road.'

After a moment, Toby said thoughtfully, 'If someone is watching the road, they'll see us coming, because there's no way I can drive any distance without switching on the headlights. Actually, they'll probably hear us before they see us. Our ride seems to have a perforated exhaust, and its engine isn't exactly whisper-quiet either.'

Emre said, 'Perhaps this is the time we call my friends.'

Harriet was anxious to get going. 'We have an agreement. We scout out the source of the glyphs first. If there's no one there, we'll go in and take a closer look. Only if Rölf Most and his people are still there do we call your friends for back-up. That's what we agreed, and that's what we're going to do.'

If Rölf Most was still there, if he hadn't yet found what he was looking for, Harriet planned to call up the *peshmerga* soldiers and use them as a diversion. While they were fighting with Rölf Most's mercenaries, she'd find a way to sneak into the caves and do whatever had to be done to seal them up.

Emre said, 'If we are caught before we take this closer look—'

Something howled, out in the mist.

Toby said, 'Jesus, was that a wolf? Do they have wolves here?'

Emre said doubtfully, 'Perhaps it was a dog.'

Harriet said, 'I think it was a man.'

They hurried towards the minibus, looking in different directions, trying to see through the mist. When Toby started the engine and switched on the headlights, there was another howl, a raw sobbing cry like mad grief, and someone ran at them. He ran very fast, bursting out of a thick drift of mist, caught square in the diffused glare of the headlights as he ran down the middle of the track: an old man in black trousers and a heavy sweater, mechanically chopping at the air with a long knife like an over-wound clockwork toy. Toby slammed the minibus into first gear and tried to swerve past him. There was a thump on the panel of the offside door and then the man was chasing after them, falling further and further behind, disappearing into the mist and gathering darkness as the minibus roared and bounced up the steep track.

Emre said, 'He was crazy. A crazy man.'

'He was a low man,' Harriet said. 'Now we know what happened to the family who owned that farmhouse.'

'Jesus,' Toby said. 'You think they got the women and children too?'

'I hope not,' Harriet said, thinking of feral children wandering the landscape, imagining a pack of them running like wolves across the bare countryside, faces blank, no thoughts in their heads but those that had been put there when they'd been turned. 'I hope they were shot. It would have been kinder.'

Toby said, 'Would this low man be able to use a radio?'

'I don't know.'

'Because if he *can* use a radio, we're probably fucked,' Toby said. There was an edge to his voice that hadn't been there before.

'We're probably fucked anyway,' Harriet said.

The track climbed a slope of stony scrubland in steep switchbacks. It was rapidly growing dark now. The mist billowed and thickened and thinned but never went away completely. They couldn't see more than ten yards at best, often much less. Harriet kept a close watch on her satellite phone's GPS, but had a bad moment when the track dipped into a narrow valley and crossed a swift, shallow river. She told Toby to stop, and spent ten minutes checking and rechecking the map and the GPS, trying to think through the solid haze of her fatigue, before she was convinced that she hadn't somehow fucked up and become turned around, that it wasn't the river that ran through the gorge beside the ancient church, but a tributary which joined it a mile or so downstream.

Emre got out, waded into fast-flowing water that swirled around his knees, and guided the minibus across a narrow chain of flat stones laid across the river bed to make a ford. The ground rose steeply on the other side, and the minibus laboured up the stony track in first gear, steam boiling from its radiator. The light was completely gone from the sky when Harriet told Toby to stop. He pulled off the track and parked the minibus in the shelter of a clump of ragged junipers. According to the GPS, they were north-east of the river gorge, some two miles from the source of the glyphs. Harriet said that they could hike the rest of the way – it should be a straight walk to the top of the cliffs above the source. Then they could spy out the land and decide whether or not they needed to call in the *peshmergas*.

Toby rubbed his eyes with the heels of his palms. 'We should stay here,' he said. 'Rest up and start scouting at dawn.'

'No,' Emre said, surprising Harriet. 'If we stay here, low men or the soldiers of our enemy could find us. Better for us if we find them first.'

The interpreter slung Harriet's rucksack over his shoulder and took the lead, using the little flashlight sparingly. Harriet and Toby were soon out of breath as they chased after him through the misty darkness, a hard scramble up a gullied slope past outcrops of rock and stands of rugged holly oaks. Before they'd set off, Harriet had swallowed two more painkillers, but her shoulder felt like it had been kicked by a horse, and her knees and ankles, which still hadn't recovered from last night's hike through the hills beyond the border, soon began to ache too. Mist soaked into her clothes, chilled her to the bone. Soon she was walking more or less mechanically. She almost walked past Emre when he suddenly stopped.

He was squatting on his heels, shading the flashlight with one hand as he shone it on the ground right in front of him. Harriet saw a bright yellow oblong the size of a paperback book leaning against a tuft of coarse grass, and whispered, 'Is that what I think it is?'

'If you think a mine or a cluster bomb, then yes, I think perhaps.'

Harriet heard Toby climbing up behind them and told him to stop, stay exactly where he was, there was a small problem. As Emre leaned closer to the little yellow package, she had to fight the not unreasonable urge to run, and flinched when the interpreter suddenly laughed and picked it up.

He showed it to Harriet and Toby, and they began to laugh too. It was an REM, a ready-to-eat meal. A ration pack of the kind dropped in their thousands by the US air force, probably part of some operation to win the hearts and minds of ordinary Iraqis.

'Cheese slices,' Toby reading the list of contents after he'd taken the package from Emre. 'Crackers. Jesus, and strawberry jello.'

There were many more REM packages scattered about. Toby, like a child on a treasure hunt, jammed as many as he could into the pockets of his flak jacket, picked up others and flung them aside until Harriet told him to stop. They reached the crest of a ridge, scrambled down a stony slope into a belt of holly oaks that reared up out of the mist, roots clutching pockets of earth among bare outcrops of rock. Harriet spotted a glow off to the right, an unfocused smudge smaller than a fingernail. They crept towards it through the belt of trees, at last reaching an apron of wiry turf at the edge of a cliff that dropped straight down into mist lit from below by half a dozen points of light. The noise of a generator came and went. Harriet took out her satellite phone, checked the GPS function, saw that they were right on top of the coordinates for the site of the ancient church and the source of the glyphs.

It was almost midnight. The mist showed no sign of lifting, and they were cold and soaked through. They agreed that they should rest and wait until first light, scout the area properly, try to work out just how many men Rölf Most had deployed, then call up the *peshmergas* and ask them for their help. Harriet didn't argue this time. It was a relief really, to let the decision be taken out of her hands. They found a rocky overhang and huddled beneath it, leaning against each other for warmth, sharing the stale crackers and processed cheese from the REM packs that Toby had collected.

Harriet must have dozed off, because when Toby shook her awake, grey light showed through the mist beyond the trees. Toby told her to keep absolutely still, saying, his mouth next to her ear, 'Emre's gone. And I think I can hear gunfire.'

33

Alfie was woken by Larry Macpherson just before dawn. The man shaking him hard, telling him to rise and shine, there was no time to waste. Saying, as Alfie levered himself out of his bunk, 'Everyone is waiting on you, so let's go.'

Larry Macpherson was fired up by something, eager and impatient, but Alfie knew better than to ask him what was going on. He struggled into a set of black overalls and asked for permission to use the caravan's chemical toilet, where he wrapped a silver of soap in the square of aluminium foil he'd torn from the waxed paper of last night's apple-juice carton. He wasn't sure if what was essentially a silly schoolboy trick would do him any good, but he hadn't been able to think of anything else – it was his only chance of fooling Rölf Most and Larry Macpherson.

In the steel mirror over the tiny sink, his face looked back at him, pale and dead-eyed. 'Now or never,' he told it.

Larry Macpherson led Alfie across the rough ground to a black Range Rover. The mist had thickened, blurring the grey light that was growing in the sky. Each of the half-dozen floodlights scattered around the entrance to the shaft drew a kind of pearl around itself. Ideal conditions for Carver Soborin, Alfie thought: the whole world snow-blind. The diesel generator that powered the lights and water pumps made a steady roar, and there was a faint staccato crackling in the distance, as if someone was letting off fireworks.

Rölf Most and one of the mercenaries were waiting beside a body that lay under a grey blanket in the blurred light of the Range Rover's headlights. The mercenary used his boot to flip up a corner of the blanket to reveal the dead man's face; Rölf Most asked Alfie if he knew who this was.

The dead man was in his forties, with a brush of greying hair, thick black eyebrows, an olive complexion. His lips were drawn back from large, yellow teeth; one eye was half-open, a horrible, frozen wink that showed a crescent of white eyeball.

Alfie shook his head, said he'd never seen the man before.

Rölf Most had a pinched, impatient look. Staring at Alfie, saying, 'You are certain? Take a close look. Study him carefully before you answer.'

The dead man looked so completely dead. Not exactly peaceful, but slyly untouchable, as if death had been his own idea, a move that had put him beyond any possible harm.

Alfie said, 'All I know is that he looks like an Iraqi. What happened to him?'

The mercenary said, 'We happened to him.'

Larry Macpherson said, 'These guys got lucky. Their patrol – their only perimeter patrol – made contact with him when they were returning at the end of their watch. Turns out he has friends, too. I understand there's quite a little firefight going on a ways down the hill.'

That was when Alfie realized that the fireworks weren't fireworks.

'My guys engaged them and they engaged right back,' the mercenary said, locking gazes with Larry Macpherson. He was a stocky, forthright man with a ruddy complexion and a wheat-coloured crew-cut. He wore black coveralls, and a long chequered scarf wound loosely around his neck. 'It was either real brave or real stupid of them, because we had them outgunned from the get-go. We're right on top of the situation.'

'Let's hope they don't call for help,' Larry Macpherson said imperturbably. His camouflage jacket and pants looked freshly pressed. The gold earring nestling in the neat black curve of his swept-back hair glinted in the high beams of the Range Rover. Sparks of reflected light spun in his dark eyes.

'There's no more than half a dozen of them,' the mercenary said. 'And we've got them pinned down. They don't know it, but their asses are already ours.'

Rölf Most said irritably, 'Stop bickering, and show him the rucksack.'

It was small, made of soft black leather, tan trim at the seams. Alfie recognized it at once and felt his stomach cramp when the mercenary produced a passport, flipped it open to the laminated back page and held it a foot from Alfie's face.

'I believe that you know Harriet Crowley,' Rölf Most said, showing his upper teeth.

'We have a passing acquaintance,' Alfie said, trying to hide the sudden surge of hope that fizzed in his blood.

'A little more than that, I think,' Rölf Most said.

'Not really. If she came all the way out here, it definitely isn't because she wants to rescue me.'

'She is too late in any case,' Rölf Most said. 'We have almost cleared away the rockfall and penetrated to the next cave. I suggest that you prepare yourself, Mr Flowers, because very soon your work for me begins.'

'Showtime,' Larry Macpherson said, staring at Alfie with deadpan cool.

34

Harriet and Toby walked all the way around the overhang where they'd spent the night, hearing sporadic gunfire in the distance but finding no trace of Emre Karin. The interpreter had slipped away in the night, taking Harriet's rucksack and her satellite phone with him. All she had left was the automatic pistol, which had been lying underneath her while she slept, stuck in the waist-band of her combat trousers; she was certain that Emre would have taken that too, if he could have done it without waking her.

'He must have gone to find his *peshmerga* friends,' Harriet said. 'He sneaked off, used my phone to arrange a rendezvous with them . . .'

She wasn't angry about this betrayal – she'd half-expected it, and now that it had happened she felt strangely relieved. Relieved that Emre had simply slipped away instead of bashing in her head with a rock or taking her prisoner at gunpoint; relieved that now that he was gone she was free to make her own move.

'And then, from the sound of it, they ran into Rölf Most's mercenaries,' Toby said. He was shivering in the damp cold air, his arms crossed over his chest and his hands tucked into his armpits.

They were standing at the edge of the cliff directly above the little mist-filled arena, filled with the diffused glow of floodlights, where Rölf Most and his men had set up camp. All around them, trees faded into misty, pre-dawn greyness. The gunfire seemed to be coming from somewhere to the north – from the direction of the farmhouse, but much closer, a mile or so away, maybe less.

Harriet said, 'There's no point in us staying here. While Rölf Most's men are otherwise engaged, we have a chance to get closer to the source.'

'You're crazy.'

'The *peshmergas* are providing the perfect diversion. It would be ungrateful of us not to take advantage of it.'

'Shouldn't we wait here? In case, you know, Emre comes back.'

'Right now he's probably in the middle of the fighting. If the *peshmergas* win, he might come back for us. Then again, he very well might not.'

She started to explain that if they followed the edge of the cliff they'd be sure to find the way down to the site of the old church, but Toby held up a hand and said, very quietly, 'Listen.'

Harriet heard the snap of a twig, the rattle of a dislodged stone. Someone was moving along the slope above them.

They found shelter behind a low shelf of rock. Toby whispered, 'This is dumb. It's probably Emre.'

Harriet shook her head. She was holding the pistol close to her face, straining to see through the mist. Her wounded arm, bent across her breast in its sling, throbbed sharply from shoulder to wrist. Her damp clothes clung unpleasantly to her skin. If the person coming unhandily down the slope towards them was Emre Karin, she thought, she'd put the pistol right in his face and ask him what the fuck he was playing at. And if it was a low man, or one of Rölf Most's mercenaries, she'd keep still and hope he moved past without spotting them. She would only shoot if she absolutely had to but she knew that, if it came to it, she'd have to shoot without hesitation. Aim at the chest, just like she'd been taught at the shooting range. Aim and shoot twice, a double tap to make sure that she took down her target. Just do it.

Her heart kicked in her throat when Toby put a hand on her shoulder and pointed. Someone was moving down the steep slope through banners and streamers of mist no more than a dozen yards away. Creeping down to the edge of the cliff with comically exaggerated stealth, kneeling beside a crooked tree that leaned into the void, looking down. Harriet was holding her breath, urging whoever it was to stand up and walk away, trying to make him move by pure force of will, the way she'd tried to make traffic lights change from red to green when she'd been a little girl.

And now he was pushing away from the tree, turning around and – *shit* – looking straight at her. Standing absolutely still, looking straight at the place where she and Toby crouched. *Do it.* She stood up and walked forward, her arm stiffly raised, aiming the automatic pistol at him, her index finger inside the trigger-guard, nestled against the trigger. He was a small, plump young man who, as she approached him, lowered his head and raised his hands above his shoulders in a gesture of abject surrender. She knew at once who he was, and lowered the pistol and said, 'It's all right. Don't be afraid. We're here to help you.'

As the three of them climbed out of the belt of holly oaks, scrambling up the rocky slope through thinning mist, Toby said breathlessly, 'Should we call you Morph, or should we call you Musa?'

'I left Morph in London,' the boy said. 'He did a stupid thing there. I am here to make it right. You'll see how, because you must help me. Just when I needed help, I have found you. Surely it is a miracle. Surely it is meant to be.'

Musa Karsu, wearing a fleece-trimmed jacket over a denim shirt, baggy jeans torn at one knee, and filthy trainers, was as out of breath as Toby and very excited, making big gestures, talking loudly until Harriet said he might want to turn it down a little, just in case any of Rölf Most's men were in the vicinity.

He'd come out, Musa Karsu said, to see what was going on. The drilling had stopped, and he'd hoped that they'd given up and gone away. Then he'd come out and heard gunfire, thought that maybe the army had found them, soldiers were shooting them dead, capturing them. *They* being Rölf Most's men, although he didn't know anything about Rölf Most or Carver Soborin or mind's i. All he knew was that he'd drawn attention from some bad people after he'd started spraying glyphs on walls in North London. He had misused the pictures – that was what he called the glyphs – and knew that he had to make amends, and that was why he'd returned to his childhood home.

'I should have finished it. But there's a little problem, you'll see when we get there, but you guys can help. We can finish this together.'

Toby said, 'Finish what? You aren't making much sense, kid.'

Harriet said impatiently, 'Don't you understand? He's found another way into the caves. He wants us to help him destroy the glyphs – the pictures.'

The boy – Morph, Musa Karsu – said, 'They tried to catch

me in London, but I was too clever, I got away from them. But they must have found out about the place where I came from, where my people came from, because when I got here they were already busy. They dug this hole, they drill away down there night and day, soon they break through . . .'

Harriet said, 'But you know another way to the source of the glyphs, the pictures, don't you? A back door.'

The boy glanced at her and said, 'There is only one way. Or there was, until these fuckers started digging.'

Harriet said, 'They're nearly there, but not quite.'

The boy nodded.

Harriet smiled. 'So we're in with a chance.'

The few hours of sleep she'd snatched had done her the world of good. She was hungry and thirsty, she ached all over and knew that her wounded shoulder would soon cause her serious trouble if she didn't get some medical attention. But she felt sharp, alert and, yes, excited. Excited and happy and purposeful. She'd found Musa Karsu, and she was beginning to believe that with his help she was going to be able to stop Rölf Most getting his hands on the glyphs.

They climbed out of the mist, reached the crest of the slope, and stopped to catch their breath. In front of them, parallel ridges saddled away towards a jagged range of mountains, with lakes of mist filling the valleys between them. In the other direction, gunfire rattled somewhere inside the sea of mist or cloud that washed against the flanks of the mountains, stretching to the north and east beneath a sky of the darkest blue where a few pale stars still showed. Something was on fire down there, a red spark flickering dimly beneath restless fog that was beginning to be burned away by the rising sun.

Toby lit a cigarette and offered the crumpled packet to Musa Karsu, who refused with a brisk shake of his head. Harriet had already told the boy that they were on the same side, that she knew about the history of his people, that like him she wanted to make sure that Rölf Most didn't get his hands on the glyphs, the pictures, whatever you wanted to call them. Now she explained that her grandfather had been one of the people who had discovered caves here more than sixty years ago, the same caves that

Rölf Most was excavating. It turned out that the boy didn't know anything about the Nomads' Club, its work at the site of the ancient church, or the time when Harriet's grandfather and Julius Ward had stayed with his people. According to him, his people had been visiting a sacred place of their own for hundreds of years, a cave full of powerful pictures, most of them too powerful to be used. He'd been initiated into their mystery by his grandfather at the age of thirteen, and three years later the Americans had come, and taken away his family.

He looked at Harriet and Toby, dry-eyed and defiant. His mass of curly black hair was held back by a red handkerchief rolled tightly and knotted into a headband. He said, 'If my mother and my sisters are dead, I'm probably the last of my people.'

Harriet felt a pang of sympathy. Musa Karsu had been forced to flee from his homeland, but he hadn't been able to escape who he was and what he knew. It had drawn him back, just as Harriet had been drawn to the Nomads' Club and found herself caught up in her family's history and the matter of the glyphs.

She said, 'When you decided to come back here and destroy the pictures, you did the right thing. I want to do the right thing too. I feel just as responsible as you do, because my grandfather and his friends discovered some of them in the caves I told you about, and put them out into the world. That's why I came here. That's why I want to make sure that what they started ends here.'

Musa Karsu studied her, looking for a moment as if he was going to disagree. But then he shrugged and said, 'We better move on. There isn't much time.'

Harriet and Toby followed him across the uneven ground. Loose stones, thin soil, tufts of grass or weeds, ground-hugging clumps of thorny bushes. Every leaf, each blade of grass, was tipped with a drop of water.

Musa Karsu said, 'My father tried to find out where the Americans had taken our family, and when he learns they were still looking for us, he took me to Turkey. It wasn't like home, it wasn't like the mountains, but it felt safe there. My people, we aren't Kurds, but we can pass for them if we have to, and that's what me and my father did. Making shoes . . . Anyway, I had this fantasy of finding other people like us, people who could help us, so I left signs that only my people would recognize. Used to make my father so angry if he caught me doing it . . .'

After a brief silence, Toby said, 'Then you had to leave Turkey. You came to London.'

'Because we had trouble in Diyarbakir. My father was arrested when the Turks thought he was someone else. He had help to get him free, but it was a bad time, and after he got out of prison, my father decided we couldn't stay in Turkey. So yes, we came to London, because I learn English at this school in Diyarbakir, and because that's where everyone wants to go, and we claimed asylum. But my father, his heart was bad. He got some kind of sickness of the chest when he was in prison, and never got over it properly. He died,' Musa Karsu said, giving Harriet and Toby a flat challenging look, as if daring them to express sympathy. 'And this social worker came to see me and started talking about putting me in care or finding a family who could look after me, because I'm not old enough to look after myself. I thought, Fuck that, I'm not a child, you know? So I ran away.'

Harriet said, 'Is that when you met Benjamin Barrett – Shareef?'

'You know about Shareef? He tell you about me?'

Toby said, 'I met him when I was chasing the story about your graffiti, trying to work up something I could sell to one of the nationals. We talked about you. He was very keen to make you famous.'

Musa Karsu laughed. 'Yeah, and also to make some money.'

'He was a good friend of yours, and he helped you out,' Harriet said, giving Toby a warning look. This wasn't the time to tell the boy that his friend had been killed.

Musa Karsu said, 'I did some stuff for someone, for a favour, right? This stupid little poster . . . Shareef saw it because he hung out in this bookshop where I used to help out, we got to talking about it. He noticed the picture I put in it, saw how it stood out. The pictures affect some people like that, even when they haven't smoked the herb. You know about the herb?'

Harriet said, 'I believe you call it haka.'

Musa Karsu nodded. 'Shareef and me thought we could work it up into something. Make a bit of money, get a bit of fame. You know, like everyone in London wants.'

Toby said, 'You weren't worried about being caught?'

'I thought I'd left all that behind. I didn't know they'd be looking for me in London. Just didn't occur to me. Fucking stupid, right, but it's the truth. I thought it sounded all right, a bit of money, a bit of fame, getting your name out on the street. I thought, Why not? I thought, Go for it. It wasn't much different from what I did in Diyarbakir, and I still had the idea that some of my people were still alive . . . And also, it felt good. Like when you get bitten by an insect, and you scratch the itch, you know? It feels *good*.'

Harriet said, 'The pictures change you. Some of it you're aware of, and some of it you aren't.'

Musa Karsu glanced at her, and something passed between them, a wary acceptance, mutual understanding. He said, 'It's true. If you take too much haka, or look at certain pictures for too long, they can enter you and never leave. But I remember the nights we danced in our special place, me and my grandfather, sometimes my father also. I remember how the blessing of Allah would fall upon us . . .' He smiled at some private memory, then said, brisk and businesslike again, 'We have to go down here. It isn't far now.'

They had reached the edge of a steep drop into a narrow valley. The tops of trees showed here and there above the lake of mist that filled it almost to the brim. As Musa Karsu led Harriet and Toby down the slope, weaving back and forth between patches of ochre soil, fans of scree and weathered limestone benches, clumps of bushes and solitary trees, descending into the cold, wet, white mist once more, he explained that the anti-American cartoons had been Shareef's idea.

'He hated the Americans, right? I mean, really hated them. They never done anything to him, but he did. He has a big thing for politics – you said you talked to him, so you know what he's like. Plus, he converted to the faith, he think he has to prove he's a real brother, more righteous than the righteous. He has his radio programme where he shouts down the unfaithful, he went on those marches against the war, even went up to Tottenham once or twice to listen to that bloke with the hooks for hands stirring up the faithful against the infidels. Me, I couldn't give a shit. I mean, the Americans started to fuck up as soon as they got here, but what do you expect? At least they got rid of Saddam. But anyway, we worked up some cartoons, me and Shareef, and I put one of the pictures around them, the one that gets attention, and we started to put them up using stencils I'd made. The cartoons, they were a piece of piss, but stencils for the picture, it took me a week to get them right. There were five of them, and I had to set each one exactly right or it wouldn't work . . .

'So then one of the cartoons got printed in the newspapers. Shareef try to seem cool when he found out about it, but I know he was as excited as me. He said we needed to step it up. Said it could make us famous, make us rich. But then I realized that people were looking for him and me. Not people from the news-papers, but the bad people I already told you about. They were watching Shareef's flat – he had to hide where I was staying. And that's when I decided to split.'

'Low men,' Harriet said. 'I saw them too.'

'Low men . . . Yeah, that's a good name for what they are. Once before, I see men like that. This is when four men came to the village, after me and my family move back there. They were bandits who heard old stories about my people, and thought we hid treasure in a cave. They threatened to kill everyone if my father didn't show them this imaginary treasure, so he and my grand-father took three of them to the holy cave,' Musa Karsu said, 'and my grandfather did something there that destroy their minds. I saw them when my father and my grandfather brought them back. The man who had been left behind, who was supposed to kill me and my mother and my sisters if something went wrong, he saw them too, and he was so scared he ran away. His friends, they didn't live long, but I remember how they were. My grand-father said that he had talked to them, talked to the part of them that could not lie. He said they told him they had been paid by Americans to find us.'

Harriet said, 'They were probably working for Carver Soborin, or Rölf Most.'

Musa Karsu said, 'And less than a year later there was the inva-sion, and then American soldiers came to the village, looking for the pictures. My grandfather had died by then – if he was alive maybe he would have turned them, you know, like he turned the bandits. Maybe all this would not happen. But it did, so now I must do what I must do.'

'We're here to help you,' Harriet said, and the boy looked back at her, an odd wary glance.

They were following a narrow track now, a crimp in the slope of bare earth and loose stones and thorny bushes. Water was running somewhere close by, the noise loud and intimate in the pressing whiteness of the mist. As she followed Toby and Musa Karsu, Harriet heard stones rattling down the slope behind her and spun around, setting her hand on the grip of the pistol stuck in the waistband of her combat trousers. But she saw nothing, only the slope of bushes and gullied dirt and stones fading into blank mist.

'There are goats here,' Musa Karsu said, after Harriet asked him if he'd heard anything. 'Also sheep, and wild animals – I don't know their names in English.'

Toby said, 'Back in London, the sheep at the party? Was that your idea?'

'What sheep? I don't know nothing about any sheep.'

Toby explained about the wrap party for the horror movie, the appearance of sheep which had each been spray-painted with a single letter, a living anagram. Musa Karsu shook his head and began to laugh when Toby told him about the fake exhibit smuggled into the Imperial War Museum. They worked out dates – Musa Karsu had already left London by then, had been travelling via train and ferry to Turkey, and then through Syria to Iraq.

The boy said, 'You got taken in by Shareef. He was trying to keep the thing going, I bet, plus he was taking the piss out of you. He should be careful, though. He might attract the wrong attention.'

'Absolutely,' Toby said, and gave Harriet a solemn look and zipped a finger across his throat.

The track dipped up and down, cut around layered outcrops and solitary boulders, vanished, reappeared, running along the edge of a steep drop to a small river, almost certainly the same river they'd forded last night. Black water flowing over and around rocks and loose scarves of mist drifting just above it. Musa Karsu walked quickly and lightly, barely touching the ground, but Harriet kept taking steps that weren't quite there, slipping on sliding stones, catching at boulders or bushes to keep her balance as she followed Toby and Musa Karsu around a bend in the river and climbed a steep, slippery path beside a small waterfall.

The mist was beginning to fade. The rising sun burned white and gold at the crest of the slope; a rainbow shimmered above the top of the waterfall where a mass of boulders had fallen into the river from the slope above, splitting it into a dozen small, swift streams. Harriet knelt at the edge of the water and drank. It was cold and silty and absolutely delicious. She'd never tasted anything better. Toby drank too, splashed water over his face. Musa Karsu watched them impatiently, and set off again as soon as they stood up.

Steep, bare rock loomed above them, fretted with dozens of narrow defiles like the folds in a curtain. Harriet and Toby followed Musa Karsu into one of them, climbing between banks of small bushes with tiny grey leaves and friable bark. The evocative scent that pulsed in the warming air transported Harriet to her grandfather's house, his smoke-filled study, the little greenhouse with its bank of electrical heaters and bright lamps. She stooped and ran her hand over one of the bushes, sniffed her fingers. Haka.

Musa Karsu mounted a pile of boulders that formed a kind of giant's staircase, waited for Harriet and Toby to catch up with him, then ducked through the cleft at the top. A long, narrow cave spread beyond, lit by shafts of sunlight that dropped through crevices or solution holes in the low ceiling. Loose rock slanted down into shadows. Cool air with a strong ammoniacal tinge blew into their faces. Musa Karsu said that it wasn't far now, lifted a rucksack from a flat ledge, and scrambled down the slope to the floor of the cave – a ribbon pinched between fans of scree and tumbled boulders. As Harriet and Toby followed him, clambering over and around boulders, the pungent ammoniacal scent grew stronger and the way ahead darker. The boy pulled a flashlight from his rucksack and switched it on; a tide of pale beetles and crickets scattered from the light across a carpet of black dung. High above, the ceiling shifted and rustled, like seaweed lifting on a wave. Roosting bats, thousands of them, hung from the pitted rock surface like clusters of black grapes.

Toby gave Harriet a big can-you-believe-this smile, and said quietly, 'Do they have vampire bats in Iraq?'

'I think that's the least of our worries.'

Musa Karsu stuffed his rucksack through a narrow slot in the floor and crawled after it. Harriet and Toby followed him into a narrow, low-roofed passage. Stone all around – a universe of stone. Here and there, the marks of picks and chisels were plainly visible where the passage had been widened by careful work, but it was a long, hard scramble, often on hands and knees. Although the black air was cool enough to fog breath, Harriet was soon slick with sweat, and her pulse thumped hard in her head and in her wounded shoulder. Gradually, she became aware of another noise, muffled and faint and far off, yet resonating through the rock all around them. Quick, urgent spurts of hammering sound. The sound of someone using a pneumatic drill.

At last the passage widened and the ceiling lifted away. They were at the bottom of a cleft or chimney so deep that it seemed like a gap between the hinges of the world, a steep slope of loose rock rising in front of them to a curtain of fluted, translucent limestone that gleamed wetly in the light of Musa Karsu's flashlight. The noise of the drill stopped, then started again.

'They're close,' the boy said. His face was half-lit by the light reflected from the limestone curtain. His eyes glittered darkly in deeply shadowed sockets. He was sweating hard, his bushy hair matted at the roots, his improvised headband soaked through. 'They work day and night ever since I get here, and before that, I think. Wait here, I must see that it is all right.'

'We should stick together,' Harriet said.

'Trust me,' Musa Karsu said. 'I will be a minute, no more.'

They looked at each other. Harriet said, 'No tricks.'

'I need your help,' the boy said seriously. 'Why would I trick you?'

He scampered up the slope and wriggled through a small hole near the base of the curtain of limestone. The little spark of his flashlight vanished; the deep cleft was plunged into darkness more complete than anything Harriet had ever experienced before.

After a moment, Toby snapped his cigarette lighter. By its flick-ering glow, Harriet saw that he was squatting on his haunches, looking utterly wrecked. He blotted sweat from his face with his sleeve, pulled his pack of cigarettes from the breast pocket of his camo jacket, and said quietly, 'Well, here we are, on the threshold of whatever we're on the threshold of.'

'I don't think he's lying. This is the place.'

'I don't think he's lying either.' Toby stuck a cigarette in his mouth and bent to the flame of his lighter. His face, pale and pinched, was swallowed by the darkness when the flame snapped out. 'My last cigarette. How perfectly symbolic is that?'

'I'll buy you one of those big duty-free cartons when we get out of here.'

The red coal of Toby's cigarette brightened as he drew on it. 'From now on I'm only smoking Turkish cigarettes. They may taste like a bonfire of camel-shit, but they don't have any of those scary health warnings on them. How are you doing?'

'I'm ready to do what we have to do.' Harriet knelt down, moving carefully in the darkness, and put the palm of her right hand flat on the floor. The cool dry rock thrilled faintly with the vibration of the distant drill. She said, 'I think we'll have time to destroy the glyphs and get out of here before Rölf Most breaks through.'

Toby said, 'We've come in the back way, and those *peshmerga* friends of Emre's are knocking on the front door. Rölf Most doesn't know it, but he doesn't stand a chance.'

'Imagine his face when he finds out what we've done.'

'He puffs up with rage, starts jumping up and down like Yosemite Sam, and above his head a precariously attached stalactite starts to tremble . . .'

Harriet said, 'I'm sorry that I got you into this.'

'I got *myself* into this. When Alfie asked me for help back in London, when he was looking for Morph, I insisted on coming with him. Poor bloody Alfie, that's the last time I do him a favour . . . Listen, if they do break through while we're in there, shoot as many as you can.'

'Absolutely. But it won't come to that.'

'I'll probably be lying on the floor with my hands over my head, screaming like a baby. Don't let that distract you.'

Harriet heard something far off in the darkness, felt a freezing hand clamp on her skull. She whispered to Toby, 'Did you hear that?'

'Hear what?'

Light flashed above them; Musa Karsu called out, told them it was all right, they could come up now. 'Be careful what you look at,' he said. 'There are pictures all over the walls. I have made the most holy ones safe, but it is possible the lesser ones might get inside your head.'

Harriet said, 'We haven't taken any haka.'

'But you are hurt, you are very tired. That is one of the ways of opening a door in your head and letting them in.'

'Wonderful,' Toby said.

Harriet squeezed through after him, emerging at the top of a slope of cobbles cemented together by limey deposits. Walls of pale stone curved away on either side and curved together overhead, lit by a carpet of flickering stars. Night lights, Harriet realized. Dozens of night lights, random constellations that defined a huge, roughly circular space easily fifty yards across, with a high ceiling lost in darkness. She was reminded of the space under the dome of St Paul's Cathedral where the four arms of the nave, transept and chancel aisles met. The air was cool and absolutely still, and the noise of the drill was much louder here, a busy resonant chatter that seemed to come from every direction.

Musa Karsu swung the beam of the flashlight across the space, and Harriet began to laugh, realizing what the poor foolish naive kid had done, realizing that their task was probably hopeless.

The oval footprint of the flashlight travelled over slick stone covered in paintings of animals – vivid, detailed, immediate, obviously made by people who knew their subjects, intimately done in red and yellow ochre, in white clay and charcoal. A maned lion six feet high. A leopard running at full stretch. Overlapping paintings of heavy-shouldered bison, shaggy-headed and bearded, outlined in thick charcoal. The head of a deer crowned with huge scooped antlers. A great bear, eight or nine feet high, standing on its hind legs. All of this was amazing enough, a treasure-house that would take a lifetime to catalogue and analyse, a gallery of masterpieces of Palaeolithic art as great as the Hall of Bulls at

Lascaux, the Sanctuary at Les Trois-Frères or the Black Salon at Niaux, as great as any discovered anywhere in Europe. But woven between the paintings was a greater marvel: a continuous band of entoptic patterns, parallel sets of riverine lines, rectangular patterns, crosses and circles made of hatch-marks, red dots swarming across broad sweeps of white clay, forming an irregular frieze roughly at head height, once or twice thickening into circular patches that Harriet was certain were glyphs. And laid across each of these circular patches were the things that had made her laugh: copies of the cartoon – grinning skull, soldier's helmet, crude representation of the Stars and Stripes – that she had seen on the wall of the farmhouse, done in the same red paint. They glistened brightly in the beam of the flashlight, as shocking as if they had been sprayed across canvases in the National Gallery or the Louvre.

Musa Karsu walked down the slope, explaining that he'd taken the idea from some crazy person who'd been obliterating his cartoons in London. 'He used black paint, but I think this is just as good,' he said, the oval footprint of the flashlight's beam shrinking and growing brighter over one of the red spray-paint cartoons as he walked up to it.

Harriet laughed again; it was so perfectly, stupidly ironic. She'd started spraying black paint over every piece of Morph's graffiti that she'd come across, and Morph, Musa Karsu, had decided that it was the best way to destroy the real glyphs; he'd copied her method . . .

The boy turned, blinding her with the flashlight for a moment, putting a finger to his lips. That was when she realized that the noise of the drill had stopped. She could hear a faint but distinct scraping noise now, metal on stone. Someone clearing rubble.

Musa Karsu whispered, 'We have to be quiet. They're very close, I'm scared they could hear us when they stop their drilling.'

Harriet crabbed down the cobbled slope, walked across the uneven floor of the huge space, picking her way between the flickering stars of night lights, walking up to a bulge in the wall where a pride of lions rendered in charcoal and red ochre stalked one after the other across slick, glistening stone the colour of old tea, a beautiful, expertly executed mural older than any civilization on Earth, older than cities or religions, older than farming, perhaps older than language. She pulled the automatic pistol from her waistband and dragged its foresight across the mural, gouging an irregular line through a masterpiece whose maker had died ten or twenty thousand years ago. But fuck it, she needed to make her point and make it as quickly as possible.

She walked back to where Musa Karsu and Toby stood, said in a fierce whisper, '*That's* what you have to do.' Saying, as Musa Karsu stared at her, his face underlit by the glow of his flashlight, 'Spray-paint is acetone-based. The glyphs are done in ochre and charcoal and clay. Your cartoons can be washed off with any organic solvent, and the glyphs underneath won't be touched. Covering them up is no good. You have to *destroy* them.'

Musa Karsu shook his head. 'I can't,' he whispered.

'You're going to have to. You too, Toby. I can't do it all by myself.'

Musa Karsu shook his head again. 'I can't. I try. I come here because it is what I want to do, because I think I can do it. And I try, I really try, and I can't . . .' He took a deep breath. 'One of the first things my grandfather taught me was to respect the pictures. When I was initiated, I sat here with him for three days. I drank water, but I did not eat. He burned haka, filled this place with smoke. I slept with my eyes open. He whispered words that burned inside my head. He showed me how the animals could be made to step off the walls. I felt them walk into my head. And they spoke to me . . .'

He cocked his head when the noise of the drilling restarted. He said, 'They walked into my head, and they're still there. I think that's why I was always drawing them. I think that's why I had to come back, you know what I mean?'

Harriet knew what he meant. Her anger was gone; she felt sorry for the boy all over again. The glyphs had drawn him back, he'd come here to destroy them and found that he couldn't – because he'd been conditioned to protect them, because they were as intimately a part of him as any of his thoughts and memories.

'I should have brought explosives,' Musa Karsu said. He was trying to look defiant, but the expression kept threatening to dissolve, and there were tears leaking from the corners of his eyes. 'Dynamite and such. Light a fuse and walk away, it shouldn't be hard. But I don't know anything about that shit. Anyway, I thought I could do it, and I couldn't. Painting over them, that was no problem. I know they're still there. But when I tried to do what you did, when I tried to erase them, I got this fucking awful headache. I thought I'd gone blind. I threw up. I think I passed out for a little while. I tried it again, same thing. But you're here now. You can help me out.'

Harriet said, 'You won't try to stop us when we destroy the pictures? You won't go crazy?'

'I don't think so. I don't think—' The noise of the drill stopped again, and Musa Karsu lowered his voice. 'I don't think it works like that.'

'This stuff must be thousands of years old,' Toby said.

'I know,' Musa Karsu said, looking as unhappy as anyone Harriet had ever seen.

She said, 'We don't have to destroy everything. Just the pictures under these stupid cartoons.'

'Jesus,' Toby said. He took a last drag on his cigarette, pinched out the stub and stuck it in the pocket of his camo jacket.

Musa Karsu said, 'I must show you something else. I must show you where the strongest and most holy picture lives.'

The floor of the space sloped down in one corner, a kind of semicircular funnel that tilted towards the mouth of a narrow pit partly hidden beneath the overhanging wall, with a low cleft or crawl space off to one side, a crookedly grinning mouth under a boss of rock. The edge of the pit was marked with regular, deeply incised triangles that, outlined with traces of white clay, looked like a necklace of sharks' teeth. Pieces of bone and glittering fragments of quartz had been thrust into cracks in the rock. The ends of some of the bones were splintered and flattened; they'd been hammered right into the cracks and crevices as offerings or to mark some rite. Musa Karsu shone his flashlight into the pit, revealing fluted, slickly glistening walls that dropped to a narrow triangular patch of floor some eight or nine feet below. He said quietly, 'My grandfather said that at the bottom of this place a man with the head of a lion guards the most holy picture.'

Harriet said, 'You haven't seen it.'

Musa Karsu shook his head.

'Do you know what it does?'

'My grandfather said that if it entered the right person, a person perfectly prepared and clean of all sin, he would be transported to paradise. But if it entered the wrong person it would destroy his mind. He said that it was the final test. Only the most holy and wise of men, or the most foolish, would dare to take it. He said that a thousand years ago a man named Nimu, a man who led our people into war and drove invaders from these mountains, allowed the picture to enter him. But although he was a great warrior and a great leader he was also vain and foolish, and the picture utterly destroyed him.'

'How do you get down there?' Harriet said.

Musa Karsu said, 'I have a rope. Now that you are here, I think I can go down there and face it. I have not taken haka, so it will be safe.'

Harriet said, 'Perhaps you could face it, perhaps you could even spray paint over it, but you couldn't destroy it.'

Musa Karsu shrugged.

Toby said, 'I'll go.'

Harriet and Musa Karsu looked at him.

He said, 'Harriet can hardly climb down a rope, and besides, both of you have spent too much time with these pictures. Like you said, they're inside your heads. You're sensitized to them, like poor old Alfie. He was knocked sideways by Morph's graffiti, but they didn't do a thing to me.'

Musa Karsu said, 'It is a very holy picture.'

Toby smiled and said, 'I'm a very profane man. Maybe one thing will cancel out the other.'

The noise of the drill started up again. It was coming from the cleft under the bulge of rock, which had been covered with red ochre and had eyes painted in black charcoal on either side, like a mask or face that pushed through the wall and peered out at them.

Harriet said that before they committed to anything she wanted to check out the progress of Rölf Most's men. Musa Karsu lent her his spare flashlight, and she edged around the pit, ducked under the rock, and found that the space opened up beyond, a short passage that sloped down towards a floor of fallen rubble and a smooth rock face – a slide that had dropped straight down and sealed off the passage as tightly as a bulkhead door in a submarine. She thought that she could see a glimmer of light shining through a crack that ran across the middle of the slide, and she crabbed the rest of the way down the steep slope, cradling the elbow of her left arm with her right hand, moving slowly towards the growing noise of the drill. She switched off the flashlight for a moment, saw that there was definitely light flickering through the crack; when she put her face close to it she felt a cool draught blowing in from the other side. The drill blurted and rattled, making the slab of stone shiver – Rölf Most's men were so *close* – but when she peered through the crack all she could see was a vague confusion of motionless shadows, a pile of rubble shored up on the other side of the slide, which was a solid chunk of limestone two or three feet thick.

The drill growled again, stopped. Harriet held her breath, heard the steady *chink chink chink* of a pick or shovel working on the far side, the rattle of falling stones. And was that a man's voice?

Maybe they had an hour before Rölf Most's men broke through, she thought as she crawled on her knees and one hand back up the slope. Perhaps a little less, perhaps a little more – but not much more.

She ducked through the narrow crevice, straightened up. On the other side of the pit, Musa Karsu and Toby were standing with their backs to her, looking across the huge cathedral space of the cavern towards the slide of cobbles that rose up to the cathole entrance.

A man stood there, transfixed by the shivering beam of Musa Karsu's flashlight. A young man not much older than Musa Karsu, wearing a ragged *dishdasha*, his feet bare and bloody. His stare was unblinking; his head moved from side to side in a sinuous loop, like a snake taking a fix on its prey, deciding exactly where to strike. His huge shadow, thrown across the fluted curtain of limestone behind him, aped his movements. Harriet dropped her flashlight, pulled the automatic pistol from her trousers and stepped forward, picking her way through the constellations of night lights.

Toby hissed her name, told her to be careful, but her attention

was on the man – the low man, he was definitely a low man –
in front of her.

'I don't want to hurt you,' she said, hearing an unexpected
tremor in her voice. 'Why don't you sit down? Sit down, put your
hands on top of your head.'

Behind her, Musa Karsu said something in Kurdish.

The man stared at Harriet with wide unblinking eyes, threw
back his head and howled, a keening wail that raised echoes in
the shadows high above, then ran straight at her.

That was when she shot him.

35

As he was lowered into the shaft, standing in the swaying bucket hoist and clutching its greasy hook with one hand, Alfie plucked the sliver of foil-wrapped soap from his pocket and pushed it inside his mouth, wedging it between gum and cheek, and felt his anxiety ease a little. Perhaps he'd never get a chance to try out his little trick, but at least he was ready. The patch of indigo sky above him shrank and darkened, a single star gleaming in its centre. Then the bucket hit the floor of the shaft with a bone-jarring clang and tipped sideways, spilling him onto the unforgiving rock floor.

Larry Macpherson hauled him to his feet, saying, 'You okay, my man? Nothing broken?'

Alfie nodded, for the moment unable to speak. The little foil packet had become dislodged when he'd tumbled out of the bucket, and he was working it back into place with his tongue, thinking that he was lucky that he hadn't swallowed it or coughed it out. Now Rölf Most stepped forward and told him to kneel. After Alfie complied, the psychiatrist lifted off Alfie's hard hat and fussed with the electrode wires glued to his scalp, plugging them into the little digital recorder and clipping it to the belt of Alfie's overalls.

Once he was satisfied that everything was working properly, Rölf Most said, 'This is your last chance, Mr Flowers. We will first test your reactions without the drug. You will identify for me the glyph that you believe to be the most potent, and then we will give you the drug and see just how potent it is by its effect on you.'

The psychiatrist was full of crazy glee, his face flushed, his eyes glittering. He raised his glyph gun high, like a king's sceptre or Lady Liberty's torch, gesturing to his little audience – Alfie and Larry Macpherson, the crew-cut mercenary and Carver Soborin – and saying grandly, 'This is the rebirth of mind's i! We stand at

the threshold of the dawn of a new form of human consciousness! We will wake thoughts that have slept inside our minds for
ten thousand years! After this day, nothing will be the same again!'

The man had the devil's own luck. The mercenaries who were
clearing the rockfall which blocked the passage had almost finished
their work, and just before descending into the antechamber the
crew-cut mercenary had passed on a radio message reporting that
his men had killed most of the intruders and chased off the
survivors without suffering a single casualty. The way things were
going, he'd survive Larry Macpherson's attempt on his life too
. . . Not that it made any difference to Alfie, who was certain that
neither Rölf Most nor Larry Macpherson would bother to haul
his carcass back to the surface after he'd been struck down by
whatever lay beyond the rockfall; his only hope was a silly trick
that he probably couldn't bring off.

With Larry Macpherson crowding behind him, Alfie meekly
followed the psychiatrist and Carver Soborin through the passage
into the first gallery. As he clambered up the ladder laid over the
slope of fallen rock, climbing towards the chapel-like hollow and
the glyph which had felled him yesterday, he clamped the little
foil packet between his teeth, getting ready to bite down on it,
tasting soap. *Showtime.*

His plan was desperately simple. Fall down in front of the glyph,
pretend to have a fit, jerk and thrash, suck soap and foam at the
mouth. If it worked out, if he managed to fool Rölf Most into
thinking that the glyph had zapped him even though he wasn't
primed with the cocktail of drugs (and if Rölf Most didn't check
the tell-tale EEG trace or decide to have him shot on the spot
for being a bad little lab rat), the fake fit should buy him a little
time. Perhaps, while everyone believed that he was unconscious,
while Rölf Most was busy with whatever lay beyond the rockfall, he could somehow sneak away . . .

Palms sweating, sick with stage fright, his mouth full of the
slimy, bitter taste of soap, Alfie ducked through the narrow opening,
and saw − *oh, shit* − that the glyph had been chiselled clean off
the pale stone wall. Only the charcoal and red ochre outline of
the bison's body was left. For a moment, Alfie thought about
going through with it anyway. But without an obvious trigger,

Rölf Most, who was grinning at him, enjoying his reaction, wouldn't buy his act for a moment.

'I have a complete record of it,' the psychiatrist said, 'so there is no point leaving the original for others to find. If only your grandfather had thought of doing this, eh? How much trouble he would have saved you, Mr Flowers!'

Alfie used his tongue to push the foil packet between his teeth and upper lip, and said, 'My grandfather was an archaeologist. He had a deep respect for the past, and the things he discovered.'

'As do I, Mr Flowers, as do I. The past lies within you, waiting to be awakened. As it will be, very soon.'

'Assuming you find something beyond that rockfall.'

'Of course I will find something,' Rölf Most said. 'You must understand that there is a consistent pattern to these cave complexes. When the initiate enters the underground or spirit world, he must pass though a membrane or gateway that separates it from daily life. He does this with the aid of communal rituals in which he consumes psychotropic drugs that help him to move deeper into his mind, a spiritual journey that is reflected by his physical passage through the vortex where we now stand, inhabited by spirit animals and minor glyphs, to the place where he fulfils his vision quest. That is what lies beyond the rockfall, Mr Flowers, there is no question about it. Glyphs more powerful than any your grandfather discovered here. Glyphs that will release our most fundamental archetypes, those reflexive patterns of behaviour that were hard-wired into our brains by accidents of evolution, which underpin everything that makes us human.'

Carver Soborin said, 'One with God.' The old man was examining the ruined picture of the bison, peering at it through the frosted lenses of his glasses, running his fingers over its belly. 'They will make you one with God.'

Rölf Most clapped Carver Soborin on the back and laughed. His affection for the old man was genuine; he really believed that his occasional pronouncements were precious grains of Zen wisdom rather than the random ejaculations of a shattered mind.

'Who knows where this voyage into inner space will take us?' he said. 'And you, Mr Flowers, you will lead the way, the first astronaut in at least ten thousand years to explore the sacred heart of this ancient temple. We will open the eye of your mind, and send you on a vision quest deep into the neural structures of your own brain. And, of course, we will capture the entire journey on video and EEG.'

'I don't feel like an astronaut,' Alfie said. 'More like one of those chimpanzees they sent up before they sent up people. Or what was the name of that dog that the Russians sent into orbit, at the beginning of the space age?'

The dog which died in orbit, he thought because there was no way of bringing it back to Earth.

A vertical cleft in the other side of the chapel-like space led into a second gallery smaller and narrower than the first, with a waist-high tidemark on the walls and fresh heaps of stones scattered everywhere on a floor flooded with water two or three inches deep, canvas hoses lying deflated among them, and everything lit by a couple of battery-powered floodlights. If there had been any glyphs here, they had either been erased by the flood or were hidden in the shadowy clefts beneath the sloping roof and its freight of stalactites.

The two mercenaries who had been clearing the passage beyond this gallery were waiting there, their hard hats and black coveralls filthy with rock dust, their grimy faces marked with white ovals around their eyes where they'd been wearing goggles. They'd heard something on the other side of the rockfall, they said. Someone had screamed, and then there had been two gunshots.

Rölf Most said that it was impossible, but the mercenaries were adamant, standing firm as the psychiatrist lost his temper and sprayed a stream of invective into their faces. Alfie stood quietly next to Carver Soborin, his mouth full of the taste of soap, the taste of failure, trying to work out how this changed things. Beginning to feel the faintest prickling of hope, now that, for the first time, things didn't seem to be going Rölf Most's way.

'It's really very simple,' Larry Macpherson said calmly, when at last Rölf Most paused for breath. 'There must be another way into these caves. Those unfriendlies your people saw off, they were a diversion. While you were fighting to hold the front door, someone slipped in around the back.'

The crew-cut mercenary who'd accompanied them underground said that Mr Macpherson might have a point: his people
had searched the area as a matter of course, there were plenty of
caves on either side of this gorge. 'We didn't have time to explore
them properly – any one of them might link up with this complex.
Or there might be a sink-hole that leads down from above.'

'This is a trick,' Rölf Most said, glaring at Larry Macpherson,
at the mercenaries, strangling the barrel of his glyph gun with
both hands. His emotions, driven here and there by the random
impulses of his mania, were as changeable as English weather.
He'd gone from euphoria to anger in a split second. 'Right on
the threshold of my triumph you step in with this silly trick and
try to fool me. You *want* to fool me. You want to steal my glory.'

Larry Macpherson said, 'There's an easy way to find out. We're
just a couple of feet shy of breaking through, and I bet you boys
have some kind of explosive charges down here, don't you? Just
in case you ran into a rock you couldn't break up with your
drills.'

One of the dust-stained mercenaries, a blond, lanky man, said
sure, they had a few sticks of C4, but there was no way they
could use explosives. 'We didn't have time to shore up the last
part of the shaft properly when we cleared it. If we use charges
to blow out what's left, the whole lot could come down.'

'If you don't use explosives,' Larry Macpherson said, 'whoever's
back of the rockfall is going to have plenty of time to rape the
place before you cut through.'

The crew-cut mercenary said, 'If they got in through a sink-
hole, maybe we could blow in smoke and send people up top to
see where it comes out.'

Larry Macpherson said, 'How long will that take? An hour,
two hours? And meanwhile your unfriendlies will be taking photographs of those glyphs and then smashing them to hell. You said
there was bound to be pretty powerful stuff in there, Dr Most. I
bet these two guys heard a scream and gunshots because one of
the unfriendlies got more of an eyeful than he expected. It drove
him crazy and his friends had to put him out of his misery.'

'That is possible,' Rölf Most said grudgingly. He was studying
Larry Macpherson and the three mercenaries with a grim, angry

expression, a pocket Napoleon taking on board the unpalatable advice of generals he neither liked nor trusted.

The blond mercenary said, 'If we use explosives, there's a more than fifty per cent chance we'll bring down the roof.'

Larry Macpherson said, 'If you do it right you'll not only clear the rockfall, you'll probably also give the unfriendlies on the other side of it something to think about. You may not kill them, but you'll definitely knock them down. It's your choice, Dr Most, but while we stand around talking about it, those unfriendlies are stealing those glyphs from right under your nose.'

'Then we will use explosives,' Rölf Most said. 'There is no other way.'

'You won't regret it,' Larry Macpherson said. He was alive with excitement, like a gambler who has staked everything he has on a spin of the wheel and is living completely within the moment. He looked at Alfie, actually winking as he pulled two black spheres from one of the pockets of his combat jacket and said, 'These are flash-bang grenades. I've been saving them for a special occasion like this. Toss in these babies after you blow that passage open, and I promise that you won't have any trouble with whoever's on the other side.'

While Toby used a broken cobble to gouge lines across one of the spray-painted cartoons and the glyph that lay beneath it, Harriet helped Musa Karsu to fasten his length of rope around a spur of rock near the edge of the pit. Harriet had told him that the man she'd shot dead had been a low man, that killing him had really been an act of mercy; she'd explained that there had been nothing left of whoever the low man had once been, that when he'd attacked her she'd had to defend herself, and she'd had to kill him because if she'd merely wounded him he would have kept coming. But the boy wasn't having any of it. He was upset and angry, and although he carried out her instructions meticulously, he worked in bitter silence. Securing one end of the rope – a weathered length of blue nylon cord badly frayed at each end – with a double hitch. Tying knots in it so that Toby would have handholds when he had to climb out. Tying a sliding loop in the free end so that if it came to it, if for some reason Toby couldn't get out of the pit under his own power, Harriet and Musa Karsu could haul him out.

There was still no sound from the people on the other side of the slide. 'Perhaps they're still shifting rocks by hand,' Harriet said.

Musa Karsu shrugged.

'I don't think so either. I think they're about to break through, so we are going to have to work as fast as we can.'

Another shrug.

They dropped the free end of the rope into the pit. Harriet held on to it with her one good hand and leaned out while Musa Karsu shone the flashlight past her. She saw that the loop and a couple of coils of slack rope lay on the floor of the pit, turned to call to Toby – and that was when the slide blew, a tremendous blast of hard noise and hot air and dust that smacked into her and knocked her onto her behind. Dizzied by the ringing echo of the explosion, she began to slide down the steep funnel towards the lip of the pit's mouth. A jag of ancient bone tore her combat trousers, scraped skin from her thigh. The automatic pistol was ripped from her waistband and dropped over the edge of the pit as she managed to roll sideways and grab the rope. The jolt as her right arm took her entire weight sent a bolt of pure white pain through her head. The nylon rope burned her palm as it sped through her slack grip; one of the knots Musa Karsu had tied in it smashed into her fingers and forced them open; she fell backwards, slammed into soft clay and blacked out for a moment, woke to find herself lying on her back, looking up at the maw of the pit.

After a moment, Toby leaned out, looked down at her and asked if she was okay. Harriet's left arm had been pulled from the sling (something grated nastily in her shoulder when she got to her feet), the scrape on her leg stung like fury, and she'd bitten her tongue, her mouth was full of blood. She spat it out, wiped her chin on her sleeve, told Toby that she was fine but that she wasn't in any sort of shape to climb out by herself.

Toby said, 'Don't worry. We'll pull you up.'

There was a semicircular hollow in one side of the pit, about six or seven feet across and full of inky shadow, with dozens of stencilled hand prints on the slick tan stone around its margin, each outlined by a ragged splash the colour of dried blood. Harriet remembered that Palaeolithic artists would often sign or mark their work this way, planting one hand square on wetted stone and spitting pigment over it or using a reed or hollow straw to blow powdered pigment cupped in the palm of their other hand, leaving a mark to show that they had been there, a particular person in a particular place at a particular time. Saying, *I exist.* Saying, *I was here.* Realizing that these prints were the marks of the men who had dared confront what must lie inside the opening, she looked up at Toby and said, 'I've found the glyph. Throw down the flashlight so I can check it out.'

Toby said, 'Don't even think of looking for it. We discussed this. If it gives you a seizure, you'll be stuck down there.'

'I'll be fine.'

'You don't know that. And now isn't the time to find out.'

'I didn't have a seizure when I saw Musa's fascination glyph, back at the farmhouse, did I? Really, I'll be fine.'

'Grab hold of the rope, Harriet. We'll haul you out of there and then I'll come down and do what needs to be done, just like we agreed.'

Harriet was burning with impatience. 'There's no time for that. Give me the flashlight, I'll finish it right now.'

'There's definitely no time to argue about it,' Toby said stubbornly.

Harriet called to Musa Karsu, asked him to help her out, asked him to let her have his flashlight, but he didn't reply.

'Rölf Most's men could burst in at any moment,' she said angrily. 'There isn't time for you to haul me up and then climb down here.'

Toby said, 'There'll be enough time if you come out right now. Just put your foot in that loop, Harriet, we'll haul you straight out.'

'I'll switch the light on and off, a quick flash so I can see where the glyph is. And then I'll scratch it off the rock, in the dark. Don't worry,' she said, and a double thunderclap burst overhead, flooding the pit with blinding light and hard sound.

Harriet must have blacked out again for a moment, because when she opened her eyes she was lying on her back, looking up at lights dancing over a segment of the stone ceiling, hearing a man with an American accent shouting harsh peremptory orders, telling someone to put their hands behind their heads, do it right now, motherfucker. She realized that Rölf Most's men had broken through, and she scrambled into the hollow moments before a dazzling beam of light shone down, travelling over the white clay floor of the pit, glittering on the automatic pistol that Harriet in her panic had forgotten to pick up. She pressed backwards into the shadows in a niche to one side of the hollow, trying to make herself as small as possible as the light flooded in around her, revealing the figure painted on the rear wall. Black and red, with the head of a lion, he stood in profile, nursing his huge, erect member with both hands, framed by a great circle of living shapes. Harriet squeezed her eyes tight shut at once, but it was too late. He was already inside her head.

As far as Alfie was concerned, the explosion that blew out the last of the rockfall was something of an anticlimax. A muffled thump, a shiver in the stone under his feet, a rolling rush of dusty air filling the crowded, chapel-like space with a choking cloud. When the dust had settled, Larry Macpherson shoved him through the cleft into the gallery, following the three mercenaries who were disappearing one after the other into the entrance of the passage on the far side.

'We're going to have some fun,' Larry Macpherson said in Alfie's ear as he steered him over the uneven floor, their boots splashing through muddy water. 'Count on it. And count on *me*. Hear that?'

Alfie heard it: two sharp bangs.

'Those boys have gone to work. And when they're done, *I'm* going to work.'

'Because there's another way out.'

'You got it,' Larry Macpherson said.

Behind them, Rölf Most said, 'Take one of the floodlights. We will need it for the video.'

Larry Macpherson switched off the nearest floodlight and collapsed its tripod stand, telling Alfie to take one end. They hauled their awkward load up the slope of loose stones, dragged it into the narrow passage. Naked electric bulbs, every one shattered, were strung from hydraulic props, just beneath a low, irregular ceiling of wooden planks. The air stank of burnt sugar and was hazed with dust and smoke that swam in lazy coils through the beam of the flashlight that Larry Macpherson gripped between his teeth. There was an awkward scramble over shattered stone, sharp fresh edges blackened by the explosion, slabs groaning and squealing overhead and shedding trickles of dust and pebbles, then a short climb through a kind of stone chute into a huge space where the three mercenaries were aiming their flashlights and pistols at two people who knelt on the floor, hands clasped behind their heads.

One of the prisoners was a teenage boy in jeans and a fleece-trimmed jacket; the other, wearing ill-fitting forest camouflage trousers and jacket, was Toby Brown. Both of them were covered in dust, squinting with pinched expressions in the glare of the mercenaries' flashlights. When Toby saw Alfie, something sparked in the air between them. Alfie dropped his end of the floodlight and started forward, but Larry Macpherson grabbed hold of his shoulder, told him to stay right where he was.

Rölf Most clambered out of the crevice and stood up, dusting himself down with fussy little slaps, calling to the mercenaries, asking them to help Dr Soborin. The blond mercenary dragged the old man out by his arms, helped him to his feet. He adjusted his white-tinted glasses, looking around with a dazed, bewildered air, while Rölf Most walked up to the two prisoners, saying to Toby, 'I believe we have already met in London. You were with Mr Flowers, looking for Benjamin Barrett.'

Toby looked up at the psychiatrist but didn't say anything. His hair and face were chalk-white with limestone dust. Alfie thought that he looked like death.

'And you,' Rölf Most said, turning to the teenager in the sheepskin jacket, 'I know you, too. Musa Karsu, who also calls himself Morph. You have come home, Musa. How kind of you – I appreciate it very much. Was it with Mr Brown's help, or did he lead you here? Does the Nomads' Club know you are here, Mr Brown? And what about Harriet Crowley? Does she know?'

'I'm working on a story,' Toby said. 'An exclusive.'

Rölf Most stuck the wide lens of the glyph gun in Toby's face, laughing when he flinched. 'I think you know that there's no point in lying to me,' he said.

'Because you have ways of making me talk?'

'A very good way,' Rölf Most said. 'A *fascinating* way.'

While Larry Macpherson set up the floodlight, Rölf Most borrowed a flashlight from one of the mercenaries and walked away across the dark space, shining it here and there, revealing glimpses of paintings of animals and abstract patterns, shining it on something crumpled at the foot of a stony slope: a man's body. The psychiatrist knelt beside it, lifted its head by the hair, shone the flashlight into its face. 'I believe I know this gentleman too,' he said, his voice echoing off the high roof. 'Followed you here, didn't he? And you shot him for his trouble. Poor fellow. Well, he did his job. That shot warned me to expect to find unfriendly people here, which is why I had to make such a dramatic entrance.'

Larry Macpherson switched on the floodlight, turning it towards Carver Soborin, who was running his hands over a big, smooth bulge of stone. Rölf Most walked back across the chamber, saying jovially, 'Have we found what we are looking for?' Then, his voice changing, suddenly choked with anger, 'What's this?'

He pushed the old man out of the way so that he could study the bright red cartoon of a skull wearing a helmet, touching it with his fingertips, suddenly bursting into laughter. He stalked over to where Toby Brown and Musa Karsu knelt, gripped Musa Karsu's chin, lifted his head and smiled at him, saying, 'More of your spray-can art, I assume.'

The boy stared in sullen silence at the psychiatrist, who gave him a playful slap and turned to the three mercenaries. 'They didn't destroy the glyphs,' he said. 'They used spray paint to hide them, but they did not destroy them. I will need a solvent – gasoline will do if you have nothing else – and clean, soft rags. We will remove the spray paint from the glyphs, and this boy will explain every one of them to us.'

Larry Macpherson stepped towards him, backlit by the floodlight's glare, saying, 'You're dead sure this kid is who you think he is?'

Rölf Most said, 'Even if I had not seen the photograph on file with the British immigration authorities, I would know him by his work. Don't you recognize it?'

Larry Macpherson said, 'He definitely knows all about these glyphs.'

Alfie was certain that Larry Macpherson was about to make his move. It fired up a nervous exhilaration that tingled between his shoulder blades and prickled his electrode-studded scalp.

Rölf Most looked up at Larry Macpherson from beneath the brim of his hard hat. 'I believe this young man knows more about the glyphs than anyone alive. I very much look forward to talking—'

Larry Macpherson shot him in the chest. He stumbled backwards and sat down as the whiplash crack of the shot chased itself around the stone walls of the chamber, and Larry Macpherson shot him in the face and his hard hat fell off and he flopped backwards, still clutching the glyph gun.

Carver Soborin gave a shrill and wordless cry and scurried towards Rölf Most's body. Larry Macpherson ignored him, turning to the three mercenaries, asking them as casually as if he was asking for a cigarette to set their flashlights and guns on the floor and take two steps back and kneel down if you please, boys, lace your fingers good and tight behind your heads.

The three men did as they were told, kneeling in the low, crossing beams of their discarded flashlights, and Larry Macpherson shot them one after the other. The crew-cut mercenary started to get to his feet, asking for mercy, Jesus Christ you son of a bitch please don't, and Larry Macpherson shot him and stepped up to the bodies and gave each of them a *coup de grâce* shot in the back of the head. He paused for a moment, as if reflecting in quiet satisfaction on what he'd done, then picked up a flashlight and aimed it at Alfie, saying calmly, 'There you go, partner. Aren't you going to thank me?'

Alfie's terror had reached a transcendent level, possessing him completely, thrilling in him as a high C thrills in a wine glass the moment before it shatters. He was convinced that Larry Macpherson was going to shoot him too, kill everyone in the place – why not? – and bathe in their blood. But the man turned away and picked up the guns of the three mercenaries, placed them in the canvas bag that one of them had been carrying, and carefully patted down the bodies, finding several knives and dropping them in the bag too.

Toby stood up, pale and trembling. Musa Karsu knelt beside him, hands cupping his face, saying something over and over in a soft hoarse voice, a prayer or a plea. Larry Macpherson upended Musa Karsu's rucksack, tipped everything out and stirred it with his boot, picking up a knife and dropping it in the canvas bag with the rest of his booty before strolling over to them, easy and confident, stepping past Carver Soborin, who was cradling Rölf Most's body and keening wordlessly, stepping up to Toby and looking at him and saying, 'Which one of you shot that low man?'

Toby jerked his head up and down.

'No need to be frightened,' Larry Macpherson said. 'I'm not going to kill you. Why? Because I need your help. To begin with, you're going to tell me where the gun is. The gun you used to shoot the low man. I have the pieces that belonged to those poor boys, but that's all I have. So I guess they didn't take your weapon off you, and that means you must be hiding it somewhere. Give it up now,' he said, levelling his gun in Toby's face, 'and there won't be any unpleasantness.'

Toby shook his head, licked his lips, said, 'It's in the pit.'

'No shit. How did that happen? You throw it in?'

Toby took a deep breath, shook his head again, and said, 'I dropped it. I was about to climb down into the pit – you see the rope? I was about to climb down when your fireworks went off and knocked me senseless. I dropped the gun and it fell in. Take a look if you don't believe me.'

Alfie felt a clean flash of admiration for his friend's coolness.

Larry Macpherson said, 'Keep talking. You got my undivided attention. Why would you want to climb down there?'

Toby looked him in the eye and said, 'Because the most holy glyph is down there.'

'What does that mean?'

'I think it means it's the most potent glyph. The strongest.'

'And how would you happen to know that?'

'He told me,' Toby said, inclining his head towards the boy.

Larry Macpherson nudged the boy, Musa Karsu, with the toe of his boot. 'Is that true? Look at me, will you? Quit praying, it won't do you no good. Look at me and answer my fucking question.'

Musa Karsu looked up, sullen and defiant and hopeless. He shrugged and said, 'Why not?'

'Why not? What does that mean?'

'My grandfather told me that a very holy picture lives in the pit. Only the most pure of men can look at it.'

Larry Macpherson leaned down, put the muzzle of his gun against Musa Karsu's forehead and said, 'Is that the truth? Think carefully before you answer. Take your time.'

The boy said in a choked, resentful voice, 'I swear on the souls of my father and my grandfather.'

'All right,' Larry Macpherson said, and walked over to the bodies of the mercenaries.

Toby was staring at Alfie, a desperate, pleading look. As if he was willing him to do or understand something.

Larry Macpherson pulled a digital video camera from the pocket of the crew-cut mercenary and walked back to Toby and Musa Karsu, saying, 'Here's what we're gonna do. You, my friend—' he shoved the little camera into Toby's chest, forcing him to take it '– are going to climb down there. You'll video this most holy of glyphs, and then you'll tie the camera and the gun to the end of the rope and I'll haul them out. You try anything else, I'm gonna shoot you. You believe me?'

Toby licked his lips and said, 'Absolutely.'

'I'll check that you've done a proper job of capturing this holy glyph on video, and if I'm satisfied, I'll let you climb back out. Then I'll use the rest of those boys' plastic explosive to bring down the roof of that passage, and we'll leave by the back way. Do we have a deal?'

Toby nodded.

'All right,' Larry Macpherson said. 'Oh, just one more thing before we get going: where the fuck is Harriet Crowley? And please don't tell me she didn't come here with you. I've seen her passport. It was found on the body of a local who I believe brought both of you here.'

Toby said, 'We were attacked by a low man, at a farmhouse a few miles away. He rushed right at us. He had a knife.'

Larry Macpherson stared at him. 'And?'

'And he stabbed her. He stabbed her right in the heart,' Toby said, thumping his chest with his fist, giving Larry Macpherson a level look that was very familiar to Alfie, the look his friend used when he was trying to fuck with someone's head. 'And he killed her.'

'Right in the heart, huh? What did you do with her body?'

'We left it in our minibus, a little way down the hill. We didn't know what else to do.'

Larry Macpherson kicked Musa Karsu and said, 'Is that the truth?'

'She is gone,' the boy said.

Larry Macpherson held his gaze on Toby for a long beat, then slowly turned on the spot, shining his flashlight all around the big dark space.

'She better not be hiding somewhere, waiting to take a pot-shot at me. Because if any shooting starts, first thing I'm going to do is kill you,' he said, completing his circle and aiming the flashlight right in Toby's face.

Toby, squinting in the glare, said, 'I'll go into the pit for you, but you'd better hold on to the rope while I climb down. I'm not too sure of my knots – I never did get that badge when I was a Boy Scout.'

Larry Macpherson turned the flashlight on Alfie, and Alfie felt a jump, a beat, a moment when everything went away. He swayed on his feet, the taste of burnt metal suddenly cutting through the taste of soap, heard Larry Macpherson telling him to get his ass over here, he could take the strain on the rope while his friend went spelunking, and knew that he'd just suffered an episode, an absence seizure. And knew too that this was the moment, now or never, when he could provide a vital distraction, give Toby a vital few seconds to grab up the gun from wherever he'd cached it – or give Harriet, if she wasn't dead, the chance to step out of her hiding place and get the drop on Larry Macpherson.

Alfie walked around the edge of the pit to the place where the rope was fastened around a spur of rock, turning his back on Larry Macpherson as he squatted down and pretended to test the knot, shifting the little foil package in his mouth, biting down hard on it, letting himself go. He banged his hip and elbow on the hard stone floor when he fell over; the pain helped him get into his act. He didn't remember any of his major seizures, didn't know what he was supposed to look like or do, but jerked and shivered as best he could, sucking and chewing on foul slippery soap, slobbering gouts of foam, his eyes squeezed shut, waiting for Larry Macpherson to tell him to quit fooling around – or worse, shoot him in the head.

He heard the man swear, heard him step towards him, felt the man's hands grip his shoulders, pulling him up. He groaned, dribbled soap bubbles, kicked out like a clubbed fish.

'Goddamn it,' Larry Macpherson said, and then cried out in surprise and let go of Alfie.

The back of Alfie's head bounced on the rock floor, hard enough to jar his teeth – he almost swallowed the wad of foil – and explode a flash of white light behind his eyes. He risked opening his eyes and saw that Larry Macpherson was struggling with Carver Soborin. The old man had climbed or jumped onto his back and was clawing at his scalp, at his face, digging in hard enough to draw blood. The two men waltzed along the edge of the short steep slope that dropped down to the mouth of the pit, the beam of Larry Macpherson's flashlight whirling around, pointing at the ceiling, swinging down and swerving across the floor, shining starkly on the body of Rölf Most, on something that glittered beside it.

Alfie jumped up, spat out the disgusting wad of soapy foil, ran to Rölf Most's body and scooped up the glyph gun just as Larry Macpherson, with an exasperated grunt, managed to dump Carver Soborin on his back. Carver Soborin started to get up and Larry Macpherson raised his gun and shot him. The old man was knocked flat on his back, blood splashed across his white jacket. His frosted glasses had fallen off; as he groped for them, Larry Macpherson shot him again, shot him in the chest and shot him in the head, and Alfie stepped up, swung the flared muzzle of the glyph gun in Larry Macpherson's face and pressed the trigger.

For a moment, the mercenary's pock-marked face shone with light so pure and bright that his skull seemed to show through.

Then the light began to strobe, a complex flicker precisely reflected in the black mirrors of his pupils.

Alfie screwed his eyes shut as Larry Macpherson took an involuntary step backwards and lost his balance. He swiped out at Alfie, missed, and fell. Tumbling head over heels down the short steep slope and dropping over the edge of the pit as Toby ran forward, shouting out Harriet's name.

Harriet had loved to play hide-and-seek when she'd been a little girl, had loved the excruciatingly exciting mixture of dread and anticipation she'd felt while crouching among the raspberry canes or hiding behind a rotting sofa in the barn, listening for the footsteps of the boy or girl who'd been made 'it', daring herself to peek out, nerving herself up to make a desperate run for home and safety. After she and her mother moved to the country, playing hide-and-seek at her birthday parties became an absolutely essential part of the day, taking place between the opening of the presents and the birthday feast of cakes and tiny triangular sandwiches, jelly and ice cream, and at least three kinds of fizzy pop. One birthday, her tenth, when she was almost but not quite too old for the game, it rained all day and Harriet and her guests had to play in the house. She hid herself in the airing cupboard, crouching under shelves of bed linen and towels next to the dusty insulating jacket of the hot-water tank. She'd draped a white sheet over herself; when the boy who was 'it' opened the cupboard door, she was going to jump up and give him a terrific fright by pretending to be a Scooby-Doo ghost.

While Harriet waited, listening to footsteps thump past the cupboard door, hearing the muffled screams and squeals of laughter from various parts of the roomy house, she became increasingly convinced that something was waiting with her in the warm, dusty dark; by pretending to be a ghost, she had somehow summoned a monster. The only way to fool it into thinking that she wasn't there was to keep her eyes squeezed tight shut and stay absolutely still under the sheet. She crouched there for the longest time, her heart beating quickly, a sick scraped feeling in her stomach, a sharp pain growing in her bladder because she'd drunk too much lemonade. Her imagination ran wild and free.

Suppose the monster had friends? Suppose they had caught all the guests and had turned *them* into monsters who were right now waiting outside, silent and somehow *drained*. Suppose she had been transported to another place (she had recently read *The Lion, the Witch, and the Wardrobe*), and when she finally opened the door, she would find a snowy wood, hear the bells of the witch's sleigh as it glided towards her . . .

When at last she heard the tread of someone approaching the airing cupboard, Harriet held her breath and tried to make herself as small and insignificant as possible. She heard the creak of the loose floorboard outside the door. The handle rattled, the door opened, and she could bear it no longer and screamed and jumped up, and, still tangled in the sheet, blind with terror, ran straight into the arms of her mother.

Now, crouching with the base of her spine pressed against cold stone and her arms wrapped around her knees, her eyes squeezed tight shut and a zoo of luminous shapes wriggling in the warm dark behind her eyelids, she felt the black unreasoning wash of that childish terror all over again. There was a monster inside her hiding place (there was a monster in her head), and there were monsters outside it, too . . .

Harriet heard a distant confusion of voices, heard Rölf Most crowing about the capture of Musa Karsu and knew that she was in serious trouble, then heard a gunshot, loud and hard, echoing off the stone ceiling. Shock drop-kicked her heart. There was another gunshot, and then she heard someone ordering people to kneel, heard three more shots in quick succession, and then another three, deliberately spaced. She didn't know what was happening up there and could only imagine the worst. Toby Brown and Musa Karsu had been executed, and at any moment mercenaries armed to the teeth would swarm down the rope into the pit and see her huddled in her pathetic hiding place and riddle her with a hail of bullets. She wanted to scrunch further into the niche, melt into the stone, find some place so deep and dark that they'd never find her, but she was paralysed by the conviction that if she made the faintest sound or the slightest movement her enemies would be on her instantly, so she crouched quiet and still, her wounded shoulder throbbing sharply, straining to understand the voices echoing above.

A man with an American accent ordered someone to climb down into the pit. She heard her name, heard Toby tell an outrageous lie about her death and felt a gush of relief that he was still alive, heard the American threaten him, and the sounds of a struggle. Then the sharp hard crack of yet another gunshot, quickly followed by two more, sounding so close that she jumped up, ready to run even though there was nowhere she could run to, opening her eyes because she was suddenly more scared of being shot than of being devoured by the monster. Toby shouted her name, and a man crashed to the shadowy floor of the pit, just two yards from her hiding place.

Electric light, a single unsteady beam, shone down on him as he pushed himself up onto his hands and knees. Toby shouted Harriet's name again, and she started towards the automatic pistol that lay on the white clay. But the man was quicker, raising his own gun and pointing it at her, saying calmly, 'Be cool, Ms Crowley. Can you do that?'

It was Larry Macpherson. Harriet looked at him, looked at the gun.

He glanced up at the rim of the pit, then pushed forward, sprinting across the narrow space, grabbing hold of Harriet and twisting her right arm behind her back, spinning her around and pulling her backwards into the shelter of the hollow in the wall. Jamming the muzzle of his gun into the soft flesh behind her ear. Saying loudly, 'Boys! Listen up! If you want Harriet Crowley to live, you're going to have to do what I say. You hear me?'

There was a whispered consultation, and then Alfie's voice said, 'Let her go, and we can sort something out.'

Larry Macpherson said, 'That's not how it's going to work.'

Toby's voice said, 'We have guns up here.'

'I wouldn't try to use them. You'll probably hit your friend, and you'll definitely piss me off. Now pay attention,' Larry Macpherson said, speaking forcefully but calmly, completely in control of the situation. 'This is what's going to happen. You're going to leave those guns in the bag, you're going to leave the C4 in there too, you're going to put that video camera in there, and you're going to drop it into this hole. Harriet will check it out, tell me exactly what's in it. If she comes up short on guns or knives or anything else she gets shot. Her life is in your hands. It's tough, but that's how it is.'

There was another whispered consultation beyond the edge of the pit.

Larry Macpherson said in Harriet's ear, 'I guess that this so-called holy glyph must be somewhere inside this hole in the wall, because I don't see it anywhere else.'

'Why don't you turn around and take a look?'

Harriet's right hand was jammed up between her shoulder blades and her left arm was useless, but all she needed was a moment's distraction; she could slam the back of her head into the man's face, stamp on his shin . . .

Larry Macpherson said coolly, 'That's just what I plan to do. That, and make a little movie, with you as the star.' Raising his voice, saying, 'You boys need to drop that bag right now. No ifs, ands or buts, just do it or I swear to God I'll hurt your friend so badly she'll never get over it.'

He twisted the muzzle of his gun into the bandage over Harriet's bullet wound and she cried out, she couldn't help it.

'You got thirty seconds,' Larry Macpherson said, 'or I'll shoot off one of her kneecaps or gouge out one of her eyes.'

Harriet shouted, 'Get out! Forget about me—'

Larry Macpherson rapped her on the back of her head so hard that she bit her tongue. A moment later, a small canvas bag slid over the edge of the pit and dropped to the floor.

'Good boys,' Larry Macpherson said. 'I hope you aren't holding back a gun on me, because if you are, I *will* shoot your friend.'

He put his mouth close to Harriet's ear, told her that he wanted her to check the bag. 'Listen carefully, do what I say, and there won't be any unpleasantness. I want you to go over to that bag and open it up, check that there's a single package of C4 explosive in there, check that they put the video camera in there. Tell me you understand.'

'C4. A video camera.'

'A small one, but it'll do the trick. There should be guns and knives in there, too. I want you to count them, tell me how many there are. And listen: if you try to use any one of them, try to pick up the gun on the floor there, or try any other trick, I'll shoot you at once. It won't kill you, but it'll put you in a world of hurt. You understand?'

Harriet nodded.

'All right,' Larry Macpherson said, and let go of her wrist and shoved her forward.

As she stepped towards the bag, a flashlight beam swung into her face, dazzling her. Larry Macpherson shouted that he wanted that light off right now, and it vanished a moment later. Harriet knelt in the half-dark, blinking away after-images and luminous floaters, fumbling one-handedly with the nylon zip of the bag, managing to get it open. She felt inside, found three guns and four, no, five knives, found a small package, done up in greasy paper, that she supposed was the C4 explosive, found various tools, a screwdriver, a small hammer, a roll of something – tape, gaffer tape. Found a cool slim metal shape that must be the video camera, here was the lens, and here was something tied to its strap, a metal cylinder not much bigger than her thumb . . .

From the other side of the pit, Larry Macpherson said, 'Talk to me. How many guns you got there?'

'Three.'

'How many knives?'

'Five.' She was trying to free the cylinder from the strap, realizing that Alfie or Toby had given her a last chance to make things right.

'No need to be nervous, you're doing fine,' Larry Macpherson said. 'What about the explosive?'

'There's a packet.'

'Is the camera there?'

'I think so.'

'Is it there, yes or no?'

Harriet finally managed to pull the cylinder from the loop in the strap. She stuck it in the waistband of her trousers, saying, 'Yes. Yes, it's right here.'

From above, Alfie's voice said, 'Don't hurt her. We gave you everything you wanted.'

'Be cool,' Larry Macpherson said. 'Zip up that bag, Harriet. Zip it up and bring it over here. And don't even think of looking at the gun on the ground.'

Harriet held the bag out to him, her head averted because she was scared that she'd see the glyph on the wall behind him. She'd only had a quick glimpse of it before, and some of it had been hidden by shadows, but that had been enough to do a number on her head.

Larry Macpherson told her to set the bag down and open it up, then sit down and take hold of the back of her neck with her good hand. She obeyed, watching sidelong as he felt around inside the bag, taking out and examining the silvery oblong of the video camera.

'All right,' he said at last, and picked up the bag and carried it past Harriet, scooping the gun from the floor, sticking it in the back of his combat pants, looking up. Saying loudly, 'You boys did just fine. We're nearly there. What I want you to do now is turn that floodlight around and shine it in the hole behind me. I want to video what's in there, so light it up good. And don't get any dumb ideas about cutting the rope, anything like that, because if you do I'll start in on your friend and I will take my time. Am I understood?'

After a moment, Alfie said that he understood.

'That's good, partner. As long as you don't cause me any more trouble, I might even find it in my heart to forgive you. What were you chewing on, to make yourself foam at the mouth like that? Soap?'

Alfie agreed that it had been soap.

'You almost had me, partner, but I'm just too sly. How about turning that light around?'

Harriet saw a glare light up the darkness beyond the edge of the pit, and shut her eyes.

'Look at that,' Larry Macpherson said, after a moment. 'Move the light a little to your left, boys, I have to get every inch of this on record. Perfect. He's well-endowed for a holy fellow, wouldn't you say? Are you shy, Harriet? Or wait, you're sensitive. Just like your friend Alfie Flowers . . . I have to admit, that stuff around him does look weird. What does it do to you?'

'I caught a glimpse of him. That was enough,' Harriet said, bowing her head and hunching over as if in distress, putting her hand against her stomach. 'Please, don't make me look at him again.'

'I want you to get up,' Larry Macpherson said. 'I want you to get up and look at the big man, and I'm going to video what happens for some friends of mine.'

'I can't,' she said.

'I can shoot you,' Larry Macpherson said. 'Shoot you somewhere painful and non-lethal, then duct-tape your eyelids open and make you look.'

She stayed absolutely still, hunched over.

'Goddamn it,' he said and stooped over her, gripped her under her right arm and pulled her up.

Harriet went with it, coming up with the canister in the hollow of her right hand, raising her hand as she hung off his grip, thumbing the button of the canister and spraying him in the face.

He roared and dropped her, instinctively rubbing at his eyes. She let herself fall, ignoring the jarring pain in her left shoulder as she sat down hard, staying focused. She kicked out and hooked the handle of the canvas bag with her foot, then scooted backwards into the hollow, scrunching into the niche as Larry Macpherson wiped at his eyes with one hand, blindly pointing the gun here and there. Getting one eye open and pointing his gun at Harriet as she felt around inside the bag, then stepping back, both eyes wide, the gun swinging up and around and firing, the noise hard and loud in the confined space as he shot the glyph and shot it again and again and again, shards of stone spattering Harriet as she frantically searched inside the bag. She cut herself on one of the knives, closed her hand around the grip of an automatic pistol, pulled it out and worked the slide. Larry Macpherson shot the glyph with his eyes squeezed tight shut, his face horribly twisted, shot it again, and then the hammer of his gun fell on an empty chamber. He threw the gun aside and reached behind him, and Harriet pushed to her feet, told him to step back and turn around, wondering what he had seen, what the glyph had done to him – her quick, partial glimpse had been bad enough.

Larry Macpherson stepped back when she fired a warning shot between his feet, but then he brought out the gun he'd picked up from the floor, raising it as Harriet screamed at him to drop it. He fired blindly towards the glyph as she shot him, screaming

into the noise and flash of her gun as he took three steps backwards and struck the wall of the pit. He was still holding the gun
and she blew a red chunk from his arm and he sat down and her
next three shots struck sparks from glistening rock above his head
because recoil jerked up her unbraced wrist and threw off her
aim, so she had to step forward, the monster staring at her, his
mouth opening and closing, and she shot him in the face, shot
him blind, kept pulling the trigger even after she'd exhausted the
pistol's magazine.

Harriet stood still among drifts of gun smoke, as if she'd fallen
asleep on her feet. Then she threw her pistol at the dead man,
fell to her knees in front of him, and began to cry.

36

Like the survivors of a mining disaster, Alfie and Toby crawled out of the narrow cave mouth into hot, brassy sunlight, stumbling and drawn, their faces and hair and clothes filthy with rock dust. They had collapsed the passage that Rölf Most's men had opened, using the plastic explosives Harriet had taken from the canvas bag before they had laboriously hauled her out of the pit, but they hadn't been able to work out how to alter the two-minute setting on the electronic fuse. They'd barely had enough time to scamper across the big cavern before it blew; the blast wave of the explosion had knocked them down as they were struggling up the slope of cobbles towards the narrow hole in the limestone curtain, and then a choking wave of dust had rolled over them.

Alfie managed to stumble down the pile of boulders and follow Toby a little way down the steep, narrow draw before his legs gave way. He sat down hard and dropped the glyph gun between his feet, nursing his splinted little finger, which he'd badly bruised during the long hard scramble out of the caves, breathing in the strong, familiar scent rising from the low grey bushes that grew everywhere in the shaly soil. Toby staggered stiff-legged to the shallows of the river, knelt, and splashed handfuls of water over his dusty face and matted hair, shaking his head, flinging diamond-bright droplets in every direction. Meanwhile, Harriet squeezed crabwise out of the cave mouth and sat down, cupping the elbow of her injured arm with her right hand, her hair hanging in rats' tails around her face. Musa Karsu stepped past her, cantered down the boulder-pile and walked past Alfie to the end of the draw, pausing there and looking left and right, cocky and confident, his rucksack slung over one shoulder.

Toby got to his feet, his black hair sticking up in spikes, water chalky with dust running down his face, pattering onto the front of his dusty camouflage jacket. Saying to the boy, 'What now, Kemo Sabe?'

Musa Karsu said, 'You said you came here in a minibus. Is that true?'

Toby smiled. 'When you tell a big lie, one on which your life depends, you should make sure that you stick to the truth as much as possible. If this is the river we crossed last night, all we have to do is follow it downstream a little way and keep a lookout for a clump of trees. That's where we left our ride.'

'I think you should go now, before someone finds you.'

Toby studied the boy. 'I get the feeling you're trying to say goodbye.'

'I have my own ride,' Musa Karsu said. 'I stole it in Mosul. A good one – a Toyota with four-wheel drive.'

Alfie slouched down the draw, the glyph gun in one hand and a grey-leaved sprig in the other, a tender, dreamy, distant look on his face. Looking at Toby, at Musa Karsu, saying, 'This is haka.'

Toby said sharply, 'Don't even think of smoking it. You're in bad enough shape as it is.'

Alfie said to Musa Karsu, 'Did your people plant it here?'

The boy shrugged. 'It is a gift. Wherever it grows, it is a gift.'

Alfie said, 'The two things together, haka and the glyphs: it can't be a coincidence. Perhaps the people who made the glyphs in the first place picked it and brought it here because it was a part of their ritual. Seeds fell, the plant grew . . .'

He sniffed the sprig, went away for a couple of seconds.

Toby said, 'Please, Flowers, don't go all weird on me. I don't think I'm up to carrying you down this mountain.'

Alfie came back with a visible start, and said, 'It reminds me of the last time I saw my father.'

Toby said, 'Morph is trying to say goodbye. We chase him halfway across Europe, and as soon as we find him he wants to leave.'

'I did what I came here to do,' the boy said. He took a deep breath and let it out, then smiled shyly at Alfie and Toby. 'It is over.'

Alfie smiled too. 'I suppose it is.'

'No,' Harriet said. 'No, it isn't.'

She stood at the mouth of the draw, her bare left arm cradled in its sling, her face haggard, at the very end of her strength.

Toby said, 'I think those mercenaries are going to have a hard time clearing that rockfall. And even if they do manage it, all they'll find is a bunch of defaced glyphs. But frankly, I don't think they'll bother. The man who was paying them is dead, and they'll be worried that the *peshmergas* will be coming back with reinforcements. In short, if they have any sense, they'll cut their losses and run.'

Musa Karsu nodded. 'You helped me out, we work together and destroy the pictures. I'm grateful you help me, but it's over.'

Harriet stepped towards him, teetering on the high wire of her exhaustion. 'We destroyed the pictures in the cave. What about the ones in your head?'

The boy drew himself up, returned her gaze defiantly. 'What about them?'

'Do you really think that Rölf Most is the only person looking for you? People were paying him to chase after you, to find the source of the glyphs. As far as they're concerned, this isn't the end of their search; it's no more than a setback. They'll put a price on your head and find someone else to hunt you.'

Musa Karsu folded his arms across his chest and considered her. 'You'll look after me, is that it?'

Harriet said, 'You'll be a lot safer in London than in Iraq.'

'Lady, I left London because it wasn't safe for me. I don't have any plans to go back. This is my place. I have bad memories, coming back here I feel a sadness for what I have lost, but it is where I belong.'

'*Hawar*,' Toby said.

'That is a Kurdish word,' Musa Karsu said. 'I am not a Kurd, but yes, I feel it. I feel there is no place where I can be safe, even when I come home, but it is better to feel it in a place you know than in a place 'you do not. This is my home. It is the home of my people, my family. The Americans came here and took away my mother and my sisters. First thing I do, I try to find them. What I do after that, that's my business, not yours.'

'I don't think so,' Harriet said. She reached behind her and from the waistband of her combat trousers drew the automatic pistol that she'd taken from Larry Macpherson's body, extending her arm and pointing its squared-off muzzle at Musa Karsu, her gaze steady as she looked at him over its foresight.

Toby took a couple of steps towards her. 'I think you're making a mistake,' he said, and froze, hands half-raised, when she flicked the pistol towards him for a moment.

Musa Karsu said, his voice thickening with contempt, 'So you want the pictures too. You are just like those others.'

'I don't want anyone to have them,' Harriet said. 'That's why you have to come with me.'

'They are destroyed,' Musa Karsu said. He stood very still, staring straight at her, defiant and angry. 'You helped me to destroy them.'

Alfie said, trying to reason with her, 'What are you going to do, hold us all at gunpoint, all the way back to London? Put down the gun, Harriet, and we can talk about this sensibly.'

'There's nothing to talk about,' Harriet said, without taking her gaze from Musa Karsu. 'You should be on my side. Your father gave his life to stop the glyphs falling into the wrong hands. This isn't any different. You know what the glyphs can do – the ones we know about. They're bad enough, but the ones we just erased are even more powerful, and the boy knows all about them. No matter what he says, I know he'll keep using them. He told me that he can't help himself. Sooner or later someone will catch up with him, perhaps someone a lot worse than Rölf Most. Imagine what would happen if they were propagated over the internet. Imagine what would happen if a terrorist group got hold of the glyphs.'

Alfie said, 'Is that really what this is about? Or is it really about *your* father? Are you still trying to make amends for him?'

Harriet shook her head. She had her back to Alfie, was still staring straight at Musa Karsu. 'It's about stopping the spread of the glyphs. That's all it's ever been about.'

Alfie said, 'And you've already done more than enough. This is where it ends.'

'If you think that, why don't you and your friend take off?' Harriet said. 'Leave me to deal with this.'

Alfie said, 'You aren't going to shoot him, Harriet.'

She was swaying on her feet, as if the slab of stone on which she stood was the pitching deck of a ship, but she kept the pistol centred on Musa Karsu's chest, saying, 'I don't want to shoot him. I want to take him back to London. I want to help him. But I *will* shoot him if I have to. I've already shot two people dead today. One more isn't going to make any difference.'

Musa Karsu said, 'You know nothing about the pictures. Nothing.'

Harriet said, 'I know plenty. My grandfather spent most of his life studying them, so did his friends, and they taught me everything they knew.'

Musa Karsu said, putting the full force of his scorn into his voice, 'If that is so, then they learn nothing, and they teach you nothing. Because all you think is how you can use them, how they can cause trouble, how they can hurt people or make them crazy like that poor low man. You study them, you analyse them, you break them down and you put them together again, but that is not how you can know them. You do not use science to find Allah. You cannot measure him with numbers. All your powerful telescopes and microscopes, your satellites and computers will reveal nothing of him. Your friends and your grandfather, I have not met them, but I know that they are fucking fools. You tell me your grandfather danced with our people one time. He knew then that the pictures are not weapons. That they are not tools. They are a gift, and the haka is a gift, both are parts of the one gift, a great gift that lets you find Allah inside yourself. All the rest is lies and perversion. It is like taking a shit in the heart of a mosque. I know this because that is what my grandfather taught me.' Musa Karsu stared straight at Harriet. 'And I am sorry for you because your grandfather could have taught you the same thing, but he failed. Instead, he taught you to hate the pictures, to fear them. And that is why you want to kill me. Because you are afraid.'

'I don't want to kill you,' Harriet said. 'I want to save you. This isn't the world of our grandfathers. It's far more dangerous than that, all connected together, messy and complicated. If the wrong people find you, they'll torture you for what you know, and then they'll kill you.'

'You were looking for me in London. So were these two, and also the bad guys. Did any of you find me?'

'*I* found you,' Harriet said. 'The world's too small for anyone to be able to hide from someone who wants to find them.'

'But if I want to try, that's my choice, isn't it? What right do you have to tell me what I do?'

'Because I'm doing the right thing.'

Alfie dared to take a step towards her, saying, 'I'm sorry.'

'You walked into this by accident,' Harriet said. 'It isn't your fault that things turned out like this.'

'I mean, I'm sorry that I have to do this,' Alfie said, and swung the glyph gun in a short arc that connected with the top of her head.

Harriet grunted, took a step and tried to take another, but her legs folded and she sat down. She tried to lift the pistol and couldn't. Alfie plucked it from her fingers and told Musa Karsu, 'You better get going.'

The boy studied him for a moment, then turned and began to walk away.

'Hey,' Toby said. 'There's no need to thank us.'

'See you around,' Musa Karsu said, without looking back.

'I hope not,' Alfie said, watching as the boy went around a shoulder of rock and disappeared from view.

'Well, here's another fine mess,' Toby said, running his fingers through his wet hair.

Alfie smiled at him. 'It's good to see you too.'

'Goes without saying. What now? Where do we go from here?'

'Before we do anything else, I think we should get rid of these,' Alfie said, weighing the pistol in one hand, the glyph gun in the other.

'Good idea.'

Alfie tossed the pistol into the deep pool at the bottom of the little waterfall, then used a rock to smash open the glyph gun's casing, shatter the LED array, snap the circuit boards and crush the little hard drive. As he and Toby gathered up the pieces and threw them into different places in the river's braided stream, Harriet tried to get to her feet. Alfie helped her up. She touched the top of her head, tried to focus on fingers wet with blood. 'You had an accident,' Alfie said. 'Just rest there a minute.'

She looked at Alfie. Her eyes crossed, uncrossed. 'You hit me.'

'You were going to shoot the boy,' Alfie said. 'Lean on me. Let me help you.'

'Fuck you,' Harriet said. She pushed away from him, drew herself up and walked away, clutching wet rock with her one good hand as she began to pick her way down the steep path beside the waterfall.

Alfie called to her, but she didn't look back.

'That could have gone better,' Toby said. 'Do you know how to hot-wire a car?'

'I don't know, I've never tried. Why do you ask?'

'Do you think Harriet can?'

'Probably. It's just the kind of thing she would know.'

'Then I think we'd better go with her. Rölf Most's goons took the keys for the minibus from me, and in all the excitement I sort of forgot to get them back.'

LONDON,
5 NOVEMBER 2004

When Harriet walked into Alfie's yard, the first thing she saw was Toby Brown firing a Roman candle across the railway tracks. It was half past four in the afternoon, the end of a cool, crisp November day, the sky lightly fretted with clouds that were beginning to bruise as light died out of the sky. Streetlamps were flickering on along the road; lights were burning under the pitched roof of the garage at the far end of the yard. Toby was engaged in a firefight with a trio of teenagers, standing on the trampled remains of a chain-link fence between two leaf-less sycamores, gripping the fat tube of the firework in both hands as it shot off red and yellow and green fireballs. Whooping and laughing, shouting 'Getsome! Getsome!' while on the embankment on the far side of the railway the three teenagers dodged the fireballs that exploded in spatters of bright sparks among the bare trees, shouting back at Toby, striking attitudes, and lobbing firecrackers, most of which exploded in the air above the railway tracks.

Everyone seemed to be having a fine old time, fireworks exploding, the teenagers shouting, Toby whooping. 'Eat my fucking fire, Getsome! Getsome!'

The Roman candle lofted a last ball of red fire, a feeble runt that burst at the top of its wobbling arc and dropped a scattering of sparks onto the railway tracks.

The teenagers jeered.

Toby tossed the smouldering tube at them and shouted cheer-fully, 'You miserable pieces of dole-bait wait there. I'll be right back!'

He turned and saw Harriet standing just inside the gate, under the big board that the developer had erected, with its idealized pastel picture, price list, and promised completion date. Said coolly, 'They were chucking firecrackers at the trains, I responded in kind, and now we're having ourselves a little war. Care to join in? I seem to remember that you're a dab hand with heavy ordnance.'

'Does Alfie Flowers still live here?'

'You noticed the sign,' Toby said, walking towards her.

He was more than a little drunk, and sweating hard in the chill air. He took a half-pint of Bell's from the pocket of his black jacket, unscrewed the cap and took a swallow before holding it out to Harriet. She refused the offer with a shake of her head, managed not to flinch as a couple of firecrackers went off, one on the heels of the other, among the leafless bushes and trees that bordered the yard.

Toby said, 'Of course you noticed it. You're a spook. I believe they actually trained you to notice stuff like that.'

Harriet adjusted the strap of the laptop case slung over her right shoulder. 'I'm no longer in the spook business – if I ever was.'

'So this visit has nothing at all to do with the glyphs, or the Nomads' Club.'

'How is Alfie?'

'He's in his caravan, you can ask him yourself. He'll probably even tell you the truth – he isn't the kind to hold a grudge.'

'Unlike you.'

'Unlike me, unlike you, unlike most of our brave island race. We're good at holding grudges, good at keeping old fires smouldering. Remember, remember, the Fifth of November, gunpowder, treason . . . all the rest of that rot. But Alfie's a decent guy, one of the best. He might even ask you to stay for our little end-of-an-era firework party,' Toby said, offering her the whisky bottle again.

This time Harriet took it from him. She warmed her mouth with the tiniest sip and handed it back, saying 'Actually, I came here with a peace offering.'

'How's the arm, by the way?'

'It's getting better. They tell me that I'll never recover the full use of it, but I'm doing physio, I'm swimming every day – it's getting to be about as good as it ever will be.'

Another brace of firecrackers exploded with whip-sharp cracks; this time Harriet couldn't stop herself from flinching.

'I don't think any of us will ever be one hundred per cent back to normal,' Toby said. He took another swallow of whisky and screwed on the cap with the careful deliberation of the inebriated before leading her across the yard towards the caravan.

Two men were working at the front of the garage, one holding the base of a long ladder while the other, perched at the top of it, was stringing up one end of a long banner that hung straight down. *ALFIE'S BIG GOODBYE BASH* was painted on it in clumsy red letters. Both men, the younger one at the top of the ladder and the older one in a cardigan at the bottom, watched as Toby led Harriet past them, past a long table set up just inside the garage, in front of the red Routemaster bus. Covered in a white cloth and crowded with beer glasses and wine glasses, plates and silverware, bottles of red wine and lemonade and cola, bowls of salad covered in clingfilm, slabs of cheese, a mound of bread rolls. There was a steel barrel of beer on a wooden cradle, and two large tubs brimful of crushed ice, with the necks of beer bottles and wine bottles sticking out.

Toby climbed the steps to the door of the caravan and jerked it open, saying, 'Flowers! There's a prize if you can guess who this is.'

Alfie was sorting through boxes of magazines when he felt the cold draught knifing into his back and heard Toby's challenge. He turned, saw his friend in the doorway, saw Harriet Crowley standing behind him at the bottom of the steps.

'I think,' Toby said, 'I'll leave you two to talk things over.'

Harriet said, 'I'm not here to cause trouble. I have something that I think you should see.'

Her right hand was on the strap of the laptop case slung over her shoulder; her left was jammed into the pocket of her fawn raincoat.

'It's all right,' Alfie said, although his pulse was beating in his throat and his palms were moistening.

'I'll be outside,' Toby said. 'The war, it is not yet over.'

'Don't use up all the fireworks before the party starts,' Alfie said. He was looking at Harriet, who stepped aside to let Toby go past, then climbed the three steps to the doorway.

She said, 'I saw the developer's sign.'

'I decided that I didn't have to live in a caravan for the rest of my life. A block of flats will be going up here by spring.'

'What about your tenant?'

'I didn't sell out completely; I gave George the freehold of his workshop. He'll have to find some other place to park his buses and his fire engine, though.'

'And you?'

'I'm buying one of those live/work places. The top floor of an old garment factory in Hackney. I move out in the New Year, which is why I'm getting rid of stuff I don't need, like these magazines. I'm spring-cleaning the past. My past, my father's past . . .'

Alfie owned a huge collection of the magazines that had published his father's photographs, but he'd hardly ever looked at them until he'd returned from Iraq. And after he'd gone through them, he'd realized that he didn't need these musty souvenirs any more. It was time to let the past go.

On several occasions since his return from Iraq he'd tried without success to explain everything to his grandmother – either the story was too complicated for her to follow or he wasn't able to do justice to it. But when he'd visited her the previous weekend, she had been enjoying a rare spell of lucidity, and although she kept confusing Alfie with her dead husband – sometimes she was lucid and sometimes she wasn't, but she would always be confused – he'd finally been able to make her understand that, as far as her family was concerned, the business with the glyphs was over.

When at last he stood up to go, she caught at his sleeve. 'You said that those things haven't changed you, Maurice. You said that you were stronger than them. But you weren't stronger, were you? They changed you, didn't they?'

'Yes,' Alfie said. 'Yes, they did.'

'They won't ever change you back.'

Alfie was surprised and touched by his grandmother's acuity. 'I know. I thought they would, it was one of the reasons I got into this. But I know now that I am what I am.'

'It's like the maze,' she said. 'Do you remember the maze at Hampton Court?'

She was remembering something that had happened a long time before Alfie had been born, but he said that he did.

'We found the centre, didn't we?'

His grandmother's face shining now, lit up by the memory of a long-lost day.

'Yes, I suppose we did.'

'You win the game when you get to the centre of the maze. But you're still in the maze, aren't you?'

'But once you find the centre, you can find your way back,' Alfie told her.

For a moment, he thought that she understood. But then her gaze lost its focus, her face slackened, and she said, 'The lawn needs mowing, and it's such a big lawn. I don't know what we were thinking when we moved here.'

Standing at the threshold of the caravan, Harriet said, 'I've stumbled into the middle of your leaving party. Perhaps I should—'

'No, no. It isn't a problem. Really. Why don't you come in, shut the door?'

She came in. She shut the door. There was a long awkward moment.

Alfie said, 'It sounds like I'm making some big changes, but not really. I'm still in the photography business. Remember the wrap party for that movie, *The Elemental*? It was a surprise hit, and a major studio wants a sequel. In two weeks I'll be starting work on it, taking continuity shots on set, pictures for publicity, that kind of thing.'

Harriet said, 'It sounds like you've moved on.'

'I still have seizures,' Alfie said. 'The atypical petit mal I've always had, and a couple of serious ones, too. Clarence Ashburton was kind enough to let me try out haka, but it didn't really work out. I mean, it helped with the petit mal, but it also gave me some very bad dreams . . .'

He didn't remember the details of the dreams, but every night while he'd been trying to reduce the frequency of his seizures by smoking haka he'd woken covered in sweat, his sheets soaked, so frightened that he'd been unable to speak, a dark feeling in his soul, a stain that shadowed him for days afterwards. So he'd given it up, gone back to phenobarbitone and cautious self-medication.

Harriet said, 'Clarence told me that he'd seen you.'

'He wanted you and me to talk. I suppose you weren't ready for it.'

'Well, here I am now.'

Alfie said, 'Frankly, I'm not sure if *I* want to talk. Also, your charming and persuasive friend in MI6 had me sign the Official Secrets Act.'

'I know.'

'So we shouldn't really be talking about it.'

When he'd finally returned home, Alfie had found that Dr Robin Cole, of Franks House and the British Museum, had left several phone messages enquiring about his research into his grandfather's discoveries. Feeling more than a little guilty, Alfie had explained the problem during his first interview with MI6 officers; they'd promised to have a friendly word, and he'd heard no more from the helpful but over-eager archaeologist, who no doubt had been made to sign the Official Secrets Act too.

Harriet said, 'Do you think that this place is bugged?'

'Actually, it probably isn't. Call me paranoid, but I have Elliot check it out every day with this gadget I bought in a spy shop. The one on Baker Street, near where my grandfather used to work.'

'You're small people, Alfie. I don't mean that in a bad way, I mean that you have nothing to worry about. They'll keep an eye on you, but they probably won't do anything else.'

'As long as I don't register on the radar again.'

'You were definitely a blip, once upon a time. Look, if you don't want to talk about this, fine. I'll go.'

'I suppose it's proof that I screwed up when I let Musa Karsu go free. Well, I'm not going to apologize for it. I still think I did the right thing.'

'They showed me the transcript of your interview.'

'Which one? There was the one when we gave ourselves up to the Turkish army in Zakho, and there was the one after the Turkish army handed us to the CIA. And then there was the one in the British embassy in Ankara. And so far four interviews here, the last one just this week, going over the same old ground to no good purpose . . .'

'You were the only one who always told the truth.' Harriet wasn't exactly smiling, but she was relaxing, no longer looking strained and severe. Saying, 'It was the transcript of your last interview. The one you had just three days ago. They brought me in too. They interviewed me, and then they made me go through your transcript, asking if I wanted to add anything.'

Alfie said, 'Something happened, didn't it? That's why they brought us in and re-interviewed us. And that's why you came here.'

'But if you don't want to talk about it . . .'

There was another silence, broken by the thin crack of a firework and Toby Brown's drunken whoop.

Harriet said, 'How is Toby?'

'He doesn't talk about it, but I think he has flashbacks and bad dreams. I know I do. Also he's pissed off by the American election and the way of the world in general. And he drinks too much, but that's not so very different from . . . before.'

There was a silence.

Alfie said, 'Would you like some tea? I have peach or peppermint or fennel.'

Now Harriet did smile. 'You're still maintaining your equilibrium.'

'I'm going to make some peppermint tea, and then you can show me whatever it is you came here to show me.' Alfie organized the kettle, a couple of mugs, tea bags. As the kettle cleared its throat and began to rattle, he said, 'I like the haircut. I mean, short hair doesn't suit everyone, but it suits you.'

'They cut half of it off when they stitched up my scalp,' Harriet said. 'I decided to keep it this way.'

'I'm not going to apologize for that, either.'

'I don't expect you to.'

There was another silence.

'At least we're talking again,' Alfie said. 'I think you said about three words on that drive to Zakho.'

'I was pissed off.'

'Actually, so was I.'

'Because I used you.'

'I was pissed off because just about everybody had been using me.'

The kettle boiled. Alfie made the tea; Harriet fired up her laptop, showed him what she had found.

It was a brief video clip, no sound, showing a rally of a new political party in south-eastern Turkey. A man in a black overcoat stood on the back of a pick-up truck, with two armed soldiers and several men in civilian clothes behind him. The man was speaking into an orange bullhorn, making sweeping gestures. A big square banner was strung above him. Red writing on the white cloth, and a photograph of the man in the suit super-imposed over a stylized blue dove, the photograph and the dove framed in what looked like more Arabic writing, but which Alfie knew, with a sinking feeling, almost certainly wasn't.

He said to Harriet, 'Where did you get this?'

'I pulled it off Al-Jazeera's web site. It was picked up by the BBC and shown once on *News 24* before they were served a D-notice. The speaker is a former community activist by the name of Mehmet Celik.'

'The man who turned you over to the *peshmergas*.'

'He's a politician now, a member of a party that's advocating the peaceful establishment of an independent Kurdistan.'

The clip ended. Harriet used the mouse button of the laptop, clicked on an icon in the bar at the bottom of the screen, and a still picture blossomed. A close-up of the banner, showing the photograph, the dove, the frame.

Alfie looked at it, looked away, blinking hard. As if that would get rid of the pattern that swam in his vision.

'I'm sorry,' Harriet said. 'It was a silly trick. I should have warned you. Are you all right?'

'It was the fascination glyph, wasn't it?'

'Not exactly. It's something new. Like the fascination glyph, but not quite.'

'But it's one of Morph's. Musa Karsu's.'

'There's one more picture,' she said. 'No glyphs, I promise.'

It was a grainy enlargement of a frame of the video clip, showing the soldiers and the men in civilian dress who stood behind the speaker on the load-bed of the pick-up. Alfie had to ask who he was supposed to be looking at. Even when Harriet pointed to the man on the far left, he wasn't convinced.

'He's grown a beard and cut his hair. Lost a little weight, too,' Harriet said.

'If it is him, what will happen?'

'Nothing will happen. Not to him, anyway. Maybe my friend in MI6 will try to have a discreet word with him, but that's as far as it will go. He's part of the inner circle of the newest political party in Turkey. It will cause all kinds of problems if he's arrested.'

'And if he happens to be close by when a bomb goes off? As they do, in that part of the world.'

Harriet shrugged. 'I was told that no direct action would be taken.'

'Right.'

'What they actually said was that they would be monitoring the situation closely. Which is spook-speak for doing nothing.'

'Right.'

'It isn't in anyone's interest to assassinate him. You should be pleased.'

'Because I let him escape.'

'Because you were right.'

They were leaning side by side, looking at the screen of the laptop. Alfie could smell the outdoors on Harriet's hair: fresh air and gunpowder smoke.

He said, 'You came here to tell me that I was right?'

'There was something else.'

'I knew it.'

'We're just about all that's left of the Nomads' Club, Alfie.'

'I never was a member. And if you're inviting me to join, remember that I'm trying to let go of the past.'

'I never was a member, either.'

'That's right. It was that kind of old-fashioned club.'

'What I'm trying to say is that it ends here, with us.'

Alfie studied her for a moment, then said, 'What does this glyph do? You said it was a new one, and I bet your spooky friends have tested it out.'

'Peace,' Harriet said.

'Peace?'

'It gives you a peaceful feeling. It calms the heart. It makes you receptive to new ideas.'

'Peace.' Alfie smiled at her and said, 'I think I can live with that.'

ACKNOWLEDGEMENTS

Although this is a work of fiction, a number of books were especially helpful while I was researching and developing my ideas, and I should like to thank their authors.

David Lewis-Williams's *The Mind in the Cave* (Thames & Hudson), and *Consciousness: How Matter Becomes Imagination* by Gerald M. Edelman and Giulio Tononi (Penguin).

Richard Rudgley's *The Alchemy of Culture* (British Museum Press), and Peter Stafford's *Psychedelics Encyclopedia* (Ronin).

Jeffrey T. Richelson's *The Wizards of Langley* (Westview Press), and John Jacob Nutter's *The CIA's Black Ops* (Prometheus Books).

Wilfred Thesiger's *Desert, Marsh and Mountain* (Flamingo), and David McDowall's *A Modern History of the Kurds* (St Martin's Press).

My thanks also to Dr Jill Cook, the British Museum's section head for the Palaeolithic and Neolithic collections, who generously gave me a tour of Franks House, and Russell Schechter for invaluable insights into the structured tedium of an average day in the life of a private detective. Kim Newman provided data storage and diversionary tactics, Antony Harwood supplied professional life-support, and as always Georgina Hawtrey-Woore gave unstinting moral support.

Graiguenamanagh